CORA

CORA

a novel by
Daphne Athas

The Viking Press   New York

Library of Congress Cataloging in Publication Data
Athas, Daphne, 1923–
Cora.
I. Title.
PZ3.A865Co   1978   [PS3501.T323]   813'.5'4   78-15426
ISBN 0-670-24116-4

Printed in the United States of America
Set in Fototronic Baskerville

For the continuity of Greece,
to Miranda Cambanis

Can you see the moon can you see it seen. . . .

—Gertrude Stein, *A Circular Play*

But surely the Revolution means joy. And joy does not like orphans in the house. Good men do good deeds. The Revolution is the good deed of good men. But good men do not kill. So it is bad people that are making the Revolution. But Poles are bad people too. Then how is Gedali to tell which is Revolution and which is Counter Revolution?

—Isaac Babel, *Red Cavalry*

ACKNOWLEDGMENTS

I thank Melba De Bayle for the central metaphor of change.

The Vivien Leigh dreams are actual, and were told to me by
Tony Harvey. I want to thank him for them.

For a grant to write this book I make acknowledgment to
the National Endowment for the Arts.

Part one

The Face appeared to him while he was playing the second game of a semifinal match in Naples. It was the face of a woman. She looked more Greek than Italian. She was with two men. The base of her eyebrows rose in a spasm of gallantry from the root of the nose, catching that moment of conflict when life engages tragedy. And the drama of cheekbone, eyebrow, and forehead ended in something telltale, the mortal mouth. No Athena appearing to Achilles in battle would have such a mouth. At his gaze, she turned one corner in to mask the too-naked flatness of her upper lip. It became a leer. He understood why he was afraid of her. Her mouth was a wound. To combat his attraction, he concentrated on the game.

His opponent was Sancho Sanchez, a Cuban enlistee in the U.S. Navy. He was good, stylish, and had a following among the sailors from the *Forrestal* of the Sixth Fleet. The Service Club in the basement of the Hotel Grili felt like an aquarium. Electric hum of neon lights, the click of the ping-pong balls, everything garish, green, jittering. The winner would go to Izmir in Turkey to defend USAREUR in the 1971 U.S. Armed Forces Finals.

Suddenly, he saw her look up at his name: TECH. SGT. DON TSAMBALIS, chalked up on the blackboard. One of her companions was pointing to it, the one with the cupid mouth. Both men had the smoky/shy look of exiled intellectuals, the Bakunins, the Orwells. The first whispered in her ear loud enough for Don to hear: *"Prepei na einai Hellenes."* He must be Greek. Her eyes, amber and large, registered no expression.

No one else seemed to notice the three foreigners, although they stuck out among the GIs. Black sailors had come out of the poolroom and draped themselves like lizards against the walls, chalking their cue-tips provocatively. They were uttering contemptuous, arcane, American sounds which dismantled space into time. The whites, a gamut ranging from Ohio hillbillies to Arkansas plebes, were catcalling:

"Hey you, dum-dum, Army, whyn't you go more lightly on that ball?"

" 'Cause it's the only one he's got! Hee-Haw, Fort Bragg!"

They hated the way he played: his ignominious, mincing backhand, his short, close shots. Sanchez kept trying to pull the ball out for a smash, but it was like pulling taffy. He couldn't get in on top of it. His rhythm kept getting destroyed. It was the principle of small boats against the armada. The trick was the wrist. Never move any muscle but the wrist. His wrist movement was poisonous, like an adder's strike. He gave nothing away with his body. He kept it hunched and spooky, like Ed Sullivan, a tubercular posture which disguised his aim.

Sanchez shot three off the table in a row.

Don realized that he was playing for her and that he was about to win. So he swam outside himself and saw everything in slow motion. Himself delivering his shots faster than his will commanded. Himself looking profane. His stance prayerful, as if beating the celluloid pizzicato to hysterics were worshiping.

At that moment he noticed she had assumed his posture, as if she were imitating. But it made everything about her inappropriate. Whereas he was tense, she was languid, he medium-sized, she tall. In fact, she was as tall as both her companions. Her shoulders were hunched over breasts which, outlined by her thin black jersey, were ample and beautiful, and made her arms seem too long. They hung down by her sides, bare, white,

4

and peculiarly defenseless. She lit a cigarette. Smoke rose around her hair, which was the color of toast, thick and irrepressible.

The crescendo of GI indignation snapped him back. Sanchez's arm yawed as he shot off the table for the last time, losing the game. It seemed less a victory than a win by default.

Don did not want to see her expression. He turned his back on her with insolence.

Sanchez came around the table to him, mopping the receding curls from his prematurely bald dome with a large embroidered handkerchief, so gallant, shaking his hand, that it was hard to remember the lovely confidence shining in those liquid, coal eyes before the game.

"Well, Ace," he said in his elegant but execrable English. "I got to hand it to you. You catch me with that bitch style of yours." Not a trace of jealousy. "I admire it, you son of a bitch, I really do. It's the ultimate in awful."

"You was robbed!" shouted his claque.

"Purse-snatched by a stiff-assed creep!"

"Shut up, you guys!" he called, and turning back from them, holding that handshake, warm and generous, his gaze was so *double-entendre*, as if he were the victor rather than the loser, that Don suspected him of a metaphoric jerk-off. Don was glad Sanchez ended with a manly challenge: "But you watch out, Ace, in the next match." He disappeared, towel around his neck, leading his school of fish through the door.

Don turned away from the spot he knew she was standing and cut in the opposite direction to get a drink from the water fountain. He drank in large, thirsty gulps. But the sensation of icy water in his throat suddenly merged with the image of her face which came floating across the watery aluminum, as in a distorting mirror. Was it a shadow? A dream in color? He saw that her hair was redder than he had thought, almost the same color as his own, but burnished with streaks of sun. It fused with his reflection. He thought, Yes, it is my face, and turned around. She was standing no more than two feet behind him.

"Congratulations," she said.

He felt surrounded yet neutralized by her eyes. They were shallow and light as if pelagoes had been paralyzed by sun. His were blue. Also, her smile should have banished the tragedy of the Face, but it didn't, it confirmed it.

"There is no such thing as tragedy," Philo had said.

"Thank you," he answered. Was he his father's son?

"Are you Greek?" she asked.

"Yes. Half. My father was born in Greece." But he refused to play the professional Greek. What were three Greeks doing in a U.S. Navy service club? "Are you ping-pong players?"

"No, we're only amateurs," answered the second one. He had a black beard and a very swarthy skin.

The cupid-mouthed man smiled. He was dressed in outmoded Carnaby Street striped bell-bottoms. Were they students, he wondered, some of the thousands who had got out since the junta?

"We love ping-pong," she said, "and we happened to be passing by." She spoke English with an American accent. Not a wound perhaps, but sensitivity so extreme as to shock. *"Isos thelei kafedaki, Michali,"* she added to the cupid-mouthed one.

"Will you join us for coffee?" asked Michalis.

The café was a couple of blocks from the Grili, near the esplanade. Scooters stuttered through soft April air, bouncing chatters of complaint from old purple-stone buildings. The dust and Mediterranean salt-smell mixed with their cappuccino. They talked about movies. They liked Torre-Nilsson, they disliked Godard. Resnais and Robbe-Grillet were alter egos. Don told them Robbe-Grillet was haunted by the Goddess. Had they seen *L'Immortelle*?

Then they introduced themselves. Her name was Zoe, which she pronounced with a Gee-Whee sound like an exhalation. The swarthy one was named Eleutheris. They called him Lefteri.

"This Sancho Sanchez," said Lefteri, "I don't think he likes playing your game."

"He hates it."

"You keep him from using the table."

The table, he told them, is a hemisphere. A leviathan treats this hemisphere as mere turf, controlling it by standing light-years away from it enacting huge spins, semaphoring, like using an earthquake to kill an ant. He had worked out his game himself, without any training, and whatever rationale he gave of it, or apologies, it worked for him. It went against all the rules of form, but the old forms were useless in ping-pong as in everything else.

After a half an hour they invited him to their rooms a couple of blocks away.

The sun was going down and Naples was coming alive in the dusk. People descended into the streets. The lights came on and music and chatter began. It was a creaky old hotel called the Sagittarius. He followed them up dark stairs. On the first floor they passed an old man sitting at an entrance desk in a pool of light. Michalis put his finger on his lips and they went by unnoticed in the darkness.

They led him down a brilliant, newly painted corridor, which jumped into being at the press of a button. Countless rooms gave off from this corridor, each the same as before, differing only in furniture, the sink dirty in one, the window shades torn in another, beds in some, broken bureaus with cracked mirrors in others.

This whizzing acreage, with lights being turned off and on, gave way suddenly to their apartment. They had raided these other rooms to furnish it, they said. It was serene, large, cozy with candlelight, some ottomans, and a divan propped on cinder blocks on an Oriental rug. There were a couple of small rooms beyond. Zoe turned on the switch of a two-burner electric stove to warm up a pot of lentil soup.

They had lived there for six weeks, they said, and nobody knew it. It was an accident. When they had come from Paris, they had seen the hotel, explored the stairway, found the empty beds and rooms, yet the man at the desk had told them there were no rooms. Being tired, they just went to sleep anyway. And then they had stayed another night, and another, and so on.

"You mean nobody ever tried to collect rent?"

"The old man's deaf," explained Michalis. "I tried to tell him the first week, but he waved me away. Once he took six hundred lire, but he thought I was paying him for number eighteen on the second floor. He kept mumbling, 'Number eighteen.' We think the owner lives in Milano."

On the doorway to the bedroom there was a poster, a black-and-white drawing of a Christ-like figure with cast-down head and chains. A legend flickered in the candlelight in English: "Come to Greece. 1969. War. Concentration Camps. Death!"

"You are exiles?" he said.

"If you mean do we like the government, no, we don't like the government," said Michalis.

"If they go back, they'll both be drafted," said Zoe.

He refused the guilt of his own passive choices, ping-pong, special services, luck, and successful maneuvering while men were in Vietnam.

After his own personal resistance, the mystic-dope trek through Afghanistan to India and back, then a year after college living with Kitty and teaching in the Frank Porter Graham Center and, when she left, those seven months in upper New York state meditating with Decker in that old house without heat or electricity. The letter from his draft board was a relief. He was twenty-four years old now and he had four months to go.

Michalis had a Ph.D. from Berkeley and was doing a postdoctoral in Paris in public health. Lefteri was studying engineering at Bologna. Michalis and Zoe had known each other from childhood and had been married two years.

"Married! But I thought you were the Three Musketeers!" He spooned the small beans into his mouth, inhaling lemon and onions.

"We are!" smiled Lefteri.

Don skipped the marriage step. He began talking about Sanchez, idealist of the right. He had been a soccer star. He had escaped Castro in a dinghy with two other Cubans, paddled the last thirty-five miles with an Australian boomerang with which he had beat back Cuban police on the beach, and landed on a polluted strand near Miami, dehydrated and starving. His two friends were corpses in the bottom of the boat. He had started a nightclub, trading on his soccer name, but it had failed, so he'd joined the U.S. Navy and become more chauvinistic than George Washington.

"You don't believe in nobility in ping-pong?" said Michalis.

"I don't believe in the *appearance* of nobility."

"Why?"

"Is ping-pong anything?"

"Then you *do* believe in nobility," said Zoe.

He hated the superiority of Troy-lovers who still measured by winning.

"Is the world black and white?"

"You don't believe a person can be noble in this world?"

"I'm a realist."

"And one cannot be a realist and be noble?"

"Americans can't be noble."

This stab at wit earned him status, and for the rest of the evening everything grew lively. They talked about student days in Athens. He told them how he had been in Greece at age nineteen in 1967 and had visited Philo's village, Metamorphosis. It was before the junta, on his way back from India. They speculated on how they might have passed each other on the street in Athens. They speculated how when he was in Chapel Hill High in North Carolina, she was in Mount Bethel, Tennessee. She had spent a year of high school on an American exchange scholarship and then returned to Athens University to graduate in architecture. They sang Theodorakis songs. He sang "Ta Roda ta Triandafila," which Philo had taught him when he was four. They asked why Americans called fathers by their first names. And where was he headed now? He told them Greece, if he won. He had a month's leave saved up and he'd fixed it so he could take it between Temporary Duty in Naples and Temporary Duty in Izmir. Presupposing he won. Philo called it Smyrna. There were two types of Greeks, Philo said: ancient and Byzantine.

This bantering changed to a mood of confidentiality. As the evening went on, he felt he knew them. They were sympathetic. He could feel himself opening up to them.

At eleven o'clock, when he looked at his watch and said he had to go, they asked him to do them a favor. Would he take a keepsake—from the christening of their child, Eleutheris, six weeks ago in Paris—to Zoe's mother and father in Athens?

A child! He could not imagine them with a baby.

"I'll be glad to deliver it, but you certainly have faith that I'm going to win tomorrow!"

"No more than you have in yourself," said Zoe, smiling. "You will!"

When he looked into her eyes he started drowning, a strange reversal, since it was usually others who lost themselves in his eyes. Half of him willingly gave in to it. The other half refused by imagining sex with her, pounding the territory of her hips inordinately and brutally.

He bid them good night. They arranged, all of them, to meet at the café the next day after the set.

But the next day his feelings were diametrically changed. He woke with a chill, a hangover from intimacy. He tried not to think of them but to concentrate on winning. They were playing the best two-out-of-three on consecutive days. Down in the game room his play was desultory. It was an agonizing game, which he lost. He wondered if he would win the match at all. This meant a day's delay.

He stood them up. He went to see *Bad Day at Black Rock* and watched Spencer Tracy spouting perfect Italian. Then he walked around the slums along the southern arm of the harbor. He remembered Merritt Mill Road at the railroad tracks during his high-school days and pretended these old women were mammy-types in Niggertown and these children with shaven heads for lice were pickaninnies. At last he went to the café. They were not there. It was empty. He found himself walking the two blocks to the hotel. He went in, climbed up the stairway, sneaked past the old man, and reached the door of their apartment. It was open. She was alone, sitting, smoking, writing something on a clipboard on her lap. There was a large briefcase on the couch next to her. How long and thin her arms were! She moved them in a fastidious way. The skin above the elbows was extremely white.

"Zoe," he said, knocking.

She looked up.

"I'm sorry I wasn't there. I didn't win after all."

She smiled and told him to come in. She looked sympathetic. Michalis was at a meeting. Lefteri had gone for groceries. She gave him some wine.

"We take turns grocery shopping. Isn't that fahnny?" The wide sound of her palate smote him as he laughed. There was no trace of ire, hidden or otherwise.

He felt longing. He wanted something, some acknowledgment. The thought came to him that she wanted him to make love to her, that she had known he would come and had left the door open on purpose, and that it was this discrepancy that was at the heart of her parthenogenesis. She had no woman's guile at all. She was as legato and straight as a boy. And her awful dignity, untouchable and untouched, disguised something.

"I feel something about you," he blundered forth. His ears, protruding like Philo's, burned in the wilderness. "I feel as if you have seen—something." His voice sounded a dark, groping sincerity. "Do you work for the Resistance?"

She said, "Why do you say that?" But her eyes did not change expression.

"Because it feels like you are beyond the law, that's all."

Philo, in his role as ethics-seeking ancient, sat in his pulpit, the tractor seat, and repeated the question as though he had not already asked it a hundred times before: "If you saw a man running fast down the left-hand path, and a minute later the policeman came and asked you, 'Which way did he go, the criminal?' would you point to the left or to the right?" According to Philo, it was from Plato.

She began in a low voice. She was the leader of a certain group, yes, she said. She kept the details vague. She talked as if it were merely a group of friends. She had organized strikes in the architecture school at the time of Lambrakis during Karamanlis. Then the junta came. She had seen her friends imprisoned and worse, so of course it was impossible to stay in Greece.

What did she do specifically, he wondered. Gestures like blowing up statues and exploding bombs in Chase Manhattan and Esso Pappas? Or did she kill people?

"I feel something too," she said. "You're like an old friend. I have trust in you."

He felt like laughing. The way she said "friend" evoked the Narodnaya Volya, the maquis. Friend. Comrade. An affectation he envied, everything he logically despised. But the temptation was larger than the contempt. He imagined himself on some mission with her, risking his life. They would be in danger. Their lovemaking would involve them totally and he would become wholly human. He would become frail and subservient to the death that would surround him.

"I would like to make love with you," he said.

Her slow gaze rested on him.

"Yes, *matia mou.*" There were specks in the irises of her smiling resignation. "There is something about me. It even makes me sick, my power over people." She used an imploring tone that put him on a special basis.

"How do you feel it?"

"No more than a half an hour with people I have never met before and they will do anything I say. . . . They will go jump in a lake if I tell them to."

He was fascinated by her arrogance, for it was naïve.

"They fall in love with you?"

"Yes."

"You mean they want to go to bed with you?"

"If it were only that—pah!"

"You mean it is love then?"

"Yes, love. Ah, it's very heavy."

At that moment Lefteri came back. He was carrying a string bag full of vegetables. He greeted them, set the vegetables on the table, and the talk switched to generalities. She talked so naturally, as if the price of

11

vegetables was of the same importance as resistance and love, that Don's guilt was anachronistic.

Philo said: "Greece is five donkeys pulling a cart. Each donkey pulls the cart the way he wants. The cart stays in the same place and the five ropes break."

What had she risked after all? If he betrayed her, she could deny. She had given no names, nothing concrete. But nothing excludes. He did not care that the backside of his awe was skepticism. The real decision left to man is the universe he chooses.

"All right then," he said when he left. "I will meet you again at the café tomorrow—only I shall be there this time, win or lose. Agreed?"

"But why don't you come here and we'll have supper?"

He did not blame her for not trusting him again, but there was a MAC flight at six, he said apologetically.

"Of course, agreed." She smiled, but he imagined a small strain in her generosity.

It was almost midnight when he got back to the Grili. There was a noise of laughter and in the corridor he saw Sanchez come out of a room with an ice bucket. He was slightly drunk, and after staring at him a moment as if the glow from Zoe had made him unrecognizable, Sanchez shouted, "Ace! Come on, it's a party!" and scooped him with one arm into a room heavy with smoke. It was ambisexual, only three or four women, several couples dancing, but the atmosphere was so good-humored, convivial, the faces of the men, the faint reek of male sweat, masculinity diffused in laughter so *gemütlich* that it felt reassuring. He felt free to think about Zoe.

"No, I can't drink anything, Sanchez."

Sanchez raised his arm fraternally like a boxer and introduced him to the group: "King for a Day! Before I beat him tomorrow, of course!" And then with impeccable tact: "Who of these do you want?"

"No, Sanchez, thank you. I want to go to sleep."

"A girl?"

"I can't cut it with whores, old buddy." He was watching a little Italian one working on a sailor's cock.

Sanchez beckoned to a blond, innocent-faced boy across the room. He whispered in Don's ear: "I would love to be nailed by you, Ace." And aloud: "This is Allen."

The boy unloosed Don's tie, and was beginning on his fly when, amid a smell of Old Spice and like a magic vision, making him erect, Sanchez appeared from behind, totally naked, massive with pectorals, his torso a plate of armor, astride, like Poseidon, the promise of his own phallus. He slid the boy away from Don, undressed him, and performed the act like a football play, placing his hands on the boy's hands. The boy's body, white and powerful with last traces of baby fat, looked impaled on Sanchez's powerful loins.

Later he mopped his curls and laughed. "You can't go, you know, like that."

"I won't spill my seed on a hotel carpet either. You know, Sanchez," understanding that only style would release him from the Cuban's hospitality, "you're the only person I can think of in the world, that I could bear to be buggered by in ping-pong."

"You're sick, Ace, but you have stature." Sanchez laughed, clapping him on the shoulder.

The next day he won in three games.

"Viva the European champion!" cried Sanchez, striding around the table looking gallant but bored. He grabbed Don's hand and held it above their heads.

Don was free to go back to himself and his protean life, survival by disguises.

The first thing he did was to get rid of all traces of the army. He put on corduroy pants and his old green sweater, folded the uniform and stuffed it in with his paddles and balls in the bottom of his pack. Then he put in the books and tied on the bedroll. It was heavy, forty pounds. But he was back in the ritual wanderer mask. Nor had he lost the knack of fastening his gear. It was like swimming, like snorkeling, like ping-pong. Once the motion is organic, it is significant. Left arm in. Pull the strap. Heave to the left. Settle the burden in the center of the back. Pioneer.

Nearing the café, he grew anxious, fearing she would not be there. But she was and he saw her from afar. She was wearing blue drop earrings which flashed like signals.

"You won!" she cried, jumping up.

"Hi, y'all," he mocked, crowing a soft rebel yell.

Yanking off the pack, he was conscious of the Face. It was whiter than he remembered.

13

"No thanks," he said, backing away from Lefteri, who had stretched out his arms to help with the gear. "I've got this system, see? I swing it." And he tossed himself, half ashamed to recognize that he was less a pioneer than an animal in harness.

At that moment he felt strange, as if he had changed in some way because of the victory and they sensed the change in him. They were embarrassed, as though he were already half gone.

He studied the Face again. There were beautiful caves in her cheeks. Her eyes wandered past him as if she were searching for something in the bullet-pocked walls of the stucco church across the street.

"Here is the coufetta," she said.

She called it a "coufetta," a silver cylindrical box tied with a blue ribbon. She opened it and inside nestled pastel, sugar-coated almonds. For some reason the sight of them hurt him.

"They look like ping-pong balls," he said. But they really looked like eggs.

"Won't you have one?" said Michalis.

"The last thing I could do is disturb their symmetry."

He felt relieved when she put the cover back on.

"Now the address." Michalis gave him a piece of paper with her parents' address, and he copied it in his notebook. "Also ours," Michalis said. Don saw that it was a Paris address. He put the notebook in his back pocket next to his passport. "You take the Number Twelve trolley from Panepistimiou; it's out past the museum on Patission."

"Okay."

They talked a little, randomly. But it was an exercise in nervous silences. He began to feel like a hypocrite. His departure was imminent. Zoe kept looking past him, scanning the church.

After a decent interval of time, he rose, put the coufetta in the pocket of a light nylon jacket, wrapped it around and stuffed it in an outside pocket of his pack. He motioned to the waiter.

But Michalis would not let him pay.

He rose to strap himself back into his pack. "Thank you for everything," he began. But he was embarrassed, putting it on in front of them. He played with the words "doff" and "don" in his mind, as if it meant strapping himself into his own name, and when he got it on he recognized he was a camel.

"Wait, you haven't fastened the pocket right!" she cried. "Turn around."

His hump obscured her. He could only see the white of her outstretched arms. She held him by the hump and swiveled him around to the proper position. He felt her touches, tiny shifts through the mass, slight movement, a pull and a pressure as she fastened the buckle. It was like a laying-on of hands.

When she had done, he turned around to say good-by. He shook hands. "Good-by," he said.

"Addio."

He pressed her fingers hard to burn off the sensation of touches on his pack. Then he strode off around the corner. But the burning in his face did not wear off until after the bus got halfway to the airport.

*H*e was bumped off his flight. A second flight followed twenty minutes later, but he was bumped off that one too.

There was a breeze flapping the colored plastic flags of the airport café and above a skyful of courtesans in purple togas caught the setting sun. Only in Richmond, Virginia, had he seen clouds so bountiful with the soft grandeur of failure. Italy was sad, rich, moist and noble, and he longed to get east. Violence had burned off history's density in Greece and left only the deadly clarity of sun and rock.

In London no more than four days ago, he had made a vow. He had vowed to find the Goddess. It was a literal vow. But what it meant he had no idea. What shape the finding of the Goddess was to take he did not know. A love affair? A spiritual experience? He only knew that he had before him one month of freedom after nineteen months of army life. He was laying himself open to signs and signals.

A staff sergeant passed by hauling a cart of what looked like bolts of cloth covered in wrapping paper.

"What's that?" he asked.

"It says, 'Household Goods.' " The sergeant looked up from a clipboard.

"Where's it going?"

"Why?" asked the sergeant, eyeing him with baleful, east-Texas suspicion.

"Because I want to hitch a ride to Greece."

"Suda Bay, Crete, and if you want to go, you better ask Assy-Brassy getting hisself stoned in there."

Behind the plate-glass window a navy lieutenant commander was drinking vodka. He leaned back on two chair legs with one foot on the table next to the Smirnoff bottle. He was elegantly balanced and alone. His face was pockmarked and he had light, insane eyes.

Seeing that he was a serious drinker, Don sat down to wait.

You had to begin with Athena. It was only through her that twentieth-century women would consent to live, as if Zeus's mind, the spear of the male, and the granny glasses of the owl could avenge what Christianity had done. In 1959 in Piraeus they had dug up an Athena and put her to one side of a door in the Archaeological Museum. She was life-size. You always did a double take. That was what the ancients had reduced the Goddess to. And that was why there was no hope in Athena. It was a corrupt religion even then. Worse than when the *thea* had been a toy. The bronze had corroded around her eyes and the white stuff made her look as if she had been crying for centuries. As he went east, he thought, the Goddess would lose her identity and become more indistinct, more threatening. He would have to fight his fear if he expected to recognize her.

The lieutenant commander was corking the bottle and rising. He concentrated on making his gait steady but casual.

Don intercepted him as he came out the café door.

"Commander, if you're taking those household goods to Suda Bay, I'd like to hitch along."

"Who are you?" focusing yellow eyes. His breath reeked.

"Technical Sergeant Don Tsambalis, sir. Army. From England. I just won a table-tennis tournament in Naples, and I'm TDY." He started for his papers.

The commander waved him with the vodka bottle to keep step. Their feet scuffed airfield grass. The commander was wearing a mint-condition uniform. His body looked like a disheveled collection of bones moving it along. He compensated for signs of drunkenness by training his eyes like tracer bullets on Don.

"Why does every off-duty military man try to look like ex-1968 civil rights?"

"It's the only way to be a pioneer." Render unto Caesar.

"Pioneer comes from old French meaning 'peon.' You're already a peon so you don't need to try."

Don was going to enjoy this.

The commander went to the cockpit of the old cargo plane, shouted something to the pilot, and then returned. "If you wanta come, you gotta sit on this stuff."

In the belly of the plane the only light came from the reflections from the cockpit and some dim bulbs burning in back. They sprawled on the brown-parceled bolts.

The commander snorted from his private world as they took off. "Do you know this here is the most expensive glassware in the world, Corning?"

"Glassware! But it's soft. What's it packed in?"

"Household goods! Haw haw." The commander's bony legs and knees shook loosely with the air bumps.

After half an hour, the commander got up to go to the bathroom. Don ripped open a torn spot in the paper to look. Persian carpets.

The commander returned in the inspirational mood born of taking a leak. "You know the only place left in the world where you can be a pioneer?"

"Where?"

"Right here in the military. You'll find the most flagrant freedom in bureaucracy. The only freedom that exists is in that place where nobody thinks it can exist. Prisons. Armies. Tolstoy knew that. Remember Pierre? For freedom you need predictable elements, strict rules. The larger the bureaucracy, the larger the freedom. Need a left hand that doesn't know what the right one is doing. That doesn't fit in with your archetypal protest psychology, does it?"

Maybe he was a genius, like Philo.

"You have to measure freedom by outrageousness. For instance, today is April nineteenth, the anniversary of the American Revolution, and here you are flying on top of Corning glassware to Suda Bay, Crete. You never thought you'd be pioneering freedom like that, did you?"

"No. What I always aspired to, was to be the first man to fly east on a magic carpet."

That was initiative, the commander's laugh admitted, knocking like a boiler. "Do you know I collect three times for the Corningware and twice for the Persian carpets? The paperwork takes more art and profits than the haulage. In this light, everything flattens out; you don't have your easy little set of values."

Don never had. But how could the commander know how he and Theo had been brought up, Philo seesawing between the values of winning and service? "Dirty liar! Filthy bum!" He could hear the spit of Philo's "t" in "Dirty" caroming out of his imagination into the present tense, vibrating with the buzz of the aircraft. It was as comforting as the muffling insulation of the carpets. Style of delivery was equal to valiance for a Greek. Philo may have had an ancient heart, but his brain was Byzantine.

Don felt in cabal with this drunk, flushed, pitted commander. The beaker of corruption was refreshing. He admired even the rottenness of his breath.

The commander began to tell him World War II stories. After the war, he had had an epiphany. He had suddenly understood that everything under the sun was new and amazing, that everything he had thought until that moment was untrue.

"We were taking these gooks off an island that was to be used as a testing area in our bomb-testing days. We had this old B-29 filled with Chinks. They were sitting in the belly just like we're doing now, only in those old B-29's the bomb bays opened right here. There must have been fifty Chinks. Somebody made a mistake and pushed a wrong button and one of the bomb-bay doors opened and a half-a-dozen gooks dropped out of sight. The rest of the gooks were amazed. First they were silent. Then all of a sudden they began to laugh. Then they applauded. Presto. Zippo. Now you see them, now you don't. Magic! That was when I understood that to embark on empathy is to bark up the wrong tree, that our whole system of morality based on the golden rule is a courageous failure, that something else is needed."

People never know when they do it. The commander did not know he had made God bark. His words turned into the drone of the airplane, nonsense abstracted into pistons' jitters, the screams of mechanical parts in pure atmosphere which released him into that territory where, events being nothing, they become stimuli for the Unseen Presence.

Philo's lips moved in Don's mind. Philo was reading a newspaper, pronouncing everything to himself. The silent words seemed magic, the answer to the secret of life, nothing to do with the newspaper article. Philo had taught him and Theo to read, lifting his upper lips high above his gums on vowels. When Philo said a vowel, Don knew it meant something about the good and the bad, the male and the female of life, but he did not know what. One day when he was twelve he heard a redneck say Philo's name: "Fahlo-It's-un-Valley." At that moment he realized the vowel was female.

"Say our father's name," he told Theo.

"Feel-Oh," said Theo.

"File-O," countered Don.

Theo was delighted. It changed Poseidon to Silo Bogsbottom. He loved anything that enabled him to escape Philo's influence and become a bona fide American.

But Don knew that was not the point. In that outrush of sound from his open gullet and exposed tongue, the promise of inrushing but empty air bespoke femalehood, possibly goddesshood. This was the moment when the pursuit of the Goddess became the germ of his life.

One day, Philo was in the junkyard garden trying to take the oil pan off a 1957 tractor. Philo was terrible at anything mechanical. He spent long hours puttering, pretending he was good, but made weird mistakes—like the time he hitched an electric hair dryer to a jug of honey trying to make an electric water sprayer, and attracted a swarm of wasps.

"Hey, Fa-ee-lo," called Theo, with an infallible sense for the insult. "You want me to help you?"

Philo's yellow eyes did not betray a quiver, but the pinpoint pupil was a laser. He stopped working and picked up a rag.

"Pour that gas over my hands," he ordered Theo.

For half an hour Theo was forced to pour spouts of gas while Philo cleaned his hands with the rag: "More. Stop." Wipe. "Again. Stop." Wipe. "Pour." Etc. Theo became the insidious enemy Philo was searching for in the cracks of his knuckles: ignorant, Anglo-Saxon dirt. And Philo's patience was endless; Theo's rage caused the gas spout to tremble. He was being forced to be an accomplice to his own self-extinction.

There was nothing for Theo and Don to do but sit spellbound, yawing between the days when they were rich as Croesus from some trade Philo had just made and the days they were as poor as church mice. Don had not known until he had seen his first outdoor café in Athens in 1967 how ingenious Philo had been. Wisteria adorned the spokes of the wheels of two tractors, two riot wheels of color at the entranceway of their junkyard garden, like giant bridal bouquets, camp chairs under the peach tree Philo had planted, honeysuckle floating from a telephone pole that Philo had instructed the electric company to put up, a tin shed built by roofing over a space between a discarded Frito's truck and an old Orange County prison-farm vehicle decorated with climbing roses. Philo had a telephone outside, although it never rang because it was shut off half the time. The ivy-covered 1938 General Electric refrigerator did work, however, and they kept it stocked with milk, oranges, and apples which they ate during arguments. They spent more time in the garden than in the house, an old two-story frame building, bare and clean. Each had his own room. Philo allowed no sign on the business, but he had all kinds of letterheads and cards printed with different enterprises: "Tsambalis Scrap Metal Enterprises," "Tsambalis Associates, Inc.," "Tsambalis Furniture, Inc.," "Tsambalis Growth Organization," "Tsambalis Trust Company." Business was synonymous with service or the common good of all men. Philo-filtered Locke, Hume, and Adam Smith was the universe.

A traitorous session in the garden, conducted by Don and Theo as a Socratic dualogue but effected as the witches' refrain from *Macbeth*, concerned how it was that Philo had ever made money at all. In the early fifties, before civil rights, he had organized Bedlow, Clyde England, and Wyvono Ethridge into a laundry-cum-dress-repair industry. But the Negroes' collaboration was too dependent on Philo's Harvard-economics talk and foundered.

Philo's left-handed buying and selling made the money. He was ashamed of it. It was impulsive. The more money he made, the more he preached bigger and better mousetraps. You don't separate artifacts from ideals. If a product is better, it will sell; it will improve the life of mankind. He bypassed the lessons of the light bulb, the nylon stocking, and the electric automobile.

The deepest concern of their treachery was their mother. What had happened to her? It was the awareness of being catalyzed by Philo that gave them the habit of clothing her absence with words. If knowing was words, not knowing was also words.

"I say she left him," Theo said at age thirteen.

"But she died," answered Don, who was ten.

"Who says so?"

"Philo."

"When did he actually say that?"

Don did not remember the exact date.

"He just turns his eyeballs up," said Theo, "and he lets us *think* she's dead. But I say she couldn't stand him, so she had to leave and abscond, and that's why he won't answer any questions."

One day, Don took the bull by the horns. It was August and very hot in the garden.

"What happened to our mother, Philo?"

There was not a flicker of expression in Philo's face. The crow's-feet, which made his light gold eyes overflow with kindness one moment and drip sulfur the next, were tracks in stone.

"She left," he answered.

"Did she leave or did she die?" demanded Theo.

Theo's tone was fatal to the inquiry, because when Philo withdrew he always left his statue.

"When you die, you leave. You're not there, are you?" asked Philo. "It's the same as leaving your mind in the bureau drawer." Inspiration came as his eyes fell on the rake. "For instance, when you leave the rake out in the rain to rust, are *you* here? Is your brain here? No. You are only bones, an outline moving."

He pointed, and Theo was forced to pick up the rake and put it in the shed.

Don leaned forward toward Philo's ear—a pole of two is more confidential than a crowd of three—and whispered, "Where is she, Philo? In Cairo, Illinois?"

The afternoon was so deadly still that when the lock of white, shiny hair fell down on Philo's olive-granite brow, Don could hear it.

"Why Cairo, Illinois?" accused Philo. His jug-handle ears stuck out to catch the answer.

He knew perfectly well why Cairo, Illinois. Their mother had come from Cairo, Illinois. She was the daughter of a judge, had graduated from Oberlin College, played the violin, and married Philo, who was almost twenty years older. And Philo called her younger son Dombey because that was what she had called him in play. One of her artifacts, kept in the linen closet, was a patchwork quilt that her aunt had made at a Cairo, Illinois, quilting bee. These were facts that Don and Theo had always known and had never known how they knew them. Perhaps Philo had told them on a day before he had become a pharaoh.

"Why did you say Cairo, Illinois? What made you say that?"

"Because she comes from there."

Philo did not answer. He picked up Grote's *Greece*, vol. ix, and focused on a line.

"Philo, she died, didn't she?"

Philo's eyes went up into his head which signified that the conversation was over.

But the memory of their mother had degenerated to a status symbol between them. There was not one photograph. Theo claimed to remember what she looked like because he was three years old and Don only a baby when she disappeared. He described her: She had black hair and she was beautiful. Don found a picture in the *Encyclopaedia Britannica*, the replica of the head of a Minoan woman stamped on a coin, which he believed to be his mother.

Besides the quilt she had left a copy of *Seven Pillars of Wisdom* by T. E. Lawrence, inscribed: "For Philemon Tsambalis, Christmas 1944, from his loving wife (of one year!)." The exclamation mark was incongruous and vulnerable. It made Don feel sorry for the lady, a disguise of his mother, who had written it. But the title itself commanded him. Threatened him not to go backward but always to face the East for pillars could be salt as well as caryatids.

His real mother was the woman behind them all. As a child, he saw her so clearly he could never forget, dark with black waving hair on cool white skin. She had pale golden eyes, like Philo's, which loved him, and she bathed him in gold when she leaned over him. But the leaning-over threatened some terrible bliss that never came to be. An embrace. He fantasized this embrace: She wore a gray, thin, ruffly dress; his head was just on the verge of being enveloped in her bosom; bosom because he had no notion of it having outlines, of being formed by two breasts; if there was flesh it was only a cool white space above a cleavage which did not show; it was an impending soft, deep, and enveloping embrace, faintly perfumed and endless; a place but not a touch; it remained forever filmy. If the embrace could have been completed, he would have known something. Thus, there was a monstrousness in her absence and in the figment of the mother who had inscribed the *Seven Pillars of Wisdom* because she was the frail copy incorporated into this greater Mother.

He was wily behind his quietness, and obstinate.

Weeks later, when the threat of questions had died down, he asked, "What did our mother die of, Philo?"

"Diphtheria," answered Philo.

About three in the morning they landed at Corfu to refuel. He decided to get off, since it was nearer his destination than Crete. He would visit Thea Vasiliou in the Peloponnesus on the way to Athens. He jumped out to find the pilot; the commander was dead to the world, his mouth wide open, his head lolling.

"Tell him thank you for the ride," Don said.

He headed for the airport building and looked for signs of the junta. A dirty white-and-powder-blue sign extolled the Revolution as he entered the glass door: GREECE FOR GREEK CHRISTIANS. The airport building was new. It echoed. Lit in garish neon on the central pillar was a poster with the junta's blue phoenix symbol.

But there was only one customs man on duty.

"I've just come in on a U.S. military plane," he said, showing his ID. The official was perfunctory, chalked his pack and waved him in.

A man in a hound's-toothed sports coat and with large gold rings on his fingers stared at him with lugubrious, sly eyes. He was smoking. His cheeks were as fat as a chipmunk's and his mouth bloomed like a wet rose around the cigarette. When he took the cigarette from his mouth, he held it between his index and middle fingers, extending his little one so that the nail showed a full inch long.

Don ignored the arrogance.

He looked for the taxis. Inert upon one of the black vinyl benches lay something that looked like a mummy wrapped up in a sleeping bag. He went out the glass door.

The night was dark. Nothing but a covey of millers battering themselves

24

to rags against the snoring neon tube. When he turned around a girl's head with taffy hair and red marks from the imprint of the sleeping bag on her cheek had emerged from the cocoon.

"Where are the taxis? Do you know?" he asked in English.

"There's one asleep under the tree down there." She had an accent. Was it French or Dutch?

The brutal chipmunk was talking to the customs man, sounds mangled by the acoustics and the night into a mass for technology.

"Hey, wait a minute!" The girl wriggled out of the bag and flashed a smile like Jeanne Moreau's. "Can I get a ride with you to town?"

"Sure."

"Go see the taxi driver then. I'll be ready in one jiff." She took her comb out and attacked her hair. He was touched by her British slang and her eagerness.

The taxi was an old Chevy with a lace curtain in the back window. He tapped on the windshield, and the driver, stretched like a dog on the front seat, awoke.

"Amesos." Hawking up phlegm, he spat out the opposite window toward a black Vauxhall.

When Don went to get the girl, the brutal chipmunk and the customs official were in altercation.

"Sto diavolo!" shouted the customs man. "I can't anoint every damn American with holy water. What do you expect me to do?"

Don could not hear what the chipmunk answered. The customs official cut him off again with: *"Coutos!* Get off my back and mind your own business, you two-bit crook, or I'll report you for interfering with customs."

The chipmunk turned as if nothing had happened, and approaching Don and the girl, intercepted them at the doorway. Addressing the girl in impeccable English, he said, "I'm driving into town. Perhaps you like to ride with me? Both of you," he added, showing teeth to Don.

"Thanks. I've got a cab already."

The girl stretched out her hand to Don, and like a ballet already rehearsed, he partnered her out the door, leaving the image of the chipmunk as a reflection on the glass.

In the cab she sat with her feet on the sleeping bag.

"My name's Annette. Good work on the creep."

"Mine is Don."

"Can I use the bathroom at your hotel?"

"Okay."

They had not got rid of the chipmunk. Two eyes of light followed them. It was the Vauxhall.

"Are you French?" he asked.

"Belgian. And you-all's from the South, ain't you, honey?" she mimicked.

She had not earned Zoe's intimacy.

" 'Scuse me, honey," he retorted, "there's a draft in here. Would you lift your feet? I want to get a sweater out of my pack."

He put on the green sweater over his shoulders.

"Did you bring sink plugs?" she asked in her normal accent.

"No. I forgot." She was an Aphrodite, and all the Aphrodites are floating around dead in the twentieth century, embalmed in *Playboy*.

Double rooms cost the same as a single room, but did he want a girl?

The road was very smooth and the driver too fast. Last time he had come to Corfu the road was dirt. Her mouth smelled of toothpaste. She had given her teeth a brush without water. Now why would she want a bathroom? Athena's olive trees passed them, tender, dusty heads in the auto lights.

"I always pick Class D hotels," he said.

"Me too."

"You're one of these fifty-dollar-per-month-budget types who boasts all the time?"

She smiled coyly, more certain of her charms. "I'll go half and half with you on a hotel room. Brother and sister and no strings."

They had to pretend to be an Athena in this century whether they were or not. He mused sadly that the olive leaves' silver was coated with dust. Their heads, fondled since Homeric times by winds both delicate and violent, it was anachronistic that they could be so old, their trunks so gnarled and gaped with ancient holes, yet their hair was always so vulnerably graceful.

"Why do you travel alone?"

"Male chauvinist."

"Well, how do you keep the men off?"

"In France, I lure them into an intellectual discussion about sex. In Italy, I tell them I'm picking up my baby from my father's house."

26

He smiled, but the monklike thing in him that strove beyond the biological to reach Woman required collaboration from *the* woman. He was an old child in church, always taking the cloth off the altar to see beneath. And was it really wine in the goblet?

He considered himself to be of that brand of men who, despite appearance or inclination, are irresistible to women. Rasputin, Truman Capote, Tyrone Power, Lord Byron, Leopold Stokowski, Charles Manson, D. H. Lawrence, and Toulouse-Lautrec, deformed, handsome, homosexual, or brave, it did not matter: they were of the moon and had in common an essence beyond malehood, a sensitivity to women. They could identify with women. The moon commanded them as males to worship women. They were aware of themselves as instruments of the moon. Sometimes the worship was transposed, as with Byron, who, the focus of extravagant worship by women, hated what he attracted. And the most male of them, Rasputin, *was* a woman and used his maleness as the sport of his womanhood, occupying both with a religious extravagance that exploded the empire.

Don's cockmanship always ended in his having to assuage the jealousy of double-y chromosomers who could not believe that slight build (he was barely six feet), those opaque blue eyes, and olive skin, that burnished red hair (unimpressive, deceptive), that sad, even corrupt face, the face of an old person or a fox, could melt girls. They took his tender manners for faggotry or fanaticism. "I'm a Latin. You've got to make allowances for that," he told them, smiling to cover an aloofness that extended even to the women he slept with, a gamut, except for his faithful year with Kitty—wonderful orgasms without soul—which ran from fourteen-year-olds to women past fifty. As if knowing women in the separateness, mating their cunts with his malehood, he could keep the real woman from forever escaping, fleeing to that realm that would always demand his worship. Escaped the woman because she could not understand or inhabit her womanhood. He had tried with Kitty, who was so smart, successful, and kind. She hated his irony, but could not bear that "more" that possessed him.

"What is it you *want* of me?" she complained.

"You," he answered once, and repeated it over and over until it was only a sound, no connection with the Kitty he knew at all.

But he knew possession of separate cunts was not the way to discovery, even though it kept him in the game.

"Annette What?" he asked.

"Annette Borlin."

Her mauve T-shirt and cool could not disguise that she was a sad pouter pigeon. She was slightly vulgar and kept touching her fake-gold charm bracelet and wetting her lips. He saw that she wanted to rise in the fluid society as Aphrodite had risen in Zeus's cut-off balls. So he ignored her little assaults, and paid respect to her masks because she had no understanding of herself. He played savior and felt responsible.

The taxi left them on the quay. The town seemed larger than he remembered. He paid sixty drachmas, and stood watching until the taxi bleated off into the night leaving them silence. The cobbles were shining with dew in the street lamps, the masts biting at angles to the street, chewing with the sea while dark housefronts watched.

Two lights crept furtively from the direction they had come, and then switched off. The Vauxhall.

"Christ, he's persistent," he said, denying the eeriness he felt and pulling her arm. "Come on. The cheap hotels are up side streets. They're so narrow he can't follow."

They ducked out from under the street lamp, across the wide plateia, around a corner, and up an alley, the Vauxhall approaching them as a huge, silent-moving shape, completely dark. Their footsteps knocked loudly in their ears. They turned right into a warren, went under an arch, and lost him.

"You got screwed by that taxi," she told him. "They're not supposed to charge more than forty."

"Look. Here's a place," he said.

It was the Xenodoheo Neraida, and it took more than five minutes to wake up the patron. He was a fat man in pajamas. While they were bargaining, Annette almost tipped over the pot of geraniums on the landing.

He decided: no gallantry. Took the first shower, cold water, soaping himself with Palmolive, then chose a bed and went right to sleep to the sound of water and rustling.

Water dropped onto his bare chest. He smiled and moved over for her. She was older than he wanted, twenty-two probably. Twenty-two was the age Kitty had decided to change her nickname to Chris. Her real name was Christine. It had affected his love but not his sexual capabilities. He always marveled what white-velvet animals girls were, and explored the hair, downy between her legs. Pioneer. He started by canoe up the Haw River. He always traveled toward the source, taking tributaries like Daniel Boone, partly to do obeisance to their particularity, even though he liked them young and desired to do it quick. Strange, he wanted them younger, the older he grew, further from the mystery.

He was rough on her. She began to tremble and he knew she liked it. But the Haw was dry, filled with sharp stones like Greek dry riverbeds, and he had to go upward on foot over endless stones in the meandering course. Every bit of abrasion increased his tenacity. If trying to find the source was the wrong direction for exploring, he knew that the Haw in its downflow emptied into the Cape Fear before it found the sea. He desired the sea beyond everything. But first, he insisted, he had to find the source.

As a pioneer he was always walking, walking on sharp stones, up smaller and smaller tributaries. It was exciting to them because he was indefatigable. In his mind's eye, he saw the Atlantic past Wilmington. He floated at Killdevil Hill with Theo-Orville, his brother. Over Hatteras it was dangerous. She was coming now. Flashing, translucent fish were under him, but though she lured him with her cascade, he kept his trek up toward the source. There were larger waterfalls. He let her third climax carry him backward, and he floated to the place he had started, no further. He opened his eyes to identify her.

She must be aware that his aptitude was endless, because he had never won the source of anyone with all his pursuits over stony paths, winding tributaries, never getting discouraged. His loneliness and stoniness were irresistible.

"God, you're fantastic," she breathed, staring at him with glistening eyes.

The source must be in some scrub-bush mountain territory. Was it Ida or one of the Appalachians? He kissed the sweat from her shoulders and said nothing. He did not care if she was sorry he strove in the wrong direction. But she did not even know. He left his eyes, a high, thin blue for her, wondering narcissistically if he looked religious. Then he sank to sleep to the lullaby of the waking town, the chatter of Lambrettas, the clinks of water glasses on metal trays, clops of donkey hooves, and the smell of baking bread.

When he woke at noon there was a note pinned on his work shirt: "9 am (or thereabouts). Meet me at the zaharoplasteion opposite the PO for breakfast."

He took a shower, shaved, put on his green sweater again, paid the hotel bill, and left. The next departure for Igoumenitsa was the ferryboat *Alexandros,* a small, white vessel with grease stains dripping from an open porthole down its white hull. It left in a half hour. A crowd cordoned by ropes had formed on the quayside. Aiming his camel's hump for the best leverage, he inserted himself midway. He could get breakfast on board. "You're letting yourself be screwed again," he heard her say in his mind's ear.

The crowd, reacting to the appearance of the gangplank, began to yell, pick up their baggage, and move.

Suddenly he saw her. She was riding a red bicycle at the edge of the crowd, looking in all directions. He waved, keeping step with the crowd and jostling them with his hump.

"Annette!"

She paused, balanced on one foot. "Why didn't you meet me for breakfast?" she shouted.

"Have to go!"

"Where are you headed?"

"Igoumenitsa."

She looked puzzled.

"Patras!"

For a moment she drooped like a pigeon. The bicycle and the consistency of the crowd, teeming and thick as oatmeal, forbade her coming nearer.

"Where are *you* going?"

"Swimming. Canoni."

Suddenly, he saw the brutal chipmunk at some distance behind her. He was dressed in a business suit and carried an attaché case. The man saw him and their eyes locked for a second. But the glance was noncommittal, as if triumph were not involved.

"The chipmunk!" he yelled, trying to warn her, but he had not confided that metaphor to her. She looked puzzled.

"What?"

Well, she could take care of herself, no doubt.

When he looked again, the chipmunk had disappeared in the crowd, and the river of people was taking him up the gangplank. Annette Borlin became clearer and smaller, her shoulders more sloping than he had noticed at close range, and now that he was no longer distracted by the bobbling of her breasts under the mauve T-shirt, he saw her as the Botticelli Aphrodite. She got on her bicycle, and the last sight, before the white metal of the ship's door got in the way, was of her blue-jeaned thighs pumping up and down as she pedaled as fast as the beak of a small bird pecking crumbs.

*H*e picked a place in the bow near the gunwales, took off his pack, and propped it against a pile of rope.

The anchor chain ground upward on its pulley with a deafening clank. The sea was calm in the harbor and the sun hot, but outside there was a breeze. They passed a grapefruit rind in the steel-blue water and a soggy Tide carton. As the ship throbbed beyond the last cliff, its horn belched a good-by moo.

Leaving the pack, he made his way past an Australian family and headed for the galley. On the stairway down, he came face to face with the brutal chipmunk for the second time.

So he was not following Annette!

Again, the man made no sign of recognition. Don pretended not to know him either. But the artificiality made him avert his eyes. He looked at the man's shoes. They were two-toned, white-and-beige raffia, the white retouched with chalky dye, and the heels elevated by iron cleats. This microscopic view got him past and, down in the hold, he sat at the empty bar and ordered cappuccino and a stale croissant.

In the mirror, he saw the shoes disappearing out the top of the stairway onto the deck, and the empty space made him turn his eyes upward to the picture of Papadopoulos grinning between two blank ovals where portraits of Constantine and Anne-Marie must have hung. Papadopoulos looked like Alfred E. Neuman. The waiter slopped the cappuccino. What was that faint odor of cologne?

He felt anxious about his pack on deck. He imagined it sitting untended, unguarded, where the brutal chipmunk walked.

"Countries as diverse as England, America, Canada, and Germany have used potatoes as a staple diet for years," the radio announcer said, quoting Papadopoulos, "and the people of these countries are rigorous. Therefore, it is apparent that the Greek people can profit by such an example."

He ordered some Papadopoulos Biscuits—they had no connection—paid the counterman twelve drachmas, and started back up the stairway. His disquiet grew as the announcer went on about the subject of potatoes, giving the government edict that made it law for potatoes to be served by public restaurants every Tuesday and Thursday.

When his head rose above the top rung, he had the sensation that the chipmunk had been tampering with the pack. He was in mid-stride heading away from it.

Don jumped forward to inspect. Quick, flagrant, he pulled the buckles open. He wanted the man to know he suspected.

The coufetta was safe in the ski jacket. He did not take it out. He shook it. The almonds rattled. Everything else was in place, his clothes, his snorkel, his mask, his ping-pong gear. He checked the outside flap again. The prong of the buckle was fastened in the fourth hole. Hadn't Zoe put it in the third?

The chipmunk was pretending not to notice, leaning on the rail, looking out to sea. He opened a box of Papastratos, took a cigarette between his index and third finger, inserted it between his rosebud lips, and placed the box back in his pocket. In a deft movement, he brought from another pocket an expensive, gold cigarette lighter, moved a finger, exploded a sinister spurt of fire, touched the cigarette and breathed in. Exhaling lightly, he pocketed the instrument, turned, and, without having once looked Don in the eye, went aft and disappeared into the lounge.

Such insolent style! Was he a government agent or a crook? What was he looking for? Why had he wanted customs to go through his pack?

He conjured up Zoe's face for a clue. The Face came to him so easily that he was struck with wonder at the uneven weights of different moments in life. Was it really a coufetta of almonds? He fantasized that he was carrying microfilm, photographs—even explosives—the accoutrements of Athena. The Face split off from Zoe bringing him to the same emotion he had had when he was with her, when he felt he "knew" her, a knowledge like love, compared to which the intervening hours with Annette were petty. Soon Annette would be swallowed up in a past he would forget. But apart from the Face, what did he know about Zoe? Suppose she had embroidered his fantasies, led him on with talk of Resistance to hide some other enterprise. Dope, for instance. He did not believe it. She could have used him, yes, but he "knew" she would not have operated from a paltry motive.

Possibilities crowded into his mind:

That the sugared almonds were really almonds. Nothing in them at all. Innocent.

That the brutal chipmunk was not following him, was not interested in his pack, knew nothing of the almonds and was not looking for them.

That the whole thing was a coincidental phenomenon upon which he was projecting his own suspicions.

That it was really true that Zoe "happened" to be "passing by" the Grili.

He went over the circumstances. When she had asked him to deliver the coufetta, he had been eager. He had looked at it as an opportunity. He had acted as if he was born to do some mission for a woman. But some unconscious layer of his mind had caught at the contradiction inherent in their meeting—had she come to the Grili to "find" some American GI to take a dangerous thing into Greece, knowing he would not be subject to customs, or had she just "happened" to be there as she said?—and he had stood her up. At that point, he had taken over the decision himself. He had gone looking for the mission. He had refused her terms and made his own. All his life he had been good at sex and control, just as he had been bad at love and ultimate purpose.

He had connected Zoe with the Athena theology, but what had Athena to do with eggs? Zoe's legato, fierce silence might be the pole of the terrible cry that Earth rang up when Athena sprang full born, but Zoe had a child, Athena had not. Zoe had given him eggs, Athena had no connection with eggs. Zoe had a wound for a mouth, Athena was supposed to be serene in her might. So who was Zoe? A new configuration?

In his mind he saw the icons as always waiting. The history of mankind was made up of conscious and unconscious molds. The process of your life settled you in some groove patterned by music, history, literature, movies, pictures. The icon of Merlin, Clark Gable, Orestes, Fatty Arbuckle, or Adonis was always waiting for you. The molds acted on the persons and the persons on the molds, an unending multiplication of statics, culminating in the death of the universe. (Even the death of the universe was an archetypal myth which multiplied itself, containing the paradoxical equation: the number of times the end of the world has been forecast equals the degree to which man does not believe it; yet this is how man becomes the servant of that death.) All encounters are ballets as artificial as partnering Annette Borlin through a revolving door, as artificial as the ping-pong ritual. And the only way to escape the icon is to go through it to the truth.

And how do you discover the truth? He, being a good critic and the son of Philo the icon-maker, could spot an icon in a second. By the process of translating psychological theory into iconography, look at Theo: Theo, who rebelled against everything Philo preached, had become the perfect icon of a husband, by marrying Ann Marie. The icon had been set up by Philo, who didn't have to have a living wife because he wore his phantom wife as armor. About all those widows, schoolteachers, and dieticians who had brought them dishes of Brunswick stew, thinking: Poor motherless boys! He had crowed: "They all want to marry me." They had, too. "Does he fuck them? do you think?" Theo had whispered when they arrived at puberty. They pretended he did, for they longed for him to marry one of them, any one of them at all. His faithfulness to their mother gave him the self-righteousness of a god. And that was what they had to escape. Theo had become what he resisted. And so Don believed the only way you can escape becoming an icon is to see it. Yet even that was not enough. The truth lay in what you did not know. He did not know the female power. That is what he called the Goddess.

He got up. He pushed his way past the coil of rope, ducked behind a canvas-covered lifeboat and positioned himself along the gunwale. The V of the prow was cutting the sea, forcing a glorious swath of foam upward in brutal arcs of purpose.

After all, how far did he want to go in his mission for a woman? Did he want to kill or be killed for Zoe? That's what it might come down to. Positions that could lead to violence could lead to shit. That was the crock that was life. He did not sit among the honeysuckle like Philo talking shit as silver lining. He had seen stupidity, violence, shit. Ubiquitous. And it was random shit that was the worst.

Miserable Brill, the master sergeant known by 127th Maintenance at Sutton Hoo as "The All-Purpose Loser," had fingered him in that dirty note pinned to the backseat of the Catalina which he had used for his suicide. Ah, that MP picture of him blown to the proportions of a toadfish with carbon monoxide! "It doesn't matter about life if a Greasy Greek can alianate the effactions of my fiance in who I invested true love not to mention more than 16,000 dollars. English girls are nigs that son off a bitch have no Consciance." How suitable, those extra alphas! Brill had not known when he had done it either. Brill was totally effectless, which made it all the more unseemly but understandable that Whatshername had sneaked herself into his barracks. The barracks were Quonset huts. Hilary Banscomb, that was it. She had been going to marry Brill, for his money presumably, which was before his trouble. He got caught dealing hash and was about to be court-martialed. Don could not remember the Quonset hut fuck either. Greed, guilt, jealousy, malice, stupidity.

He threw the coufetta out of his skull. The spout of water ejected it upward. It fell back into the sea and was ground through the ship's passage of water and left to float in its wake. It floated for many years in the Mesoghion, between the two shores of his imagination, and the child whom Zoe had named Free was grown up, an old man, when the silver cylinder washed ashore. The almonds were destined to be eaten by his own descendants. The tragedy lay in the fact that they would be unaware of the connection. So the child's fate would be lost as all modern men's fates are lost because they do not understand their connections.

He did nothing. His identification with the ship's engine throbbing gave his outward being a languor which disguised the resolution beneath. He was committed beyond any experiment in self-betrayal. He would deliver the almonds as he had promised.

First, he would go to Metamorphosis to see if Thea Vasiliou were still alive. Then he would go to Athens.

Nevertheless, when he left the prow and took off his green sweater to lay down on the coil of rope for a siesta in the sun, he felt that he had merely been too lazy to throw it overboard. He rested his head against the rope, closed his eyes, and lay with his arm holding the pack.

He had lost or shaken the chipmunk. He took a bus from Igoumenitsa to Ioannina, then on to Patras, where he spent the night. The next day he was in Kalamata. It was an ass-backward way to get to Metamorphosis. The sun, the dry, hot air had taken effect. He thought wryly that it was less his transfers from one rattletrap bus to another that had made him lose the chipmunk than the fact that the burning air of the mountains had scorched his imagination. Now that there was no danger, he liked the feeling of carrying the coufetta. It gave him purpose in a luxurious void of freedom. He never let his pack out of sight for long. When he was carrying it, he imagined the nest of eggs and remembered the feel of her fingers. The Face was behind the hump accompanying him.

Although the distance from Kalamata to Sparta was not far as the crow flies, the road was so bad no buses ran. People told him he'd have to go around by Tripolis, ninety kilometers out of the way. He did not believe it. He asked others. At last someone told him there was a minibus that went over the Taygetus mountains. It took him another hour to find the bus station. It was a room facing the dry riverbed in a back section of town.

When he went in, a woman was staring at him out of a gloom caused by large wine hogsheads blocking the window. She looked like an English-woman, plump, with a pink, schoolgirl complexion. Or a Renoir. At least forty years old. She rushed toward him with a gaze beautiful but inane, pointed at something behind his head which she recognized and which filled her with joy. He started to look back to see what it was when he realized she had a cast in her eye, and that she was looking at him.

"Are you going to Sparta, too?" She breathed too eagerly.

He hunched his shoulders and said: *"Nicht englisch."*

It was an American accent. Ignoring the fact he was German, she went on: "Of course I don't understand Greek too well, but . . ."

The perfect coiffure of black, wavy hair made a frame. Yet her features, her mouth a bloom, an enticing hollow between the two buds of her upper lip, dissolved into one another. She defied outline. Everything about her was intent, intimate. The aim of her gaze being off target, it was like having a lopsided flashlight trying to ferret you out, defying what it sought. He jumped inside his skin uncomfortably.

He went to look for the clerk. He faked a German-accented Greek. The man was dirty, sullen, and bored. He confirmed what she had told him.

The woman had turned and was reeling uncertainly toward a line of chairs by the window. Her legs were beautiful, shapely, but ludicrously small for her bulk, so that she teetered with each graceful step as if she might tip over.

For the first time he noticed that there was a third person. A youth of seventeen or eighteen. He was sitting in the row of chairs following her moves with suspenseful black eyes. His face was handsome and eager, clustered with rich, black curls.

He jumped up as if to save her, catching her elbow with his hand, drawing her to one of the chairs.

"Excuse me," he breathed, delighted with his catch. "I speak to you because you are stranger and I can teach my English."

Don took off his pack and sat down to straddle a chair. In the shadow of one of the hogsheads he was a Nazi spy.

"You are first English stranger I have ever talked."

"Oh, is that so?"

She was kind. She was refined. One of these middle-aged ladies who travels the world oohing and aahing over everything and staying in the best hotels. Her beauty swallowed up the views she probably painted in watercolor badly, her helplessness prevailing over donkeys, bellboys, peasants, and poppies.

"My name is Pavlos. I like very much to help you."

"Oh, thank you. I don't think there's very much to be done, except to possess our souls in patience." Her eyes searched as futilely as a lighthouse beam, but he was safe.

"Soul." Pavlos sighed, and moved nearer to her.

"When does the next taxi go?" she asked.

"Oh, it is not taxi."

"What is it?"

"Minnie Bouse."

"What?" she asked, looking shocked, her interest caught at last.

"Minnie Bouse." He faltered as if something were wrong.

"But— Why Minnie Mouse?"

"Because it is micro. Little. To Bouse what Minnie is to miniskirt."

She appreciated this. Her laughter made separate notes like bell peals.

The window behind their heads revealed a parade of nuns. They crossed the steel footbridge carrying wool bags and broken-down suitcases and poured into the street. A Papa leaning on his staff brought up their rear. He was old, tall, and cross-looking, with a yellow beard cascading from his chimney-pot hat. They swarmed among some parked gasoline trucks and headed for the minibus door.

Their footsteps made the woman turn around. When she saw them she jumped up excitedly. "One, two, three, four, five . . . There are nine of them!"

The first nun to enter, a crone, stared at her, incredulous, through gold-rimmed eyeglasses.

"Kali imera!" she breathed rapturously. *"Piges sti Sparti?"*

A second nun, white-faced, sickly, with the beginnings of a soft-black mustache, raked her with a pronged stare, picking up each detail, robin's-egg-blue suit, gray Hush Puppies, white purse, nylon stockings, before she forked the feasible culprit, Pavlos.

"Sparta, Sparte, Sparti," repeated the woman trying out endings. Was it coincidence, her conjugating the unconjugational? He felt suffocated.

"Nine in one fell swoop!" she was saying to Pavlos. She was slightly intimidated. "But I can't make them understand. I don't speak good Greek."

"Do you like the Beatles?" Pavlos was as defiant as if he were guilty and uttered the words just as the Papa entered.

The Papa flapped his robes in a grace note. He sucked in the scene. The lady turned an admiring gaze on him, which he discarded with a flick of his snake eyes. He went to stand at the end of the room by a bag of wheat, staring, both hands on his staff. The aimless movements of the nuns, which he paid no attention to, bumping against each other like animals, setting broken valises on the floor, choosing chairs to unload themselves on, filled the room with expectation and a smell of old wool and cheese. Having arrived, they acted as though they had fulfilled some purpose and that the next step was up to the clerk or God. The Papa made no move either.

In his corner, Don felt safer than ever, for Pavlos and the American lady became the cynosure of the Second Waiting. They were the center of a vacuum, untouchable, focal until someone committed himself about the minibus. It was sadistic, the suspense.

The Papa turned his gaze away from them, patient as a martyr. His disagreeable expression turned aggrieved, suffering. He was frail.

The sickly nun opened a bag of walnuts and offered them. A fat nun cracked one between her teeth. The sound cleaved the universe like a gavel and it was followed by coos, desultory tatters of conversation. No one looked at them directly. The noises were a disguise for killing time, a dance around the canyon of silence.

"Why don't *you* ask them?" the lady suggested.

"What do you think of the Grateful Dead?" Pavlos persisted. He tried to scrunch himself into a ball to hide from the accusing eyes behind her plumpness.

"I don't know pop groups."

" 'Tangerine' is my favorite."

In his corner Don had no favorites. He felt his habitual, suspect tenderness for all principals. "Pythagorean!" Philo had sneered when he had first consciously taken up his position of being uninvolved.

But Pavlos looked at his shoes between each sentence, his suit faltering.

"Excuse me," he said getting up.

"Goody! You're going to ask!"

He looked more as if he were debating whether or not to take a leak. He drew worry beads from his pocket and began strolling the length of the room, clicking them behind his back. In a calculated decision he turned, bee-lined for the Papa, picked up his old spotted hand and pecked it like a kernel of corn.

This charade of unknown quantities corresponded to that parade of motives, a universe of refusals as taut, as well balanced as Pythagoras's music of the spheres. He was galvanized. Something was about to give, to break.

It did not. Pavlos did not ask. Obeisance constituted absolution for the future. He returned beaming. "Make lah-ve, not war." The lady could not disguise her disappointment.

The action only increased opposition, and the nuns began to whisper as they stared.

The stalemate was broken by the arrival of a farmer with baggy trousers, a black armband, and highly polished shoes. He entered the office expectantly, looked at the clerk, and said loudly to no one in particular, "What? Are they going?"

"Dir-r-rty, ignorant priests. They have lice in their beards." Philo imitated them, standing on the tractor seat as if it were a pulpit, pee-pah-pohing the ritual while he swung an imaginary censer through the blossoms. He was a monotone, couldn't keep a tune. Don and Theo ate these performances up, clapped and whistled. Philo was right, most of them smelled of garlic or newly cobbled shoes, but it did not mitigate that exoticism. It was like finding out what you always knew but in a totally different way from how you knew it.

The farmer tiptoed to the Papa's ear, whispered obsequiously, then clapped to the clerk: "Come on, thirteen is plenty enough!"

"Why didn't you say you wanted to go to Sparta, Papouli?" The clerk pretended to be offended.

They were ignorant, yes, but it was blossoms of faith to decorate the narrow mind.

Everything turned into a hubbub. The nuns rose in black waves. The clerk pushed out the doorway. A shouting started in the street. A minibus pulled up screeching. The driver jumped out, clapped hands, and ordered everybody to take their baggage aboard.

Don threw his pack over his shoulder and came out of his spy nook. Immediately, he was caught in the traffic of nuns pushing and battering with their baggage.

Two rivers formed. One plucked Pavlos up, separating him from the lady and churned Don like flotsam out the doorway toward the back mudguard of the minibus, where the sickly nun was waiting in a backwash. The second caught him with a wedge formed of the fat nun who, driven from behind, rammed between him and his hump counterclockwise past their conversation.

The sickly nun was lisping a warning into Pavlos's ear, "Be careful."

"Of what, *kalo gria?*"

"You know what."

"I don't—"

"Decency. You are a decent Greek boy. You know right from wrong. She is a foreign woman and doesn't know any better, so it's up to you. Do not disgrace your family and country."

Shoved past them, out of hearing, Don found himself plunged headlong at the lady, who was fumbling in her purse. To avoid hitting her he twisted himself and pulled himself upward into the canlike interior of the bus. The lady bounced in his wake. She turned twice, a movement which precisely coordinated with the pendulum swing of the crone's woolen bag, which administered a spank to her backside. She was spanked up the two steps of the minibus and catapulted into the window seat across the aisle from him. He feared for his Germanhood. Too close.

By that time, pouncing for the best seats had begun. The fat nun snatched the seat next to the lady, but even that was ineffective as a barrier. How long till the lady recognized him and pledged allegiance? They were both Americans, conjugators, and epithet-indulgers.

Pavlos was defused. They drove him toward the backseat and barricaded him in a corner with a turret of valises topped by cheese in newspapers.

The minibus started its motor. To get out of the city it careened, hooting its horn, between trailer trucks and donkeys. In a few minutes they were on the Kalamata plain. It was hot. The nuns spread out. The crone and the sickly nun occupied the seats behind him. Beads of perspiration popped out on the fat nun's face and she fanned herself with her handkerchief. The sickly nun sighed. The crone gazed out the window and wiped her eyes. The only people who looked cool were the Papa, and the lady herself, who smiled dreamily in the seat behind him.

The minibus climbed up into the mountains, passing a forest of evergreens, a logging camp, and a herd of goats.

Don recognized what was going to happen before anyone else, even before the sickly nun, who was a territorial preemptor, who conceived her goal piecemeal, not gestalt. Each step, done out of necessity, spread like melting butter, requiring a new step.

The first step, she sighed. The second, she rearranged her luggage in the aisle, switched the valise, shoved the woolen bag under the left buttock of the fat nun, who did not notice. The third, she looked longingly toward the American lady. The lady, unconscious of her intention, smiled back, but the sickly nun took it as an affront because of the cast in her eye, a secret signal of derision to the crone. The fourth step, the sickly nun remarked that she needed a window seat or she might faint. The fifth, she suggested she switch places with the lady since two fat people on one seat caused spillage. The fat nun paid no attention. The American lady did not understand. Here the serious ploy began. The sickly nun opened a newspaper containing cheese. She cut a slice of bread and handed it to the Papa. She cut a second piece for the lady just at the moment the minibus swerved. The Papa's mouth was open to take the first bite, but the bread and cheese fell to the floor. The wooden cross flipped out wildly from his neck. The minibus jammed on its brakes and the sickly nun was foiled. They had arrived at the village of Artemissia, five houses, a whitewashed toilet, a plane tree, and a horse fountain. It was a rest stop.

Don jumped out and walked down the road to stretch his legs. The mountain silence was punctuated by far-off sheep bells. The shade was cool.

When he returned, the nuns were flocked around the toilet and the lady was bathing her face luxuriously in the fountain. He waited thirstily for her to finish. The spout gurgled. Drops fell. She drank from her hands. Just as she lifted her face, he caught her gaze. She turned into his mother threatening him with the embrace. But it was a blue color, not gold as it had been when he was a child, and the irony was not lost on him that he was looking for the Goddess in Greece when that main mother force he had not known was un-Greek. Delicate woblets of fat trembled at her throat. The memory rose of when he had gone to Cairo, Illinois. Her mouth was open like a fish and drops shimmered on her nose. He wanted to identify her expression, thinking if he could call it by name her features might be burned into his mind. But despite the perfect nose, the hint of dimples in the round cheeks, he knew the minute he looked away everything would be indistinguishable. For there was a flowing which forbade the separation of the features: the cast in her eye was a metaphor for the fact that you could not identify. It was not comedy, tragedy, nobility, banality. It was not even enigma. At that moment, he had an epiphany about the Face.

At odd times in the histories of generations and nations there is thrown up an individual who is an embodiment of the race's wound. The sorrows of the North are different from the sorrows of the South. Deirdre's sadness has to be seen as a long-shot, the grace of Tara's harp, the sloping shoulder, the weeping willow, the bended neck. "Gracefully lost," or "Turned to sorrow." *Sorrow*, not *Tragedy* in the North. Philo scoffed at Sorrow, miscalling it Tragedy. Northern adversity in its mode of strength is granite and ice, crag-faces, jutted jaws, eyebrows of frost, not tragedy, but endurance. Thaw after a freeze renders this vision soft and wan, gracefully lost, disappearing in tears.

Only in the South can tragedy be achieved. It is because of the sun. The sun glazes. The sun makes forms clear. It glazes sorrow. Bronze, ceramic, it achieves form. Zoe's face was achievement in the flesh of the form of Tragedy.

In Greece, emotions are not valid until they are shared. Emotions in private are despised, considered miserly. To call sorrow sincere because you did not share it is to be a hoarder counting his gold. To expose is to exalt. To squander is to celebrate. To yield up sorrow is to make nobility real.

She was picking her way back toward the minibus shaking the drops off her hands and teetering. She passed Pavlos, skulking alone by the wheel, but he did not speak to her. As soon as she disappeared, Don lowered his head and drank enough to cross seven Saharas.

When he got in the bus, it had happened. The sickly nun had established a beachhead. She sat in the lady's seat, her valises stacked on the fat nun's seat in a barricade. Her mustache twitched.

The lady stood in the aisle with a shocked expression. She opened and closed her mouth several times, and then said in Greek—her voice was husky, her accent terrible—"You are welcome to my seat." She added in English: "You ninny." Her expression was quizzical rather than angry. He was not sure he had heard correctly.

"Me zaleezie," whined the sickly nun as an excuse.

The lady kept standing.

"Me zaleezie," the sickly nun repeated.

"Zaleezie? What is *zaleezie?"* asked the lady to no one in particular. She liked juicing this word in her mouth.

The fat nun standing opposite wove her finger around her temple to indicate that *zaleezie* signified dizzy.

The sickly nun repeated it once more, but her confidence was faltering.

"Den pirazei," said the lady, rhyming. She smiled almost shyly. "Feel free, you little orthodox crow," she crooned in English, and then she tipped her head slightly and uttered a peal of laughter.

"You should be ashamed, taking that lady's seat! You, a member of Evangelismos!" cried the fat nun.

The sickly nun half got up and pointing to her mouth aimed retching imitations to the ground.

"She will vomit unless she gets my seat? Vomit then, you poor little curd-faced church loon," said the lady in English. In Greek, however, she said, "It is your seat." She laughed some more.

The sickly nun was unnerved by this sympathy and English. She sweated. She made more excuses. Then she began dismantling her fortress.

"Den prepei," said the lady, to indicate that it was not necessary for her to move.

But the sickly nun caved in as if hexed. She toppled across the aisle with her baggage. She took her old seat in defeat. She hid her nose like a mole and ordered the window opened wider as if she were breathing her last gasp.

Five minutes later everyone was settled.

The lady continued to laugh secretly on the way up the mountain, little peals of infectious laughter. The road turned to dirt. He felt the minibus grow smaller in the rarefied air and the world dropped below them. But she continued to move her mouth silently. Was she practicing epithets? The road wound in tiers.

This episode had changed the status of the lady. The Papa turned around to look in her face. He stared at the O of her mouth, at the pulsations of her fat as she melted into the motions of the minibus.

"What is your name?" he asked in Greek.

"Cora," she answered giving him a smile, but returning her gaze to the olive heads going by outside.

"Kori. What a beautiful name! Where is your husband!"

"Dead." Her expression was serene as ever.

The Papa crossed himself. *"Doxasi O Theos!"*

The nuns swayed to and fro, like eggs in a carton. A cliff soared above the minibus.

"How many children have you?"

"Two. A girl and a boy."

Zoe did not have a baby, he thought suddenly. She had lied.

"Bravo. What are their names?"

"Corey and Eleanor."

The Papa mouthed the names, the mole at the base of his nose wobbling as his lips moved. Eleanor was a beautiful name, he speculated, but Corey could not be the name of a boy, since in Greek it meant "girl."

"They are grown up," she said in a non sequitur.

Zoe did not act like a mother. Not one atom of her was maternal. *That* was what was discrepant, not Athena.

"How old are you?" asked the Papa.

"Forty-seven."

When women became *miteres,* they spread, lost their outlines, became consonant with the earth and elements, lost themselves in *being.* They did not act.

The bus lurched toward the top of the mountain. Hair rose on the nape of Don's neck at the height. He had a feeling of floating. The light of the sun flattened the depths to nothing. This lady was in a game with the universe as strange as his own.

He did not like the look of the Papa's eyes. Sly, intriguing, a dirty yellow to match the rolled bun of his long yellow hair.

"Stop the raping of women," he had written in answer to the question Miss Cohen had asked in the Junior High School Questionnaire: "If you had a chance to do one effective act in your lifetime, what would it be?" Miss Cohen had responded with the appalled expression of one who suspects she had been insulted and spent the rest of the year trying to find out if he had been traumatized as a child or if someone in his family had been raped. How was she to know about Philo?

"Come with us, Kori," said the Papa, after the long silence of a reptile. "Come and be a nun."

"Where?"

"To Triandafila. We are going to sing the Seventh Mass."

The nuns began to laugh.

"Where is Triandafila?"

"The church at the crossroads above Mistra." His smile made his yellow goat's beard dirtier. "You like to be a nun?"

"No, I don't think so."

"Don't you want to be a nun?"

"No."

What could Don do with his protective instinct now that he had sealed himself into Germanhood? He willed the Papa to stop.

"At your age, it is good."

"I would have to wash floors."

"No floors. They would do it," he said, indicating the nuns. "To be a nun is a good thing. You have good food and live where you see the sun and birds and devote yourself to God."

"Poly kala, but I do not think I will."

The Papa gazed into her eyes.

"Kiss this cross," he ordered, picking it up from his breast, holding it out. "Kori, kiss this cross."

Don't do it, Don willed, trying to send the thought into her mind. Don't subjugate yourself.

She looked at it. She considered. The cross was made of wood. It was smooth and dirty, polished by people's mouths and hands. If she kissed it, she would have to bend her head near the Papa's narrow, crowlike breast, would have to take it from those ancient fingers, trembling with impatience, those dirt-engraved fingernails. Don't do it, he willed.

She took the cross. She looked into the Papa's eyes for a moment. She closed her own. And then she bent and touched it silently with her lips. When she raised her head, her eyes, which were supposed to be looking at the Papa, were focused on him.

"Who named the world?" asked the Papa to the captive congregation.

A nun crossed herself.

"Did I name the world?"

Nobody answered the Papa.

"Did you name the world?"

No one answered.

"Did I name the beasts? Did you name the beasts? Did you name the mountain? Did you name the air?" He went on in rhythm. "No. Man did not name the beasts. Man did not name the mountain. Man did not name the sky. Man did not even name himself."

Had his mother named him Dombey? Why, then, had Philo called him her name for those years?

"There sits on your left shoulder a spirit!" shouted the Papa. "Whose is the spirit?"

The nuns knew. They were bursting to tell.

The Papa frowned.

"That's the devil," the Papa told them. "The spirit that sits on your left shoulder is the devil."

"And there. There!" The Papa pointed to Cora's right shoulder. "There sits on your right shoulder another spirit. He is the Angel of God. He is God Himself. From your left shoulder, the devil whispers in your ear that you are a great man. But the good spirit talks of God. What are you?" asked the Papa, looking at Don.

"Nothing." The Papa answered his own question. "Did you name the mountain? Do you name the sea? Do you even name your own name? No. Only God names the bee. The bee could not exist except that God named him. And God named the air. He named the minibus. He named the flower. He named water. Nothing exists except that God names him."

The bus made a 180-degree turn, brushing thistles at odd places until he could not tell whether he was going up or down. Gorse brushed the windowpanes. Silver, green powder puffs.

The Papa began to sing in a whining voice. It was a hymn with the same format of solo and chorus as the "Great Ship Titanic." But with the Byzantine scale. The fat nun took over the solo from the Papa and the other nuns joined in, belting refrains as the bus climbed again. It gathered momentum. The song dismantled the sound of the motor giving the illusion that the singing was what suspended them in the air. They were hanging in space as they moved. This attenuation was accented by a sheer boulder which hung out over them from above.

At the top of the mountain the radiator began to steam. The driver drove down two tiers and stopped the bus on a hairpin turn. Instead of parking against the mountain, he turned the bus horizontally across the road.

"*Brakes etsi-ketsi,*" he explained, balancing his hand in the air. "This way minibus can't go over the edge."

Loose stones dropped from the back tires. It was a thousand feet down, and the minibus was blocking passage.

"All right, *paidia*. Water. Water for everyone!"

There was a stream. The driver filled his gallon can. The nuns got out.

Don followed Cora up the mountain. She was standing on a spot some distance away, gazing off the edge.

"You should never have kissed that cross," he said.

She turned in surprise. "You said you didn't speak English!"

"I'm sorry I said that."

"What possessed you, passing yourself off as German?"

"I was afraid you'd latch on . . . you know how tourists do? Why did you kiss it?" he repeated with a winning smile.

"I actually believed you were German."

"I would never have kissed it."

"Well, you're probably arrogant."

He reminded himself that she was middle-aged, and the middle-aged, with less posture to defend, are shrinking into essence.

"When you kissed it, what did you think about?"

"How old the wood was."

"Just about its being wood?"

"I thought of all the elements," she told him gravely. "Rock, gold, silver, iron, and wood. That wood had white grains through it. Also I thought of whether that pope's hands were greasy."

"And all the other mouths that had kissed it and hands that had touched it?"

"Wood holds history better than other elements, if it's kept for a long time. I don't care for history though," she said. "Making initials in trees. You can just see trees when they grow old turning into people. But you can't see rock growing old, so it remains inhuman."

"What are you, a geologist?" He waited for her to say "housewife."

"I'm a free agent." Little doughnut rings of fat pulsated around her neck as she wopsed this phrase in her mouth, and her eyes crinkled when it came out as clean as wintergreen.

He might as well have had this first meeting with her beneath the sea upon a topography of boulders, grasses, and fishes, for his recognition was on an oceanic level.

"Rock doesn't care about names or initials. I wish it *had* been a rock cross."

"You can't wear rock around your neck. You'd drown." Yes, he knew her. Insane people can travel more easily in foreign countries than sane ones, because they carry their own worlds. Deliberately, he stripped her down. "But go on. Why rock?"

"It's more basic. It has very slow currents, so slow that you think it isn't alive, that it's permanent."

"Where do you come from?" He suddenly decided that it was to be a friendship. Friendship demands introductions.

49

"Near Boston."

"And what do I call you? Mrs.—?"

"Ellison. But you can call me Cora."

"You can call me Don." He told her just enough to let her know he was a soldier and to explain Philo and Theo.

She became conventional.

"I have a son about your age. Nineteen."

"No," rejecting motherliness, "I'm twenty-four."

"Eleanor's husband is an architect. They have two children and they made over this old carriage house in Brookline. You remind me of my first boy friend," she continued. "He wanted to be a playwright and he was a genius. Or maybe he wasn't. Very intense, though. We were walking through the woods one day and it began to rain and then it came pouring down in sheets. I said, 'Let's go home and find shelter,' and he said, 'You want to be Emily Brontë, don't you?' Would Emily Brontë go in just because of a little rain?"

"*Did* you want to be Emily Brontë?"

"No. Well, maybe I wanted to make myself into the picture he had of me."

"Maybe *he* wanted to be Emily Brontë."

"Poor darling, he became a newspaperman." She said the "darling" like setting birds free.

"What made you come to Greece?"

"I came to look." She wopsed it up in her mouth again, rinsed it through her eyes like a spin dryer, and it came out elixir.

She was also escaping him by improvisation. She practiced a waltzing step which made her tipsy-turviness scarier than ever, ten thousand feet in the air.

"A friend of Corey's who just returned from a motorcycle trip through Baluchistan and India and Ceylon always answered that when tribesmen surrounded him like ants. They always understood. Do you know when I went to the Chase Manhattan Bank just before I left New York that the head of the savings account department told me he envied me, and that if he didn't have to work, he'd go? He thought the children were right, and he had this lifelong ambition to go to those caves and live."

He could not tell her that Matala was now dotted with little dried piles of shit. The world's hippies defecated where they stood. He liked her excited way of walking, her generosity, her irony, her sense of wonder, and her hands, flirtatious as wings. Classical habits of womanhood.

"I tell you what let's do. Let's have a picnic!"

He was a sucker for enthusiasm.

She pirouetted toward the minibus. "Get my suitcases down," she ordered the driver. "Those white ones!"

The driver abandoned the radiator. The nuns began to cluster around to see what was happening. Pavlos, sitting on a stone by the stream, got up.

"Do what she says!" said the farmer with the black armband. He cuffed the driver and pointed to her luggage.

The driver climbed up and pulled the suitcases down, the large one and the small. White. Matching. Expensive. Wouldn't he know!

Cora spread a cloth across the road. She positioned the larger suitcase toward the mountain, like an altar. She summoned everyone.

"Sit down!" She waved.

The nuns lowered themselves, curious. They stared.

She lifted the lid of the large suitcase carefully. She took out six glasses wrapped in some scarves, and produced a jar of Peter Pan peanut butter from a blue negligee.

"I have peanut butter!" she said, turning toward him triumphantly.

She unpacked a knife and took a Kleenex-wrapped loaf of bread, which she gave to the man with the black armband.

"Cut the bread," she told him, and he obeyed.

Her movements were delicate and her voice had a husky ring to it. They were transfixed, the nuns, even the Papa, who sat on the gallon can at the edge of the cloth. It was an awe of silence.

The sickly nun inhaled the smell of the peanut butter, and the hairs of her mustache twitched slightly.

"Why don't they talk?" Cora asked softly, and she made signs for them to take their portions.

She spread peanut butter on a piece of bread and gave it to the Papa. He bit a round chunk and tasted it. He was silent. She looked anxiously. His tongue cleaved to his palate, and he finally broke the mask of his face.

"Very tasty."

The nuns laughed.

Beyond the mountain, above the peak, the silence had an actual consistency so vast that their small litany, the suitcases, the sounds of their voices seemed tiny.

"Why you!" she cried suddenly, staring at Don. "You knew everything I said! Every nasty name I called her!" She put her hands on her knees and gave way to laughter so contagious, giblets of fat joggling beneath her neck and arms, that all the nuns, the Papa and even Pavlos began to laugh.

"*Yah sas!*" he said, raising his glass.

The nuns raised their glasses too.

The silence became louder, almost like a roar.

"What is this?" Don asked. "It's good!"

"Kool-Aid, oranges, and Sprite. I made it up myself!"

A taxi catapulted upon them, screeching around the bend from where they had come, barely able to stop in time. Its front tires spun dust at the edge of the picnic cloth. The nuns levitated in the cloud like dervishes, and scattered, screaming.

"You almost killed us, donkey!" cried the driver.

The taxi driver apologized. He was young, thick-torsoed, with a smooth, creamy face. He backed the taxi up and poised one arm out the window, watching, the motor idling.

"Offer him some peanut butter," said Cora, for the minibus driver was threatening to report him for reckless driving, and the man with the armband was cursing.

It was fishy. Any other Greek driver would have argued. After all, it was they who were blocking the road. He merely sat there, mild, hairline slightly too low, staring. What was he looking at?

The nuns were washing the glasses in the rain barrel. Cora was wiping them. Two nuns took up the tablecloth and shook it.

Cora repacked the glasses in the scarves, bending over her white suitcase with concentration. She closed the lid and snapped the hasps.

Don felt as if he had known that taxi driver in another life. His shoulders were powerful, swelling in knots under a see-through shirt. There was a name on the tip of his mind for that genus of men he belonged to. But before he could say it, he found himself following the driver's eyes.

It was Cora's white suitcases.

She was running alongside them, entreating Pavlos with the small one and the black armband man with the large one to be careful. The minibus driver was squatted on the roof holding out his arms. Pavlos sent the small one up. The larger suitcase was more difficult. The man with the armband swung it to Pavlos. Pavlos hurled it upward with its own momentum. As it rose, passing from hand to hand, Cora's own arms rose involuntarily. An oblong stick-Jesus ascending vertically. Those bad old religious movies he and Theo had watched for free laughs in the basement of the Carrboro Baptist Church. Heaven had stars. It reached the minibus driver's hands at its apogee.

Richard. That was the genus. Lion-hearted. Barrel-chested. Burton.

Was it merely the kinetic image that lured Richard or was there something as enthralling in that white suitcase as the coufetta in his knapsack? Strangely, it was next to his knapsack that the minibus driver stashed it. Richard's gaze was too benign. His skin too smooth, too white.

"The end, *paidia.* We're ready!" shouted the minibus driver, stretching to his full height to pull the last knot of the rope. Then he jumped down, and they boarded the minibus.

The taxi followed the minibus for a long way. Twenty-three kilometers from Sparta at a wayside cross marking the intersection of a dirt track the minibus stopped, and the taxi passed.

This was the place of exodus for the nuns. They made a ceremony, alighting, all filing past Cora and shaking her hand.

"Come to Triandafila," the Papa adjured her once more.

She smiled and bid them good-by.

They were like crows dropping off a perch, standing to wave when the minibus left. In the distance, they were a covey.

An hour later, just at that time before the sun starts down, they arrived in Sparta, a new, flat ugly town with cement curbs. The mid-dividers of the broad boulevards were filled with red dirt and picrodaphne which glowed incandescent-red with sunset.

Anxiety filled him. He noticed the heat.

"Where will you stay?" he asked her.

"Oh, I'm going to Mistra. There's a hotel there called the Byzantium."

"And after Mistra?"

"Maybe I'll go to Zakynthos. Agios Dionysos had a cave there. They've got his bones preserved in a glass case."

She looked, as she stood in the street, the same as she had the first moment he had seen her, her face fresh, her egg-blue suit an extension of her eyes.

He carried her two suitcases to the local bus station and put them in a battered old bus labeled MISTRA. There was only one other occupant, a blue-uniformed schoolgirl. Cora took the first seat so she could see everything.

"I don't have your address!" he suddenly said, seeing the driver coming out.

She wrote it slowly in block letter with flourishes, taking so long that he had hardly time to get off before the driver, pulling the starter, turned a string of connections into full throttle. Don jumped off. The only thing he could see as she disappeared was a dot of blue behind the mud-specked window.

He found a Grade C hotel called the Menelaos run by a fat man, a Jehovah's Witness who was extremely repulsive because of the refinement of his wrinkles and the smooth-as-cream consistency of his fat.

"God led you to my hotel," he said in English, double chin swinging like an udder.

Don took a nap and that afternoon went to the museum. It was yellow stucco and smelled like all Greek museums, cool, musty marble. He was the only one there. Birds in a back garden filled cypress trees with squeaky chatter.

A primitive statue of Helen, rigid in archaic-idol pose, stared at him with a terrible sneer-smile. Her forehead was low, her face clay, her jaws crude. Such limited intelligence, all flesh, no soul, scorn rather than communication, reflected the terra-cotta triumph of Taygetus. He did not believe her. This did not launch a thousand ships. Every generation tries to make a new Helen.

That night he went to the movies. *Fahrenheit 451* was playing. Bradbury and Truffaut, following Socrates like Philo, carried the little flame of inquiry against the vast chaos of ignorance, walking around in the forest, like their escaped readers, beyond the boundary of total destruction, committing to memory the classics of literature. As if that would save civilization! Noble! He wanted to weep for all the ineffectual decencies. The squeaks of literature from museum cypresses. He felt horny. But it was profound loneliness, and all he could do was eat a plate of macaroni.

When he got back to the hotel and climbed the stairs, he noticed a strip of light under his door. He did not stop to think what it was or get out his key. Reflex, he pushed the door. It opened at once.

The scene took his breath away. His shirts strewn across his bed, his sneakers on the floor, his uniform thrown on the rug crossed with ping-pong paddles. Stuff scattered everywhere. The brutal chipmunk was leaning over his deflated knapsack.

He leapt up. For a second he rocked on his heels. Then he grabbed his attaché case from the bed and scuttled backward to lean, hips abutting the sink, as melodramatically as Tallulah Bankhead.

"Ti theleis?" asked Don gentle with shock.

"You know what I want." The man's words were slow. A treadmill of calculation.

Don felt hate. The man was larger than he. In a fight, no match though. Office bureaucrat with fine hands and feline walk. He'd kill with a pistol. In a brawl he'd squash like a grape. But he'd let him pace him. Slow, then.

"What do you mean, I 'know'?"

"You know everything you pretend not to know, Sergeant Tsambalis."

The audacity was unexpected. Fortunate for slow motion or he would have smashed immediately. But the restraint, like his ping-pong hunch, shot acid to the roots of his hair.

"You followed me from Corfu!"

Accusation fondled, controlled. How did he know his name? How had he got in? If he had picked the lock, why hadn't he locked the door behind him? Or had he wanted to be caught? The French doors to the balcony were also wide open.

"I'm going to call the police," Don told him.

The man made a motion toward the balcony.

Don jumped him. He didn't smash his face though. He chopped him in the left rib and consolidated his move by thrusting his right elbow into his neck, pinioning him right there at the sink, against the mirror. The chipmunk's hips were outthrust like an invitation. Instead of throwing away his attaché case to use hands, he pulled it up over his chest, as if his breasts were naked and he was modest.

"What do you want, son of a bitch?"

The worm on the pin, enticing wriggle. Red started from each pore and spread like a star. Each hair of the mustache glistened. Did he shampoo it?

Don inhaled in a scientific way, as though he were analyzing chemicals. Clean smell of Mennen's. He jammed the man against the sink with his hip, feeling the pelvic bones, the dampness of the body, the mash of the man's buttocks flattened by the marble, and he was getting a hard-on of hate.

Concentrate on details. The pupils of the eyes, large. The eyeballs aping their own pupils, slowly beginning a distension from the sockets. There was something lewd about the bulge. Tentacle of veins in naked white.

He pressed the neck harder, repugnance overtaking hate. He had to kill him to get rid of human squish. But a face stared at him, dead blue in white kill. Himself in the mirror. With despair—he had not recognized himself—he tore the attaché case out of the man's hands.

Catalyzed by freedom, the man did not move. Don riffled the attaché case before his eyes. Give him his serfdom. Laugh. It was empty.

The man pulled his lapels together, clipping back his dignity. "I advise you to be more careful about your friends," he said. The trouble with sparing aggressors' lives was this endless continuation of hypocrisy. "At any time you should feel like calling the police, feel free to do so. You'll have all their cooperation."

"Get out of here before I kill you."

In an indulgence of returning violence, to rid himself of his own hatred, Don slammed the man through the open door and down the staircase. He heard him catch himself on the banister at the same moment he locked his door. There was an additional clatter. Something fell. The attaché case?

The action was premature, based on the assumption that if there was nothing in it, the chipmunk had taken nothing.

He went for the one pocket in his knapsack that he was sure the brutal chipmunk was after. He felt. He was trembling. But he knew before he opened it, for he could not feel its hardness. The coufetta was gone.

For the first time since he had left England, Don felt that his life was taking on a significant shape. He had looked on these months of TDY as an exercise in freedom, but the burden of freedom demanded faith in the world as metaphor and the ability to recognize the signs. It had ended up as anxiety. He did not want to have to decide what to do. He wanted to know. He wanted the state where psyche and the objective world are the same.

Here was an act. An act committed against him, an act which forced him to react. Any action reassures one's being, for it belongs to the realm of cause and effect.

It was at last obvious that he had been delivering something more important than sugared almonds. What? That the coufetta had been stolen proved its value. This awareness was compounded by the fact that the burden he had dreamed of throwing away had been wrested away. Nothing could have been more calculated to guarantee his commitment.

What if Zoe had used him? He speculated on his weakness. What was it the Face reminded him of? What had he tried to evade? Zoe behind the Face was noble, even though he did not believe in nobility. He tried to remember everything about her, about all three of them, their conversation, their manners, any chance remark or gesture that would give a clue. He recalled Zoe looking at the bullet holes in the church opposite the café. Had she been checking to see that no one was watching? Then why had she made a ceremony of handing him the coufetta? What if he had eaten one of the almonds?

There were too many questions. The one thing he knew was that the chipmunk had followed him from Corfu and that his suspicions on the boat were justified.

He had three options:

He could go to Athens, find Zoe's parents and level to see what would happen.

He could hunt the chipmunk down now. Either get the coufetta back. Or beat the truth out of him. But he had waited too long. The man had a car.

Or he could report to the police. He knew he would not report to the police. It was too open a gesture. If the chipmunk was government, it would only be a matter of time before the bureaucratic arms meshed. At the same time he saw a discrepancy. Why had the man been scared by the mention of police—yet had threatened to go to the police?

He could, he supposed, write at once to the address Michalis had given him. He felt unreal. He was sweating. His collar was wet. He smelled of cologne. The man's flesh was on his fingers, soft and masculine. He palpitated with the life of that jugular, his clothes reeked of that sweet mortality.

He pulled them off, ran naked to the bathroom, What hope, that cold freezes hate! It was lust he was washing out of his pants, his shirt, even his socks.

When he threw himself onto the bed, he fell into an insensate sleep. His bare feet, a pattern of triangles picked up from the bathmat, faced the streetlights coming through the still-open French doors of the balcony.

He woke very late next morning, unsure where he was or what had happened, but fixed with one idea: to find Cora. Only when he saw his clothes still soaking in the basin did he remember. He hung them on the latches of the French doors in the sun.

The sun was a glare in the sky. The twelve-thirty bus had left. The next one was at two. He drank some tea and stuffed himself on meli kai voutiro. What had the chipmunk meant, his "choice of friends"?

For the first time since he had been in Greece he bought the *Athens News,* and he pounced on the little newsprint, the errors, "Culture Notes," "Music Review," as if its lifeline to the world of Europe and America negated his situation.

GREEK NEWS IN BRIEF: While Vassilios Alexopoulos, 60, was watering his garden at the village of Platanos, Pyrgos, on Sunday, he found a turtle and threw it away on to the street. At that moment, a 70-year-old woman, Eleni Sofianopoulou, was passing outside. The turtle fell on her head and she fell down, unconscious. Alexopoulos, thinking that he had killed the woman, suffered a heart attack and also fell unconscious. They were both taken to a doctor and their condition was reported to be improving.

He had a sense of déjà-vu when the bus ground into Mistra, though he had never been there before. Cora had been here. Cora had seen it. It was a pretty crossroads, dominated by a plane tree that cast a deep shade. Magnified off the looming mountain hung the ruin: houses, roofs, towers.

He went from the blinding stucco street-front into the arched lobby of the Byzantium. The man at the desk nodded. He knew Mrs. Ellison. But he did not know where she was. She was *exo.* She had left.

He felt alarm. *"Efige?"*

"Ochi."

At the ruins then. He climbed through the avenue of figs, planes, eucalyptuses.

If the aura of crime in Mycenaean digs, heavy, gray, brutal stones, gold drinking cups as big as a man's head, had given way to the glory of line in classical times, had been picked clean by subsequent history to rear up white as bones for debouching busloads of tourists, it had reappeared in Christian ruins. Christians hid in holes, exulted Philo, dir-r-ty caves behind mountains, savages so scared they didn't dare come out to go to the bathroom, they did it inside. Byzantine churches were made up out of chewed old pieces of marble columns and capitals pasted together with mud and dropped like turds on old sites holy to gods and goddesses. Mistra had been occupied by Turks, Franks, Venetians. There was a pink tinge to the stones, as if the blood of Christian horrors reduced by the

Turks to this crumbling confusion had been thinned out and become ethereal.

In the House of Theodorus he heard footsteps and rushed outside. But it was not Cora: it was a German in shorts, red-faced, puffing, a camera slung around his neck.

At the House of John, he searched in silence. Then a lizard scuttled into the cellar. He stood at the House of Sophia. The air felt eternally thin. Arrows marked the path upward.

He arrived at a ruined fortress house full of pitfalls. Holes dropped into dark, deep basements. High, worn steps led upward to floors without walls. He imagined a woman Humpty-Dumpty falling off and the smell of thyme overpowered him.

It was larger, more exotic, more daring, more tragic than Pompeii. He looked off to the village far below, to the roof of the Byzantium Hotel which mimicked in terra cotta the plain of Menelaus. How far could a man go for a woman? The clay, sneering Helen of the museum was brushed by his mind and he felt some presence that was gentle, like the memory of his mother.

He was above the Pantasseion, a walled complex of churches and courtyards where the nuns lived. Was Cora there? She could have been anywhere—at the House of John when he was at the House of Sophia—anywhere where he was not.

He descended behind a church alongside cupolas and roofs, until the path came into a shaded courtyard. A faucet trickled water. The sound, domestic and eternal, bounced against the whitewashed walls, and squawking hens clicked in flutters across the paving stones in front of him. A bell rang. He went into the dark church, smoky with livani, and lit a candle. Suddenly, he was aware of eyes upon him. An old nun was staring.

The grandeur of the nuns' apartments contrasted with their domesticity. Blue blinds stared over a thousand-foot drop. A nun was shouting into a wall telephone in a room of country-poor furniture, tables and chairs. On the floor by the white counterpaned bed, another sorted rice.

Had she seen a Mrs. Ellison, he asked, and he described her fat, her way of walking.

The nun yawned. Flies buzzed around the chaff spread on brown paper on the floor.

No, volunteered a third nun twisting strands from a ball of sheep's wool.

She had to shout. The telephone communicant was arguing about who was going to collect the cheese at the village.

It must be cold in the winter. How did they keep warm? Did they believe in God? Did they love God?

He decided to go to the top.

He ascended above the roofs again, followed the arrow past a rotted window in a ruined wall. A stone fell, dislodged by his heel, bounced down the mountain, and disappeared in the pale-gold silence. Cicadas thrummed. He was going up into the fiercest rays of the descending sun, and he indulged in victorious fantasies of finding Cora at the crown. He ripped his pants on a thistle. A tongue of blood turned into a poppy.

He had to change rhythm. He was growing careless. He took hold and concentrated. He breathed strongly. His ears recorded the even intervals. He timed his footsteps to his lungs. He paced himself by achieving temporary goals, an outcrop of rocks here, a clump of gorse there, a ruined wall . . .

When he reached the fort wall, he stopped. He had thought it was the top of the mountain, but it was only the end of the ruins. Sweat breeze was lethal gold, and he luxuriated, as if the trickles down his temples and the back of his neck and his wet hair were Midas-solid. At least mercury.

He called: "Cora! Cora, are you here?"

She was not, of course. He was only occupied with formalities. Covering geography by the book. She could not possibly have climbed this high, this precarious route.

A cart track led upward over a rock covered with thyme and thistle. He could not leave it. He had a greed for sweep. He craved dizziness as the ultimate power. He had thought it would go to a gentle plain, but in fact it led to a plateau of grotesque rocks, where there was nothing but sky. Taygetus stretched westward, and below him hung the ruin, the churches, the palaces, the houses.

He heard a scream, high-pitched as wind through which there were gasps of low, mocking laughter. It lasted about a minute, and when he became aware of the silence, he found that he was ten feet from the place he had been standing.

There were high boulders to the left.

He looked to the right. There was no one.

"Who is it?" he called. Again, formalities. "Where are you?"

The faces of the rocks looked back at him, but they would not give themselves up to him. In the retrospect of a few seconds the causelessness was worse than the scream itself. He knew that in a matter of minutes he was going to panic. The pumpkin-colored light was already converting, in memory, to fragments of brain inside his skull, freezing them into the same shapes as the staring rocks.

He loped, pretending carefully, and choosing his route carefully. He was aware of being cold, but his face burned. When he crossed the fort wall into the ruins, he felt safer, yet he held the panic inside of himself tight as treasure. In his descent, he entered the shade. Night was beginning, and the mountain obscured the setting sun.

It was too late. The gates were locked. He had to climb again, to find the caretaker to let him out. The man was an old Greek with the mustache of a shepherd, but he was dressed in shorts and an English workman's cap, and he smoked an English pipe.

He hurried back to the Byzantium Hotel.

The clerk told him: *"Efige."*

Gone.

"Did she check out?"

"Xero-ego?" How do I know?

The hotel bed was the bed, covered with a worn, white counterpane. The hotel floorboards were the floorboards, worn from a history of country travelers. The hotel wardrobe was the wardrobe, looming at an awkward angle from the wall, because the floor slanted. The French blinds were the French blinds, dusty and mute. They were not the faces of rocks. They even cheerful, for the hotel room had integrity, and the morning sun was new and cared nothing for the fight that had taken place there.

To feel unreal is to feel irrelevant. He could not escape. He could not find Cora. He rejected chase for the chipmunk. It was clear that he should go to Metamorphosis. It was less than thirty kilometers away. When in doubt, do *something*.

He had been looking at the glint for seconds before realizing that the coufetta was being struck by a surreptitious movement of the blade. The sword was the sun shining beneath the wardrobe. He reached down and got it out. The blue ribbon was intact.

The instant he had seen the chipmunk, the instant the man had scuttled to the sink had been the instant it had made its escape. It had taken a being beyond them, become a verb, rolled, fallen, freed itself of giver, taker, carrier, and thief. The inappropriateness of its berth guaranteed limbo, but the sun moved. It did not make it less irrelevant, it only startled him that he had so misread the signs. He must be careful of paranoia. Floating not on a sea, but on a floor beneath a wardrobe in a room in an old hotel.

Everything was changed. Not the irrelevance, nor the maze of war between presence and absence, but the fact that he was given a second chance. This time he did not put the coufetta in his pack. He put it in his shirt pocket.

The bus let him off at the cart track. He began walking the two kilometers. He could see it in the distance, ten or twelve houses sprinkled like dots on the mountain knoll, imitated far below as red rock islands in the Messenian Gulf.

He went straight to the house, unhooked the portal latch, and entered the garden which was laden with lemons and red roses.

"Thea! Thea Vasiliou!" Aunt! Wife of Vasilios! But to him it meant: Goddess, Wife of the King. In 1967 she had been eighty-seven years old.

No answer.

"Thea!" he called up the stairway, pretending she was not dead.

"Christos kai Panagia!" she had muttered when they told her that he was her baby brother Philo's son, all of them crying and rocking, but not daring to touch him until she did. She had just arrived on the donkey. She had been in the horafi and behind the saddle waved the crown of grapevine leaves and chorta that Tasia's grandchildren had picked for the goat's supper. She did not let them help her down.

"Philomen, paidi mou, agori mou." My boy. "Xanairthes." You have returned.

Her hand raked his cheek gentle and dangerous as a thistle. She took his head in her thorn fingers, stroked his hair, his ears, and his eyes until, unable to bear this enthronement of his blood, he grabbed her black rags, kissed her ecstatic yellow tears, and squeezed her skeleton hard, breathing her smell, sour as feta and glorious as vasilikos.

"Adonis," they corrected her, "not Philomen."

What did she care? Married thirty-five years to Vasili. Vasili dead another thirty years. No children. Philo, first child of her father's second wife, and the others afterward, all were her children. She had known he would come.

"What is blood?" Philo scorned them as if he were trying to keep them from going to look for their mother in Cairo, Illinois. "It's the chemical that binds donkeys to the same cart. *Och, kako moira, kako popatha,*" clasping his hands together, raising the fists up in front of his eyes, and swaying from his hips in imitation of old Greek village ladies. "My mother, my father, my wife, my children. Tribes! Same old lousy Aeschylean tribes killing each other, beating each other over the head, the sister stealing the nuts when the brother's not looking, the brother stealing the figs."

Then why had he sent the shoes in 1944?

"A box this big!" He saw the red-dirt hieroglyphics etched in her palms, her knuckles standing up like volcanic outcrops. "The shoes just fit Tasia's husband. He wore them for five years."

"Thea!" The stairs creaked. Beneath, on the loom where she wove, was a half-finished rug, purple and red. Integrity. His mother's quilt. The white tassels.

Their celebration of him sprang to fire with bottles of retsina poured from the hogshead under the house where the donkey and goats were tethered. They killed a goat. He ate the eye. The gas-pump lamp flared. He tried not to get drunk. Yes, he looked like the photograph of Philo in 1911. It could be him, Antony, Adonis, Dombey, Don.

Did he have a picture of his mother? No. And never to have seen her! They wept. It was God's will, *paidi mou.* Black, black it is where we live! All of them mothers, even Tasia's husband, with his sagging guts, his pork face, who touched him worshipfully. They gathered in their hands the glory of his American youth resurrected as harvest of Philo's life, a new Philo, more powerful for mixing with an unknown mother.

Steve had shouted at him on construction the summer after his junior year at Chapel Hill High: "Hold those trusses up, you goddam half-breed."

"What do you mean, half-breed?"

"Half-Greek and half-crazy!"

She was dead.

"Thea!" he called. He thought he heard a moan. Screams, moans.

"Paidi mou, agori mou, chriso mou." My child, my boy, my golden one, she

had said when he was leaving, his same knapsack stuffed with olives, cheese, a bottle of oil, a bottle of wine, bread for the road, and a little tapeta he took home for Philo, who put it on one of the fake-marble tables. "This is the last you will see of me. It is so far. I will be dead before you ever come back. God sent you here before I died, Antony, Adonis, to crown my life. You come. I go."

What does it feel like to be old? he had failed to ask her, curious beyond grief. The hair stood up on the nape of his neck. To share in these exalted forms was unreal. He was being crowned a man and he could not believe in it. What is a man in this day and age?

"Let's find out," he had told Theo.

"How?"

"By going there."

"Cairo, Illinois?" Theo panicked at the thought that finding her was possible.

"Thea!" He reached the top of the stairs. There was a corner room with a wooden door half-open.

Crossing the Wabash in moonlight with steam rising out of the river, out of the lush banks, a cliché. He thought he was still in the South, but the Wabash did not flow into the Cape Fear, it fell into the Ohio, into the Gulf of Mexico. The roads hadn't been fixed since the forties. If you want to go into America's past, go west. Cement plates tipped every-which-way, banked in the wrong direction with old-timey electric poles, old-timey gas tanks with shoulders. He had to look in the telephone book to see if there were any Wylers left. There were four. He called them all up and found one family, some distant cousins, they thought, who vaguely remembered old blind Judge Wyler on Mapes Avenue. They tore the house down for a Baskin-Robbins ice-cream store. Were so glad to be connected—he worked as a clerk for Chattanooga Feed—to the Wylers, who back in 1874 had a member in the U.S. Senate, that they made Don stay to dinner. He stuffed himself on chicken and dumplings enough to last for two days. His money was getting low. He moved out of the cockroachy Hotel Graham. Slept in an abandoned railroad station where he could hear rats at night. Mama, look at me now. I am in your town. Would you let me sleep in a place like this? How could you have come from this place? Did you ever take the train? Were your footprints ever left on these boards? His eyes streaming with tears, proud Mick McShane, private eye. At the *Weekly Gazette,* an alcoholic copy editor sent him to an old ex-postmistress who had lived on Mapes Avenue.

Of course, she remembered the Wylers. Louise was always playing Chopin or Mozart when you passed on Sunday afternoons. Good family. Only child. Never stuck-up. Red hair, crooked mouth, refined. Boys fell in love with her. She went to Oberlin. Then she married some Italian gambler and died leaving two or three children."

"Died of what?"

"Scarlet fever's what I heard. Some disease nobody ever dies of." Nobody could believe Louise Wyler was dead, but on the program of the high-school reunion she was an asterisk.

And her mother and her father?

A year later, her mother had died. The old judge had been blind forever, but they found out he was in debt. Hospital bills. The bank just let him keep the house till he died and then they sold it to Baskin-Robbins Ice Cream and it was torn down.

He bummed home fifteen pounds thinner.

"Well, I found out," he told Theo.

Theo trembled. He was afraid.

"What?"

"One, she's dead. Two, she had *red* hair and played the piano, not the violin." And he gave Theo a smart-ass gift: "Ann Marie has red hair! Haw haw!"

"So do you!"

He did not recognize the white rags, bones, hair in the bed. He had never seen her without the black mandilli. Something in the shape of the beak spoke her pride. He recognized the yellow eyes.

She recognized him.

"You!" she said, tears magnifying the recognition.

"Yes." He put his pack on the floor by the bed.

"Christe mou!"

He thought she was saying: my golden one.

She lifted her arms to him. *"Christe mou, chrise,* untie me."

The sheet had a yellow spot where she had spat up. A spider lowered itself onto her hair and danced a jig on the curl. There was an enlarged light in her eyes.

"Don't you see I am tied, darling?" She pointed to her left wrist where

66

crusted blood formed a bracelet around the toadstool rotting on her bone.

"Are you here alone?" He flung himself down into the stench.

"Under there. Look."

There was a torn strip of dishcloth lying under the bed in the dust.

"Oh *Christe mou, chrise,* I knew you would come."

"Who am I?"

"I know you."

"I am Adonis, Antony," he repeated, insistent.

"They beat me to keep me from dying." She laughed.

"I am here, Thea."

"Yes, *agori mou, chrise mou. Efharistimeni poly eimai.* It pleases me so much that you have come."

They came home at noon in a grinding tractor. Frightened, celebrative cries of welcome.

"You are back! Adonis, Antony! Like old times. We have been in the fields. So much work! Now is the time we hoe the vines. You cannot get workmen!"

They did not touch him as before. They had electricity. In their bedroom they kept a blue electric light burning perpetually before the Panagia.

"We are killing ourselves like dogs. Workmen won't work. They want a hundred drachmas per hour."

"Why do you tie Thea Vasiliou to the bedstead?"

"Did she tell you that?"

Tasia turned frightened mole eyes up toward her husband and wrestled silently with the potatoes for the feast with which they would celebrate his second coming.

"Lies. We don't tie her to the bedstead."

"You leave her alone all day."

"*Paidi mou,* we have to work in the fields. No one to help. Listen."

Tasia's husband bunched three fingers together for the sign of the cross, but ground them in Don's chest. "Sometimes she is in her head. Sometimes she is flying around outside it, like swallows in a nave. Did she know you, for instance? Well, what do you expect? She is in the other world, without giving her bones to this one. She wants earth and paradise the same minute." He sighed garlic. "Things are different now, *paidi mou.* We have electric light. She tried to light the electric light. She stuffed a plastic bag in it for a wick and then lit it with a match. She almost burned the house down."

In the silence of the sun, when they were gone back to the fields, she confided, "They tied me by one hand because they think I will burn the house down, because my brains are too old. I forget, but I am not crazy."

She cried in the afternoon. "I do not like hilopites. That is all they give me to eat."

"Thea!" he whispered, agonized into her weeping.

She was not there any longer. She looked bored. Was she asleep with open eyes?

"She is filthy," he told them that night. "Why don't you wash her?"

"It's all lies, *Adoni mas*. We do wash her."

"Then why is she filthy?"

"Sit down, *Adoni mou*. Tomorrow we kill the lamb. Remember what a wonderful time we had? Tomorrow, we feast again."

"Bring me the basin and towel."

"It is not right for a man to do that to a woman. It is for a woman to do."

"Then why don't you do it, Tasia?"

While they were gone to the fields the next morning he took off her nightsack. She cried tiny yelp sounds, like a dreaming dog, and he found a hard green turd underneath her, embedded in the sheet, jade in a mine. How long had it been there?

She yielded to Jesus Christ, gave up her body and her shame to the name she kept muttering.

He plucked at the yellow wads of flesh soft as flour, nipples knots in parchment, hair between her legs frightening wires, took up her backbone to carry her to the chair, setting her down like the tail of a fish on a plate. Breathing her feces. I love humanity, the lady confessed to Father Zossima, but I cannot bear the individual.

His nostrils flared like a horse and he sweat. He worked like a scientist. He propped her backside on the chair. He laved her with a wet, soapy rag, watching great wet spots enlarge on the floor. He draped her with towels and left her to sit watching him from her shroud, like an animal. Then he ripped off the sheets, hauled the mattress outside, beat it in the sun to prepare a new bed.

Was love a matter of the environment? Could you condition it? Could you train yourself to the habit if you did it every day? Not temporary, but everlasting. Not duty, but love. After hundreds of years of the question: "Can you feel the love in my fingers, in my hands, defecating, dying humanity?" could you love and throw it away? Suck my sore, Jesus. Lick my leprosy, Jesus. Fuck my feebleness, Jesus. To hell with humanity. It always knows love.

But he would never, he thought, be able to make love to a woman again.

Carrying her back to the bed he smelled the soapsuds. Pride? No, death. He refused the lavishment of her eyes. His was the same blood as hers. He was of the same blood as Philo. Someday he would die like this. Philo was right. He refused the humble intimacy sprung on helpless blood which runs only to stop, ecstatic only to keep running. There was somewhere the blood ran which no one understood.

He had to leave or stay there while she died forever.

The baked goat lay looking up at him from the plate. He ate nothing, but he cut off a piece to take up to her like a farewell gift.

"They feasted for their gods, the ancients," said Philo. "But the trouble was that they secretly hid all the meat under their coats and gave the god the fat, the bones, and the farts."

"Thea Vasiliou, I have to go now. I am leaving. And I bid you farewell."

"I thank you for coming, *chrise mou. Sto kalo.*" Her lips wrinkled around the meat.

"Remember that I will come back."

"I am coming with you, *Christe mou.*" Her gums smacked and shone with the oil from the goat. Soapsud smell gone.

In the roadway with his pack on his back, he warned them: "Feed her three times a day. Keep her clean. If I find that you have left her alone in the house, if you ever tie her to the bedstead again, I will—"

What would he do?

*T*he next morning when his bus got to the practorio in Sparta he saw Cora in a line of people. She was trying to get on a bus.

"Cora!" he shouted.

She turned. "You! What on earth! . . ." Her face was alight.

"God, it's good to see you!"

"Didn't you go to your grandmother's?"

People's heads turned left and right following their sentences like a ping-pong ball. She had no notion she was plugging up the line.

"Where are you going?"

"Delphi. Oh goodness! I'm stopping up the whole line. I've got to say good-by."

"Wait."

"Good-by."

"Save me a seat."

She waved something. He heard the word "numbers." He rushed into the office for a ticket. When he came out and got on the bus, Cora was standing by her seat like a ballet mistress. Everything was fooforay. All the passengers were standing, shouting. The driver was waiting, his foot poised over the gas pedal.

When Don jumped in, the doors smashed. Tympani. The driver accelerated. Overture, first gear. First movement, second gear. The people burst into applause, and then pointed for Don to sit down next to Cora.

"Isn't it superb? Everyone switched seats for you!"

She was dressed in a smart beige outfit with a topaz around her neck. He was slightly intimidated. No robin's-egg blue.

But they had to pay tribute to the gesture. Fifteen minutes of recitative: Answer: "Mistra." Question: "Which is more beautiful?" Answer: "Forty-seven." Question: "How many mothers do you have?"

Free at last, he began, "I looked for you everywhere at Mistra."

"You were at Mistra?"

"Yes."

"When?"

"Friday."

"But I was there!"

"I couldn't find you."

The victory delicious to taste, he hoarded, replayed the frustrations, for they aggrandized the meeting. The bus motor palpitated "fall in," "fall in," 4/4 time for Pinocchio who had left Gepetto behind.

They talked about inconsequential things. Where had he been going, she asked.

"Athens, I think."

"Do you often go somewhere where you don't know exactly?"

"No, because of the army. But on the other hand my four—no, three—weeks of Freedom," he decided, "decreed that I devote myself to waste."

"Oh yes, isn't it marvelous when you don't know where you'll sleep at the end of the day?" The motor turned to 3/4 time, "Fall in with."

He felt neither hypocritical nor tentative in his intentions. An assault in motion. All he had to do was to find the dotted seventh of opportunity.

He allowed her to talk about nature, about deserts, to make remarks like: "I always thought it miraculous how the wise men found Christ by the stars. I did not understand that stars, like the sun, were the medium for desert people of directions, weather, etc.," certain of her and of his patience. How much was he going to lay on her? How far confide?

"Think how removed I was! I thought twinkling must be a sign that took the place of beckoning, and if a star could not beckon or talk, how could a man know, even if wise?"

The bus arrived at Delphi at noon and he took charge. He carried her two white suitcases to the Electra and told her gently, "I won't stay here, because I always stay in cheap hotels." So straight. He felt like hosanna-ing.

He registered at the Hermes. Congratulating himself on his good fortune. No tributaries. No fast plays. He did not have to make love or consider sources.

At four o'clock he picked her up to go to the ruins. He insisted they go all the way to the stadium. He walked slowly. She puffed. The alkaline smell she gave off when she collapsed on the rock at the top was so clean it was an augury. Everything was about to be clarified.

"I wasn't so winded the last time I was here."

"You've been here before!" he said, shocked. "When?" This piece of information was not in his calculations. He could brook no disturbance of the friendship he had set his mind on.

"On my second honeymoon!" she answered impatiently.

Why should she act as if he ought to know? "My first was during the war. You couldn't go anywhere then." He felt suddenly reassured, as if, like a first lover's quarrel, it proved his ownership.

That night after dinner she wanted to see his room. She came in with an excited, curious footstep, peeking. He felt excited too, as if there were something in himself which he had overlooked that was more important than the signs which had preoccupied him. She noticed everything, the way he hung his clothes neatly on nails in the wall, his shaving kit from one, his ties from another, his knapsack on a third. The Cold-Water All.

Her room in the Electra was a combination head shop, mother's sewing room, and boutique. It vibrated with smells: musk, lilac, water glasses of daisies, toothpaste, and Moondrops. She had taken everything out of her white suitcases and used them for tables, placing on one vials and bottles of perfume, on the other the glasses they had used for the picnic. The hotel owner had given her the best room, one with Persian carpets.

"Now you'll stay for coffee."

She ordered hot water from below and they sat on the balcony. Behind them, her necklaces and earrings, which she had hung on hooks, made everything shimmer. She laced a string of elegant, fake pearls upon the railing and they winked in the moonlight. A scarf, hanging on the French door behind him, moved in the night breeze, forming a mysterious presence which was of her, but not herself, to preside over them as they looked down from the mountain over the black concave, the lights of Itea and the huge expanse of the Corinthian Gulf.

"After we got back from the ruins this afternoon, I took a nap and dreamed of Vivien Leigh," she said.

V for Vivien Leigh for Vowel. In his sophomore year of college, in English 24, he had first discovered Chapter 25, "The Virgin and the Dynamo," of *The Education of Henry Adams.* It was through Pynchon's *V.,* whose anagram for the classic female designation: V for Virgin, Venus, Vagina, Victory, Venery, had ignited his earlier epiphany about the vowel being female, but had failed to flash the vision he now saw so clearly. V upside down becomes A, the primal and widest vowel, the sound of Ah, the sound which opens the names of all the goddesses: Aphrodite, Artemis, Astarte, Isis, Athena. The wider the vowel, the nearer the Goddess. Vowel movement, Philo called it. He doubled the V to make W for Woman, and deduced from the Adams/Pynchon theory a metamorphosis from vowel to consonant which signified the distortion of primitive harmony through the will of Man to control Nature to the distortion of earth by the technological civilization.

She began to recount the dream:

"I was in this small screening room and a man asked me if I knew what was the biggest hit movie for all time. When I told him I didn't, he said the star was Vivien Leigh. I said, 'How can this be? Vivien is no longer alive.' At that moment a film started on the screen. There was Vivien in this beautiful gown. I was captivated. The man said these were clips of a film that Vivien had been making, and that they had taken them after she was gone and made a new film. But the strange thing was that in this new film, she dominated everything completely. Then the dream changed. It looked like Shubert Alley at night. I could see the marquees of many theaters and they were all lighted up with Vivien's name. Every single theater was playing her films!"

It was the sign. He felt a calmness invade him, and everything was natural.

"Cora, have you ever been haunted by a face?"

She leaned forward the way people do at the beginning of stories.

"No, let me tell it a different way," he said. "Ever since I've been in Greece, I've been embarked on a mission. I don't understand what the mission is exactly, but listen. I want your opinion."

He told it, and in the telling the events became smooth and bald to him as bones. Zoe. The chipmunk at customs. How he had picked up Annette. How they thought the chipmunk was following. His suspicions on the boat, and then catching the chipmunk red-handed. Finding the coufetta again. Suddenly he saw he had been placing too much emphasis on his own perceptions and not enough on fact.

Her face was spellbound. She was delighted. But her reactions were banal. He was disappointed, and yet, had he not everything to gain from the banal?

In her multiplicity of Coras, her scarf, her pearl necklace, he felt her dead center, a being cold, unimpressed with the trappings of their epic journey. That was the moon of him, that dead center which he addressed and from which he would exact responsibility.

"You should never have let that brutal chipmunk go!"

"I know it. Stupid."

"But how amazing you found the candies again!"

The stupendous concave of the night absorbed these comments and gave back silence.

"Why didn't you go to Athens immediately?"

He felt the beginning of excitement.

"I had to see Thea Vasiliou." Her name too began with V. "I was right there."

"If it were me, I would have gone." She went back to the trivialities. "I wonder what that chipmunk was looking for!" But though the territory was the same he had traveled, she merely touched the mystery on a factual level.

"Personally, if I were you, I'd go to Athens this minute and deliver it. You could go right from here."

"I could go," he said evenly, "but now that I've found you, I don't feel like leaving you."

"Don't be silly. What do you want with me?"

He felt like a flame in ice, a baked Alaska.

"I'm too old for you." She laughed. "Have you got the coufetta with you?"

"Yes." And he reached inside his pocket.

The silver was warm from his body heat. He held it in his hand for a moment before he opened it, making a catechism. If he had opened it while he was alone, it would have been a betrayal of Zoe. In the presence of Cora, it was a dark communion. The eggs, multicolored pastels, nestled together just as they were nestled when Zoe had opened it in Naples, safe.

He smelled something sweet and sharp as Cora leaned over to look. It was her hair, a peach smell, her head bent down next to his face. He saw soft whirls of glistening black.

"You mean you've had this coufetta all this time and you never cut one open to *see?*"

"Be careful," he warned, as if it were an explosive.

"I don't want to *eat* it!" she said, misunderstanding the territory of desecration with which he was tempting her.

She went to fetch her jackknife from her purse.

He watched her fingers. She chose a lavender one, and for a moment she held it in her hand, admiring it. Then she placed the point of the knife against its middle and bore down through the porcelain sugar coating.

At that moment he saw Zoe's face quite clearly, the tragic exclamation point of the eyebrows which ran counter to the benignity of a goddess.

Cora applied one deft push, and the halves fell apart in her palm, the meat of the nut revealed. She examined, and then picked up one of the halves and put it in her mouth.

The bite of her teeth was perfect, even, white, as transparent and exotic as her pearl necklace imitating it against the darkness was unconscious.

"Mmmm! I love candied almonds. How sweet! How subtle!"

She gave him the other half, and he ate too, his excitement vast, as if Cora's chewing caused the sweetness, mellow and pale, in his mouth. It was not the taste of Tragedy. This was what he sought: transformation! Cora, her mouth closed, chewing, moved a smile in the movements, the spokes of her eyes flashing his victory in being able to hold in balance this tension between tragedy and desecration, between protection and invasion.

"It doesn't prove anything though," he told her.

"True."

"It could be in one of the others."

She picked up another one, held it tentatively and ate it. He waited, calmer. He watched as she wopsed it, tasted of it, balled it in a fold in her cheek. Her eyes changed expression suddenly.

"I taste the nut. So there's nothing in this one either!"

They laughed.

"We can't eat them all," she said. "There'll be nothing left to deliver. So you'll have to go to Athens!" She rearranged the candies so the holes would be less prominent. "What do you mean, haunted by a face?"

"The face of Tragedy," he said, in the eye of the calm at last.

"Whose face? Zoe's?"

"Yes."

"What did she look like?"

He described, not Zoe, but the Face. It was complete, he told her. It was unquestionable. It had the incarnation of a statue. No matter what expression Zoe had, the Face was perpetually Tragedy.

"You're in love with her, maybe."

"Who, Zoe?"

"Yes."

"I only recognize her face. I don't know her."

"Then in love with Tragedy?"

"Doesn't one have to prevent Tragedy? If you can see it, you're involved. You have to do something to prevent it."

"Face of Tragedy," she mused. "Darling, that's bunk."

The teeth of pearls hit by a breeze tinkled and flung a fragment of something in his face. Bunk, said Philo. There's no such thing as Tragedy. He had not told her about the rock's scream. He had tempted her to eat Tragedy because he knew she would be unaffected. His footstep on the moon was secure.

"And I thought you came from this grateful door-nail generation! How amazing. Here you are, a feelie!"

3-D, Smello-vision, Feelo, feelies, feelie. Feel-Omen.

"How old you are!" she marveled.

"What's wrong with feeling?"

"You're aggrandizing the mask over the proscenium arch."

"In other words, my feeling is fake?"

"No, arbitrary. You chose it."

"How else than by feeling can man return to humanity?" he asked with his lip curled. He accommodated to the cliché by mocking the words.

"In this copy of *The Wandering Jew* my father had, the first illustration was of a woman kneeling at the edge of a cliff bordering on an endless ocean, her arms stretched out to the expanse, and the last illustration was an engraving of a man, kneeling at the other end of the world facing that endless ocean with his arms stretched out. That's how I always saw Tragedy."

He waited.

"I don't see faces," she said. "All faces meld together in my mind and I don't believe these interpretations of masks. You can look at a face one minute and it might be Tragedy, but if you look at it the next minute it isn't Tragedy; it's Comedy."

Telling him Eisenstein's theory of montage! "Christ, you're merciless for a kind woman!" he said.

Faces did not meld to him. What he saw was a pushing, a shape pushing out of its shape, people struggling to push outside their forms.

"Well, you go on ahead and cultivate Tragedy, darling, if you want to. But you know what these figures should be doing instead of stretching their arms out like that?"

"What?"

"Pee-peeing over the edge, joining their waters with the waters."

She was a cathartic in that powerful night. Everything was subtly twisted, superficiality becoming depths, heartlessness hope.

Don did not talk about joining up with her. He wanted Cora to think it was just one of those things that happens on a trip. For all she knew, he would split tomorrow.

It happened casually. She made a remark the next morning at breakfast: "Nobody should ever go to Delphi without being certain the Pythia can answer their questions."

"Do you have questions?"

"Just because a person is old doesn't mean they don't have questions."

"Height makes you feel great," he said, changing the subject.

"Yes, I'm sick of ruins."

"Let's go east then. Instead of following sites, let's go where the temples point."

"Go where?"

"Close your eyes," he said, taking her to a map on the wall.

"But you have to go to Athens."

"Point to a spot."

She was delighted. She squinched her eyes shut and wove her hands around as in a spell. Her blind forefinger stabbed Skopelos.

The nearest ferry port to Skopelos was Volos. The beckoning of the V again. He bought the bus tickets.

With her he would have to become a tourist again, but so what? He could use this state of comfort. Her presence, if it did not divert him from the Face of Tragedy, promised his camelhood passage through some eye.

When they got on the bus, he told her about V. Its significance. "I am hunting for the Goddess," he said in just those words. He was astonished at himself for doing this.

"Your vocation? Hunting for the Goddess?"

Did she use "vocation" to mock him? Or was it instinct?

"But how will you know?" she asked.

"When I find her? How can I not know?"

"No, I mean how are you going about it?"

"By signs. Like your dream of Vivien Leigh."

She was inspired, he could tell. But the effect was that she was reduced to a kind of thoughtfulness. He was driven on, protected a little by the fact that it looked like a come-on.

In a few minutes, he had pressed up to her and was saying in a phony bass voice: "My Vocation can become your Avocation." And a song came to him which he sang in her ear:

"Oh I want an Avocado
I can call my own."

A paper-doll advocate, music from her era.

"An Avocado others cannot see
You are the Avocado eye
Avocado of my I—"

She didn't like it. He could tell from her smile.

"All right, we'll give Votive offering to V from the Ablative." He turned it off.

An hour later he said to her, "Do you know how they have made the Goddess die?"

"How?"

"By putting her in museums. When you put something in a museum, you are safe."

She was agreeing with him, he felt. So he zeroed in. "In the days when the Goddess lived you played with her like a doll. You put her in a niche so you could worship her properly, and moved her around under geranium trees in gardens."

"Oh, I love dolls! When they were growing up, I used to play with Eleanor and Corey's dolls."

He was right.

At a stopover in Thebes, she picked up the initiative. "Even though you are against her desecration by museums, are you against going to them to look at her statues?" she asked wryly.

"No. But this is Oedipus's city."

"They'll have goddesses."

She was making something happen for him.

In the museum she saw a small Aphrodite, a common Hellenistic one.

"I wish I could make a niche for her. I'd love to take her out of that glass case and play with her."

He did not laugh. The statues were coming alive within his obsession and had begun to operate in relation to her. She did not suspect that she was a jukebox into which he was sticking the dimes. He was too dedicated and assiduous. He treated her in an efficient, tender manner.

But holding the tickets he had bought, he walked too fast for her and she had to run.

"You're going too fast," she said.

He slowed down, whereupon she ran ahead of him with her bouncing gait, and it was she who chose what they should look at instead of he.

"Look!" she called.

It was a blob of clay, very small. He had never seen one like it before. Primitive. All breasts, her neck created by a pinch of fingers. 1500 B.C. Above her nose, her dark eyes, thumb indentations, stared with a doleful power and melancholy grace which smote his heart.

Cora was gone. Had left him alone, acting as if she didn't care whether he looked or not. Her enthusiasm past, she was dawdling in front of another case.

Eight hundred years between this goddess and the dead-idol Helen he had seen in Sparta. The primitive does not exclude refinement. The later, calm, skilled Athena was a creation of philosophers. Going east as they were, what was going to happen? Was he going to track back from parthenogenesis to fecundity? Athena, Aphrodite, Hera, Artemis, Isis-Sibyl; that was the chronology backward.

He had competition for Cora, for she attracted people as honey attracts bees. Greeks are touchers—herding, handling, leaning, and pecking against each other in buses like animals, strolling arm in arm, holding children's faces in their hands like dishes, and they found in Cora a talisman which, like the chandeliers in Kennedy Center, they needed to feel.

In the bus station at Lamia a lady nudged her daughter and approached Cora with outstretched hands. Her eyes crinkled with welcome. She hesitated for a moment, then, smiling, began to stroke Cora's plump arm. Cora smiled back breathlessly. Questions followed, the usual ones, but they belied the energy of communication beneath them. Finally, the lady laughed hopelessly, took Cora's chin in her hand and waggled it back and forth, as if even this gesture could not quench the yearning fire, past language, and the only thing they could do was to recognize in such a gesture that planets had touched each other in this station in Greece.

Most of the touches that people gave her were like butterflies which pause, petal on petal, and fly off without language. He identified with her just as he had when she drank the water and kissed the cross. He imbibed the touches too. People came from Dallas banks, London shops, Hamburg factories for such touches, so great was the desire for connection. But he could float beyond, because she was there to enact and receive it for him.

They were on the last lap of the bus trip to Volos, where they would catch the ferry.

"I remember these Virgin Marys sitting in huge, fake seashells on the lawns of Italians' houses near Milford, Mass. I used to see them going for automobile rides with Eleanor before traffic got so bad. The seashells were painted vulgar blue— See what's happened? I can't think of anything but V. Virgin, vulgar— And here we're going to Volos!"

"You paint, don't you?"

"My father was a painter. He did portraits and still lifes and taught at the Massachusetts Academy of Art and Painting. Of course, no one would look at his type of painting in this day and age."

She had bought from the dime store a box of Circus Water Colors for children, she told him, made in England. She hadn't painted since she was a junior in college. She had done three watercolors on this trip: one of the tower in the Vatican where the smoke came out when they elected a pope. She had sent it to Tit (Letitia) Harrow Cowley in Kingsport, Idaho, because she had run across her address in her book after twenty-six years and remembered she was a Catholic; one of a sailboat in Brindisi which she sent to Eleanor; and one of a mountain in Ithaca with an earthquake-ruined house in the foreground. No good.

"I knew you painted," he said.

"How?"

"I just did. I don't know how."

A match scratched on a bargain, the trembling light ignited between them and cast possibility into gargantuan and ludicrous patterns on whitewashed walls in their minds.

The rest of the afternoon the commonest sight or sound became a signal between them. A man said something just outside a village past Lamia.

"Did you hear that?"

"Yes."

"What did he say?"

"I don't know exactly. But it sounded like 'Take a vow.' "

"That's what I heard too. A vow! I forgot how I used to be!" she cried. They were looking at each other as if it were the key to the universe. "How marvelous you are! You're making me remember. Why, this is the way I used to be when I was a child. The world held a secret. The secret was life, and I knew I would learn what it was when I grew up. I used to play in the pools in the rocks at low tide on the beach below our house, and I named every cranny in those pools the names I knew in geography, like Sweden and Europe, and Greece. I knew nothing about being able to die. Death wasn't true. You couldn't lose any individual atom. Magnets went beyond life. They would gather, bunch, palpitate around that for which they were meant, so even if you changed form by dying, the individual essence came together again!"

She began to talk the way people talk in buses. When her husband was dying, she said, she had taken up with theater people. After sitting with him in the hospital all day, she met the second-stringers (there was always an imported star, Carol Channing, Mary Martin, Florence Henderson) of the casts of old, worn-out Broadway musicals playing at the North Shore Music Center, in the dim lights of the Horn of Plenty at night. Since she had no ambition to be an actress, she became their mascot, mediator, and conspirator. They ushered her into the world of sequined gossip, ritual jealousies, character worship and assassination, and masquerade. She revived in that false glitter whose crucibles and emblems demanded no obligation. The actors brought her cookies, wine, and expensive cologne to give to Dwight, just as if he were not dying. Their rituals were balanced on their shrewd knowledge of the world as delusion. They were midgets trying on the clothes of giants, but their make-believe, scenery, and costumes were an improvisation larger than the play. Her respect was enormous. She was forced in turn to play all her different roles, so that it became a world in which the rising and falling of protean changes, from life to death, from black to white, were always visible. Everything else was transposable. Anything could be anything else. She did not mind that her children and her friends were shocked. She let them believe she was half out of her mind. Dwight's death could be enjoyed at last, for the actors dared to enter into it, and the more banal, empty-headed, and ludicrous their performances, the more reassuring. One obscenity traded for a larger obscenity whose goal was to endow.

Thea Vasiliou now more than three hundred kilometers away on the bedstead. Was the spider whose web he had destroyed lowering itself at this second on its resurrected spin? How could he be so happy?

"Freaks knew me, recognized me," she said, gazing raptly beyond the top of his head. "And I recognized them. There was a blind, sissified beggar who played an accordion with one finger and sold shoelaces on the corner of Tremont and Boylston. I kept giving him dimes, doling them out, until he boasted that he had a sighted wife and seven rollicking children, two in the university, and that he came to work every day in a Cadillac and lived in a big house in Mattapan. Of course we laughed. And once in broad daylight I saw this robbery. A young Negro broke the window of a typewriter store, walked in, took the money out of the cash register, and when he saw that I had witnessed every move, he stepped out

82

through the shattered glass, grinned, and said, 'If the pigs come, tell them I went the other way.' "

"And did you?"

"I didn't tell them the opposite direction, but I pointed up an alley and said I thought I had seen him crouching down to go into some low place."

"Did you do it to save him?"

"No, I did it because I was beyond the law."

The coincidence was so startling that he reacted with a blush. How could she have guessed Philo's obsession with Plato's question? Was she tempting him—Partner, say Me—to that realm, beyond the law, which refuses to identify criminal outcasts and judge?

Her husky, lovely voice was musing her fate as witness, the one who sought and was sought by these freaks, hunchbacked hospital attendants, actors, ladies who cursed nonexistent people in public libraries, religious fanatics, store-front Santa Clauses.

In one day of travel his disorientation in space and event was so acute that he was still hanging in the Vatican of Apollo at Delphi at the moment the blue sea lapped their feet on the boat from Volos. She talked of Aphrodite. Bang, smacked the wave on the bow. It was a nippy afternoon. Bang for Thea Vasiliou, the foam gushed joyously.

The boat landed at four in the afternoon at a small harbor on the back end of the island. Everything was bright. A town called Glossa hung over their heads upon a mountain tied to the sea by a ribbon of road. Don took one look and knew this was it.

"But this isn't Skopelos where the balconies and those churches are! Shouldn't we go on?"

No. It was here that he would get to know her. For there was nothing but a quay, two hotels, a dozen village houses, and the road winding upward from the plane trees. Bounded by sea on three sides, by mountain on the other, she was his prisoner.

"No, let's stay here—at least for the night!" and he picked up the two white suitcases and started walking along the beach to the larger hotel. "Look! It's called the Abra!"

The name settled it. How could she resist? It was large, pretentious, crude, and filled with pictures of saints, for it was run by a priest, and it was filled with sea drafts breathing.

He stayed at the other hotel, the Flisvos.

"I hope it doesn't have fleas," she warned.

When they had unpacked, they went for a walk up the mountain. They arose in ascents of thyme out of golden dusk on the sea. Glossa hung out above them, its white houses perched tipsy-turvy from one level to another. The name *Glossa* started it: it meant "tongue." A tongue sticking out of the mountain to mock, or a language into which they were going? Pure, nonsensical, bleached in the day, abstract in the coming night.

"O," he said recklessly.

"As in what?"

"Cora."

"No, Don."

"Know?"

"Gnorizo."

"Roar?"

"Blow."

"Olive?"

"Omen."

No, he did not want Philomen to butt in now.

"What color blue is Cora?" he said, changing the game to pronunciation.

"Light blue," quickly, delighting in pastel.

"Isn't that strange, seeing as how it's a long O?"

"Yes, and you're dark blue."

"It really does make blue darker when you lengthen the O," she marveled.

"And if you double the O, you are near," he whispered. Peekaboo, Sutton Hoo. Doom, bloom, dark room.

It was growing dark. From the tiered road a stone path plummeted directly downward, cobbled like the yellow-brick road in the *Wizard of Oz*. They went down through the descents of thyme over the moon which rose below them out of the sea. Past donkey droppings. There were sounds of invisible dogs announcing the birth of night, and fig trees became presences in the darkness. The streetlights came on along the quay far below and twinkled under their footsteps, like promises refusing to be extinguished. The path became more and more illegible.

Suddenly a rooster crowed.

Both were instantly alert, for the "doo" after its "doodle" was dropped.

"Did you hear that?" he said, trying to see into her eyes. It was too dark.

"Cock-a-doodle," it repeated, its voice hoarse.

Far away, another rooster crowed in response, this one crescendoing to a young, shrill, and perfectly complete "doo."

"It must be old and can't help it," said Cora.

"Don't make excuses for it. It's insane," he said mercilessly. He improvised from it: "I do. Vous do. Voodoo."

A goatbell thudded like a dreg of music. Something was close. A house? Something breathed. He had to be careful, for he felt her pleading in the silence next to him. A pang of tenderness offset his brutality. But it was only a donkey tethered to a fig tree.

The rooster crowed the stunted call again.

"See? It's defective!" he said. "Feebleminded." He was driven on. "They should invent a musical Rorschach for roosters. That would prove it!"

She wobbled like a jelly imp, about to stumble, and he took her arm to steady her. The smug Calvinism of his purity, his perfectionism made him merely more brutal. But he could not glory in it, though he was holding her with a tightness designed to handle weight, because she was light. Too light. Her fat demanded that she be heavier.

He had to be careful. Why should he turn on a rooster as traitor just because it would not say "doo"? What did "doo" prove?

*T*he next morning trucks full of peaches inundated the town. Three of them stationed themselves at key intersections.

"Look!" cried Cora. "They're only ten drachmas a case! Incredible! We can't afford not to get them!"

"How are the two of us going to eat a whole case?"

"We'll give 'em away."

A tangy smell pervaded everything. It was so celebrative that he picked up the case she pointed to and put it on the ground by the table where they were having breakfast.

He ordered coffee.

Each peach, huge, pink, soft, was wrapped in bright-green tissue. The extravagance gave to the morning—it was only eight-thirty, the sea lapping at the legs of their table, the day extraordinarily bright and calm—a delusive quality. He knew his interlude with Cora was limited. As long as he carried the coufetta, something would be hunting him. But it felt endless, the day enveloping them in the smell of the peach, an eternal present tense. He watched her peel the first one. The juice ran down her exquisite white fingers. The pulsations of her fat infected him. Flies buzzed.

He picked up the knife and asked, "Cora, do you feel old?"

"No."

"Middle-aged?"

Something crept over her face, covering a retreat with the movements of peeling. A morass faced an iceberg. He liked her ruthlessness. It justified his faith in his psyche.

She rose to the occasion.

"I have arrived," she announced, "having fulfilled the duties or expectations of a woman on earth, to the state of Vagueness." (Was she feeding him V?) "The state of Vagueness is the Second Age, the Age of Agelessness which people call Middle Age. It contains the same dynamic of checks and balances as youth, but the energy which was once devoted to survival, status, and reproduction is now devoted to cosmology. Beginnings, death, God, and Process."

He cut a half-moon slice. A couple of tourists passed by. A striking, tall girl with hair white as sun and skin as tanned as earth, who looked like a photograph negative. Her tanned, silver sugar daddy, thirty years older and one foot shorter, struggled against his cocky black pants and sandals to keep up with her lope.

"Look at that giraffe," Cora interrupted admiringly. "She must be six-foot-six."

"What does it feel like to be a woman?" he asked.

"What does it feel like to be you?" she retorted.

"Like seeing through ether." His gears were smooth. "Man is puny. You have to take the pain of men and generations and do something to alleviate it."

She didn't say anything, so he asked, seriously, "Is there anything new on earth, Cora?"

She hugged herself, delighted. "I haven't thought of that question for years! No," she decided, "I feel as if there was something new, even though I have done everything."

"You haven't died."

"Yes, I have. Dwight died."

"Did you love Dwight?"

"Yes, but I don't know what love means."

"How did you die then?"

She thought but did not answer.

"What does it feel like to die?"

Still she could not answer.

The word of the peaches was spreading. A woman shouted to a fisherman to get some before they were all sold.

A girl with a black mandilli hauled a case down for the periptero man, and a peach fell onto the road.

"What did it feel like to menstruate the first time?"

"So that's how it is."

It took him a moment to understand that this was how it felt. The dimes were paying off. He stopped peeling and started eating.

" 'So that's how it is' is the feeling of all revelations," she said. Although she had known the facts of life intellectually before the age of thirteen, the day the blood came it was a great revelation. But once it had happened it was nothing. All great revelations end up feeling like nothing, because the distance in which recognition can occur is demolished.

"Oh, I amaze myself!" she cried, relishing this particular recognition. All vital statistics, she pondered, such as being born, sex, having children, and dying are new until you do them, and then, what you know about them is exactly nothing, and that nothing is what makes you old.

"What did your first orgasm feel like?" He had eaten his bowl of peaches. She had hardly touched hers.

"You are shameless, aren't you?"

He wanted more, so he picked up his knife again. He did not even give her the benefit of a glisten toward her gesture of convention, for he was serious about sex, unlike the dirty old Papa in the bus.

"So that's how it is," she repeated.

The revelation, an opening up, imitated her body. She had had her first orgasm before she married, just from touching. Portals opened to portals ad infinitum in a vast extension of desire and at the hilt either the earth or the sky entered a rush of outward demand and banished in sensation any hope of definition. That's how mysteries are protected, she told him.

"What does it feel like to have a baby?"

When Eleanor was born, she thought she had shit the *Queen Mary*.

"Did you still feel: 'So that's how it is'?"

"Of course. The act of birth is humiliating."

"It must be a learned humiliation then, since it's natural."

Suddenly, she rebelled against his questions.

"If you think you know from this 'Meet the Press' interview what it feels like to have a baby, you're crazy." Nevertheless, she could not stop talking. Mankind should never have made a distinction between human and barnyard blood, she went on. Her baby, Eleanor—she left him outside while she went into the palace of her mind to enjoy her colored rooms, gold, malachite, lapis lazuli—was an electric flower, a butterfly of flesh, alive, an entity to itself, sacred. Too much to understand, since being ripped apart by one's own cataclysms and ejecting blood and placenta demanded Another Attitude. What should that Attitude be? She didn't know.

"Do you really mind my asking you all these questions?"

"It's foolish."

"But do you mind?"

"No. No one's ever dared ask me before."

A gust of wind caught the green tissue wrappers of some peaches carried by a hunchbacked man and scattered them like confetti.

No, she liked it, though all he was getting was history. She had lived in an inner world for years in Chelmsford, Massachusetts, where Dwight had run a computer-parts company, her psyche an extravagant, winged thing flitting among parking lots, refrigerators, and glossy magazines. People told her she was "original." Her charm saved her from being taken seriously. No, she loved mean questions. What did she care what he thought? She had never cared what anybody thought.

A schoolboy with a shaved head passed by and spat a pit in the dust by their feet, juice dripping off his chin.

In her life she had connived with marriage, motherhood, had bought stuff at the A & P, taught her children to read, driven them around in a station wagon, smoked, learned jewelrymaking, quit smoking, and read novels while she cooked. She knew everything, but what was that? The mystery asserted itself and grew larger.

"Are you finished, Cora? Let's go to the beach. I'm going to teach you to snorkel."

She popped the last slice in her mouth and jumped up, delighted.

"But you've got to be sure I don't get sunburned. I get sunburned very easily!"

He ran to the Flisvos to get his stuff, and by the time he got back to her hotel, she had packed a picnic in her small suitcase. He carried it like Red Riding Hood. The rising glare of the morning was unreal and he stepped on a peach when the bus came. A squashing muck of flesh. Flies got in the bus with them.

He wanted her to stop. But she could not; she was on a machine of memory.

Watching Dwight die in the two years between Eleanor's first child and Corey's graduation from high school began the process of her washing her hands of marriage and motherhood. In the black night, Dwight tried to capture the life he had never lived. He held her hands while he was having convulsions. Long ago, he had reacted in shock to her true nature and built his mind's defenses into implements and sold them (wheel bearings, parts of cameras, computer parts), his worldly success a proof that his reality was true, and hers false.

The bus turned a loop and the sea shone below them.

Gaping folds had appeared in Dwight's pale, sweaty cheeks. He gasped, "What is this?"

Death agony, she wanted to tell him, an endeavor he had refused as Life. The disease became palpable.

How could she talk like this in a bus? Was she moved? Did she tremble? He looked carefully to see, but she was calm. Serene, even.

She had never fought the role of happy wife and mother, but sung the refrain. They were happy with the accustomed, expected, habit-ridden, domestic happiness not often seen in America. She cringed from him. "I don't want to go," he begged. Why didn't he say "die"? she asked herself. Go, do go gently but fervently into the good night. Dylan's terrible advice from the delirium tremens of his own initials. Clasp your disease. It seems like strangling, but it's a barber pole. That optical illusion twirled Dwight's soul out—he had made a tiny, not a large sound breathing—and she thought again: So that's how it is.

Agios Nikolaos. He almost missed the sign. The muscles of his jaw were tired, he had clenched them so attentively. He jumped up, calling for the bus driver to stop. And they were left in the dust and the silence, the sea a hard blue. They climbed down the steep path to a beach which formed a perfect half-moon between cliffs. Sand. She liked sand. Rocks, he liked rocks. There was not a soul. She spread the picnic cloth, smoothed it with cat movements and placed herself upon it, covering her arms, putting on her straw-blue beach hat.

It was the sight of the donkeys in the Plaka and old black crows of women carding wool from sticks around their droppings that formed the symphony of her netherworld with Dwight. In 1952, he took her for a second honeymoon. The streets of Athens, except for Stadiou, Pan-epistimiou, and Akadimias, were dirt. In that union of their sexes she could still hear the penumbra of roaring that seemed either the sea or the moving of stars and galaxies in the living night. People were starving. Hacks of bodies were still left from the civil war, and she got pregnant with Corey.

Too late Dwight wanted to explore her nature which had shocked him. He fought, loitering to confiscate her life and make it his. Since he would not embrace his death, she embraced him. This automatically protected the children. Love vanished. She held something in her arms which she had to remind herself was the carcass of him. Her menopause began. She started going to movies. She noticed the hot flashes with pleasure. *So that's how it is!* she thought to herself, never having had to identify a hot flash before. Her sense of wonder began to return.

It was easy to get rid of motherhood. Just as easy as to be a mother, half a mind, wiping bottoms, changing diapers, going over homework, staying up during colic. Ignorance helped.

Philo blew a fuse when he found Don reading Faulkner. He grabbed the book and read out loud: " 'You got to stick to your own blood or you ain't going to have any blood to stick to you.' "

"A drunk redneck who can't write English. Half-baked potatoes! If you want to read something good, read Henry James."

"But it's required reading for English eighty-three!"

"I think I'll go over to that university and 'require' Pope Pius."

Then why had Philo sent the shoes in 1944? They say people know when they are dying because the blood goes out of their feet. Shoes for blood. If Thea Vasiliou had the same blood as Philo did, so did her sister Tasia. But he rejected Tasia's blood. Living blood is a testament to God. No wonder the ancients sacrificed. Blood that speaks and will not be heard by man is God hollering for the sacrifice.

He looked at Cora carefully to see if she believed what she said, or if she were trying to convince herself. He could not tell.

"When Dwight died, I washed my hands of Corey and Eleanor. They were shocked."

They began to court her. They wrote her letters from the framework of Panthers and ecology, but they didn't understand the ecology of poo-poo or carcasses. She went to their parties. But their proselytizing, their uniformity of beards and assumptions bothered her. They had become moralists. She was disappointed with their direction. She had hoped for help. She was eager. She had this lust for life. She grew intact in her ruthlessness and forced them, she supposed, to become adults. Having spent a lifetime realizing the fruitlessness of moral propulsion to achieve moral goals, she watched them headed up that futile path. "Like you," she said looking at him. What had they to offer her?

For instance, they had forgotten her age! Fat and light, she looked a child. But to be treated as their peer . . . to be confided in. She was wary. She too forgot how old she was. She acted like people in the movies, inhabiting her territory of dreams and designs. They wanted her to confide in them back.

She was tempted.

She told them, "Here I have lived all this time, here I have gone through the menopause, and yet I am the same thing I always was. I have this nubile belief in the possibility of everything. I have this polarity. At once I have done and seen everything, and at the same time I don't want to repeat all the things I have done and seen. I might as well die. But I don't want to die. I am untouched!

"Corey inhaled bravely, as if I smelled like rotten oysters. As for Eleanor, she turned red and swallowed a lot, in little gulps that must have made her burp. She said, 'Your menopause must have come early, Mother. Dad's death must have brought it on.' It is unbecoming to tell your children your truth, for they see you in their future, and it's terrible to believe that the mystery expands with age."

Yet there was value in having shocked them. She felt as though she'd hit some nerve. She saw the roasted dogs and fried fugitives of Pompeii crystallized at the moment of their flight. She saw Dwight's eyes condemned to rove the galaxies forever in the instamatic camera (his design) which rode the satellite. If lava opened faults, what must death open? Where was Dwight? She wanted him back for a moment to ask, the him of his undergraduate days in the canoe on Pagoda Pond talking Plato, or after Eleanor was born when he pushed past her to get his yogurt out of the refrigerator. "Where are you?" she asked impatiently.

She was sexless, like a child. If you have no age, you have no sex. Done with daughterhood, done with motherhood, what could she try? Fatherhood? She laughed. It was a spreading and a consolidation all at once. The quality of No Age was hard as a mountain of rock. But the quality of No Sex was as vague and endless as the sky.

But this was not what he wanted from her. Three questions and she had materialized a mountain and a universe. Spilled her guts in the bus. Greeks didn't need to know English. And she treated her children like penguins from Antarctica. She committed bad taste with the elegance you use to arrange flowers. No wonder he had pretended to be German.

He stared at the cliff which formed the left arm of the beach. The sun accentuated its serrations. He looked into the sky to find the end, but there were only dots of blue, and then he looked at her. When she felt his eyes she turned and gave him a smile of recognition. He flushed, embarrassed.

Her fat was hazy as a nimbus, its consistency beckoning collaboration. He watched with awe the delicate woblets of her upper arms, her plump breasts rising over the green jersey sworls of her bathing suit. Her pale-blue straw hat quivered.

"I'm going swimming," he said, getting up, taking his mask down to the water's edge to clean it with sand.

"We have a guest," she said.

An uninvited guest, a butterfly. He hated butterflies over salt water. There was something suspicious about it. The waves bleated: "Guest, ghost, host," at his feet. You must always serve the guest, for it might be the Lord. Be a host to the Lord. By serving the Guest you share in the divine.

But the butterfly was albino! Blind and attracted to the sea-wetness of the mask, it fluttered toward him, so he put the mask on to protect his face.

"Oh, you look like a priest!"

He saw himself suddenly through the oval glass from the O's of her orifices, her mouth O, her eyes O's, a plastic, black-rubber spaceman-priest, nose spying like Kilroy over the codpiece of corrugated black rubber, obscenity sealed in a vacuum, the snorkel as a periscope from his brain.

But it was a moth, he saw, not a butterfly! And she was the lost lady, the love of his youth, a frozen cameo come to life in the pulsation of those albino wings.

He pretended he could not speak, though his mouth was not on the tube, pretended to be dehumanized and separate. But above, his burnished hair ruffled in the breeze, and his torso was vulnerable.

He wanted her to look at his cock. He wanted to look at it himself, as if to prove something, but he couldn't without leaning way over, because the mask limited his peripheral vision. So he gave his balls a tug, like tightening a belt, ate the tube, sucked air, and entered the sea from the rocks. The waves drew him in gently, and he gave way to total passivity.

Below him the seabed fell steeply, laying beneath him a vast and dangerous topography completely hidden from the world of air. He was an airplane floating at the top. His sense of distance disappeared and everything became magnified. The only sound in fathoms of silence were sharp crackles when waves broke on rocks.

The noon sun illumined the blue. It breathed. Plates of rock thrust up by ancient earthquakes formed caves and rogue palaces where octopi hid. Between the rocks and sand bottom, loose seaweed moving in the deep undercurrent gave the illusion that the rocks were moving, that the whole undersea world was unreal.

He realized a city of fish was moving toward him. He did not move. But they were ghosts too, large, silver, reflecting the soft colors of the prism. In slow motion they lazed below his chest. Their tails barely moved. Their eyes were jewels. They did not recognize him. Pushing the universe with their noses, atoms of purpose, they surrounded him in a colony so large that he could not see the end of it.

He rolled over, doubled up, and sent an invisible death ray into their midst with his toes. A star exploded in a million directions from his center, and he was purged.

He lifted his head out of the water to look for her. There she was, far away, sitting on the white cloth exactly as he had left her. But he saw she was looking for him, staring in his direction, her hand shading her eyes. He waved. But she could not see him. It touched him, that shimmering speck of blue.

It pleased him that by exerting a few neck muscles he could change his entire universe.

When he lowered his head again, grasses beckoned to him from the bottom. There were some seaweeds which looked like toadstools. One blue-green one winked at him lewdly. In the sea he understood the evolution of species. There were fishes which were in markings the replica of birds, and seaweed the replica of plants. Suddenly, a fish which looked like Ernest Hemingway nosed out from under a rock. A species of blowfish. It had a beard.

He had reached the cliff that formed the beach. There was a fault in it, as if a thunderbolt had cleft the earth, which gave way to an underwater cave. He swam in. He indulged himself looking up against the sky, high red walls hung with thyme and poppies, buzzing with bees, and below where the walls refracted the light, turning red into a violent pink.

Inside, it became even darker. He pushed behind a narrow passageway. The cave was deep. A grotto. Below, the mirror world of purple, pink, moved, undulated. Balancing on water, his fingers touching rock, he discovered an arena of small canary-like fish. Large, mournful black eyes wasted in their faces. Their cheeks were soft and full and they had sleeves and tails which were elegantly embroidered like tangerine lace. They looked at him, so that he became aware of the massive space he occupied and the fact that his vision depended on his tenuous balance.

The canary fish began to dance. They waltzed against the black velvet backdrop in couples. They did not move their bodies at all. Their movement was made by the currents of the sea. The sea danced them up and down, slowly, deliberately. Vast swells filled the aperture, raising the level of their stage set. One small fish was linked by some strange suction to the side of another. Were they mating? The others danced as couples but with a thread of water each from the other.

He raised his head and saw the beads of grasses waving against the sky above, the shriek of some swallows darting, and he heard the groaning and sneezing sound of the water going far underground where he could not follow. The noon sun reflecting on the surface threw a spotlight on the wall, and with the movement of the water the light was again refracted on the opposite wall.

He looked to the light below. His motion frightened the canary fish. He saw them for a fraction of a second, and then they vanished leaving only the velvet backdrop of black water.

The light continued to refract upon their empty stage, and shimmered in spots upon the bottom. It was shocking, a mass of pink and purple stones.

Suddenly, he felt that everything in the world was supremely beautiful, more beautiful than the imaginings of any human being, for the fish, though he could not see them, were there somewhere, behind the rocks. It was a gift he had been given to see them at all. When he left, they would come out again and begin their waltz anew.

How could he share this happiness with Cora? Back there in the sun she was still shading her eyes, a blue dot, looking at the surface of the sea where he had gone. He decided to take her back a pink stone. He dove. But the stones were all welded together, an ancient earthquake ceramic. Solid mass, integral. He surfaced.

He lifted his head. He tried to absorb every light, every stone. The huge boulder which formed the overhead roof was poised precariously at the vault which gave way to the blinding blue sky. At that moment he realized that never again, not even at this very second a year or two or more years hence, could the sun be in this position, at this angle, to penetrate the sea-cave with this particular light.

When they got back the town was flying with rumors that the peaches were poisoned, that they had been injected with glycerine by the Resistance on a railroad siding, that Germany and Denmark had rejected these shipments and this is why they were being dumped on the Greek populace of the villages, who didn't know any better. The trucks were still there.

"I don't believe it, do you?" said Cora.

"No."

"We'd be dead, if they were, as many as we ate!"

But it was bravado. The far-fetched exudes the smell of truth. They noticed for the first time that the boxes were stamped in English block letters: W-E-S-T G-E-R-M-A-N-Y.

They questioned one truck driver directly.

"Why are you selling these so cheap?"

"How do I know?" the man answered with a shrug. His face was dumb, but there was an ill glint in his eyes.

"Are they poisoned?" asked Cora.

The driver screwed the point of his finger into his temple to indicate that someone was crazy, answered: "Koutamares," baloney, and laughed loudly. But an hour later he was gone. The other two trucks had vanished too.

In the town, among the rotting peaches, the clustered flies, and the persistent, thrilling tang, arguments broke out. Evidence was cited. The old man in the third house from the pier had died in the night. The ice-cream man's wife had symptoms: diarrhea and a temperature of forty centigrade.

"Don't believe any of it," the periptero man told Cora confidentially. "It's scare tactics."

"Scare tactics? By who?"

Shrug.

"Revolutionaries?" she prompted him, unafraid of being thought stupid.

"Maybe. Who knows? But the old man, he had three heart attacks before this. And the ice-cream man's wife, she's always having fevers. These people, you know are a little naïve. They'll believe any fairy tale."

A fisherman mending nets overheard.

"We are not naïve. Who are you, trying to act big with the tourists? I'll tell you it's no fairy tale. My wife is very sick from those peaches. One of the skins is stuck in her intestines."

"If it had glycerine, she'd be dead."

A little girl with dirty hands began to cry.

"You're scaring the children to death!" the periptero man swore.

"Why would the trucks leave if the peaches weren't poisoned?" retorted the fisherman.

"Because you can't sell fruit ruined by rumors."

"Are you telling me that old man isn't dead?"

"A man with three heart attacks has one foot in the grave. Peaches don't cause heart attacks!"

"Yes, they do!" screamed the fisherman. "Indigestion leads right into heart attacks. And then: kaput!"

"How do you feel?" Cora asked Don.

"Fine, I think. What about you?"

"Fine. I'm going to eat some more."

"Cora, don't!"

"Why?"

"Because, who knows?"

"Balooey," she said.

In the furniture store, the priest who ran the Abra had a fight with the owner.

"Communists. Hooligans. Revolutionary gangsters!" he inveighed.

"They put a needle in each one and filled them with poison!"

"Papooli, forgive me for saying so, but I do not believe it is true. You know that I am a practitioner of free enterprise and that I'm not a Communist, but we must be careful about spreading rumors. I've eaten at least forty. Look at me, Papooli. I feel perfectly fine. In fact, it's even cured my bursitis!"

"Be careful, *paidi mou,* pride goes before the fall. You may be the next one."

Their objectivity flaunted, hilarity invaded their anxiety. Cora became reckless. They talked about how it was a question of facts, yet how could they get the facts?

"If I could only get a newspaper," he said.

The town, as far as they could tell, splintered into two groups. The people who believed the peaches were poisoned were pro-Papadopoulos. Those who believed it a rumor, were the opposition.

At six o'clock the bus from the capital brought the evening newspapers, and among them was an *Athens News* left in the front seat, like an answer to his wish.

"PAPADOPOULOS PROTESTS!" said the headline.

He read the article aloud. " 'It is absolutely baseless and false, the rumors of extremists poisoning the crop of peaches. We view with astonishment the fact that any European government could believe the open letter of a few Communist hooligans. Not only is it an outrage that the governments of West Germany and Denmark back down on their contract, it is ludicrous that they could believe such a fantastic shibboleth. Even if the revolutionaries could have injected the glycerine with a hypodermic needle, it would have been impossible to inocculate so many. How many days would it have taken? There were over a million peaches in the boxcars. We want to assure any Greek citizen who may be worried that there is no reason whatever to lose confidence. Even if the thugs could have done it, it would have been impossible to affect the whole shipment, but those dupes would say anything to discredit the Hellenic Fatherland!' "

"There, you see?" said Cora, after they finished laughing.

"Before I knew the peaches were poisoned I felt fine, but now that Papadopoulos tells me they're not, I feel a little sick."

"Well, I feel fine."

"How many did you eat?"

"Twelve, at least."

"I ate more than that."

"Foo, you're a bit of a hypochondriac."

"Isn't it strange how the words themselves can actually affect your organs? Now the priest, out of patriotism for Papadopoulos, is going to believe they were not poisoned. And the periptero man will probably get sick."

"And the furniture man will die and prove the Papa was right."

"What if we met each other, having lived our whole lives up to this day, this hour, only to die on this island of poisoned peaches?"

That night he could not sleep. It was not his stomach. It was his head. He felt that his brains were inflamed and pushing against his skull-cage. Blood beat in his temples, and he wondered if he had fever, like the ice-cream man's wife. He wished he had a thermometer. Cora did, but he did not want her to know. If he had no fever, she would be contemptuous.

At the same time his mind was very clear, and he delineated the positions of his different realities. The truth of external events: the brutal chipmunk existed; Zoe existed, Zoe whose coufetta he'd agreed to deliver; the chipmunk had ravaged his pack; Thea Vasiliou was dying in Metamorphosis. None of these facts jibed with his fantasies (the Face was his fantasy; Theo and Philo were his fantasy, as well as externally true). But there was a third reality: the realm of unexplained phenomena. Were the peaches poisoned? What was the external truth? The scream at the top of Mistra came back to him. Who had screamed? Why?

He was lying on his bed in the Flisvos. He ran his hand over his face and felt the stubble. He smelled peaches. Peach fuzz merged with a woblet of fat above Cora's right buttock.

His cock sprang up to the feel of his hand. Damned if he was going to jerk off in bed. He got up, dressed, and went out.

The moon was full. He strolled out on the pier, his hands behind his back, wishing he had worry beads. The Greek slang for cunt is *"mouni."* The double-O sound again. But there were no features on the moon's face. It made him afraid, for it was bright and exceptionally low. He stood on the far edge of the cement quay, his feet planted at the edge, and he concentrated, trying to penetrate its facelessness. The water lapping below his shoes slapped the stars. Gusts of café music drifted from the esplanade.

He aimed, thinking of his semen, boundless and noble, as the agent which would split the moon into liquid fragments, which the waves would carry as signals all the way to America.

The meeting of two lights makes perfection. One of his games with Theo was to walk away from The Hill by night on the railroad tracks to the overpass where the highway ran. They sat on a bank smoking hash, waiting for the train. "Waiting for the Train," it was called. The lights of the swishing automobiles moved across the treetops. The crickets made war with their muffled roar, grew loud, stopped, or began again softly. After a while, the train whistle blew. This is what they had lived for. The noise of the wheels on the track emerged from the crickets. The suspense killed them. At last, the train rounded the curve and the great headlight came into view. Everything was suspended in expectation of the supreme moment when the perfect headlights of an automobile would meet the perfect eye of the train. In the thousands of times they had waited it had happened only once. The automobile had approached, its lights crazy on the leaves. The train was a slow, giant eye. The automobile paused. At the moment of its entrance on the bridge the two converged and the glaze of light formed that perfect line of recognition where the pupil engorges the teacher. Then both vehicles had gone their separate ways.

There were footsteps somewhere far behind him.

"Oriste!" shouted a man's voice.

Damn the timing, to have his conquest of the Mediterranean and of the whole Atlantic beyond the Strait of Gibraltar mistaken for masturbation! He turned around and saw two figures struggling along the rocks, one fat and dumpy, the other tall. The dumpy one must have had leather soles, for he was slipping and grunting. There were visors on their caps. Policemen!

The moon was still smiling numbly, its face still undecipherable.

He was willing, at last, to be caught. It felt fated. He had no more fight left. He tried to act nonchalant. He thought of it as fastening Absence, putting his hollow bamboo away, but Papa Dope Payola was a masturbator, too. Look at his silly smile! Apologize for nothing. Initiate nothing. The only hard thing on him now was the coufetta, which he felt automatically, in his right breast pocket. If they searched him, it was all over. For a fleeting second, he thought of throwing it in the sea.

"Good evening," he said.

"Good evening."

"Did you call me?"

"Yes."

"What do you want?"

"Would you come with us, please?"

"What for?"

"We would like to ask a favor of you."

He did not like the politeness. It felt sinister, particularly since he could not see their faces, only the illuminated visors which split the moon's face into two halves, imitating Cora's peach slices. Even more sinister was their ineptness, like some Greek Laurel and Hardy they teetered and slipped on the rocks. The fat one started sliding once, and the tall, lugubrious one grabbed his hand in a wild parody of the canary fish, himself balancing like a tightrope walker.

When they got to the esplanade safely, they became even more polite, asking him to walk slightly in front of them, so reverent or fearful of him that he felt the coufetta might explode against his chest.

Please, they said, Alphonse and Gaston, motioning him into the lighted seaside office. They took him to a back room, and motioned him to the best chair. An oval picture of Papadopoulos grinned from the white-washed wall.

He sat down.

"What can I do for you?" he asked in a phony voice, crossing his right leg over his knee, holding his ankle. He even cleared his throat.

The fat one cleared his too, straddled a chair, leaning his arms on the back, his guts and family jewels deposited in a heap. He acted embarrassed.

"Ah, hum," he began after a silence. "There are three *copelles, touristes,* up on the mountain, camping. One small with breasts and belly—" He gestured in the air around his body. "One medium-size, and one tall as a Turkish minaret with magnificent . . ." and he gestured again from his body two arcs of boobs.

There was a nasty silence. What was he supposed to do, laugh?

The tall, lugubrious one spoke with twitching lips. "Unfortunately, ergh, hugh hough." He also cleared his throat. "We can't speak English." A scowl appeared in the net of his thick, black brows. "Get him an ouzo!" he ordered the fat one in a bark.

The fat one took a bottle from beneath the desk, opened a drawer for the glass, poured, and asked him if he wanted water.

"No. Straight."

"We know you speak English," accused the tall one, still scowling.

"Because of your"—the fat one handed him the glass, gestured hips and breasts again in a lascivious waltz—"little pink porpoise at the Abra. Very discreet you are. Very discreet. We need someone discreet, you understand."

"We would appreciate it very much if you would translate for us."

He knocked off the ouzo and handed the glass back for more. Since when could Greeks not use sign language? And the fat one was a master.

"Could I have a glass of water, please?"

For he had to ingest the description of Cora at the same moment as he realized that the Turkish minaret was the giraffe.

"Since your Greek is so good . . ." the tall one with the ugly scowl continued.

He knocked off the second ouzo and took a sip of water.

"Come on, eh?" the fat one said conspiratorially. "It's not just an act of the barnyard, you understand. We like finesse. Look, we've packed a picnic, everything!"

What timing! Had they suspected, and rushed to get to him *before* he had spilled on the moon? But the fat one's greed was giving him his second hard-on. He examined the stuffed string bag full of bread, cheese, two roast chickens, and two bottles of retsina. The fat one was cataloguing: "If you'll do it, you can have the one of your choice."

"I want the tall one," he said immediately, knowing the fat policeman's face would fall. It did.

There is a different reason to fuck a woman each time. One of the bad reasons is challenge. Beneath the uniform of the junta's police lurks the soul of a hippie. If the hunters knew the hunted, who would be the quarry then? He felt the same refreshing beaker of corruption as on that day which seemed so long ago now, when he had been a pioneer with the drunk navy commander on the way to Suda Bay.

In the darkness, they started up the same cobbled donkey path he and Cora had taken. But when he saw that they were going to approach the girls' camp from below, he took charge.

"You can never approach women from below," he said to them. "Either come down on them from above, if it's on a mountain like this, or at least approach on the same level."

"He's right! He's right!" croaked the fat one, his voice silky with saliva.

"If you come up from below, they'll step on you with contempt."

"Or they'll get scared," Don said, growing excited, contaminated by the greed of the fat one. "They'll think you want to stick your horns up their ass."

His filthiness had worked. He had them in the palm of his hand. He tried to hear the sound of the rooster again. Nothing. Only the noise of their elephantine footsteps. They left the cobblestone way and went through a grove of olives. They were a few tiers above the camp. In the moonlight, they could see everything distinctly.

The girls had arranged their sleeping bags in a circle, but they were still sitting up. They looked like land-mermaids, the body bags forming their tails. The giraffe was even combing her hair.

"Quiet. You stay here. Let me go first," he whispered.

Stepping toward the circle was like stepping off the white night.

"Hey, you chicks," he yelled. "Knock, knock."

"Who's there?"

"Dewdrop."

"Do drop in, I suppose."

It was the giraffe. He went forward, so she could recognize him. He let the moon light his face completely, sauntered up, and said in a natural voice, "I don't want to wake you up or anything, but my name is Don Tsambalis and you've seen me before in town; I was sitting at the café when you walked by with Sergius, remember?"

"Well, you do look familiar."

She looked like Jane Fonda, but was dressed with fussy naïveté, puffed sleeves. It touched him. He had picked the right one. The other two were dumb-pretty, unmemorable. Their mouths were already open and receptive.

"The fact is that I wouldn't be here on my own, but I've been commandeered by two locals that you have bewitched. They wanted me to translate for them. They're over there by the olive tree. They've brought a picnic and everything—roast chicken, wine. They may even have a transistor radio. Anyway, they've got designs on you."

"You don't?"

"I play it as it lays."

The giraffe ignored the pun. "We're Canadians," she said. "I'm from Vancouver."

"Oh, really? I'm from Halifax. My mother was an American, though, from Cairo, Illinois."

The minute he said it, he wished he hadn't. But prowess demands the style of Epimenides, the Cretan, who said that all Cretans are liars.

"Let them approach," she said.

"Elate!" he shouted, waving.

They looked even worse in moonlight.

"Oh, I forgot to tell you," he said, "they're policemen. But don't let that worry you: it's even better. You've got a hold over them if you don't like them. All junta cops are afraid for their jobs."

Another lie, for if they raped them, they could manufacture any excuse and get away with it.

They were bowing and scraping, smiling lubricious smiles, and they sat down and opened the string bag. For a while, he translated very formally while the giraffe injected epithets:

"Keystone Kops. Rosencrantz and Guildenstern."

At last sign language took over, and leaving the other girls to take care of themselves, he devoted himself to her.

"Where is Sergius?" starting in on her father complex.

"That's not his name."

"Aristotle?"

"Nestor."

"No!" he said admiringly. He decided to make no moves, though. Having stuffed himself with chicken and retsina, he was now horny, even hornier at the prospect of its being the first time in two years that he would make a girl so much taller than he was. The large, firm, fruity breasts atop the sheer length of her were superb. A girl with a father complex also has a brother complex. He would be her brother, he decided. He let her tell him about Nestor. Nestor, she told him, was going to take her to Skiathos on his forty-five-footer (yacht, not cock, he translated), but meanwhile she was stuck with these friends of hers from the convent school. Frankly, sleeping bags and camping were not her style.

"Let's go for a walk, I've got a joke I don't really want to tell in front of your friends," he said, meaning the one about Jackie being the only woman in America who could kiss her Onassis. She liked it.

"No reflections on your style," he said, selecting the first olive tree out of sight, and bringing her down on the ground gently.

"Oh, I'm so glad you're not an American!" she breathed, making the word very dirty.

He looked up toward her chin. Feeling slightly guilty, he tried to imagine her mouth, invisible to him as a balcony above the concavity of skin. Her tongue would lie inside the mouth like some alluring monster.

She twined about him, enveloping him. He took off her clothes, marveling at her thinness. She was an armada, like Sanchez. He would have to begin with far shots.

He and Theo had wanted to deposit their first week's profits from the Tsambalis Bright, the laundry which Philo had lured them to incorporate, in a bank. Philo hated banks. He would not enter beyond the front door. He stood next to the big white wall waiting. He scorned them as they went inside to open their first account.

Mr. Mango was counting up the cash, scratching his hearing aid with his forefinger and writing the sum, $69.43, in the savings book. It filled them with pride. Mrs. Faith Shafter-Lowestoft was having a check cashed by Elise Eversill.

The siphoning up of phlegm in Philo's chest and larynx fit perfectly with the sound phenomena of banks: hushed voices, clanks of cage-grilles, squeaks of chairs. Theo and Don picked up their book and headed for him just as it had reached his tongue. The fact that he was dressed up in his natty brown suit, shoes polished to a high shine, his white hair bestowing upon him dignity, made it incredible to the people who actually were witnesses.

It happened in a split second. The explosion was loud, not clean like a shot, but prolonged, very large and liquid, and with a whistle of wind through water. If it had been done in a spittoon it would have been accepted, but on the wall it froze the audience in disbelief. They occluded it. Elise Eversill stared at it. Mrs. Faith Shafter-Lowestoft turned around to see what she was looking at. Mr. Mango, not having heard it, observed it like a Punch and Judy with less belief than the others.

The wad at eye level resembled an underdone fried egg, pale yellow in the middle and snot-loose at the edges. It dripped slowly down the blank plaster, forming little divisions over the pebbled grain. After a suspended interval, it arrived at the new green wall-to-wall composition carpet, where its welcome consisted in complete absorption and an enlarging, dark-green wet spot.

"I have made my deposit. Have you made yours?" said Philo, disappearing through the revolving doors.

"Does orgasm always make you hysterical with laughter?"

He opened his eyes through his jerks and giggles and sobered immediately. "I'm sorry, darling." Cora's word.

"Don't be sorry about anything! You're fabulous, you sleaze. You've got leadership to your very foreskin." She smiled generously. She would have fallen in love with Philo.

With the entrance of every new coed into their junkyard garden, Philo conducted an initiation ceremony. He told them a joke about the professor at the University of Tennessee who asked a coed why she had come to college. The answer of the coed was: "To be went with." Years of cringing at this terrible joke had not stopped Philo. He was the arbiter and judge, and he often warned them: "I don't want any floozies in any of my rolling stock." He was stuck in the twenties and girls were either "coeds" or "floozies." If a girl laughed at this joke, it meant she passed the test, and was a coed, not a floozie. Another test was smoking. If a girl smoked, Philo would say nothing, but he would sniff, cough, wave his hands in the air, and make innocent remarks such as: "It's strange. Don't you smell something awful, like garbage?"

But the junkyard of automobiles was a bad magnet for college students. They called it "The Oriental Archive." Theo was once forced to slug Bob Rhodes for calling Philo a curator. So Philo made Wyvono Ethridge build a ten-foot-high barbed-wire fence around it, upon which he planted morning glories. This cut down the number of condoms. The fucking of his first girl, however, took place in the Rolls-Royce, a discard of a millionaire Negro slum lord who had wrecked it by driving it through the plate-glass window of the Hung Wu Restaurant. Philo liked to flirt with the floozies and coeds Theo and Don brought home. But he made them cook, carry trays, and wait on him. He flattered and teased them. He liked the smart, beautiful ones who gave him a run for his money—girls flocked after Theo—and was ultimately as remote as a hermit.

One night, one of Theo's rejects brought the university chancellor's son to the Rolls-Royce where they smoked pot, drank Almadén, and left a mess. Philo blamed Theo.

"You're to blame yourself!" retorted Theo. "You flirt with all these floozies to inflate your ego."

After that Theo devoted himself to Ann Marie and chemistry and never brought another girl on the place. "That Ann Marie is a sourpuss with German bones," said Philo. "Is he going to marry her?" Philo was too superior to commit sex and too strong to talk about it. A bit like Saint Paul, whom he despised. He was really worried, however, because he could not bear the idea of his favorite son marrying a homely woman. "Well, how's Miss America today?" he would ask Theo sarcastically, as though the packaged icon would discourage him. But Don noticed in those days that Philo's eyes were moist and cheesy, as if, having ingested and incorporated their mother from Cairo, Illinois, about whom he would not speak, she had begun to speak out of his eyes.

*T*he next morning he checked out of the Flisvos. He chose an olive tree two mountains away from the girls' camp. It was on a terraced plateau high above the sea. He hung a mirror on a branch to look in while he shaved, and he hung his clothes on coat hangers from another branch. He had even bought a second-hand rug for the ground, and a sleeping bag to make a sofa. There was a well nearby for water.

As soon as he had made the house, he went to get Cora.

"Come and look," he said. "I want to show you something."

"How do you feel?" she asked.

"Fine." He had almost forgotten about the poisoned peaches. "No effects at all, in fact. What about you?"

"Phoo! I told you they weren't poisoned."

She was speechless at the sight. She clapped her hands together. "What is this?"

"A new conception," he said triumphantly.

"You have taken up your bed and walked!"

"This is just to show how a person can be a free agent." And it came to him, as he made her sit down on the sofa, how to explain it. Outdoors was indoors, yet the fact that it was a tree made it have a center. It was a fantasy of a house. You could use anything, branches, leaves, ground, anything that needed to be used. Just as personality pushes out of a face, the concept of shelter pushes out of a roof. A roof recedes to the depths of the sky. The domestic becomes infinite. The tree itself is the presence which makes the house alive, because it is cool in the fierce field breeze of noon, warm and protective against cold night dew. It is bountiful with olive blossoms, and it makes a good storage house for anything: food, clothes, sleeping bag, books.

They sat a long time.

"I had another dream last night about Vivien Leigh," she said.

His skin gave a sensation of tingling.

"I was in front of this churchlike place and a taxi pulled up and Vivien got out. I had been waiting for her. She had on a dark-green dress, almost black, and a pageboy bob, and we embraced each other like old friends. We went into the basement of the church and it was a room with seats and a stage like a theater and a man was playing the piano. A couple of people went onstage and sang some songs. It was an audition. I told Vivien that it was a musical version of a book by a friend of mine, and that I had written the music—"

I am the friend, he thought.

" 'Guess what, Vivien, I can't even read music!' I told her."

"Can you?"

"Yes, in real life I can, but in the dream I couldn't. She was absolutely amazed."

The word "amazed" played upon his ear.

"She couldn't understand how I could have written this music. I told her how."

"How?"

"I hummed each song and somebody—the dream didn't tell, it wasn't important—wrote it down for me."

"That's how?" Was *he* writing it down?

"Yes. Vivien thought it was marvelous that I had done such a thing for a friend. Then I understood why I was there. I wanted her to play the lead.

'Vivien,' I told her, 'I want you to play the lead.' She did not say a word. She simply went up to the stage, picked up the sheet music, and began singing."

"Is that all?"

"Yes."

"Then she *was* going to play the lead?"

"Yes."

Vivien Leigh as the Goddess! The degradation to movie star pleased him. Vivien Leigh's emanations went from Scarlett O'Hara to Blanche DuBois. Yet Vivien Leigh, he suddenly recognized, looked like the Minoan woman in the *Encyclopaedia Britannica.*

"Do you identify with Scarlett O'Hara?"

"Oh yes, of course! Tara. Tara. Tara."

Tara was Heaven of Irish mythology. Vivien had come to Cora to tell her to play the lead.

"It affected everybody of my generation. I was thirteen years old when they were looking for the person to play her. I read everything I could about her. Vivien tried on costumes that were still warm from the body heat of other actresses. She knew that she was to play Scarlett, for Scarlett is the one indisputable modern heroine. After all, tomorrow is another day."

Variations on Vivien, he improvised with glib enthusiasm. He had made the vow in London. Vivien came from London. The Goddess he expected to be Greek, must be, of course, American. His mother was American. The reality comes from Greece who never feared to anthropomorphize (Philo anthropomorphized for fun, giving life with his left hand, taking away with his right), but the icon is American. Northern.

"And do you identify with Blanche?"

"Yes, I identify with her too. I have always depended on the kindness of strangers. Don't, don't hang back with the apes. Do you know what happened to me once? I took Corey to see Vivien Leigh on the stage, in *Ivanov* by Chekhov. It was the last thing she did before she died. We sat in the second balcony. It was in New York in 1960 something, Corey was only ten or so. Five drunk people came walking down to the best seats in the orchestra. They were all dressed up. Evening gowns and tux. And guess what! They had an ape with them. A girl ape, all dressed up too, in a blue pinafore with a clean white apron. There they were in the third row. The ape sat on one of the women's laps and was on its knees looking at the audience over the woman's shoulder and making faces. Just before the curtain was about to rise, people started hissing and shouting, 'Get that ape out of here!' "

"Did they?"

"Yes. The minute I saw the usher come, I said to Corey, 'Let's go!' And I grabbed his hand and we ran down. Can you believe it! We sat right in the ape's seat! From there we could see Vivien up close. She coughed like this." She imitated a tubercular cough, delicate and refined, more like a rattle than a cough. He was galvanized. "Next day Earl Wilson wrote about that ape in his column."

"I know why you aspire to rockhood," he said. "Rocks have impartiality to offer. They are merciless. When I was ten years old, I got hung up on Purity because I knew there was no God. Philo always made jokes about old ladies, prostitutes, and helpless cripples who got converted by Saint Paul to the opium of religion, so I was ashamed to believe in God. I looked around to see what to believe in, and what I saw was that everybody, including me, wanted Freedom. So I thought: God is Freedom. Then I analyzed Freedom and saw that on earth Ultimate Freedom leads to killing. The only reason you think 'Freedom' is because you don't have it. There are obstacles. If there are obstacles, get rid of them. If the obstacles are people, kill them. If you are really free, then all it means is that you don't see the ants you step on. Thus, the world is based on to and fro, in and out, killing and birth. I wanted stasis, permanence. I saw permanence as purity." He waited. "Have you ever kissed a rock?"

"Yes, I have." Her voice was low and attentive.

"What's the main thing you noticed about it?"

"That it doesn't kiss back."

"Yes, they're sexless. Well, I adored the sexless! At the age of ten I used to play World War Two with Theo. In and out, of course. While I played it, I could see myself playing it, and I thought: There is a boy who is a fool. But I, Don Tsambalis, am a rock next to that boy, the fool. I am superior to all the fools and the in and out, down and around, about and beyond. I am pure and everlasting! At the same time I reveled in prowess and wanted to kill Theo with that stick—and did—and the more I killed him, the more I wanted to find a solution for the in and out, the to and fro, the killing and the birth, because I was sorry for the power of weapons."

"And if he killed you?"

"The same. Of course later this led to sex and to the difference between men and women, but I knew from the beginning, fucking and killing were a lot alike, so this is when I started in on my categories of Purities."

"What were your categories of Purities, darling?"

"First, I loved stuffed animals."

He liked conning her, liked her laughter.

"After stuffed animals?"

"Animals."

"You mean you believed they didn't have any sex?"

"No." Though Theo told him Keith and Kevin Howard had fucked Estes Mangum's nanny goat, and boys were always boasting about hens, he had blocked his mind. Even seeing dogs screwing had been a matter of surprise, that they did it in the open air without scruples. "But they weren't neuter either. I anthropomorphized them."

"And after animals?"

"Next to animals I loved boys."

"Were you a homosexual, darling?"

"Not really. I didn't desire their cocks and I didn't desire to be screwed by them. But I adored them. Like marble figures. Because they resembled me. Some might have been bigger, better, or stronger, but they were never as good as I, because I was purer. I could not find one boy purer than I was. If they were pure, they tended to be weak and to adore me, and I let them, but I had contempt for them."

"Were you cruel?"

"I am cruel, I think, don't you?"

She shrugged.

"What did you love after boys?"

"Men. You see, a young boy is more sexless, that's why I didn't love men as well as boys. Of course, maybe I'm lying when I tell you that I never arrived at wanting to kill with arrow and sword or to screw women. But this leads directly to the difference between men and women. I associate malehood with purity."

How much was he performing, how much laying it on to make her collaborate in his discoveries? He threw caution to the winds.

"Woman is classically impure compared to the male. For instance, women smell more than men. They smell of slicking snails, sulfur, earth's bowels, minerals, decayed seaweed, shellfish molting in sea-pools. Females go in and out more than males. Biologically, they exist simply in terms of going in and out, for the act of being caressed is the act of taking in, and the act of caressing, as females do to children, is the same as holding to the bosom. Look at the difference between the ultimate female acts and the ultimate male. The female takes the penis into the genitals, into the womb and re-creates it there only to have it push out as a baby which she again takes in, to her breast, and repeats this in-and-out movement ad infinitum."

He was not one to separate the kernel from the cadenza. He was enjoying this.

"In mythology, men with their thousand hoes and arrows plow and hunt, caressing in an orgy of creation, the Goddess splaying out every surface of her body with extravagant messages to take, thrilling man to worship while he sucks her, milks her, plants her, thinking her to be endless, because she has no outlines. I can certainly share a homosexual's repulsion; I have been hunting for a mother all my life, and unable to find any outlines. Always that something hot, moist, sticky, loving."

He noticed little pink veins in her cheeks. Was she shocked? He laughed up his sleeve, but was dead serious. He could feel his wrist muscles tighten, as though he were in the middle of an outstanding volley.

"A man, on the other hand, has outlines. No wonder Saint Paul thought women dirty. He could not find outlines, therefore he cast her out as a possibility for truth. She was just a big Isness, an unacceptable Isness who up to then had been worshiped. Hey! Isness Isis!"

She smiled, despite its being a bad shot. He rushed on, for he felt he was coming to something.

"She hasn't even got an outline for the part of her that does the contracting in and out. A cock is pure outline and bears witness with length, breadth, strut, and angle of erection." In improvisations, you shocked to be serious and insulted to be true. He despised the snobbery of smallness. "This is where purity comes in. Because if a man is just pushing out, the one-dimensional action of the killer-fucker, well, you could just say 'Fuck!' and be done with it. But outlines hint at truth. What is the truth? Now all men know that ultimate malehood, hunting, war, arrows, swords, guns, and screwing women is nothing—"

"But you do them," she interrupted sarcastically.

"Don't get me off my point!" he punned. "All men know that making a woman a female is not enough. When a man does it, he pushes out his essence (the seed goes out of his cock, the ego goes out of his head), but he *himself* is taken in. But the male doesn't want to be taken in. He wants to take in, too!"

But he does take in, he thought.

"But he *does* take in," he told her out loud and felt suddenly as if he understood the truth of God.

"Classically, the male takes in through the head." He spoke in an exploratory voice looking past and through her. "Milton put Adam's head next to God; God was thought; God could not ensconce anybody in moist heat and sticky kisses and the feel of flesh, all those undeterminables that have no outline and therefore cannot be a source of truth. Man as outline demanding outline, demanding Truth, not Isness. That was the mistake, for the taking-in through the head, and constructing from the head, all the domain of the male—reason, words, ideas, categories, no matter how constructively translated from killer deeds to good, humanistic deeds, to buildings, books, airplanes, railways, churches, and power plants—is the big delusion. Abstract to abstract."

He understood why it was that Christianity was the male religion, not the female. It was the only one which offered "taking-in" on a *physical* basis.

"Unless a man can take in physically, like a woman, he will be condemned to being taken in himself to the woman-land of moist chaos. Fearful. You cannot separate flesh from the meaning of being. The male has to take in physically to make spirit known. And the only way a male can take in physically is to take in a wound. Spear, sword, bullet, nail."

She looked not incredulous but merely as if she were bent on getting it straight.

"So the only way to be male is to go beyond the act of killing to ultimate martyrdom?"

"Yes. The strongest, freest soul is the man not afraid to take in the ultimate wound."

"And the ultimate purity of malehood is man's belief in God?"

"Yes."

"And God is the ultimate in Freedom?"

"Yes."

"That's not what you described."

"What did I describe?"

"Death. Your God is death. Also impotent, for any act with such a God is impotence."

"Motto: Don't commit suicide if you don't believe in God," he mocked.

It was very late and the sun was going down when they left the tree house. He was in a quiet mood, not brooding, but contemplative.

The sky had turned purple, and there was some dignity in the vision of the sea that he did not want to disturb. They ate at the café under the lights with the music of the bouzouki fading and falling behind them. They made small talk.

As they ate, the Canadian minaret passed by with Nestor.

"Look, the giraffe, again!" murmured Cora.

She saw him, and they exchanged a long and distant look, as final and complete as those horns of ships passing each other on the Aegean. Again the lights made her look like a photographic negative, her lips white because of the lipstick, her long, tanned arms black.

In slow motion he walked Cora back to the Abra, and he walked upstairs with her for coffee. On the balcony he saw the sky as a dome fully ripened, like the peach. The stars were not yet out, and the lights shone on them from her room.

After the waiter had brought the hot water and they had finished their coffee, she took up her knitting, and asked, "Did you ever talk to her?"

"Yes." He could see two hairs shining against the back of her neck, not more than two inches from his wrist.

"She puts too much lipstick on," she said. "It makes her look exactly like that goddess with the broken mouth in Lamia."

"Yes," he said, and touched the two hairs.

She turned around, shocked.

He strengthened his hold on her neck, leaned down, inhaled deeply—she smelled of peaches—and kissed her.

"What are you doing?"

He felt the sensation of coolness even after the kiss, but her lips, wet and innocent, were amazed. He unfastened the tiny buttons of her collar. Her knitting slid to the ground. He cut off the lights inside.

She fended off his pressure, but he took advantage of her motion, increasing the pressure on her neck, so that she was lifted out of her chair and into the room as if by his will alone, and her breasts slid out of the cloth. He had her down on her bed, her head above him on the counterpane. The balcony was a frame for the sea beyond the streetlights. Undoing her clothes was like opening a seashell. Her soft stomach throbbed, pinkish white, and he touched it with his forefinger. An objection rippled in her flesh.

"Don't speak," he warned.

He looked at her for a trace of Tragedy.

Her shoulders sloped, but her nakedness was too innocent. There was no trace of Tragedy. No trace of Sorrow. Her cunt was fairy fur, each breast a bunch like some lily pad on a wave, spilling whichever way he pressed it. She was all round, soft, tighter than he had imagined, but pliant, offering more to touch than to look.

He lowered his head, to merge, to feel, to go anonymous. He kissed her mouth first, and the peach taste thrilled him. He transferred it to her nipple, still tasting the peach. He worked it in his mouth. Sometime long in the past Corey and Eleanor had sucked it. He listened for the licking sound of the sea against the stones. She was giving up, turning into a vast breathing. But she was very slow, so he too became slow.

The more he sucked on her nipple, holding the spilling cup in his two hands, the larger he became against her, melting, feeling extremely tender. Suddenly, he knew he did not want to fuck her; he wanted to take her with his mouth, like liquid. He became filled with yearning, a longing to separate pride from purpose (conquest), so he moved his lips and tongue down into the soft, silk lining. Something threatened in her, something peripheral to the real. First, it was a contraction in the vast softness. She began heaving. He knew she was going to come to him, so he pushed his cock in.

He came. He spent his entire being in that push. And what was it? Nothing. A mere hit on the surface of the sea.

Later, when she got up, she didn't speak. She was putting the hairpins back in her hair, picking them off the pillowcase one by one. She dressed. He tried to figure out what her emotion was.

He could see she was not embarrassed. She was not angry, either. Her cheeks were very rosy and there was a glow in her eyes she could not disguise. Her mouth bloomed full. It was wet, almost purple where he had licked and taken from it, and he wondered if she were smiling, but he could not tell. He had never seen her so luscious before, so beautiful.

The next morning, she said, "Go to Athens."

"No, I won't," he answered evenly.

"You've got to deliver that coufetta. You're wasting time, marking time."

"What are you trying to evade? You want to get away from me?"

"Ridiculous," she said. "You act as if no one were after you. You act as if you know what you're doing."

"Are you worried about me? Or yourself?" He had to think fast. "I am not about to leave you, Cora. No." But he could not stand her contempt either, as if she were a Lotus Eater. "Don't you understand? I love you."

"You are romantic, extravagant."

But her eyes said something different from her words, so he pressed his advantage. "I—or you—may be nothing in ourselves, but we are at the service of something sacred. . . ."

"You mean you're not going to deliver the coufetta?"

"You let me worry about that."

"What about that man following you!"

"No man is following me now. I've shaken him, for God's sake." And since she was unconscious in falling into that woman's game of tempt and withdraw, he moved even faster: "There's a boat leaving for Skyros at ten. Let's go."

Everything pointed to a showdown between them. But what was there to show? He refused to admit that there was any discrepancy between his pursuit of her and the role he had cast for himself. If he could fall so easily into this mission for Zoe, then it was just as plausible that Cora should fit into it as that she should not. That's how you measure faith. He had to operate the polar sides of himself simultaneously, to allow destiny to pull him along without defying it, and, at the same time, to exercise his will in its details.

In fact, to allow destiny took more will. The will to be elastic, spongelike, to spread, to accept disparate currents. The curbing of his aggression in ping-pong was not female. It involved restraints, crunching, hunching, reining himself in. But this destiny demanded his will to the other side of femalehood; it required a loosing of his inchoate self. She personified it. He recognized that, having spent himself last night (a failure, he decided), he would have to trap her, to pin her down.

On the boat they were uncommunicative. He kept looking at her, but it seemed as if she were smiling a secret smile.

The town of Skyros hung like a hammock between mountains. The new hotels were situated half a mile below on a newly developed beach. He booked her into the Xenia, made a date to come for her at seven, and started on foot to find lodgings, to explore.

On the beach he saw a sign with blue-and-white letters: "Keep This Koast Clean." He felt afraid, as if he might never see her again.

The road turned into an old, cobbled way. It led to a small square, from which a double stairway led upward to right or left. A sign with red letters said "Sto Brook," and an arrow pointed to the right. A brook at the top of a mountain? It did not make sense. People looked out at him from the windows. An old lady crocheting lace on her doorstep smiled at him, and a fit of love smote him so sharply that he felt like weeping.

"Kali Imera."

"Welcome to Skyros, *paidi mou,*" she told him.

The houses stacked like boxes in the rising gold light were capped by a monastery. The afternoon was cold and windy. When he got high enough, the surface of the sea filled the horizon in three directions, an infinite and alien blue, some other world from where the wind came. On the street, he passed a man carving a chairback. He came to a new sign with the same legend: "Eis to Brook," but the vermilion lettering on this one looked like blood dripping.

He stopped for a cup of coffee, left his pack at the kafenion, and started upward again. More signs. Two. He followed them.

Immediately below the monastery the ground leveled off into a square, bare and flat, with planted trees, and in the middle stood a statue of Rupert Brooke, naked, his bronze body molded to a viscous green. His face, intended to be soulful, was romantically bankrupt, moronic. One shoulder sloped. It was the long-shot of the North! Sorrow. But the sculptor had made the eyes those blinded bulbs of ancient statues, and in this incongruity was revealed the feckless collision of North and South. A mongrel!

No wonder Christianity ended in social service and the ethics born of reason.

"If I should die, think only this of me: That there's some corner of a foreign field/That is for ever England." From the kingdom of God to the kingdom of England.

Poetry of the North, like sorrow, has to be private to be valid, opposite in conception to the poetry of Tragedy, the Greek drama, which was religious poetry, social poetry. And after the classical age, only the Church saved the poetry of Tragedy, freezing it in litanies as its content, unguaranteed, went corrupt. The last public poetry became ballyhoo in Ireland, gilded cruelty in Germany, troglodyte visions in eastern Europe, white-lit guilt in Sweden. Shakespeare revived the chorus, but only witches spoke, and the message traversed the centuries like sinister sabbaths of beggars, ending up in T. S. Eliot begging a mercy as milky and ingrown as corneas imprisoned in lead.

Someone was staring at him. It was a woman in black carrying her washing in a blue plastic tub on her hip.

"Brooke's ashes there—over there—" She pointed to a distant stone cropping out of the sea, and she smiled shyly, on her upper lip a faint growth of mustache. *"Sti thalassa!"*

Keats, Shelley, Swinburne, Brooke, singing the poetry of the individual. In the name of sincerity. Separate. Church services died. Ethics against litanies. Actions not words.

He looked at the steep and lonesome rock in the sea where she pointed. He imagined the ashes dissolving in the waves. Oh Rupert Brooke without a church.

Then he looked at the statue. From Rupert's figleaf dripped some white substance which long ago had stained the green mold. Ephemeral. Perennial. God lost from his worship. Each of us individually must take the guilt that Christ died for. Without the chain of celebration, we alone are to blame. Purists, moralists, we have shattered Christ's victory, and the weight has fallen on our shoulders alone.

When the woman had gone he took out his pencil and a piece of paper.

"Dear Cora," he wrote, sitting at the base of the statue. "You are only half a mile away and I shall see you at 7 o'clock. But I imagine: 'What if I never see you again?' 'What if you go back to America?' "

But he knew it was hypocrisy, that it was he who might go to Athens and never see her again.

He creased the paper, tore the fold, crumpled up what he had written and put it in his pocket so he would not litter Greece.

"Dear Cora," he began again on the paper which was left. "It is very lonely here this afternoon because you are not here. I am trapped in my solitude and my love and I do not believe in poetry any more than you do. So where shall I place my belief? I am in a dying afternoon, light gold and growing thinner and thinner, leaving only a horizon and pure pale light. The wind is cold and comes from so far away it is another world. Only the alien blue is mine. The people of Skyros are very kind and gentle, but the wind has scoured them and scooped the soul out for itself, leaving us only philoxenia and Rupert Brooke. Now I see the world as dead.

"The Greek world is dead (the world of categorization, manners, and the processes of reason). It led to chopped forms and schism. The Judeo-Christian world is dead. (The world of the absolute All. Ye shall worship no idols, only Me. God is Absolute, Pure, and No Form. Moses gave ethics as Law.) .

"So where is living? You talk of the goddesses—"

Was it a mistake to go hunting these goddesses in every museum on every island? He couldn't finish it. He folded up the paper and put it in his shirt pocket, next to the coufetta.

Walking downward to the kafenion to get his pack, he talked to Cora out loud. "I touched you," he said.

There was a small blond English girl sitting in the café with a swarthy Greek.

No, I did not touch her, he thought, turning Cora to third person. In the English girl's green-and-white-with-key-pattern bag there was a copy of the *Athens News*. He sat down at the next table and ordered coffee.

Suddenly, he leaned over. "Excuse me. Could I borrow your paper for a moment?"

The girl imitated a kitten, tipping up her face adorably helpless.

There was a sinister flash of gold from the Greek's mouth as he scowled.

"Of course," mewed the girl with a lavish smile.

"Sex Change in Fishes Studied" ran the headline.

An Australian zoologist has spent the last three years sitting on the sea bed watching fishes change their sex.

Mr. Ross Robertson, a 28-year-old postgraduate student at Queensland University, said this week he discovered that the cleaner fish, a small, iridescent wrasse, is capable of changing completely from female to male within three weeks.

The Greek couldn't speak English. They were talking French.

He said that the male cleaner fish has a "harem" of five or six females to each of which he pays regular attention.

Almost immediately after the male dies, the chief "wife" begins displaying all the aggressive characteristics of the male. And within three weeks is sufficiently male to fertilize other female's eggs.

He folded the paper lengthwise and returned it to her.

"Thank you."

"Not at all."

She was overacting. Greece must have made her lose all sense of proportion. Ravishing. Breathless. Pretty. Preening.

"That man is no good for you."

"What?"

"Where did you meet him? On the boat?"

"No. I—"

"I wouldn't trust him as far as I could throw a piano."

Her lip quivered and her blue eyes showed a perplexed alarm.

"Get right up from there now."

"But I can't!"

"How old are you? Seventeen?"

"No. Nineteen."

"Tell him I want to swap my *French Lieutenant's Woman* for your *Tess of the D'Urbervilles.*"

She stammered his exact line to the man in French. Both titles sounded good in that language, but especially Tess D'Urbervilles with her faltering accent. A dark cloud lowered itself onto the man's already low forehead.

"Tell him you'll see him later."

She did. The man shrugged.

"I don't care if you do see him later, but he's a sleaze," he said, propelling her along double-time.

"I thought there was something funny about him!" She was gasping in tiny, relieved flutters.

"You should be careful who you get in with. In fact, what are you doing traveling alone?"

Now that he had her, what did he want with her? She was twenty-two if she was a day? He had neatly picked up his pack as well as her, and he sidestepped her to a hotel that appeared on the street they had entered. The Skyros Hotel.

"I can get it out for you right here, or, if you want, you can help me register for a room."

"Get what?"

"*The French Lieutenant's Woman!*" She was blushing.

"What?" he said pretending shock. "You haven't read it already, have you?"

"No."

He registered. They climbed the stairs. Big double bed. He leaned down to open his pack.

She leaned against him crooning familiarly, "What are you doing?"

"Getting the book."

"I'm not terribly fond of reading, really, you know."

"No. But you ought to read it."

"Why?"

"It shows you how to be an authentic woman and how not to take up with crummy characters."

"Oh you! Why do you keep on with all that stuff?"

"What? *The French Lieutenant's Woman?*"

"Yes, you naughty great liar. Anyway, I don't have *Tess of the D'Urbervilles.*" She was reverting to kittenhood, rubbing herself against him.

"I know that. When I lie, I always do it by telling the truth out of context. That's the easiest way because people automatically don't believe you, and doing it like that has great suspense. Like this book which also has suspense, although you may be disappointed in the ending because it's preaching freedom of choice and all literature has taught us to believe in the inexorable and inevitable."

"I hate boring things. Are you sure you want to give it to me?"

"Yes, I do." He sat on the bed. She sat on his knee.

"Why?"

"Because I'm sick of giving anybody anything I don't believe, and because you need it. I can spot what people need immediately."

She took the fingers he had just snapped and placed them on the cloth of the halter, between her breasts. He tried to find her breasts through the cloth. He pulled the whole halter off. She had no breasts at all, but tiny soft bumps, like white doorknobs, with extraordinarily high, tight nipples.

"I have to meet some girl friends on Tinos and the boat is leaving at four-thirty," she warned, unhooking her leg from his knee and girdling his waist with it. It was extemely lascivious, the feel of the hotness of her vagina in waves on his jock, yet she was as light as a vine. He took off his pants, stripped her completely, and screwed her to kazoo.

"Oh, you're good, you are," she said, cuddling him with satisfaction.

He got her to the boat just on time, her bag heavy with *The French Lieutenant's Woman,* her psyche reverted to quivering virginhood, her glance clinging to him from her waving tendril of neck. Something was déjà-vu about it. He knew the Greek sleaze was hiding behind one of the smokestacks and so his attention kept wandering from her.

The ropes were cast off. The boat hooted and moved off in a moil of water against the dock. He looked again and saw the two figures meet. Now he knew why the déjà-vu. Annette Borlin.

Back in his room he made up his bed and finished the note to Cora.

"Who is She? Do you know?" He thought of signing it A Don Is, but rejected the cleverness and wrote "Don."

He gave Cora the letter at dinner. She read it in the bamboo restaurant with the wind blowing yearningly, crackling the paper, making the light bulbs swing, casting their shadow-monsters on the whitewash. He thought of it as a test rather than a declaration and told himself: "I don't care what she thinks." But the blood roared in his ears and he plumbed her expression for reaction. She took a long time, concentrating as if it were Shakespeare. Then she folded it up, gave him a glittering, generous smile, and continued smiling in silence afterward.

The next morning, early, he walked down from the Skyros Hotel to pick her up and they boarded the ship *Niki* bound for Mykonos.

They walked around the second deck.

"Look what's happening to the Goddess as we go east, Cora."

"What?"

"She's becoming that prototype with the twenty-four breasts and arms stretched out based on Artemis/Sybil."

"Yes, and she's spreading out and getting fat and she's clay!"

"She's always accompanied by a cow now."

"A cow! That's not a cow, that's a bull!" She placed her hands on her knees in her familiar gesture and broke down in laughter.

Beneath the heat spreading like a paste across his face and neck, he registered a shock of memory. When he was four years old, Philo had brought home—ostensibly as a companion for his dog, Jack—a German shepherd mongrel which he named Leo. The friendship did not start well. Jack had a ruff like a lion and a habit, bored and gentlemanly, of following Philo everywhere, stopping when he stopped, looking away when he delivered polemics. He was standoffish. But Leo's large, emulsive, ebullient, and slavishly affectionate tongue licked him to tolerance.

Leo, being the younger dog, bounded with energy. Don identified with him and took him over. He trained him to heel and shake hands. One day, Theo discovered Leo to be female. Don was heartbroken that he had identified with a female. But it was of such importance that they had to tell Philo. It took three days to work up the courage. They kept stalling for "the right time." It turned out to be supper. Theo announced, "Philo, Leo is female." Philo was chewing on a piece of liver with onions. He looked at Theo, put his eyeballs up in their sockets, and moved his knife from the left side of his plate to the right, without once stopping the rhythm of his chewing, even when they knew it was masticated enough to swallow. Theo repeated the news. They waited. But he kept on chewing. Without acknowledgment, the fact had no truth. It became the mere order in which you thought it: Leo, who is female, is male.

Philo never said a word until Leo became pregnant with sprouting milk-filled dugs and a litter of German-shepherdish puppies, living proof of the Greek ideal of progeneration—head or womb, what does it matter: "You will have to get rid of these puppies," he ordered. They knew the ominous meaning of "get rid of," and in a feat of entrepreneurial ingenuity they avoided it. They sold the litter door-to-door for fifty cents per puppy and continued to call Leo "he."

"And other wild animals like tigers," added Cora, still laughing.

A sense of freedom burst through his chagrin. What a fool he was! What conceit! He felt stripped, washed, cleaned, and he looked at her with amazement. Beyond her head were two plaques, which read from left to right: "Constructed and launched in Glasgow, 1897" and "Reconstruzzione, Italia, 1952."

From the glow of this glance she told him softly, "I had another dream last night."

A delicious danger threatened.

"About Vivien?"

She nodded. Vice, the clench of his fists. Viciousness to counteract

Vowelhood. Victory, he hoped, to rise out of their conspiracy. He waited. Her voice was breathless but full of suspense.

"I found myself in this ground-floor apartment, kind of decaying. It was in an old mansion in a city. Two men had been there and gone. And then Vivien came. She said I'd been neglecting her, that she missed me. Then she disappeared. The two men came back. One said he had a letter for Vivien." (His letter, last night, of course.) "And asked me if he could leave it. I said yes, so he did, and left. But the other man took the letter and began reading it. I was shocked at this invasion of Vivien's privacy. I grabbed the letter away from him. The next thing I was running desperately to find Vivien, so I could give her the letter. I ran into a store filled with shoppers. In the distance on a kind of raised split-level floor I saw her. She was waving to me, surrounded by a great ring of light. I rushed toward her. But the shoppers were milling around and when I got there, she had turned into someone else. Someone I didn't know."

Her privacy? His letter? What part of her was Vivien? Suddenly, he noticed that her voice had been out of sync all this time.

"The Greeks killed the Goddess."

He thrilled at the accusation in her eyes.

"But the Jews—" he argued.

"It was before the Titans that the Goddess prevailed, back before the year fifteen hundred B.C. And that's what we've been seeing in these museums. The myth of the Titans could only arise after the Goddess was murdered. In fact, the Greeks made Rhea the culprit, you know. They said she instigated it, remember? They said she made Zeus, her own son, kill Cronos."

Such talk, heedless, inaccurate, belonged to their cabalhood. Philo was the Greek murderer.

"He killed our mother," said Theo in that boardinghouse room on McCauley Street after he had run away.

"What do you mean?"

"Philo killed our mother by his sheer existence."

Cora, his wizard other-soul, was so close that he felt a snip in his brain. He was on the brink of understanding the scream. Homer was a great apologist of her murder, and Athena was her death mask. He compared Athena's face with Zoe's again, but again that difference: Zoe's face was human and tragic, Athena's was divine and dead. After, the Christians had taken over. For, having been murdered, she kept appearing everywhere. Especially in Christianity. Fragments of faces multiplied. V turned W, which upside down made Man, Machine, Mind. It begged for Vowels. "Vowel Movement Makes Meaning!" He heard Philo.

"He's a great man, Don, old buddy. Never forget that. He squashes from pure idealism." And Theo took the bag of figs Philo had sent as a peace offering, tossing it from hand to hand as if it were burning him.

It was dark when they passed through the Strait of Andros and Euboea. A Greek in shorts with a domed forehead and owlish, horn-rimmed glasses told them:

"That's Yaros, where they keep the political prisoners."

"Why did he say that?" she whispered when they were alone. "They never talk about that gratuitously."

"He was boasting that he's not afraid."

"Maybe he was threatening."

"Threatening me?"

The wind which had begun in Skyros had increased during the night. It tossed the ship. Its quality had changed from loneliness to capriciousness. Yet the moon rose quite calm and innocent. Her insistence on danger gave him a feeling of being sucked into something, succumbing. The waves were jittery, and foam flecked the deck creamy and phosphorescent.

"Yes, you." Cora had to struggle to keep her balance. She looked drunk, arms flailing the air, feet seeking footing against the wind and leaping bow.

He took her elbow to steady her. The wind was cold so he made her wear his nylon windbreaker with the hood up. He led her to a coil of rope, thick, dry, perfect for sitting on. It appeared as if he had chosen it for the rape, and to rape a monk would save him from murdering a goddess.

The danger put them into a state of hilarity. They understood each other perfectly on this level. She was charming in the peaked hood, and she knew it.

"Do you like love?" he asked, ravished.

"Of course."

"I love love." He even thought it was funny he could talk like this when he knew he was going to commit rape.

"As evidenced by your note."

Her dry tone delighted him further. What he would do was pounce when she least expected, no lead up. She would laugh, thinking it would be wrestling, like children or angels. Yes, they fitted together. She wanted rape, he knew. And he wanted outlines. The dark shapes of boxes and a Volkswagen with a plastic cover like the V of her hood pointing upward toward the moon and plunging downward into the sea.

The ship was on the back of a huge, untrustworthy cat, its waves raised against the enemy. They were coming near to Tinos, a dark hump with scattered lights.

"Tinos. See?"

"Are we going to land?" she asked.

"It looks so." And he contemplated doing it while they were docked, in full view of those lit monasteries on the dark mountain whose aisles and pillars were ornamented by the discarded canes, trusses, crutches, and hearing aids of those crippled, blind, and diseased faithful who had been disgorged by ships like this. Prince Philip's mother had died up there before one of those burning candles. They had taken the carcass to Buckingham Palace.

He would put his hand over her mouth, stifling the scream the Goddess would try to make through her mouth. They would be in shadow.

Men came in silhouettes, shouting, not three feet away from them, but the docking was very tricky because the wind whipped one way one minute and another the next. It was done with ropes. The hotel windows looked out at them scared, and the houses clung above, each to the next.

A crane started moving. It was not propitious. The men tied the Volkswagen beneath each wheel and lifted it into the air to deposit it on the quay.

"The lights are twinkling," mused Cora as they watched passengers leave the ship. And then she improvised during the next hour on the word: "Tinkling, dinkling. No. Dunkling." The childish words were strange on the back of this slippery, evil black monster which did not want to be known by those lights.

The men cast off. The ropes slattered across the water. The lights faded away and they headed into a black sky pierced with stars. The morning star had risen by the moon and was pulling the prow along. There was some music far away in the saloon, but most of the passengers had gone, the men had gone, and lit by a fleck of phosphorus, they were alone in a vast breath.

"In and out," he prompted, as if it were the name of a song he wanted her to sing.

"In and out, in and out," she said in time to the ship's listing. "Oh, aren't you glad we didn't land there? That we only deposited the Volkswagen? But now we have only the stars, darling, and the blackness in and out, in and out is the real form of the Goddess. Although the stars are trying to disguise her by twinkling. See, round and above us so close, she is the sky. Down and under, she is the sea. In and out she breathes, and we are in her breath. We cannot escape."

She took his head in her hands. Her fingers moved down across his ear to his shoulder. The stroke was quite deliberate, yet he could not believe it. The ship listed. She used the motion, unbuttoned her blouse and gave her breasts to him.

He took them in his hands and fondled them. He extracted her flesh out of its cocoon of clothes deftly doing away with buttons, zippers. She lay in full pride naked, except for her head still encased in the pointed hood, her arms resting lightly on his arm. There was a half-smile on her face, belying his shock, and he took the hood off her head. Was she seducing him because she had known he was going to rape her?

This lovemaking was different. She began rubbing his chest and arms lightly with her breasts, her thighs. Her movement mixed in his mind with the long rocking of the ship, and her flesh was soft and silky, diaphanous, as if she hovered over him instead of touching him. He concentrated on sections of her body. It required that he look the moment that he touched. He looked at the curve of her buttock. He followed it with his hand. But this surface began to escape him, for the balance swayed in both of them as the bow plunged and the moon's light moved.

Then it focused on the concave at the base of her left nostril, where it curved to the corner of her lip. This curve expressed two things. The first was the tenderness for which all men dream. The second was the sneer of the Goddess and the sphinx. He took her head in his hands, moving it one way and then another to decide *which* it was, stroking it, worshiping it. But it too disappeared, slipping out of his hands as the stern sank behind them shifting his gravity downward.

Her billows were transformed by the moon to slippery planes. The position known in one second fled away in the next. He could hold on to nothing. Like water or silk she escaped from his touch.

These details, understood by his mind only to elude him, suddenly became quick. He had to give up visualizing just to follow her motions. Before she had been slow. Now she was quick and light. She was outrunning him, twisting herself, changing to the opposite direction. The senses of sight and touch became confused.

At the moment her nipples hardened, she was all around him as if the moon had widened itself to become the sea.

"We're fucking in public, Cora!" he cried, scared.

"Sh-sh-sh."

Waves of moonlight splashed in his ears. Pale light blistered him. Her familiar mouth became unrecognizable. He inhaled some perfume mixed with salt spray. He could not isolate one action, he who had worked up dry riverbeds, conscious of stones; he was trying to chase her movements as they grew lighter and longer. At a sudden moment he opened his eyes to identify, to name it one last time. Something very slow and deep came from a pause in her. He had to adjust himself. His ear was on the heartbeat of night. Stasis was near, but it was not stasis. She quivered. He felt that something definite was almost in his hands.

He was at the height of his power when she overwhelmed him with a dark withdrawing. He lost himself trying to find her, and when she pushed the gift forward on him, it was as if the bow had risen too. It took a long time to throw himself away. She did not make a sound, still rising as the bow plunged downward back of her. He began to sob in her neck, holding her breasts still in his hands, like crushed flowers. It seemed beautiful to him, this waste. He was assailed by a sense of wonder for waste.

The next two days the pattern of their relationship changed. He never left her side. He stopped the charade of going to a different hotel. He slept with her at night. Minutes were so freighted that they contracted into hours the feeling of days. Time became white. She had no age to him. They did not talk. They existed in a realm of silence and sensuality in which they were melded and looming and everything about them diminished. Sometimes they made comments, but they were mere reminders of an individuality which had become submerged.

The boat stopped at Paros for a few hours.

"I want some candy," she said.

It was past noon. The wooden doors were shut by law. Imperturbable, she found a bonbon shop with its door open a crack and slipped in.

"We are closed," said a woman who was sweeping in the darkness within. She gave them a significant look.

"Ah, look!" cried Cora, her roving eye spotting a box of fancy sugared fruits. "Wouldn't it be possible for me to buy just that one with the red bow, please?" She smiled unselfconsciously.

"But it is forbidden."

Cora prepared to go.

"The law," said the woman, faltering but fascinated. She raised her hand.

"Wait," closed the door completely so that the light of noon was blocked out. "If the police catch us—"

"We will hide it in this newspaper," Cora said, her pupils shining in the darkness.

With the sounds of the street shut out, the conspiracy against the unknown bloomed and tourist Greece became the Greece of political prisoners, decadence transposed into a truth which the gaiety and whitewashed walls obscured. The woman eyed the door furtively, handed Cora the box, whispered good-by and, when they left, pretended not to know them.

Against this danger, when they had gone through a warren of little streets, Cora sat down on a little wall surrounding a tree and chewed a sugared apricot.

"Doesn't it bother you to be slumming in fascism?" he asked.

"I'm not the one who didn't deliver the almonds." She chewed carefully, looking beyond his ear with sparkling eyes.

"If we get caught all they'll do is put us out of the country. But if she gets caught, jail."

"Balooey. Does it help not to know?"

"Is eating candy knowing?"

"It's better than being a hypocrite."

He was ravished with admiration. He bent down, kissed her, and in the kiss seized the apricot out of her mouth.

It was she who noticed the signs of the junta: the phoenix rising out of two bayonets.

"Those aren't bayonets," he said, but she insisted. "Greece for the Greek Christians and nobody else," she read. And laughed.

They reboarded the boat for Naxos. They entered towns and departed from them by the island boats, changing universes on whim. Nothing by decision.

Did she know? To be insouciant and know was a strange power. Or did she not know? Was she blind and superficial?

"All the time I thought I wanted these nymphets, I was a mother-fucker," he mocked, waving the flag of his egotism above the surface, for he was rendered up by the silence of the sea and sky to a state of nature.

On the boat, apropos of nothing, she referred to her seduction on the ropes as the Second Coming. She said she had seen the captain in the glass booth above them, his face lit and pale in the reflection of the dials. Don's scalp prickled.

"Did he see us?"

"Of course not. He was steering."

"You saw that and said nothing?"

"Tell you, darling, when you were so shocked at making love under the open sky?"

"You're crazy, Cora. But tell me what the captain looked like from down under me."

She described him so vividly that he saw first Hamlet's father, then Philo, then the Presence. The Presence was the turning inside-out of Absence. It happened to him usually when he was looking at great views. He felt the Presence in the sea when he looked through his mask. Once, when he had been hitchhiking in France and had been picked up by a French couple near Grenoble in a cardboard Citroën with two cylinders which stalled in the Alps, he had felt the Presence. The French couple had, too. The whole world went gray, and snow fell. It was overpowering, and they were afraid. And another time that same trip, on a stretch between Cannes and Nice, when he had got out of a car he had decided on whim to go swimming. He climbed down from the road and the moment he was in the sea, he felt it. Cars were traveling along the Corniche above, people sitting at roadside cafés, a few swimmers, yet everything was so clear, so powerful that he knew it. It was a wonder that the people in the cafés, the swimmers, the people in the cars did not freeze at once in its power, which was electric, thrilling, or ecstatic. Yet in this case it was their unconsciousness which proved the Presence, and the silence of the trees, the bluffs, the stones, the waves which the Presence inhabited.

"Fortunately, I don't have to bother with children any longer," she was saying, changing shape under his hands.

A penumbra of her flesh like the sea always surrounded him, flowing through his fingers, sinking into his collarbones. A breast across his mouth like sliding silk. A sail of belly billowing against his legs. He drew from her while she sailed on past him, leaving her perfume. Then she turned around and surprised him by alighting upon him like a bird.

That night he dreamed that she was his daughter, an unreliable child of five years. In the dream he was wickedly thrilled, and he raped her in the hayloft of a barn which moved. He woke into another dream in which he discovered that it was not a rape, that she had seduced him, and he understood that the second dream was the truth of the coil of rope. "Theo and I always wanted a little sister," he told her in the dream, "because if we had had one, then Philo could have let our mother go and loved you in her place. Then we would have had a female in the house, and we would have known what that meant." But the fickle little girl opened her mouth and said the following words:

> "Fickle, fuckle, bet my buckle
> You don't know what
> The dunkling stars of Tinos say."

The actual words were notes of laughter, although in the dream she was not laughing. Incest was thrilling. His dream confirmed him in the knowledge that she was himself and he her. He had no need of resistance against Philo, like Theo, who picked Ann Marie to marry, finishing forever Philo's great expectations and patronage. (No woman is good enough for us, raged Theo. He patronizes, the girls cook dinner, he criticizes. What does he want?)

On the Island of Ios she came running to tell him she had another dream about Vivien. He was jealous, he was galvanized. He was dependent, he was envious. Why was it the messages came to her?

"I had just been to a play and gone backstage to this dressing room which had light bulbs and mirrors going from the floor to the ceiling. Also a long staircase like the one in Twelve Oaks. Reporters and photographers and flowers and noise and flashbulbs were going off every minute, and all of a sudden Vivien was at the bottom of the stairs in a long dressing gown, and she ran to my arms and ordered all the reporters and photographers out and turned to me and said, 'I have been waiting for you to tell me what you think of my performance.' I said, 'Vivien, it is one of the best things you have ever done.' She smiled her happy-little-girl smile and then told me confidentially, 'You know Katharine Hepburn is doing her play at the theater across the street and she is waiting for you and me to dine with her.' I heard the hubbub of reporters outside her dressing room and said we'd never get through that crowd, but Vivien laughed and said, 'We'll go by the underground passageway.' She opened a door and said, 'This leads right to it,' and just as I tried to see where the door was going, I woke up."

At last the Goddess was living through Vivien, through Cora albeit. But now something was going to happen. Literally. It was leading somewhere. Underground passage. It frightened him. To counteract the implications he pretended that they were psychological: that the Vivien-feminine part of Cora was about to go through some underground passageway to enter the Hepburn-masculine part of herself which represented the independence that Athena-women thought they must inhabit for the modern world.

But she interrupted: "That's not all. I went to sleep again."

He was too frightened to laugh.

"Guess what."

He waited.

"It took up right where it left off, but instead of being a door at the end of the room, there was a curtain. She pulled the curtain aside. Underneath was a door the same color as the curtain, cream-colored. 'Vivien, what is that?' I asked. 'That's the underground passageway.' And she laughed. When she opened the door, I saw this huge tunnel, shaped just like a subway tunnel. We both looked at it, laughed, and then started to go into it. And I woke up again. This time for good."

"I love you," he said, giving up, burrowing his head in her breasts, her belly, rocking her in his arms. "I love you. I love you." The banality of the images confirmed the reality of the Goddess. Cream-colored doors. Movie stars. Underground passageways. Stage doors. Shubert Alleys. If a thing is worth dreaming, he thought, it is worth dreaming badly. Americans slumming in fascism, the Goddess appearing in the trivial; in these days, in these times the only appropriate underground passage to knowing. Only in the extreme can there be knowledge. Her flesh smothered his awe of the passageway and made possible the fact that it was going to happen. Then it endowed him. He reveled in its generosity. What it meant was that between them, her being was the confluence. He focused on her flesh. She focused on her flesh, too. He focused on her dreams. She was in the center of her dreams. His reality gave way to her reality. It made sense to him now at last, and the very delusiveness of Greece, pretending to be the same Greece under the dictatorship, reflected the dangerous reality which connected her dream messages with the increasing nearness of the Goddess. He felt the growing sense of knowledge as power and, like a giant, he lay this power before her.

"I worship you."

"That's what's wrong with the world. People have no place to put their worshiping instincts." She had a preoccupied expression. "That's why technology has made material the fantasies of those who invented it and the atomic bomb is a debasement of people's power to worship."

Had he said these words she was playing back to him? He laughed.

He sucked her nipples, thinking again of Eleanor and Corey and of time itself, of the years she had spent nourishing and cherishing these two people, strangers to him. He tried to taste the juices, in awe, as if she knew the process of which she was processee, and as if he could know it by tasting. He made her tell stories of their growing up. Had she breast-fed them? Yes. He loved her for her mother-love of them. He saw her whole. He tried to mother-love them himself. Then he tried to be Eleanor and Corey loved, working his lips and tongue around the same purse of flesh, feeling it grow hard with wonder that he was a stranger and a man, not her child.

The element of insanity in her psyche that aggrandized the role of performer—"You're an actress," he accused fondly. "Only actors can perform the sacred. I found that out. The holy can't appear except as performance"—he recognized as truth. Her arrogance made his mouth water and her outrageousness fed his passion. Hair rose on his arms. She was like aged movie stars who watch their old movies and refer to themselves as "She."

"Do you think of yourself as 'She'?"

She paid no attention. She was too caught up with the Sacred and the Holy. "The difference between you and what you are doing is how conscious you are. If you are what you are, you're blind."

That afternoon she took up with a man in a store where she bought writing paper. Impulsively she accepted his invitation for them to dinner at his house. When they arrived the whole household had been turned upside down, everything cleaned, glasses polished, the best silver and napkins set out. It was not a rich house. It had no electricity or plumbing.

135

They sat in the courtyard to a feast: stuffed eggplant and rabbit stew; aunts, uncles, cousins, children, grandfathers gathered in the night around the flare of the gas lantern breathing in the sight of her, feeding on her smiles, toasting welcomes. Faces gleamed in wobbles of light. Suddenly, she had to go to the bathroom. The lady of the house led her out across the courtyard to a cubicle. Everything stopped. Dead silence.

When she came back, the conversation turned to strange happenings. The host told of Agios Nektarios raising to life a woman on some island who had died two years ago of cancer, appearing three times to her husband. Another man told how when his father died, a little dog had appeared, and how he had kept the dog for five years—until it was run over by a car, and how he believed that the dog had been five extra years of his father's soul remaining on earth. Somebody asked where the soul goes when you die.

For dessert the host brought out a bowl of juicy, fresh strawberries. Cora cut her finger with a knife. Women rushed for bowls of water, bandages. In the flurry there was the strange sound of footsteps.

A goat entered the courtyard, its eyes solemn, its nose sensitive and sorrowful, its horns curving gracefully behind its ears. It paused just long enough for the smell, deep as chocolate, to draw the horrified gaze of the company to the platform of its back which bore, as abstractly as the platter bore the decapitated head of Saint John the Baptist, a mound of steaming excrement. The host kicked the goat. The goat dropped its load and scrambled away.

And they left, piled with strawberries, Cora's finger in a bandage, greetings and vows ringing to some strange silence out of which Cora smiled until they reached the old medieval wall. Then she gave him the strawberries, put her hands on her knees, and succumbed to gasps of laughter.

"What is it?"

"I know who done it, who done it!" And she told him how it was pitch-black in the "place," not enough light to find the hole, even to know whether it was a sit-down or a kangaroo, so she had stood up. The eggplants had been responsible. And just at that moment there had been a bonking sound, something fell, and the thing that she thought had been the place began moving. But it was too late. It fell on the goat's back, so what could she do but leave it? To think that it had come full circle, that frail aim, to demonstrate that even poo-poo is holy. "I'd like to sculpt with mine," she improvised, "I would mold it, mix it with olive and poppies and do wall-paintings. I always think of that when I see that Bernini throne in Saint Peter's."

She disappeared behind the wall. It was two in the morning.

"Cora!" he called, a sudden taste of desolation.

She stepped out naked from an arched doorway with her arms stretched toward him.

"You fool! The police!"

"They're all in bed." Her voice was as chatty and domestic as if they had been in Heritage Hills Development.

The streetlights exaggerated her breasts. Her legs followed a perfect curve from her nexus of fur down to her delicate ankles. She had aristocratic calves. Quietly he knelt down on the cobblestones and stroked them. Then he threw her clothes half over her, and still carrying the strawberries took her through a narrow street to the beach.

Her palm was sticky with blood, but the moonlight had drained the color to the paleness of moth wings. He turned it over and over thinking of the "Sto Brook" signs. Then he took her on the cold velvet sand. He was beginning to sense her outlines. Beneath her plump, white sloping flesh the merciless palpitation of wings which were elongated and hard, which made her weightless and quick.

"I never want to go back to reality," he breathed.

"I haven't left it."

"How inexact and silly you are, Cora. Also, you're too universal."

"I'm practicing free agentry since you, darling, were given to me for that."

"If you're too universal, you go insane."

"Balooey."

Their beds changed at night but were always the same. In the center of her generosity was a kernel of distance. He changed strategy.

"Have you had any lovers in your life?"

"Besides Dwight?"

"No. Besides me. Have you?"

"Well, yes."

He believed she was lying.

"Who?" She was silent. "Who? That guy who egged you to be Emily Brontë? Did you sleep with him?"

"Yes." She yawned, pretending to be sleepy, smiling. Her mouth was open so wide he could count the small perfect teeth forming the amphitheater of her palate.

"What was he like?"

"A dolphin. Too smooth, too slippery, very nice, of course, but the opposite of his itchy, feverish soul."

Was she speaking of him? "Who else?"

"Edward Livingstone."

"Who is Edward Livingstone?"

"He sold house plants, then he gave that up and got a job in social work, in a settlement house to do good. Corey was still only ten."

"You lived a double life!"

"I told you that."

He was repelled. He was regressing. He was being tempted away from himself.

"Do you think I am a good lover?" he asked.

She gazed at him curiously. "You are superb, darling." She broke into merry laughter.

Though his jealousy was vinyl and glass-tubing, it was real enough to make her capricious. She created new lovers to tell him about. She went on an automatic machine of confession reminiscent of her Dwight-death talk. There was a doctor called Holden Henshaw, a name she had plucked from Salinger-influenced Corey, probably. There were two actors, friends who fell in love with her consecutively, Paul and Sylvan, both narcissistic men who told her to become an actress. A construction foreman who worked on high buildings, who had heavy eyelids, and was Italian. She said she had slept with Sterling Hayden, a sad man who thought only of sailing, whose muscles looked like strings.

"What did Dwight say?" It was the nadir, identifying with that suffering Lindbergh of a man.

"Are you crazy? You think I'd tell him all this?"

"You were unfaithful to him!"

"Yes, I was. But I was faithful to him, too. I was an excellent wife."

This remark converted him. She was the only sane person in the world. He was humbled. How he had prided himself on giving her freedom when she was always free! She was a flatterer. It was not the lovers of whom he was jealous; it was more profound, the richness of her experience and her dreams.

They went on to Amorgos, where she had the fifth Vivien dream. She told it to him in the hotel lobby. But she swayed to the left and the right as if she could not get the proper position.

"This time in the dream I was not myself, I was you."

Triumphant amino rushed to the roots of his hair. "Me?"

"Yes. I was on a movie set with Laurence Olivier and Robert Mitchum and we were her three leading men. We had a scene with her and then, when we took a break, Vivien came to me, took my hand, and walked some distance away, and we sat on a love seat. She had tears in her eyes. 'Don,' she said. She called me that."

He wanted to laugh, but she was frowning, absorbed. He tried to spearfish her gaze. If only she would look *at* him rather than beyond.

"Did you feel you were me?" he asked.

"I accepted it, yes. Though I knew I wasn't. But you know how you accept that in the real world?"

The real world in the dream world of telling? He felt a rush of love for her for refusing the distinctions. Who else in his life had dared?

"And she said, 'Don, Larry has just told me that he is divorcing me and I can't bear it. What I want you to do is: As soon as he gets the divorce, I want you to marry me. It won't matter that you love me only as a friend, and I love you only as a friend. It's just that I can't bear not to be married. Do you understand?' "

The familiar fragments of orange terror cracked in his skull. She does not love me. She loves me only as a friend.

"But then I said, 'Vivien, what I don't understand is this: is this really happening in real life or is this part of the film script?' Vivien said, 'This is real life.' The next thing I knew, Olivier, Robert Mitchum and I were riding in an open limousine, like Nazi officers. We were chatting as the script called for, and we were turning our heads to the right and left to greet the watching people. I wondered where Vivien was. Then up ahead I saw a figure being transported in the sidecar of a motorcycle. The figure was dressed in the red costume and hat of a cardinal of the Catholic Church. I wondered who this actor was. The figure turned around, smiled at me, and waved to me to come on. It was Vivien! And that's where the dream ended."

He did not laugh. Greece had lured into the open the tourist posing as the Nazi spy, and from the minibus office the Nazi officer rose up out of her dream like a declaration of the junta's reality.

After dinner they walked to a deserted amphitheater in the moonlight. He stood in the pit and watched her pose ten rows above him in the ancient emptiness. She kicked off her shoes and started a dance. She bent to the right and then to the left. Arms spread, fingers delicate as wings—there is nothing more liquid than a fat graceful person—she floated. He understood what enamored him. Her paradox was to be female in form against brutal straightness of being. The paradox of others was femaleness of form against fake-maleness of intellect, and their being, all those bright argumentative college girls from NYU to Carolina, was inchoate, soft, mush-modern.

Suddenly, the sense of danger rose like steam from the moonlit fragments of rubble. He knew this time that she would fall.

"Be careful!" he shouted

But she lost her balance before it was out of his mouth.

He ran toward her. Leaped up. Caught her at the third row. Broke her fall. He had the sensation of a soft, slow-motion weight bearing him down. He tightened his arms around her body and tried to retain his own balance. But he fell too. He struck his shoulder, skinned his elbow. They rolled down onto the stones of the pit. He tore off her clothes, took her hot, milky droops in his hands. She was excited, liquid in her cunt, and he got it in under her so fast that she threw her head back. When he opened his eyes a Bacchus with a broken nose grinned at him from the ruins of the royal box.

The evidence of evil at the base of Greece germinated some necessity in his mind. He was not sure what it was, except that the blasphemy in their love demanded a counterweight. He reached out in limbo for a hallowing act. And it came to him the next day at noon.

They were walking the blinding streets after lunch. The town, typically Cycladian, now deserted, was perched high on the mountains, the air perilous blue, the sea a flat plate below, and the atmosphere speechless. They came to a whitewashed chapel overlooking the sea.

The cardinal of her dream, the red of his robes melding into the blood paint of the "Sto Brook" signs, was beckoning to the church, of course. Synthesis literal, from dream to act.

"I want it done in a church!" he whispered, insistent on sex in the passive voice as a warranty of automatic monitoring by Vivien at last—or by the Goddess herself. He could even, in his mind, see the dome, see their act below and the Eye above.

He grabbed her arm and rushed her inside before she knew what was happening. There was a smell of frankincense and livadia. It was black as pitch. What if the priest walks in? he thought. But no. The priest would be snoring in his own house, his greasy mouth and nose oscillating.

Blind, he backed her up against what turned out to be a throne chair in the men's worshiping pew, pulled her blouse apart, took her breasts in his hands and kneaded them. Her perspiration was cool. He pressed his own cold, sweaty flesh against her, rubbing the moisture to a squeak, and when he pulled up her dress, her pelvis was thrust forward by some carved knobs, and his gouge was so glorious it made the whole row of wooden seats squawk in reply.

She gasped.

He came, groaning in her ear, "I love you. Witness!" to the Eye, yet unsure of who or what it was as separate strands of her hair plastered his mouth. V for violent vision.

Yet there was a deep hilarity in his rutting. For the poles: the evil of Greece/ the divinity of Greece, the blasphemy of sex/ the immanence of love, the impossibility of identification/ the necessity of identification, made of the act a transcendence and a travesty at the same time.

She pushed him away with all her might.

"Get away from me!"

She tottered, her breasts out and bouncing around her open blouse, heading down the chancel to the iconostasis. He was still gasping with laughter, dizzy, but melting also, for he had felt her alkaline beginning to agitate around him. He zipped himself up in a wonderland where it was the farce that proved the hallowing.

Suddenly, the street door opened and the priest entered. He was beefy-looking with a large black knob of hair. She did not see him.

What was she doing? Bowing and scraping to the icons. She was even whispering to them affectedly.

"Cora," he ventriloquized in F sharp. "The red cardinal has entered the church. Do up your blouse."

But she paid no attention to the warning.

He went to greet the priest to divert him. He swooped forward, his hand

141

outstretched, placing his body between those eyes and the body of Cora. Block the view. He talked about the all-seeing Eye in the dome, praising it as if the painting were unusual.

The priest warmed to him.

As Don talked, a corner of the priest's mouth unfroze and crept sidewise like an octopus arm. It stretched until it reached his left ear and there was a scandalized jiggle of his bun of hair.

He turned.

Cora was returning up the aisle, her left nipple revolving in a series of signals, her face utterly unconscious.

"Good-by," he said to the priest, giving a final shake to his hand, and he swept Cora out the door with a smile. On his retina was an impression of the mouth, as if three or more octopus arms had formed, one reaching toward the right nostril.

He rushed her round the corner and up an alley, where he buttoned her blouse. They collapsed in a frenzy of laughter.

After they calmed down, they packed and took the three-o'clock boat to Samos.

How far they had drifted to the east! They were less than fifty miles from Izmir. In some dim field of his consciousness was a nod of recognition that he had yet to return to Athens to deliver the coufetta. But he had, he supposed, raped her at last. He felt in his hilarity hallowed, any misgiving buried in his joy.

"I didn't hurt you, Cora, did I? In the church?"

"No," she said.

But she was far away, and he was ravished by her, could think of nothing but her. What was she feeling? What was she thinking?

"What are you thinking?"

She told him. She was thinking of him in the church. He was blind. He confused romanticism with devotion. He imposed his will. He was a theologian, extravagant in his arrogance, who believed the form was it, the litany was it.

Instead of being angry, he could not get enough of this. Could not get enough of her. He opened his hilarious vision to her: "You should have seen that priest's face!"

"I've never liked Charlie Chaplin. People are big, not little."

Her inconsistencies, stuck in a place midway between his gizzard and his belly, merely led him on. She would not join with him to laugh in this case. She was preoccupied. By what?

"What were you doing with those icons?"

"Speaking to them."

"About what?"

"Private things. I don't know what. What do you want to know for, darling? When you know, I can tell you."

How ironic that former vision he had had of the middle-aged woman on her last fling, upon whom he would spend the full power of his youth.

"Eleusinian mysteries." She laughed to herself. "Thinks worship is done by graphs."

She kept changing forms. A snow-star. A goose-maid. An iridescent blowfish. A pink porpoise. She was a triangle stretched inside his body, the hypotenuse balanced against the other two sides, one stone, the other water.

That night the moon streamed upon their bed in the town of Vathy on Samos.

"Do you love me?" he was driven to ask her.

"Of course I love you." The effluence of generosity, not the essence. "I adore you, Don."

"Then marry me."

She sat up in bed and laughed so merrily that he stared.

"That's what your dream means," he said insistently. "You want to get married."

The moon on the round bubbles of her breasts shook. Her nipples were invisible in the shadows. There was some pale fur in another dimension.

Something expanded deep inside him. His erection complete, he sent the semen back to its source, becoming cruel. He took her breast in one hand and with the other pulled the nipple out to make a boat in a lake. He placed his finger in the niche. She suspected nothing sinister.

It was not him she wanted. She wanted something toward which he could go only as her Partner. Her demand was insatiable; yes, as insatiable as his. She for goddess, he for goddess in her. His only chance was to flush her out.

"I want to tell you something. My name is really Adonis," he said with effort, remembering a photograph of a Chinese religious mystic in the act of being sacrificed. Where his chest had been bared, there was a square piece lifted out, cut like a piece of cake, half off, tubes and gristle still attached, the priests falling back with their bloody swords. His eyes were glazed with the pupils focused on the ecstatic It, leaving the world only the whites.

She said nothing.

He probed the niche further. A drop of woman dew came from her vagina. She uttered a moan. The drop rilled down her thigh. Good. Meanwhile he did nothing, merely withdrew his forefinger from the nipple. He wanted to bring her to bay like a wild dog.

Instead of begging she went into an orgasm. She thrust herself back away from him and he was furious. Her breath was large, sweet, and exciting. He tried to be studious, but the flailing mound of flesh, reminding him of when she had fought the air like a drunk on the Tinos boat, made him mad with envy.

She opened her eyes and looked straight at him and did not see him. Then she went into a second orgasm. He thought of masturbating. She was so far away he imagined a ghost in the linings of her sex.

Giving up, he cried her name. He pushed into her full of hate and foreignness. The moment he did so, he felt the transversal of himself inside her. The ghost attached itself to him, a bladder of identification, thrust him away, then pulled him back. He was a giant murdering the ghost. He kept up this seesawing a long time, wanting to take what was left of her after she had been rolling with the moon. But he grew, taking and taking. She returned. He gave back, or she took; they became confused. It was beyond love, marriage, future time. Just at the top of such power, he felt he had become her.

*T*he morning was calm, and every now and then a little breeze from
the sea riffled the pages of her guidebook to Samos.

"Hera was born under a willow on the edge of the Imbrassos River," he
read, seeing Embrace. He was wide awake. She usually got up before he
did, but he always got down to breakfast first. Such domestic details filled
him with pleasure. He took his first swallow of coffee, noting, relishing the
cornstalks along the street beyond the hotel café. They rustled. Orna-
ments. Fertility country. There was an old *Athens News* lying on the chair
next to him. He picked it up. In the middle of the "Greek News in Brief"
column he read:

> Corfu police announced on Thursday that the body of a 25-year-old
> woman identified as Annette Borgnes, Belgian tourist, has been washed
> up on the rocks beyond Canoni. A red bicycle belonging to the firm of
> Maranga from whom the bicycle had been rented more than 10 days ago
> was the clue as to the identity of the female, and it was at first assumed

that she had been camping, but further investigation brought to light that she had earlier been in the company of an American tourist who has since disappeared. Police are trying to discover whether the woman simply drowned, or whether she met with fowl play.

Cora arrived, carrying her blue floppy hat in her hand. Her sleeves brushed the back of his head. She hung the hat, pole into crown, on the empty chair, announcing full of enthusiasm, "I found out the bus goes at eight."

He snapped the page over, but she was pouring her tea and noticed nothing.

Borgnes—Borlin. It didn't say whether the American tourist was a man or a woman.

She picked up the guidebook and began reading between sips.

"Look!" she exclaimed. "There's a tunnel on this island! The Eupalinian Tunnel!" She read out loud: " 'According to Aristotelis, constructed at Polycrates's expense, based on the laws of correspondence, discovered by Pythagoras!' "

He looked at her lips. But her voice was dubbed in language of waves and bees.

He needed to look at the paragraph again. The spine of her guidebook flashed: *The Famous and Romantic Island of the Aegean, by N. S. Raptou.* RAPTOU superimposed upon RAPTURE.

"Vivien!" she whispered.

He reached reflex for the coufetta. It was there, warm, loudly beating his heart in his shirt pocket. To be called an "American tourist." To be pronounced "disappeared"; the state of Disappearance being the state of Cora. He felt her still against him, her flesh incredible under his hands, her shoulder sliding along his chest, palpitating until something in an erratic gesture pulled the fowl out by the legs. It was a plucked chicken with the face of Annette Borlin, water dripping from its beak.

"Let's go there from Hera's Temple. It's right near by."

The date of the newspaper was April 29. Today was May 4. Five days' old. Annette Borlin had been murdered. The chipmunk had done it. He rolled the newspaper into a tube and tapped it like a riding crop against his legs under the table.

Cora rose, wiped her lips, and picked up her hat.

"Come on. We must hurry to get that bus!"

"Let's take a taxi," he said. He couldn't afford to get stuck off in nowhere at the Temple of Hera, where there might be no buses or taxis.

"Are you crazy? It'll cost the earth!"

He had two choices. To go to Corfu and report to the police, or to go to Athens and deliver the almonds.

She turned around, teetering with such surprise it made him stop. He waved her on. He followed upon her precarious bouncing walk as she brushed by the cornstalks oblivious to Whose accoutrements they were, listened to her excited chatter of the virtues of buses and unpredictability, and did not think of the plane tickets until they were on the bus. He was in the fat nun's seat, the bus groaning up the haunch of the mountain. They had to get back before two or the airline office would be closed. But was there a plane today? He borrowed the guidebook. Planes three times a week, it said.

She took it back to read about the Heraion and the tunnel. They were both on the south coast, not much more than a mile from each other. The tunnel was enterable at one end only, the other being blocked. As for the original Temple of Hera, it was the largest the Greeks had ever built, 354 feet long, 175 feet wide, with 134 columns, such a vast display suggesting an Egyptian influence which had earned it the name of the "Labyrinth."

But the chipmunk could not have murdered Annette! He had been on the ferry to Igoumenitsa with him!

"Look!" cried Cora at the top of Mount Karvounis. Below, the mountain range fell gently to a vast plain and the estuary across which loomed the peaks of Turkey.

But it need not have been the chipmunk. ESA, KYP, any of the government or military police agents could have done it.

"Micro Asia!" she whispered, trying out the words, taking his arm and holding it against her.

He saw Annette pedaling the red bicycle along the blue waves, wheeling onto the plateau headed for Ephesus. Samos to Turkey was the same geographical formation as Corfu to Epirus.

"Here. Right here the Great Goddess originated, Artemis over there, Hera right here. And to think Pythagoras! No wonder he did not deny her. This is the spot she lived before religion and science split! And Vivien led us!"

The road descended. Annette's mauve breasts bobbled, Asia's purple peaks suddenly obscured by oleanders and large willows. Dead, he tried to realize. The tarmac followed a deep gorge clinging with herbage. At the bottom was the Imbrassos River. He tried to re-create her white-velvet animalhood, but he could not isolate his body or his senses from Cora.

"Which tree was she born under, I wonder?" mused Cora. They had missed its source while they were looking.

The riverbed was dry. He tried to feel sorry. He conjured her vulgarity, her Jeanne Moreau smile. Everything was unreal, Samos green, the air insubstantial, and, when he looked at the newspaper he was concealing from Cora, he saw strange monkey pawprints of sweat.

The road to Pythagoreia branched off, and they came down, passing a cow grazing near a stunted fig tree, onto the plain. Two or three miles beyond were the ruins. They got out and stood waiting for the bus to lumber off.

There was a gateway. Nothing else but the sea and the marsh ground covered with poppies. Cora tottered forward in several directions at once, her face galvanized at the sight of the megalithic pile of stumps and stones.

One lone column stood. In Herodotus's day the columns were feet at the sea's edge. Now they were a puzzle of stones which had to be put together.

The coufetta was the only conceivable reason to have killed Annette. They thought she had it. With Cora in the distance, he stole another look at the paragraph. Burned it into his mind. Then he shouted to her, "I'm going for a swim!"

He walked past some stone storehouses where Austrian archaeologists kept broken shards and noseless faces. The beach was a meager, narrow strip of sand bleating with small waves. He dug a hole and buried the newspaper, then took off his clothes and placed them on top of the hole. He folded his shirt with the coufetta in the breast pocket and put it carefully under his pants.

The moment he ducked his head, he knew he would go to Athens. If he went back to Corfu, the police would hold him as a suspect and they could do anything to him.

The water, calm and too warm, stretched westward from his skin through the Cyclades, touching the neck of Eboieia, the breast of the Peloponnesus streaming through the Corinthian Gulf to Corfu filling Annette's mouth, nose, lungs. When had they killed her? Had it been the very day he left for Patras? The newspaper said ten days ago. Thirty days hath September, April. Add three. The day after he had left.

When he came out and dressed, his clothes clung to his wet body like petals. At first he decided to leave the newspaper buried. But walking toward the ruin he got stumped on the question of why they had killed Annette if they knew he had the coufetta. The chipmunk had known. He had seen it in his hotel room in Sparta. So he returned, and dug up the paper, as if it contained the answer. He shook the sand out, folded it up into a small square and stuck it in his back pocket. He went to find Cora.

But she was not in the ruin. She was sitting near the stone huts in the garden of stones, shading her eyes, and staring through buzzing yellow grass at the lone column.

He recognized something. It was the edge of the continent. Across the estuary on the continent of Asia Sibyl stretched out her arms not in yearning, like the picture in *The Wandering Jew*, but in power.

"I love you, Cora," he whispered, bending down, both hands on her shoulders, trying to claim her eyes. But death vibrated in the heat. He felt a cramp like a sob rise in his gut, buried his face in her neck, extinguishing it. Above, he imagined her unmoored eye roaming behind his head for the pineal gland of the temple. He yanked her up with a laugh, and staved off her suspicions as far as the gate. At that moment a taxi came out of nowhere, wandering aimless as a fly.

"Vathy!" he shouted, hailing it with one arm.

"No! Pythagoreia. Aren't we going to the tunnel?" She looked stunned. She had prepared herself on the altar of the Heraion.

"We're going to eat first," he said, pulling her into the seat next to him, "at that restaurant by the art school overlooking the sea. It's too hot now. The tunnel is closed. I've got to do an errand too. We'll go at four, and after we see the tunnel, then we'll have wine on the quay in Pythagoreia and watch the sun go down behind the mountains."

"Oh, you amaze me," she cried, making him feel that it was easy.

No, the chipmunk had *not* seen the coufetta that day in Sparta! He went over it again. The moment he had opened the door, the chipmunk had jumped. The coufetta must have rolled under the wardrobe at that moment, *before the chipmunk saw it.* That same day, to calculation, Annette had died. The chipmunk must have concluded that he had slipped it to Annette.

They reached Vathy in half the time it had taken them to get to the

149

Heraion by bus. He paid the driver and walked with her to the lobby.

"Go up. I'll meet you at the café in half an hour," he told her.

In the Olympic office, the clerk told him the flight to Athens left at seven that evening, and the airport was on the south coast, not a stone's throw from Pythagoreia.

Cora could not come with him. With him she was in danger. But the idea of separation was mechanical in his mind, as he postulated different versions: she, remaining strong, separate in Samos till he finished the business and returned; she, remaining strong, separate, going to Izmir, where they would reunite in a week; she watching him win the final tournament before they went to visit Ephesus. He booked and paid for one ticket.

All his limbs went into the service of the cold energy packed like a ball in his brain. The muscles in his elbows and knees were tiger springs, his fantasies, born of that one euphoric certainty, the airplane ticket, truer than human frailness. His prerogative for returning to Athens would be whim. He could not tell her about Annette. "I have decided to go to Athens on whim," he would say. As he headed for the restaurant, he planned the five and a half hours. He would pack. They would visit the tunnel.

She was there before him, standing behind one of the chairs in the street, her hat fluttering slightly. Something was wrong. He was intensely aware of the hat's blueness. Her hands were trembling, too, and she moved nervously from foot to foot. He felt like a stranger trying to pick up a woman whose irresistible come-on was the sole necessity to take a leak.

"What's wrong, Cora?"

"Someone has gone through my things."

The breeze flapped the tablecloth.

"They must have been looking for—"

" 'They?' " The anger jerked out of him in Philo's intonation. "Who is *they?*" as if she had invented this complication to foil him. He resented her trembling hands, the crushed look of her face.

"How do I know? Go look at the room. It's a shambles!"

He left her, ran back through the alley to the hotel and up the rear staircase. Midstride, he realized she was a sitting duck back there in the street, an open invitation to whoever was watching, more provocative than Annette, her quivering blue hat a bull's-eye. He turned again to go back, but at that moment she appeared around the corner banking like a Bumpo-Cart.

The room was not a shambles. It was not flagrant like Sparta. Her emery board was lying on the floor by her shoe. The tag-end of her slip was caught like a tongue in the shiny jaws of a zipper. Her mirror lay on the floor, the empty ceiling staring from it. They had gone through his pack also. His clothes were scattered. The mouth of his snorkel was stuck in a sneaker. Nearby lay a girdle he had never seen her wear. It was so familiar, imitating her deflated body on the hotel floor, that he picked it up caressingly.

When he looked at her, there was a tear brimming in her eye. She was attempting to repair the bed, smoothing the wrinkled counterpane. It was the first time he had ever seen her cry. He took her in his arms, and the motion broke the tear and made it roll down her cheek.

"Don't humor me. I was a spoiled girl." She took the girdle out of his hand, ashamed. "They're only things, after all." She hid it under the blanket and stood like a culprit to block the sight of what she had done. "And they didn't take anything valuable," she continued in the chatty voice of women buying at flea markets. "There was my jade ring. They didn't take that."

All that was left to him in the face of her bravery was her smell. It clung to him.

The hand he saw rummaging through her underwear was hairy, blundering, clung with detritus, sticky as a bladder, blind as a yahoo. He tried to conjure the face, but it was a painting by George Grosz, the paint in brown daubs thick as excrement. He applied an eraser furiously, but it rubbed down to the white hide and crossthreads of the canvas and became a hole. So it could not have been the chipmunk.

"You are coming to Athens with me. I'm going to deliver the coufetta."

He began packing immediately, gentle and efficient—his actions were to persuade her, not his voice—smashing tenderness under his clothes at the bottom of the pack.

"Come pack, Cora," he urged softly, his certainty atrocious.

For a few moments she was unresponsive; then, as if he had claimed her fate, she began.

He looked at his watch. There were fifteen minutes yet before the Olympic office closed. It was not absolutely necessary to get her ticket in hand to get on the plane, but he was dealing in *faits accomplis.*

Her movements were strange and benign, her face not numb or terrified, but merely thoughtful, her hands folding and wrapping, fluid. Things disappeared into the white suitcases like magic. She was far more efficient than he was, and in a paradox sprung from the knowledge in his chest, untellable, he became jocose. His mask and snorkel would not fit!

"Look! My mask and snorkel! There's no room for them!" he said. "Can you put them in your case?"

She smiled. "Give them here."

She was completely his now. She could not leave him, even for a second, or she might die.

He did not call the porter. He carried the bags himself. She gave the room a last look. They paid in the lobby and walked across the street to the Olympic office, where she made no protest as he bought the ticket. She, like the moon, had gone in, and he felt his power to be uncanny and relevant, while her freedom was infinite and irrelevant.

"We'll eat," he said, putting the tickets in his billfold. The stones of the pavement were white-hot. They outlined their bodies, their baggage. They were targets in the sun. They were surrounded on an island. These were the logistics, and he thought of the drunken commander's universe of the "freedom of prisons."

He ordered macaroni.

"Macaroni in this heat!" she exclaimed with a laugh. They were the first words she had spoken since the hotel.

His senses speeded up. The strands of macaroni quivered in the dead light. The tables were being vacated, people around them leaving, for it was almost two-thirty. He reversed the rifle site. He trained his eyes on the deserters one by one as they walked the shady side of the street camouflaged among the shadows of cornstalks. Soon they would be asleep. When they disappeared, his projectile vision was so keen that he saw behind the shiny olives of the salad, behind the stones of the blinded buildings. He wanted it to come out, that lurking threat behind the noon emptiness, those eyes behind the shuttered window, that person behind the stone.

He felt lethal.

He pretended to be a slob. He slurped up strands of pasta while his mind raced. He staked out the taxi driver, a man with three gold teeth and a fierce mustache, leaning in a half-snooze against his mudguard, who looked expansive, dependable, potentially jolly and whose car was a Ford, and he bargained him down to three hundred fifty from five hundred drachmas. They got in the taxi pared to the bone, three pieces of luggage, the coufetta, and their two bodies.

As they cruised up the mountain, all four windows open, the sun sucked them, a crucible of doom behind the searing air blowing their hair, all vegetation turned in against its heat, the oleanders and willows which had been dewy earlier now torporous and weighted. It did not diffuse rays; it soaked up everything—rocks, leaves, earth, buildings—leaving no consciousness in matter, rather building a locus of subversive power in the sky. He fed on this, like some aberration. It was a paradox, deadliness attracting him, that flat, white sheet, solid as lead. But as long as he was climbing toward it, exposed, he felt in that state beyond safety, reckless yet precise, poised extravagantly and in perfect balance as if on an invisible scaffolding.

It was somewhere after the turnoff to Pythagoreia that he felt the change in her. It was almost audible, like the click of a switch that makes you turn a corner in your mind. She became gay, even gleeful.

"I amaze myself! What a fool!"

"What?"

"It's balooey! What do I care about those suitcases? It's a mere matter of the mind! Here I am free, and resisting it!" She made the clinking little laugh to herself that she had made to the sickly nun.

They were crawling along the dirt road, circling the mountain. The sea came into view, glazed below them.

"It's like a lesson. It happened to tell me something, Don, before I became trapped and petty."

They came out on an immense gravel plateau in nowhere. The land was chunky with rocks, barren, and spotted with gorse and small cacti.

"Do you think it will be the same as the one in Vivien's dressing room?" she breathed.

Time collapsed. He was shucked down to childhood. Annette receded to unreality. He leaned forward, interested only in the details. The stupendous silence of heat ate the sky and the past. Above sat the mountain, not large but compact, hunched like a griffin. Yet the plateau—he was aware of it as a liquid arena of light, aware of their sitting in the taxi, he and she, nothing but he and she, approaching that face, their horizons condensed in the reflection of the sea—was more like a stage than the dressing room of the Goddess.

"Of course it could be, but *is* it?"

A ruthless mischief floated out from the tops of her pupils. He inhaled it, wanting to laugh, and he felt he was looking out from the whites of her eyes. She was making little clucking noises of suspense in her throat.

"There!" she cried. "That's it!"

A stone portico was pasted upon the façade like a Western movie set.

"But didn't you say it was cream-colored?"

"It *was!*"

"This is green."

"So what?" She rattled her beads. She made giggles of excitement.

"But—" he began, full of anxiety on the one hand, for the details had to be exact, and, on the other, of antic suspense.

"It's been painted!"

"Painted since the dream?"

"Do you think dreams stand still?" She threw him a conspiratorial glance. "Balooey. Dreams don't stand still, any more than time."

"Painted *since* the dream? Or *in* the dream?" He had to test her to the extreme.

"How do I know?"

He laughed, for he did not need the argument, everything was telescoped. This place. This time. All else effectless.

"I've always hated literal people." She snorted.

In the distance, back of them, from the direction they had come, there was a minibus. He noticed it for the first time. It was parked and three or four tourists, finished looking at the tunnel, were getting into it. They were little dots in the distance. The minibus started away, but he couldn't hear the motor. It was some trick of acoustics in that amphitheater of sodden light which sucked the sound in the opposite direction.

"See, the doorway is on the left. That's the exact location—as in the dream!" But Cora's voice was cautious.

A calligraphy of dust rose from the back wheels of the minibus, puffed against the glazed sea, and expanded until its message became illegible.

She was too busy to notice. "Yes," she murmured. "The exact direction she pointed."

"She?"

"Vivien!"

Her fingers poised on the taxi's door handle as they pulled up. She threw open the door. She jumped out. Waves pulsed off the naked rock like flamethrowers.

"Keep the bags locked in the trunk," he told the driver. He jumped out after her.

From the doorway toward which she spun in her teetering hurry, there emerged a creature who looked like a spider. It was the guide. He was very old. Knobby knees stuck out from the dirty British shorts he wore. He held a flashlight in his hand.

The driver was saying that he did not want to come into the tunnel. He had been in a thousand times, he said. He would wait in the shade of the doorway.

The old guide grinned excitedly at the sight of Cora. There was something ghastly about the flashlight. Profane promises.

"Fine," Don told the driver. He headed after Cora toward the old guide, whose mouth, he saw, was toothless.

Suddenly, before his eyes, following the guide, Cora disappeared inside the mountain. It was as if she had been swallowed up.

He had to duck, the doorway was so low. He itched to laugh. At the same time he was reluctant to leave the sun, no matter how poisoned, for a flashlight. It was a shock. First it was black and then it was cold. Earth and mold. He was blind. He felt his body swollen, his hands molten, groping. On his retina glowed that last fatal imprint of rocks and cacti, burning in his sockets like coal.

He heard Cora asking, "Is this the aqueduct?"

Sweat rolled from his temples coursing coldly down his cheek and into his collar, a replica of his journey from doom to unreality. He shivered. It was clammy.

"Be careful," the guide warned in a chortle. "Hole. Fall."

"Cora!" His eyes became accustomed to the light. It was a small chamber gouged out of rock. An opening led inward.

The second chamber was larger than the first. He stood up straight. It was a relief. From the sound of her voice he estimated they were a hundred feet inside the tunnel.

He had to duck again. Bent double, he proceeded at a crawl. The tunnel sloped downward. He felt like a snail, his antennae sliming the walls. Cora's shadow cast by the flashlight trembled before him; it looked like a bowling ball with a thumb stuck in it. When he caught up to them, her real body was so small it was a surprise. He moved close, almost touched her, soaked up her warmth, strange in the darkness, and smelled her faint, familiar, milky perfume.

"It's leading somewhere, even though the other end is blocked," she whispered, groping for his hand.

"Where?" He thought of someone pursuing them to the blocked end.

"All tunnels lead somewhere." She squeezed his hand and let it go.

"To Katharine Hepburn."

"Meandrios escape from other end," said the guide, "from citadel occupy by Persian. Come past here. Zoop. Escape to sea. Herodotus tell."

"Tunnels are always for something," she mused. "Treasure."

Prisons, or cemeteries, he thought.

Earthquakes had caused the floor to subside in potholes, the guide said; rockfalls had happened during the ages and broken the ceramic tiles of the water-trench. "Feel here," he said. He made them stick their arms down into the aqueduct. It was at least three feet deep. The conduits, where the water had flowed, were shards.

The old guide pointed the light at the ceiling to show them chisel marks.

The gouged walls looked silver, a domestic sculpture of time frozen. It was the punctuation of slaves. He could hear pick-axing, talking, pick-axing, eating. Fifteen centuries old. But it seemed yesterday. Where were the workers? He wanted human grandeur in chicken scratches.

"The guidebook said it would take fifteen years for a thousand slaves working every day to finish it," said Cora.

"Numbers are things," invented Pythagoras, and he felt himself drain out of his skull, pass up into the chickens' feet, which turned into the roots of trees. Fifteen centuries ago he was catapulting out of this tunnel, out through the mountain until he stood poised on the sun, looking down to the very spot they stood this very minute. Goats had eaten the trees to nubs, left the roots to rot, the wood to drop off. These were the imprints of historical process: the human merges with animal, the animal with plant. Not, as Philo said, echoing the false longing of those whose conviction it was that man is civilized, "First came the ape, then the barbarian, and then came man."

They walked inward for about a quarter mile. A frail procession: the guide leading, Cora in the middle, Don at the end. He surrounded, but did not touch her. He occupied the spot of warmth she had vacated before, hearing the filmy rustle of her dress, strange slithers of silk.

At last they came to a huge place where the tunnel opened out. He stood up from his hunching. He stretched. But the space widened between him and Cora and it disturbed him.

"Where are we?" he asked.

The guide was having trouble with the flashlight. Don could hear him shaking it. The batteries thumped. The light went out.

Their blindness, without the confines of walls, became palpable. How large was the place? How high the roof? He imagined the space to be more dangerous than density. He focused within the volumes of blackness on Cora's breathing.

When the light came back on, he saw that they were standing next to a black railing in a chamber about twenty feet high and over thirty in diameter, whose ceiling gleamed like coal. A frieze of marriage. The guide was the preacher. Caught in torchlight at the altar.

Cora rushed to the rail, leaned over. "Look! A hole!" she screamed.

The guide trained the light, a faltering pulse which crept around the mouth-shaped O perimeter.

"A bottomless pit!" she exulted.

Speleologists had recently been lowered down on ropes, said the guide, and it was more than a mile deep. There were other openings, many natural tunnels. In fact, it was so deep that no one had ever reached the bottom.

"Boo!" called Cora down the hole. "Cock-a-doodle!"

The hair froze on his arms.

At that moment the light went out again.

"*Ga moto!*" the guide swore, shaking the flashlight. "*Sto diavolo! Christos kai Panagia!*"

"The dame has lost her shoe," she went on. "The master's lost his fiddlestick and don't know what to do."

Didn't she understand what she was saying?

"Get a match!" he barked to shut her up, and he went forward until he touched her elbow. He felt it was not Cora at all, but someone embedded in her, like a Pythia in a person who utters answers to secrets in gobbledygook. What was she doing? Strange whiffs of cold air pulsed against his face. She was swinging one leg experimentally over the void.

"I don't have a match. But I have a cigarette lighter!"

It was one of those quixotic traits he loved, that she should carry a lighter though she did not smoke. He heard her fumbling in her bag, her fingernails tapping on hard objects, the shishing sound of Kleenex, and suddenly she lit the flare, and there was the beauty of her leg en jeté attached to nothing. And shining, floating eyes as she called for something to burn.

He thought of the *Athens News* and reached for it.

"You have a newspaper?" she cried. "Darling, how could you have guessed we'd need it!" and she attached the lip of flame where he unfolded it over the hole. A wing of fire ate the sockets of her eyes. Without the knowledge of death, there is no death.

"Beautiful," she breathed, swinging her leg out again, en pointe.

It struggled like an angel trying to ascend, then exploded into a mass of flame, singeing his fingers. He let go while her leg was still in extension. She pulled back so quickly that her shoe flipped off. It sailed upward through the flaming sheet. Light thrilled the sides of the well. Sparks ejected. Shreds of fire followed its trajectory.

Such was the perfection of the downward fall of the burning newspaper in its coordination with the upward thrust of the shoe that he was reminded of the train headlight with the automobile headlight. The shoe hung for a second of a grace note, toe pointed upward in its galaxy of sparks, at its apogee. Then it reversed direction and plunged downward. It crashed through the last tatters of the newspaper fire below and bonked off an edge of rock. The light disappeared. Seconds later they heard it ricochet again, but though they listened for a final sound, there was none.

"Vivien was wrong!" she said, her voice strange, as if a hard rind had peeled off.

He felt as he had when she told him the Vivien dreams.

"Her birthday fell on a great religious holy day in India. They threw all these different-colored powders in the sky like fireworks. She grew up in India. It was her mother. Her mother told her every single birthday, 'See, Vivien, the whole world is celebrating your birthday.' And then she grew up and six months before she died, she said, 'I don't believe the world will celebrate my birthday anymore.' "

She had moved away from him A cold vacuum sucked off his skin on that side, and he felt fright as if she had disappeared down the hole with Vivien Leigh.

"Vivien, you are wrong," came her voice from somewhere below.

He felt downward and touched her hair. She was kneeling at the edge of the hole, holding on to the rail.

"What are you doing?"

"India is the only country in the world where the living Goddess is still worshiped in the flesh. Don't you understand? All those people knew. Everybody knows."

"Take my hand," said the guide in a threadlike voice. "I don't need light to go out of tunnel."

Their journey back was like a procession of moles, with Cora in the middle again. But this time she limped.

"Why don't you take off your other shoe?"

She paid no attention. She was babbling to herself as she had done with the sickly nun.

"I heard her mother's words. It was literally true."

He felt she was a prophetess, limping and crippled, whom he and the guide had to tow. Was he pushing her? Or was she propelling him along?

"It was the fireworks. Of course she believed it when she was a child."

"If you took off your other shoe, it would be easier. You wouldn't have to limp."

"I can't."

"Of course you can."

"To be an actress is nothing. But to leave the Goddess in films! It's operating in heaven right now. It looks like a freak of fate, but the Goddess made me dream the tunnel to see Vivien's celebration of her. Oh, I amaze myself!"

"Then your feet would be even and you wouldn't have to go in and out and up and down like this. I'll carry your other shoe."

"I can't. It hurts. The floor of this tunnel is too sharp. These rocks hurt my feet. And, Don, darling, I'm not going to Athens with you."

"What?"

They were climbing upward. He imagined light.

"You have to!" he said.

"Of course I don't have to."

He could tell she was smiling.

The path climbed more steeply and they reached the large inner chamber. He stretched for a second, but bent down again immediately to follow her out. The greasy light of the outer chamber changed the consistency of the walls.

In a second they were outside. He shut his eyes against the glare. The onslaught of heat made him realize he had been chilly. He opened his eyes slowly, squinting. Everything seemed smaller. But the horizon had expanded beyond imagination and the bushes, rocks, mountain were subsumed by space itself.

The taxi was not there, it was far away at the entrance of the plateau. But there was another car. Two men got out of it.

The first man looked familiar. As he walked toward them, his footsteps drew a line separating the plateau from the sea, so that it looked as if he was walking on water. In addition, the sun glittered off his head like a halo. He was the perfect emissary, clean and deadly, smiling a kind of greeting. It was Richard. Lion-hearted. Barrel-chested. Burton. His brow seemed lower and more benign than that day on Taygetus when he'd stared down on their picnic with the nuns.

He had to get rid of the coufetta. He returned the greeting, raised his left hand, using the wave to disguise the motion of his right as he took the coufetta from his breast pocket. He palmed it carefully so the sun's rays could not reflect off the silver, scanned the rocks, chose a large outcrop with several holes in its base, aimed, and threw for the largest. Then he circled to the right, keeping Cora at his back. He did not think Richard noticed.

The second man was far away but approaching. He was old, or middle-aged, with pants belted across a thick paunch, waffling like a spinnaker against his thighs and crotch. Richard was close. Instead of the see-through, he was wearing a flowered print whose petals moved sinuously with his powerful pectorals.

A cobra of joy uncoiled in his spine, the arch of unleashing a primitive attack. He was aware of that moment before anything happens, when intentions are still unclear, when something peripheral to the real occurs. Everthing seems in slow motion. Knees tensed, he shot forward to meet Richard's downward swing.

He caught Richard's arm in both hands, and made a quick half turn. He threw him off balance.

But Richard held on. They grappled. Richard was heavier, more powerful. Don had to be agile. He unfooted him. Richard imitated his motion. Their two bodies revolved in a dance. There was a series of transformations: the surrounding horizon whirled in a circle, the sea burned into the mountain, the little guide in shorts passed through his field of vision, Cora turned into the mountain, the mountain turned into the sea.

Richard forced the dance to a halt. He pulled a knife. The blade was a hooked shape, like a Saracen's nose. He got hold of Richard's raised arm and squeezed it until it paralyzed the knife to a glint in the air, and waltzed him again.

Cora went by his line of vision twice. The first time was the moment the shaggy man overpowered her and she was staring from the drunken embrace with her mouth open. The second she was rolling like a ball, having just been flung away by the shaggy man whose crotch was in full sail, one leg lifted at a right angle as he ran toward them.

The knife plummeted down past his cheek toward his esophagus, but he felt nothing. He broke his hold, and two fists together reamed Richard's neck downward and Richard's face upward. And he heard something crack in the bones below the flesh as the low, creamy brow bounced under the impact and the body hit the ground like rubber. I always was a good fighter, he thought, tasting a split second of victory before he turned, tensile, to face the other one. But there was no time. He did not even get a look at him before bones shuddered at the base of his own skull, as if the mountain had simply risen three feet behind him.

Part two

awake. I am lying on pavement stones. The sun is beating down. How have I gotten here? It is a ruined courtyard. The worn, mud-yellow stones exude merciless heat.

I sit up. I am weak. Why? I look at myself. My hem is ripped. There's a hole in the shoulder of my robin's-egg-blue suit. I notice my elbow is bloody. There's a rag around my knee, a dirty bandage. I rise. I try walking in a circle. I limp like a newborn animal.

It is huge, deserted like a crumbling Venetian fort. Odd-angled walls stretch against the light. Beyond, a mountain rises. The processes of my mind are fragments, associations, not memories. I am far off. It may be Greece, but this has no reality. I know only the words "far off" and "here."

All at once I think: I'm going to get burned in the sun. So I go to the shadow of the wall and squat down.

What time is it? I look at the sun to see, but it blinds me; then I think of my watch and it is a surprise that I am wearing it as usual. It is running and it is 3:05. My heart sinks. I was sure it was morning. I cannot bear to miss anything important, and I know now that I have missed my birth. I suddenly believe that I have been born again in death. How can I begin death after it has begun? While I was lying there, my ignorance must have been drying in the sun.

A half an hour passes. I have gathered strength. I begin to explore.

There is an archway that leads from the courtyard. I follow it. The stone path goes through some broken walls, past some picrodaphne whose blossoms have grown old and brown and dropped off. I pass a dungeon. A hole stares up out of weeds and rusty bars. It is empty. There are two or three dungeons. I go down one. I stick my head into a black doorway hole. I smell ancient meat, gunpowder, defecation. It is crimes. I call "Boo" into the blindness. I have some memory of this sound, but I don't know what.

Suddenly, a stairway leads me to a field which slopes down to the sea. The sea is lost. It is not friendly. The sun is dead upon it. The sun sucks it upward as I watch and suspends it in an artificial plane, not like water but like a plate of mercury; the sun is robbing it of its gravity.

But I am determined. I am determined to go to the water.

I go through a copse of pines which gives off a perfume execrably sweet. Pines smell like this in July. Is it July? Goat droppings punctuate the way. But no goats.

The sea is getting closer. It licks and breathes fierce, dry thyme. The sun burns me but I do not sweat. I come to an area of rocks which look like the inverted footsteps of a giant. I follow these footsteps. There is a steep drop. I scramble down and come to a lion lying at the edge of the water in stone. I step on its back. The waves crackle at my feet.

I dip my hands in the water. It is cool. I wash my face. I drip. I notice I am wearing my Hush Puppies. I rarely wear them. How strange! I take them off and stick my feet in the water. The tiny waves tease my legs mischievously higher and higher, to my knees. I pull my dress up, laugh, pat the water, splash some at a bird. The water sneezes, showering drops in the sun. I take the bandage off my knee and wash the wound. It smarts from the salt. The water revives me. The coolness makes me ecstatic. I wash my elbow. The two wounds are bad scrapes. I look at the slices in my skin. It looks as if I had been dragged behind a chariot. I want to get rid of the bandage. It is dirty. I hate it. I want to burn it. But I have no matches, so I stuff it into a crack of the rock to hide it from my sight.

The sea's familiarity with me contrasts with its sheer space and silence. Far away, three or four miles, there is a series of islands which form a harbor. This fort in which I sit is one of the arms of the entrance to the harbor.

I move the islands in my mind. I make chess pieces. The farthermost is a table, formed out of a huge fault, a hole the shape of a cathedral door whose sides form its legs. The next is the Hunchback of Notre Dame. The third looks like an eagle. The land formation is delusive. Mountains are connected to necks, pelagoes are mouths. Land and water move across one another like bellies and arms. I cannot tell what is outside or what is inside. Perhaps I am a child playing in the pools left by the tide and Mother is sewing curtains on the long porch in the house, which is out of sight up above.

The islands form a giant stone woman! She is stretched out on her back facing the sky. Her bosom is large and merciless. She folds her arms upon it. Giant! She made the footsteps, and then lay down to disguise herself as islands!

I am pleased I read the chess game rising from her stone mind. She doesn't acknowledge my delighted experimentation with her metaphors though, those spaces, absences, presences. I try to rouse her attention. It is futile. I laugh. I think: She likes it. I have enormous respect for her.

Old rules don't apply here, I realize. I can take my clothes off. I do. I fold them neatly, place them in a niche, am careful to remember my watch. I put it in one of the Hush Puppies.

My feet are too soft for the spiky, lava rocks. How naked, white, and dumpy I am—a plump, featherless duck! I stick one foot in and feel the coolness, then I turn around to go in backward, squat down and aim my buttocks in. A wave slaps them. I laugh. I search with my foot, find a shelf and ease myself in carefully. Delicious. The water reaches the linings of my sex. My fur is like the seaweed. I pick some of the real seaweed, wash myself, and throw the seaweed on the water. Then I push myself off the lion's back and begin swimming. It is as calm as a bathtub. I rejoice in the rotund shapes of my motion and the sea's insouciance. I close my eyes. A faint breeze spurts wave caplets. My breasts bobble. My nipples grow tight as starfish.

All at once I think: It's deep! I grow afraid and imagine a monstrous fish below. I look down. It is black. I pull myself out and am ashamed. My body jiggles with fear. The water tumbles out of my orifices. One drop spills out of my belly button. Another drop falls elegantly from my ear and rills between my breasts. I reach for a towel. There is none. I wonder at the inconsistency of my reflexes—I did not look automatically at my watch—but I do not want to be logical. For I am enamored of this new existence.

I stand up and swing my arms in the vast space. The sky is spectrally pink. How long have I been swimming? I look at my watch. Almost five o'clock. An hour and a half!

Though the sun has cooled, the heat retained by the rocks bakes me dry. I dress, refreshed, to return to the courtyard. Already, I think of the courtyard as my center.

But before I leave there is the matter of the bandage. I do not want to take it and I do not want to leave it. I hate it. I pull it out of the crack and wash it in the sea, rubbing it fiercely between my hands to rid it of blood. Then I stretch it on the rocks to dry in the sun, pinching one corner into a crack.

In the grasses, just at the edge of the pine copse I am suddenly thirsty. It is because my body is cool and refreshed, and I feel this tremendous new energy. Like a dedication to sweet water not salt water. The first thing I will do is drink water.

The world is new in the slendering light, the evening air intense and fragile. I turn to look at the stone woman. She is plum-colored. The goat droppings are amber, ethereal excrement, celebrative for my new existence. I am moved.

Perhaps I am not a physical body at all!

In fact, everything in the courtyard seems different. The shadows are long and point east. My mind thinks backward. Am I tired—or is this just the lingering of old physical sensations? I sit down by the wall facing the stone woman. I look at myself to see if I sweat. Yes, there are drops on my forearms, but they could be dust. If they are liquid sweat, then I am a body that must replace liquid. The stone woman grows dark as a silhouette while I grow light, my very hairs astral gold. And the ball of sun which is casting these questions is plummeting behind her bosom. I fear she will disappear when the sun goes. I want her to stay.

I am sleepy. Perhaps the act of breathing can make me forget water. I take five slow, exploratory breaths. I count. They accomplish something strange. They give me possession of space. The horizon of the sea is mine.

The table is mine. The hunchback and the eagle are mine. The mountain is mine. The bosom of the stone woman is mine.

The outer limits are in fact my internal organs. The sky is beating my heartbeat. The sea is flowing my breath in liquid form. The ebbing sun is moving my blood in its last warmth.

The darkness comes on like a cap to deny every distance that I cannot achieve. The stars and moon promise a new concept of distance. All my thirst is gone. Night closes my eyelids. I recognize roofs. I am slumped down flat in the new dimension of these peculiar breaths of the open sky. The stars and moon are not yet in dominion.

"Cora!" he called, pushing himself up against the chamber wall, looking around.

The old guide, flustered and jerking, approached with a basin of water. It slopped over the brim and splashed down the knobby knees into the broken shoes. The old man knelt down to help him, but he was afraid, and instead of touching him, he sniffed and reached out tentatively, as one reaches out toward a dangerous animal, with trembling hands and glittering eyes.

"Where is she?" Don asked.

"You're bleeding, kyrie. Don't move."

"What did they do with the lady?"

Because the old man did not answer, he thought Cora was dead, killed in the struggle, and he got to his feet, turning the basin over in his hurry to get out of the tunnel. How had he got in here? Had the old man hauled him? Blinded by the sun, he stopped at the doorway, and hung on the lintel waiting for the waves of blackness, of liquid heat, of chilliness to coalesce. When he opened his eyes, he saw that the two taxis were gone. The sun had passed its zenith and the empty plateau was an orange color.

"Where is she?" he barked, turning back.

The guide had filled the basin again and was fussing with a rag. The sight of the rag, of blood spots on the earthen floor, of the mud on the old man's knees and the stubborn glint in his eyes above his frightened mouth, sent Don into a rage of impatience. He gave the man a shove which sent him bouncing off the wall. The basin overturned a second time. He kicked it. The sound was like a cowbell. He hung over the old man for an answer.

The man cowered on one knee.

"They take her. The police."

"Nobody's going to hit you. Take her where?"

The toothless mouth, lips flapping, looked like a grin below the metallic eyes. He fought the impulse to smash him again.

"I don't know."

"And what about the other taxi driver. *My* taxi driver?"

"He drive away."

"Did he go with them?"

"No. He went before."

"The lady was hurt?"

"I don't know. They carry her between them. First she talk, she argue, then she don't say nothing."

Don sat down to think. He checked his pockets, found his wallet. His money was intact. So were the airplane tickets. But what about the coufetta? The moment he thought of the coufetta he thought of the baggage, his gear, his ping-pong paddles, her suitcases, his mask and snorkel.

The old man eyed him so greedily he suspected him of mind reading.

"Police? How do you know they were police?" he asked slyly. The weak are prey of the weak. He was stalling to gather strength. He felt a throbbing sensation in his head and a prickling. He moved his hand up to explore, and his fingers found a wad of ripped flesh and hair at the back of his skull. Blood mixed with earth on his fingerpads.

"They told me." The old man began fussing again, filling up the basin from a plastic bottle of water he kept with food and blankets in a mound by the doorway. He made five motions to accomplish what one would have done. Jerks and starts. "Are you criminal?" he asked, crawling toward him. Yet he acted as if he dared not touch him.

"Give the rag to me."

There was a wound on his forearm too, two lips of skin hanging limp, the slit so neat it must have been the knife. He ran the water over the head wound. It stung. Then he washed the rag, wrung it, and held it tight over the two lips of skin, binding the wound together with a knot.

"Have you got any more water?" He spoke more gently now, for he had to divert the old man until he could find the coufetta.

He pulled himself up, and while the old man was jiggling back to the plastic bottle, went out to scan the land. He retraced his steps from the mouth of the tunnel to the spot where Richard had attacked. He found the rock where he had aimed the coufetta, but the angle of the sun was so different that it made the holes at its base unfamiliar. He bent to look more closely. He was not sure it was even the same rock.

The old man was standing at the mouth of the cave staring.

"It is dangerous, *paidi mou,* to stand in the sun."

"Is this where I fell down?"

"Yes."

"You hauled me out of the sun then and saved my life?"

"The man that falls at one's door might be Jesus Christ or Barabbas."

"I'm sorry I pushed you, old one." But he had to get rid of him so he could look for the coufetta. "There's a clock inside the tunnel. Could you go look and tell me what time it is?"

The old man pointed knowingly to the watch on Don's wrist.

"I know I have a watch. But it is fast. I need to know exactly."

"I check for you then." And the old man disappeared in the tunnel.

Kneeling down, he found the hole. The coufetta was lodged neatly inside, deep. It was turned in such a way that the sun could not penetrate or betray its whereabouts as it had in the hotel room. He pulled it out, shook it, rattled the almonds. He opened it. They were untouched. Carefully, he closed it and had just returned it to his breast pocket when the old man came out of the rock.

"Six-ten."

"Did the police search me?"

The old man nodded.

He had almost an hour before the plane left, he calculated. He went to wash his face and hands. He debated going back to Vathy, but, by this time, with the methods of transport they had at their disposal—automobile, plane, boat—Cora could be anywhere, Athens or Timbuctoo.

When I open my eyes—such a slight movement!—my two white suitcases are sitting in the moonlight of the courtyard as naturally as if it were Grand Central. One is a parent, one a child by its side; impeccable and forlorn. I am dreaming, but even the dream annoys me, for it brings doubts, memories, as if I am after all a physical being, alive somewhere.

Memory brings motive. The rules of continuity, memory, ontology, cause and effect. How did the suitcases get here? When? Who put them here?

I must have died in some violent way. My arm, my wound, my scraped knee, my weakness are a sign of violent death. Maybe I had a heart attack, like Adlai Stevenson, and fell down in the road.

No, I do not want to be reminded of earthly existence anymore. I want this total freedom from thoughts of Greece, Don, America, Dwight, death, Eleanor, Corey, etc. I want this total freedom of unexplored birth.

So I shut out the suitcases and fall upward toward the moon into unconsciousness.

In the morning, when I wake up into the vast cold, everything is overwhelming, thrilling. The state of sleep and the state of wake are dwarfed by my new existence. Mount Elias is blue with dewy chill. The sun has not yet pushed out from behind; only pink and golden rays have thrust out; they mint the cold stones. I call it Mount Elias. I don't know why. And my stone woman lies facing morning, the calm sea ringing her with gold.

I try not to look to see if the suitcases are there. I swivel my eyes in a 180-degree arc, but the corner of my eyes catches them in the same position. They are smaller, though! Their white hide reflects a shyness which has, in fact, made them blush. I look, look away, look, look away, not to will them away, but to understand.

What I understand is this: some keeper has left my suitcases here to tame me. He knows I will have to open them.

I sense myself as a big caged cat. I go into a corner of the courtyard and pretend not to see them. I look. After an hour, I give way to my curiosity. I inch toward them, sniff, circle, able up close to see the expensive weave of that laminated material which I bought in a fit of snobbishness at Abercrombie & Fitch for $250. How vulnerable they are in the sun! I am tender. I feel the values that no longer apply.

Does the stone woman care? No. The sea palpitates but gives a glazed eye. I feel terror. These artifacts possess some power. No matter how much I stall, I will open them ultimately.

The promise of the dawn which had thrilled me with its coldness is now repellent. I think: Maybe there's a bomb inside. But I do not believe I will be killed; I believe the past will be opened up to me, and it is the benignity behind my suitcases' appearance that is repulsive. Who merges with keeper? Keeper keeps keys.

I open the big one first, press the hasps with my thumbs. How familiar the action feels! I peep in the crack. The first thing I see is his snorkel and mask.

Why?

Who was he? He may have been my son, or he may have been Anthony Perkins. Suddenly, I imagine that he is the master mover behind the return of my memory. Why else would he have left his priest's utensils?

All my things are there: my traveling iron, my white shoes, my underwear, my fat cupid brassieres, my pants, my jersey, my blue sweater-dress, my beige suit—and one blue shoe. But they have been plundered. Pillaged for no theft. Some fool has wrapped my drinking glasses in tissue paper. I had neatly packed them with my underwear. I can see the exact route those looting fingers took through my neat packing, like the path of a typhoon. My circus watercolors have tipped over and ruined my nightgown, transformed it, by green-and-brown splats, into a polka-dotted clown suit.

I want to hang up my clothes. Let the wind unwrinkle and purify them. But I have no coat hangers. I could drape them over the walls, but the wind will blow them to the ground. I think of dirty French and German campers hanging their dirty undershorts on pine trees.

I shut the suitcase with a bang.

Am I in Greece then? Not in the New Existence? Why? How did I get separated from Don? Did I really not have a heart attack? Am I really alive on earth, a physical body with a daughter and son who were dead when I arrived in the New Place?

The minute I face the fact, I am thirsty. My gullet without saliva is strings. The strings draw down the corners of both my eyes when I swallow, and I have no tears. I think: If I had tears, I could drink them and quench my thirst. The liquid would go as far as my fingertips. I would then be generous and give sweat as an offering to the sun. I swallow again, wopse up my tongue, my mouth-linings, and the secret pockets between my tonsils and my teeth, and manufacture the beginnings of a fountain of gorgeous and silky saliva. Salvation!

Suddenly, an avenue opens to me. I can die! I am elated. I decide to die.

I try dying for four hours. I deny my thirst. I deny my hunger. I feel myself becoming visibly thinner. I concentrate on the hands of my watch. The sun commands the hands. The sun watches me. Dry my fat quickly, I entreat him, for I realize I will die less fast than lots of people because of my fat. I regard my fat somewhat as I regard my blushing suitcases—with tenderness.

No one would believe a plump person would have such reptilian passion as I do, would exercise such pride to fight the sun. I think that dying by sun will, although fierce, be easy and ultimately painless. I am getting sunburned. I do not like the idea of redness, so I desensitize myself and try to think a step beyond the one where the flesh comes off and exposes the pomegranate. I think dehydration. I imagine myself salted, a dried codfish. I smell myself as a dried codfish. I kick my metaphor. White strings. Full stop. I am flat. If anyone wants to eat me, I will be good.

My father—or is it my husband?—has called together a meeting. The house is not our house. It is a Victorian house with a round turret. This is the place we always meet. Although we are aware that the meeting room is round, no one is aware that the place is a tower.

There is a young man at the meeting. I am in love with him, but he is not in love with me. Perhaps he is a divinity student. Perhaps he is a homosexual. I only know that, like many strange persons, he may have the secret to life.

The readings are to begin. I am taken by surprise. I did not know I was to read my paper. I am not sure. I am flustered. This is a tremendously important meeting, because the young man I love is here.

The name of the group is the Euphoria Society. It is a newly formed society, created by my father to practice something connected with the mystery of why things move and change. My father believes that there are certain people who have more energy than others. It is the energy of these people which changes events. Therefore energy is *good*.

Therefore these members of the Euphoria Society are all people who have this excess energy entitled *Euphoria*. They are meeting here to practice it. It is practiced by means of reading papers. Each paper is a revelation in itself and will lead to the revelation *of* itself. That which each of them had more of, and of which they are a member.

Thought, dream, or hallucination is beside the point. I am arrived at a state where I am profligate with my realities. I do not have to name them. My switch from memory to fantasy is a demonstration of the insignificance of my New Existence. It is irrelevant whether I am a physical body or not. How doctrinaire I have been!

I decide not to die. I am Euphoric! I decide to accept the Universe.

Now that I have decided to live, my thirst returns in force. I am hunched over my suitcases. I am famished. Also, I feel the heat of pain. Having taken off my jacket to dehydrate more quickly, sleeveless, backless, I see I am swollen to scarlet. I realize the danger I am in. For I have imbibed the fierceness of sun and my flesh burns gaudily, challenging the Enemy from whom it has taken its weapon.

The sun makes a hollow sound as it starts its descent behind the skirts of my stone woman. I laugh at her protecting it, since I now contain its fire.

I rise on fire. I totter up the crumbling stairway, past the dungeons, down through the pine copse to the sea. I half-run, half-laugh. Pain reinforces my dedication. I refuse to die. Nothing shall make me die.

I am going to eat those shellfish Italian tourists scrape off rocks. I am at the giantess's footsteps. I realize I have no implement to scrape the shellfish off with.

Yes I do too! My brooch! The pin end. How ingenious I am!

But I have to go back, for the brooch is pinned to my jacket, and I have left my jacket with the suitcases. I start back. These changes of mind and direction only increase my dedication. Each is a test. I am as fierce to live now as I was to die, for the lover-enemy who was to dehydrate me is now in me. I have stolen him to make me live.

I push my fat up the hill. I love effort. I have the fat for effort. My fat, the stumbling block to a fast, dried-fish death, will make me live. I have moisture to squander.

I pretend to be tubercular, so that I can banish the sun and wash floors in damp, cool, wet medieval dungeons. Vivien, not Jennifer Jones, should have played Bernadette. As I plunge out of the pines, I cough, cold and clammy, increasing the liquid in her phlegm where the bacilli live euphorically, proliferating water-albinos. Her soul has to go into air because she turned into water. She floats around me. Her cold and watery death is my life. My fat contains water which will save me. My fat will save me.

I find the brooch pinned, as I knew it would be, to my robin's-egg-blue suit. I snatch it. I turn again toward the sea. I run through the stone archway, across the field, through the copse. I am a fat animal full of water. I am going to cut out fat little sea animals and fill myself with their water. I no longer feel the pain of the sun. I am merciless.

I arrive at the lion's back. The seaweed is deliciously cold. I throw off my clothes and lower myself into the water. I begin my search.

I float at the edge of the water, combing the seaweed with my hands. My mouth is underwater. It is three minutes or so before I find the first shell. It is brown and reflects the sunset, blushing like my suitcases this morning.

I try to pry it off. I have to be careful. I do not want to break the pin. I insert the point between the rock and one petal. I wiggle it. I breathe carefully. The breath of the sea snorts in imitation through holes in the lava rock. I am deft. I have always been good with my hands. I feel like a safecracker, with powdery, delicate fingers. I lift upward. There is a sucking sound. How tight it clings to the rock for safety! But it clicks and then falls into the palm of my hand.

The meat tries to hide itself. Beneath its wet-brown, its bed turns to mother-of-pearl. I put it in my mouth, bite it out of its shell with my upper teeth. I dislodge it, until it is a little lump of meat upon my tongue. I mince it between my uppers and lowers. It is tough. Tiny squirts of juice slip out among my taste buds. Sweet. I have to chew it a long time. If you are starving, eat slowly, I remember. I swallow.

Cool meat adjoins the hot linings of my esophagus and stomach. My linings, which have been working on my fat, hot and old, are used to consuming their own moisture. The cold sea meat is a surprise. They cannot believe this freshment. They do not have to work to eat themselves up anymore.

Cool energy travels out the nerve linings of my arms.

I grow used to searching; I grow used to finding. I find many more. I learn to become skillful at prying them from rocks. I eat so many of them that I lose count.

As I eat, the sun disappears and it becomes night. I pull myself out of the sea, my hunger quelled, my thirst quenched. I know that I can live for many weeks on the sea animals.

But I must find water.

I return to my courtyard in the saffron light of night and lay myself down on the cold stones, balm to my burning flesh. There, without further ado, without pondering the stars and the night, I sleep.

In the rue de Grenelle they sat around Zoe's desk holding each other linked by arms, hands, waists. Zoe's left arm was around a man named Fotianos, her other around Lefteri. Half-filled wineglasses stood on the desk. Their eyes were closed. They did the singing like a prayer. Something flowed from Fotianos and throbbed through them like blood, redeeming them, swelling their pride toward their eyebrows in a spasm that made them feel victorious over tragedy.

But Michalis, standing apart by the window where he could see the headlights and streetlights below, knew the delusion, knew that Zoe knew. She herself was going back to get Lampris, and could not bring herself to tell him.

Zoe raised her eyes and saw that he knew.

"More wine, *paidia?*" she cried gaily, and came over to him.

She thought of pretending, but she did not. "All right. I have decided to go," she said.

"Why?"

She did not know why.

He accepted her decision, as if his wife, brave as a flag, warm, wrenching, soft, bitter, sometimes vicious with love in bed, were not this person.

She wanted to reassure him, but she despised him for not having faith in her faith. She had no court record. They had no evidence. It was safer for her than the rest of them. But that was not why.

"Promise me one thing. You will not go to see your mother."

"Do you think I'm some kind of fool?"

"Promise anyway."

"I promise."

Why? she wondered, for he had struck on something. He knew her too well.

A white stone. A bare cypress. The sea. Her mother.

She was restless. He had suspected because she had become suffused with wine, not the Coca-Cola she usually sipped from the wineglass; though she could hold wine, she never got drunk. And he had seen her eat impulsively, as though she were starving, tearing the flesh off the chicken, joking, swallowing without chewing, talking. But it was not for Lampris. It was not because he had failed with Lampris or succeeded with Fotianos. She had planned it from Alpha to Omega; it was no one's fault that Trigc had turned evidence against them.

It was not because she was sick of it either, sick of the French who looked like birds and thought like woodpeckers, sick of her photographic memory, her impeccable judgment of people's capabilities and limitations, her split-second timing, her genius for allocating the right segment to the right person. It was not because the first flush was gone, nor because she knew now the junta would not fall in one month's time. Michalis thought she thrived on danger, lived on death by a hair's breadth, but he it was who looked with cold fear, as if her indomitability were cracking. She was going out of her skin.

In three hours she and Lefteri would be flying the Ionian Sea. There was a lot to do before she left, even though she had fixed everything, made stephada, lasagna, crème caramel, which he loved, covered a notebook with the numbers and times of the stops, and made codes for contingencies.

She took his arm and they went in to the baby. He had kicked off his covers and lay spread-eagled on the pillow. She put him back, kissed him, told Michalis where to get the Pampers, a friend of Aphrodite's with PX connections. Then they went to the monitor room. She thought of him there while she was gone. The first time anyone but her would know the plan from Alpha to Omega. The first time anyone who knew it would be actively involved in its operation.

She trusted him above everyone.

He disapproved. For their success had been in her planning, and her devotion which commanded devotion unto death. He was right.

She felt sorry for him.

Why then? She saw herself flying and in her mind she became a gull. A white stone. A bare cypress. The sea. And suddenly she was in the Fokianos Negri, five blocks from her house, where her mother was cooking dinner, fish, for her father, with no suspicion she was so near.

It did not make sense taking Cora and leaving him.

"Well, old one, thank you for saving my life. Is there anything else you should tell me?"

"Best policy no talk."

"They told you not to talk?"

"Best policy."

"Is there a bus that goes along this road?"

"Yes. One at six-thirty, to Pythagoreia."

"*Lipon*, then, old one, good-by."

"*Hairete.*"

The sun was reddening on the sea. He felt the old man's eyes following him, but he did not look back. He felt humpless without his pack.

In a quarter of an hour he reached the dirt road. He had to walk up and inland away from the sea. The main road was asphalt. The bus came by when he had been walking only minutes.

It let him off at a wire fence. The airport was a jerry-built cinder-block building. This was the point beyond which he had not been able to imagine.

"And I'm not going to Athens with you," she had said, as if the Goddess had overtaken her, inhabited her just as she had refused to inhabit his imagination past the Eupalinian Tunnel. He was unnerved, as though the Goddess were abandoning him because Cora had been shorn away. Why did she decide that? he wondered. And then he thought of decisions. He thought of his decision not to take the coufetta on the day Zoe had scheduled. So it could be his decision, no one else's. What difference did it make? Was there any significance in that?

A few people arrived in taxis to take the plane: a businessman, a woman whose husband and children were seeing her off, an old woman whose son was taking her to Evangelismos Hospital in Athens. No one with any clue or connection. But they looked at him with the distaste the bourgeoisie cannot disguise for filthy hippies.

The DC-6 standard features, its contours and carpets, its muffled acoustics disguised the real extent of his ruinous state, dirty rags, torn clothes, bloody head, and he settled by reflex into the Olympic blue seats noticing only that the white antimacassars were slightly greasy. A minute later he fell asleep.

He was awakened by the stewardess serving coffee and three Saltine crackers in cellophane packets. He was starving. He crammed the crackers in his mouth, gulped the coffee down, and went to sleep again.

When the vibration changed, he jumped. He reached out for Cora, but the seat was empty. They were circling over Phaleron Bay. He looked down and saw a city floating underneath, supernatural with wine-dark turrets and outcrops in the condensed sunset. It was the destroyers, aircraft carrier, and support vessels of the Sixth Fleet. A million lighted portholes, like diamonds. They upended to divert attention from the humps and blades of the dense and complicated abstraction of three-ply guns and radar screens. In that second, sunset became night, and the feast of its lights behind which he thought of Sanchez—which bead was his cabin?—

grew small and fragile against the expansive blackness of the sea in night. So that ahead, the city of Athens, beckoning with the outstretched blue arms of lights on the Glyphada runway, promised the embrace of Cora again, the color of its lights more yellow, more vast, twinkling along the shoulders of Hymettos, the tiny temple glowing on its head in celebration.

He decided to take a taxi to Omonia and from there the No. 12 as per Michalis's instructions. But when he looked at his reflection in the mirror of the airport café, his burnt-orange hair, the dried blood caked on dark-olive skin from ear to collar, his pale-blue gaze rising from the tatters of his shirt, his sleeve hanging off the ripped seam, the tear below the knee of his pants, he knew he could not appear demented like that at anyone's doorway. He ordered the taxi to take him to Katrantzos.

It was past eight. The stores were beginning to close, people swarming into the streets, the Athens night going into high gear. Could he make it before Katrantzos closed? He sat in the taxi, floating between stoplights on the long boulevard of Sigrou, leaving in the wake of licking tires and screaming buses the salty dust and stink of landfill from jetties in construction, new boat basins with cement lamps encroaching with green and bulging myopic gazes upon the vast darkness of the Saronic Gulf. Through the back window the Sixth Fleet levitated to pinpoints.

Katrantzos was closed. He dodged through the crowds of Omonia to make Prisunik, where he slid in under the bell and bought a cheap shirt and a pair of jeans, a razor and toothbrush and paste and soap. When he finished it was past nine-thirty. The Parthenon glowed frail as bones above the clamor. But where should he change clothes?

He felt weak under the force of his obsession—not an inch of time left or Cora would die, an inch of time and Cora would appear full-fledged, a genie of faith sprung from the touch on the coufetta of Zoe's mother—he knew he could not get to Zoe's home before eleven.

He looked for a hotel. The places in Omonia were full. The Palladium in Panepistimiou was also full. Tourists had converged early. Even the Y had no bed. He felt light from hunger, but kept reaching up to feel for the pack that was not on his back. So he went to a pension on Valaoritou called the "Home." It was run by a painted barge of a woman called Mme. Guaracci, who growled in three languages and who remembered him from four years before. He'd had an accident in a taxi, he told her. Her eyes glistened with suspicion—where was his baggage?—weighing the possibility of a brawl, but at length she let him have the sitting room on the second floor. It had a great French gilt mirror and cellophane flowers on the wall. It was ten-thirty, and he fell into a drugged sleep on the overstuffed divan.

The next morning, at nine-thirty, he woke into the somnambulistic emergency again, drummed to a dark, steamy consciousness in a shower where a cockroach crawled between the faucets. He cleaned his wounds, feeling nothing, and replaced the bandage on his arm. He put on his new clothes—the pants were too big—and entered streets which smelled of fresh bread and exhaust fumes. He did not stop for breakfast. The city swarmed, freshly pink, cool, everybody going to work. The traffic was crisp and the soaped surfaces of his body jumped to the auto horns.

There was a crowd waiting for the No. 12. He squeezed into line next to the guardrails. There was an OTE across the street. He wanted Philo's voice suddenly, the cleanliness of Philo's insults contemptuous of all obsessions. The last time he had telephoned, three months ago, Philo had not said, "What are you wasting your money for?" as he usually did about transatlantic calls. He had not even referred to the English as barbarians. "You are in England?" he had asked in an unfamiliarly fragile voice.

"Yes. I'm in Ruislip."

"Where's that?" That trace of the old contempt mitigated his worry somewhat.

A No. 12 came and the crowd inched forward, but it was so packed only half the people could squeeze in.

"Who told you to join the army?" he remembered Philo saying, as if he had not been drafted. What was he supposed to have done, go to graduate school?

He managed to get onto the next No. 12. But he was forced to stand on the back deck until the bus turned into Patission. Then he wormed his way to a free strap where he hung wedged between a factory worker with a briefcase and a fat woman with a string bag.

"Ping-pong is a feeble-minded AristoCat game," said Philo as the brakes shrieked. The man's briefcase cut into his ribs. Philo liked Walt Disney.

Morning lottery sellers threaded their way through milling crowds, their masts of fluttering blue coupons unfurled above heads like sails. They were barking the same bark as when Socrates walked the spot. "He wants one of us to be famous," said Theo, who had disqualified himself by becoming a physics professor and getting married. So it was left up to Don.

"Dirty Pythagorean. Sits contemplating his navel and lets the world go hang." But Ann Marie diverted Philo's attention from fame. "Don't *you* marry a sourpuss eight feet tall who never smiles. German blockhead."

Don tried not to listen. "What are you talking about marrying for?" bristling under the unspoken demand. "If you want somebody to get married *you* do it."

"I'm too old," Philo retorted, his head wagging in mendacious triumph. "Nobody would have me!"

Beneath a movie marquee announcing "Icy North Pole Cold," a crowd picked over a cartload of shoes like vultures. It was too early to telephone: it was the middle of the night in Chapel Hill.

"Pea-brained hedonist. You no-sense sensualist with untied shoelaces for brains."

In '67 after he got back, he had tried to get Philo to go to Greece for a visit.

"I'm not going any place with a dictator." The junta had just taken over. But Philo had a dozen ratiocinations. He kept talking, as if sending shoes in 1944 had fulfilled the contract of his blood connection. The truth was he was afraid of his past; it might destroy his illusions.

The bus rammed forward and Don had to jump to keep his balance. They were inching toward the archaeological museum.

At the museum a lot of people got off, but just as many got on.

What was the demand Philo had laid on him that had brought him to choose the vowel over the word, the female over the male, rhythm over reason? Why was it he who had to discover the secret of life? And what was this synthesis between ethics and the inhuman universe Philo had forced him to make?

The bus went up through Kipséli, past streets with the names of islands to a square in the Fokianos Negri district. Everything became soft as feta cheese. He got off at the next stop.

He was not sure of the direction. He consulted the paper Michalis had given him. He walked a few blocks and got lost. It was not until he had spent a quarter of an hour that he asked a passerby. He had to retrace his steps.

A few more wrong turns and he found Barka Street. It was a quiet residential street with apartments and separate houses. Number 9 was an old two-story peeling stucco building with crumbling walls. It was attached to a five-story apartment building under construction. The door was blue. He tried to ring the bell, but it was too rusted to push. He knocked.

Tit Harrow (now Cowley), who had moved from Kingsport, Idaho, seven years before, walked down the driveway to her mailbox with its lettering: WALT COWLEY, RTE #3, TALHSEE, FLA. A mockingbird sang in the white oak. She opened the grained envelope with the foreign stamp and recognized at once that the watercolor was Saint Peter's. Thin tissue paper protected the wrinkled brown and yellow surface and the note said:

> Dear Tit,
> This is where the smoke comes out. It has done this thrice in our lifetime. Do you remember our discussions of Pope Pius and popes in general in the smoker in Piltdown? Love always,
>
> Cora

Letitia Cowley felt the consistency of her life stop short in the morning. She smelled the Chesterfields, saw the peeling white windowsashes, the maze of pink Vermont snow, and continued up the driveway. She did not so much see Cora Simonds as hear her laughing out of that beautiful pink complexion. Had Cora Simonds really lived twenty-six years since? Some lopsided gaze poked through Letitia Cowley's world to render the mockingbird, the heat, the driveway, the geography of her marriage and children unreal, and the feet walking back up the driveway were bearing some strange woman with gray hair.

The next morning I wake at high noon. There is something inapropos about it. For, although the sun is merciless and fierce, there is a red glow in the sky and the heat comes from the wrong direction. The sun pretends to be rising!

I am raging with thirst and hunger. I think of the juice of the sea animals, seize the brooch again, and begin running toward the archway which leads to the sea. At that moment I remember that I have always carried a jackknife.

What a fool I am!

The jackknife is in my large suitcase. I turn around toward the suitcase, tear at the hasps, open it. I throw Don's Plexiglas mask onto the stones. I tunnel through the clothes, throwing them out on top of it. My fingers strike a cardboard box. Ritz crackers! And peanut butter! I forget the jackknife.

I open the peanut butter and dig in with two fingers until I have scooped a great gob. I stick it in my mouth. What delicious muck! But my mouth is so dry that my jaws stick. Dry peanut butter clogs the dry linings. I try to manufacture liquid. I cram Ritz crackers in over the peanut butter. I cough. My tongue is half-stuck to my palate. I blow crumbs. I waste, dishonor peanuts, do not care, think of fodder, imagine saliva, swallow, and eat until my stomach grows huge. Then I have to shit.

I go to shit in the corner of the courtyard. And I have nothing to clean myself with. So I do not clean myself.

I return immediately to the peanut butter. I eat more. I gorge.

When I have finished with this ravening act, my being is disfigured with thirst. I sit in the courtyard and burn. I am in pain, the skin of my body inflamed. I look at the stone woman, as if she might tell me where water is. She is young and pink, fresh in this zenith of noon-fire. I think how she protected the sun last night behind her skirts. I grow mad with desperation. Where shall I go to find water?

I get up, leave the empty peanut-butter jar wide open and totter away from her. The sea is no good. I want sweet water. There is a rotting roadway which leads into the heart of the fort, eastward toward Mount Elias. I follow this road.

I pass walls. I walk upon a dirt path along rising ground. Ahead of me I see a church sitting in a clump of cedars, a Byzantine church in the center of this acreage of castle precincts!

Churches always have water. The faucets in the Chelmsford Congregational Church basement leaked. They needed washers. I gulp what the children of the First Sunday-School Class used for fingerpainting and discussion groups made coffee with.

As I approach, the red cupolas huddle into themselves. I pass through some stinging nettles. A cedar tree introduces an archway which leads to the entrance. I rush into the courtyard.

The door is open. I smell a cold and musty breath. I plunge into the darkness. Bernadette! Oh water! I grow excited. I plan how I will drink, and what I will do with the water after I drink. I will wash all over. Then I will wash the floors of the church on my knees, sloshing. Then I will cough my praise and thanks for water.

The first thing I see in the church is Jesus. He is hovering over me in the All-Seeing dome, staring at me. I ignore Him. He is too melancholy. He leaks melancholy.

The font, I think. There is a pail on the floor near it, a rope attached to its handle. I rush toward it. It is empty. The font is also empty. There is dust in its marble bottom. I run my fingers through it and the dust sticks to the film of peanut butter on my fingertips. Jesus is still looking. Melancholy is heavier than tar, agony is heavier than oil. He dooms; He does not quench.

There are others there who watch my every move. I do not know their names, but I recognize the Panagia. She is younger than the stone woman, a stocky peasant girl made of ignorant wood. I pick her up and look behind her. Pictures often hide safes; she may disguise a spigot.

She does not. There is nothing there. I feel so sorry for her that I kiss her wooden mouth, but my lips are too dry and they click.

I hurry into the little room behind the altar where women are not allowed, for I think the water may be hidden there. They always store holy water in the most sacred spots. There is a rickety table covered with dust. There are four empty, dusty bottles, and some olive-oil candles. But there is no water.

When I emerge, I am surrounded by them. I try to believe they are dead. I refuse to look at them. I concentrate on the carved wood in which they are framed. The old gold paint is dry. The wood is dry. The dust is dry.

Jesus follows me with liquid chastisements, but I know His fate was vinegar. My fate shall be water. I am not fire for nothing. I cast Him off, ignoring His pleas and the pitiful droop of His neck.

I rub the walls with my hands. I decide to lick the wall. Bernadette made the fountain that way, and then the church came. I am pleased to know the correct order; shiny pipes are the latter blasphemy, for they disguise the spring. The wall tastes salty. I am amazed. The wall tastes of peanut butter.

I stand among the icons in the balmlike stillness, a strange, dry, burning, and alone figure, and I believe that they are teasing me with a promise of words. Words like Water. Then I see that they are begging me to speak. I begin to think in yea's. Yea, though I swim in the valley of memories, Yea though I water the valleys, etc. No cups runneth at all. My Jesus-pity sunk at the bottom of my stone past, my present is fire. I stick to my present.

Nevertheless, they affect me, for they keep staring, and I know I am expected to accord their shapes and forms my recognition of their sainthood. Saints are dry. They want to make me a saint too, and I fight the red paintbrush arriving at my lips. I shall not scream for the past. I imagine the icon-painter dipping his brush in water before he points the brush at my lips. It is strange to drink from a paintbrush.

I begin to sob, but I do not produce tears. I only shake, and I am afraid I will fall down upon the floor like an epileptic.

At that moment I recognize the one who can save me. It is Elijah. His chariot is flames. Hosanna! I shall surpass water with flame! Elijah's beard is fire too. Mercy is not rain, it is fire, as molten, as liquid as water. I bow to Elijah. I take his strength.

I quit the church. I am too full of worship to be disappointed that the church had no water. I look up in the sky. The sun has quit pretending at last. It is high noon and he is in full glare.

I am quite calm now. I take a cobbled pathway to the north. I pass through a boulevard of tall cypresses. Everything is very stately.

There is a place in the recesses of my mind which knows that I must find water or die. It knows that my blasphemy is necessary but incomplete. Despair waits for me, so that all my discards in the church, Jesus and the Panagia perhaps, may sometime become useful.

There is a flash, a suggestion in my calmness that water is always found inadvertently. It is like that speck, perhaps a mote, in the corner of an eye to which the divining rod points at the moment least expected.

I walk northwest toward the main entrance of the castle to survey the lay of the land. I estimate it to be three miles in circumference. A high parapet surrounds it. The entrance gate is a thirty-foot wrought-iron portal. Locked and immovable.

I must climb the parapet in order to see. I scan the walls for a stairway. Half a mile to the east I see one. It takes me more than thirty minutes to get to it.

I climb. It is dangerous, for the stairway is broken, there are gaps like teeth, and stones crumble away behind me and ricochet to the earth. Near the top a lizard looks at me and then scuttles away.

At the top I am anesthetized by light. I am so high I feel no danger. Yet the parapet in this place overhangs the sea by more than a hundred feet.

How safe I am, suspended!

The castle is surrounded on three sides by water. Waves foam on the lips of the shore below me, but it is like toothpaste. The sea congeals in my eyes. The ripples do not move. It shines, a polished corrugation of glass. I attach the sea's horizon to earth by an abstraction.

I walk the parapet to its headpoint. My footsteps are neat and perfect. There are cuts in the wall for gun emplacements. The eastern section of the castle is a city of ruined houses, platforms, blocks, and cells, a warren of dugouts most of whose roofs are fallen. I shall look for water there, I think, for if there was once habitation in this place, there may be a well or cistern. I arrive on the headland. It is a mammoth platform. Armies could have stood here to man the harbor's entrance. From this vantage point my stone woman is flattened out, and in disguise, white as death.

I see my courtyard. It is one among many. There is even a part of this western complex of yards that is roofed.

A solitary speck now, I head at last for the one side unbounded by the sea. For there the portal gate leads outward. I am unaware of time, though more than two hours have passed since I have begun my exploration. I am exposed, but feel nothing; the calmness of my fire has neutralized the sun's blaze.

I reach the portal gate. A dirt road leads far into the distance and disappears in white rocks at the foot of Mount Elias. But as far as I can see past this ribbon which connects the castle to the mainland, it is a land of rose-colored mountains. There is no sign of life. I see no village.

I am aware of shimmering signals, dark and silver. I focus my eyes. They are the leaves of a thousand scrub-olive trees which are catching a breeze I cannot feel. Their shimmer is returned in secret code by the needle glints of the sea. It is an emanation of landscape so graceful and so loving that it is incredible to discover that I am a prisoner in this place.

A woman came to the door.

"Good morning," he said. "Kyria Diamantes?"

Her expression was remote, diffident, with a trace of suspicion.

"I have brought you a keepsake of your grandson's christening. I am a friend of Michalis's and Zoe's."

She was tall and bony with one pigeon-toed foot. Her hair carefully curtailed in a net had once been black, now was bluish gray. It took a moment for her to ingest it. She made a grimace of a smile, half fearful, half joyous.

"My name is Adonis Tsambalis."

"Ah, *perasthe.* Come in."

She led him to the parlor through a small hall smelling of dead flowers, furniture polish, and boiling chorta from the kitchen in the recesses of the house.

Only nerves tied her to earth. She walked unevenly, half jerking, half sweeping past the tables and coat stands, her reflection darting at him from a huge gilt mirror. He looked for traces of Zoe in her face. But he found none. The flesh had sunk in below her thick glasses, and the only feature holding the shape of former years was her nose, large and still strong. It was heavily powdered but unevenly, so that red pores showed through, giving her the appearance of used-up grandeur.

"Sit down," she said in a high, slightly cracked voice, pronouncing the words assiduously and pointing to a large overstuffed chair with antimacassars. But he did not.

A Byzantine table filled the room with dark mahogany, and its carved intricate edges, curlicues of a bygone era, made such a powerful picture of the mother's notion of beauty as the main influence of Zoe's childhood that it wounded him to shyness. There were books behind glass in Greek and Italian. And across from this bookcase, a sideboard with a small mirror secreted in its huge diaphragm concealed Zoe behind its opaque stare.

"What is it you have brought?"

"Ta coufetta of almonds." He took out the silver cylinder.

"Oh, you were there at the baby's christening?"

Before he could say "No," she took it and with a jerky motion brought it close up to her eyes. She turned it over sidewise and lifted her glasses to inspect it. And he saw her eyes. They were hooded, gray with milky spots. Cataracts. Half-blind, she rotated the silver to make it glint, murmuring to herself as if he were not there, and she interrupted with token amenities: "My husband is in the study. I will tell him you are here."

But she made no move. She searched for something in her pocket. She was wearing a brown dress with beige flowers, of that sheeny silk material that genteel Greek ladies wear in the afternoon, and she found a crumpled perfumed lace handkerchief. But it was not to weep—not even in a weak moment of surprise would she weep. She dabbed her forehead and her cheeks—it seemed an affectation—while she continued to revolve the coufetta, holding her glasses off her nose.

189

I have delivered it, he thought.

"Sit down," she said again in the sharp voice, letting her glasses down.

She disappeared through the faded gold drapery of the double doors. He waited for the feeling of the historical moment.

He was a spy again, now alone in Zoe's house. Low voices murmured far inside. He spotted a photograph of her in the sideboard and went to look.

She was only thirteen or so, wearing her school uniform. A portrait shot. She looked exactly like herself, but with a child's vulnerability that hypnotized. Thinner. More boy than girl, more naked, trying to hide her mouth with her characteristic leer. She had a ribbon in her hair.

There were three other pictures. One of an older girl with smiling black eyes and oval forehead. Her sister? She had not mentioned a sister. Then a wedding picture of that girl and a heavy-lidded blond boy in a black suit. Flowers adorned. The third was a recent picture, glossy, of two small boys and a girl, none older than nine. They were dressed up in Sunday best, bowlegged in a cobbled street.

He listened behind the pictures and the furniture for some hint of children's games, afternoon laughter, some careless phrase from the past era of knee socks and calculus exams. Had she really been poor and escaped from the room during the German occupation to keep from eating cats? Perhaps, but he saw their prosperous past, some tradition of doctors or diplomats or fortune made at sea.

The mother returned clutching at the coufetta and said, "You have not sat down! Do sit down please and forgive me. It's such a surprise and the house is in an untidy state. My husband will be here in a moment. I have not offered you anything. What would you like?"

"Nothing, thank you." He sat in the overstuffed chair.

"Lemonada? A little cake?"

"I am fine as I am." The polite Greek: "I don't want," bothered him.

"But you must allow us to show hospitality. It is not often we have visits." But she was thinking of Zoe, of the coufetta, and she turned to the doors once more to call impatiently, "Panayotis!" "You have just come from Paris then?"

"No. From Naples."

"From Napoli?" She was surprised. "Then you saw her in Paris before you went to Napoli." She did not utter her name.

"No, I met them in Napoli." He felt immediately he had said the wrong

190

thing. She had not known they were in Naples.

"They had the child with them?"

"No. I have not met the child."

Uncomfortable, he explained how he had met them at the ping-pong tournament. He described how they had become friends. "And since I was coming to Athens they gave me the honor!"—he made it appropriately flowery—"to bring this keepsake to you."

She followed his words avariciously. Far from telling him what he wanted to know, she was using him to fish for information. What did she want to know about her own daughter?

"You came to Greece by boat or by plane?"

"By plane to Corfu."

"Then you have just arrived!" Hope. Palpable joy. "You were with them just a few days ago!"

"No." Her face fell. "I have been in the Peloponnesus visiting my father's relations." And he felt the days with Cora a full denial of what she sought from his flesh, his eyes, as if they alone made Zoe alive for her.

At that moment, the father came into the room. He was handsome, frail, older than she, with silver-white hair, and at the doorway he pulled his shoulders back and jumped forward, simulating the steps of a much younger man, stretching out his hand to him genially.

"Welcome to our house."

While they exchanged pleasantries, the mother retreated into a thoughtful silence. He was aware of her, of her hooded eyes, of a brooding fear that was keeping her alive. Did she know what her daughter was involved with?

"Come now. Let me see it," said the father, turning to her.

Instead of giving it to him, she opened it up with a jaunty innocence reminding him of Zoe's same gesture. The candies, gay in their pastels, trembled into the empty spaces, clicking like beads. But she suspected nothing.

"Take one," ordered the father, and, as Don hesitated, he picked out a green one to encourage him.

He chose a yellow one.

The mother picked out a rose-colored one.

Before the father, who held his green candy between his thumb and forefinger, muttering some words in such a low voice that he only distinguished the word: "Anna"—before the father could raise the candy into the air flourishing the words: "To our grandson, Eleutheris," the mother had put hers into her mouth. Then she grimaced and left the room.

A picture of Cora's teeth coincided with a sharp stinging beat in the wound in his hair. He tasted again the sweetness of the sugar, the mahogany aftertaste of the nut.

He pointed to the picture of Zoe. "How old was she when that was taken?"

"Ah, Anna!" The old man sighed. But he did not pick up her photograph. He picked up the other girl, so young Zoe continued to stare at him from the frame while her father uttered a monologue. "Since she has gone, the children live with Ioannis's family near Megara. Of course, we would like them here, but we are too old, and my wife is sick. See?" He pointed to the three children, singing their names: "Ioannis, Panayotis, and Aleka. We see them most weekends. And of course it is tragic, but children belong to their father's family."

"Zoe," he insisted.

The old man was deaf!

He pointed once more to Zoe's picture.

"Yes," sighed the old man putting the pictures back. "Life is *agonía*. But Greeks have a talent for pain."

He took a step forward to cry in the father's ear: "Stop. You must tell me everything about Zoe, who she is working for, who the enemy is who tracked me. Someone's life depends on it."

But the father was crooning: "During the war it was hard. We escaped to the mountains and the children had good milk from goats. Since then times are better: we have food, we have quiet, we have peace. But we do not have our children."

And knowing now he could not shatter that poetry for past grief without shattering their present life, whether the old man was truly deaf or deliberately so, knowing even that if he left this house there was nowhere else to go, he let the moment slip.

The mother appeared in the doorway carrying a tray which bore a bottle of lemonade, two clinking glasses of water, her best plates, and a chocolate cake. He was starving, having had nothing for breakfast. But he drank the water first. He took a large bite of chocolate cake. They watched him eat in silence.

"Your father was born in Greece?" she asked as if returning to a conversation.

"Yes."

"Then that is why you speak Greek. You are Greek." She offered him another piece. "And your mother?"

"My mother is dead. She was not Greek, and I never knew her; she died when I was a small child."

Justice—or was it purpose in these litanies? They made those formal murmurs of sympathy that are congealed for lifetimes in churches and anterooms. And he suddenly thought that Anna might be Zoe's sister and that she was dead and that was the tragedy.

He tried not to look at the third piece of chocolate cake, although his hunger was more voracious than ever. He stood up.

"I have eaten," he said.

"Will you write your name on a piece of paper?" she asked. She went to get a pad from the drawer of the sideboard. He wrote it. She took it, looked at it through the side of her magnifying glass. The same clinging glance she had laid on his flesh, as if he were the only link left to Zoe.

At the doorway Don shook hands. "I know you must miss Zoe," he said, hesitantly. He felt no shame for his execrable taste.

"Ach," the father said. "Far away she is. As far as America, where you come from."

"I thank you," he began, reluctant. They had either foiled him or they knew nothing.

"Paidi mou," said the old man, "we want you to know how grateful we are that you brought us this sign from our daughter."

There was a throb in his hair.

"We welcome you at any time into our home. It is to you we owe the pleasure of bringing her presence as near as possible from her exile so far away. We miss her presence and her friends. Come again, anytime. We welcome you. And go well, with our best wishes."

Was not this the point he had desired from time immemorial, the void where God would take over?

As he walked through the streets named for islands, he passed under a pepper tree and a little breeze moved overhead rustling the feather leaves. An impulse took him to run back again. He had not pushed them enough.

Instead he boarded the No. 12. When he got off at Stadiou, OTE was in full gear. Cleaning ladies pushed wet mops along the marble floor to a row of plastic chairs. The people awaiting international calls had to lift their feet for the mops.

His footsteps made clean round prints of O.

When I wake, I am amazed at the plate of food beside me. I am back in my courtyard, unaware of how I got here. There are two bits of meat on a pile of rice. It is warm. I feel it with my hand. It is served in a chipped crockery plate. But it is not food I want; it is water.

The grease on the meat shines and reminds me of water. I put it into my mouth and lick it. The grease lubricates my mouth slightly, so that I can chew. But I cannot swallow. There is no fork, so I pick up the rice in my hand and swallow it without masticating.

I am burning. I am still determined not to die, yet I am in greater danger than before. I don't know why, but I am.

I see that my courtyard is a stage and that the stones of the walls are staring at me. Perhaps I was misled, having fooled Paul and Sylvan about not wanting to be an actress, but Vivien did not lead me here for nothing. What I know with certainty is that Elias is watching me too. I hate him for not giving me a fork, and not knowing I need water. How could he have brought me food, not water? I grin at the crowds.

Watch me eat then, so that you may be ashamed. Gobble, Cora Burnheart, gobble, swallow lick.

"Elias! Elias!" I call him. The sound of my voice is a mew, far away, pitiful-sounding. It doesn't contain the force of the purpose that surrounds me.

I realize for the first time how alone I am. The watching stones keep him out. They can give me nothing, that crowd. But to him they give protection from my eyes. I know that he is back of them somewhere, and that his eyes are human, even though he is my keeper. Perhaps he is in collusion with them!

"I want water!" I shout angrily.

The word rills down the cliff of my brain. I begin to sob. The sobs turn into retching.

I stumble feverishly up to the corner of my courtyard which is my poo-poo place. I deposit rice grains in bile. Every time I retch my skin screams. Some separation is going to be accomplished, like that of a snake or a silkworm. The crowds watch me from my wall of purpose. Great suspense. I can retch no more.

I am still hungry. I totter slowly back to the plate.

I decide not to eat here. I pick up the plate, start upward toward the east doorway to go eat in the church. It is blasphemous to eat alone. Every action of our physical life is sacred and must be shared. I am going to give part of my food to Elias, to the Panagia, to Jesus, and it will be blessed, and then I will be able to eat.

But I stumble. I fall down; a perfect stage fall, my knee, my elbow, my shoulder, in that progression. I break neither my bones nor the plate. I do not even spill food off the plate. I simply slide it with perfect equilibrium onto the stone platform next to my face. I am too weak, too feeble to go to the church. I lie beside my plate. After a while, I wonder if they are still there, if they still expect me to go on. I think how my aspiration to rockhood has arranged itself about me as an audience of stones.

Some time has passed—it feels as long as a day—when I think: How did the plate get there? I have been thinking about the wrong things: i.e., the stone audience which is my wall, or I would have wondered about this before.

At first, I assume that Elias walked here while I was asleep and set it beside me. I see him doing it in my imagination. I shudder at my vulnerability under his gaze . Then I grow angry that I had not waked up to see him, to demand water.

More time passes. The passing of time has become so discrepant that it causes me anxiety, for my watch ticks and goes, but it is at variance with the sun's positions, so I know that I have never gotten it set correctly. I worry that it may be afternoon when it is morning, or that I will think it is late afternoon when it is late morning. Anyway, the passage of this section of time gives me the idea that he was not inside my precinct at all.

Where was I sleeping, for instance? Up against the wall. The plate was set near to my face, also against the wall. If somehow he could have inserted it, as most jailers do, through a hole in the wall, it makes more sense. To think of him walking across the expanse of the courtyard—from where did he enter it? which door? had he come from the church or the sea?—is not logical. The food would have cooled if he had, for instance, entered the castle through the main gate.

I rush to the wall where I sleep. I touch the stones and push on them. Sure enough, although most of them are intact, giving way only enough to send a scatter of old dry mud-cement on the paving stones, there are two which come right out in my hand. Cleanly, too. They are oblongs, as large as two fists, heavy, weighing maybe six pounds apiece. I set them on the ground by my knees, excited. When I look through, though, there are more stones behind. I reach in and give one a shove. It moves. I push further. It falls, a shaft of blue sky pierces through, but I do not hear where the stone falls. Nothing. If this is an outside wall, as I think, then the stone may have dropped thousands of feet to the shore, or onto the ribbon of land which connects this island to the mainland.

How did Elias get up here then? Is there some sort of platform out there? Does he climb a ladder? Or is it part of the warren of buildings, and not the outside wall? If this is true, why did I not hear the stone when it hit the ground?

I know how to find out. I will go up the parapet again until I come to the spot over my courtyard. From there I can look down the outside wall to see if there is some way a man could climb up to put a plate through.

I feel the other stone at the far end where the sky looks through. It too is loose. But I do not push it out. Instead, I grow scared that I have upset the balance of nature with my discovery. I set the two oblong stones back in, shutting out the sky. The wall looks as it had before.

But instead of moving away from this wall, going up the parapet to check on the hole from outside, I do not move. I sit quietly and contemplate the wall.

I give myself many reasons for making no move. Night is coming. I see that the sun has lowered, and soon it will set. I must not get caught on the parapet at dusk; I might lose my footing. When I think about the sun, I realize a whole day has passed since I ate the meal that Elias left. I have spent this whole day in my courtyard and not once gone down to the sea.

I cannot move because I am tired. The feeling I had in the morning of some incipient separation is stronger now. I can feel my skin smoke along the seams of my long-sleeve blouse. I am wearing my blue sunshade hat, but the sun is raging in my eyes like coals, on the backs of my hands red as the claws of a lobster, and on the hair of my arms and legs, which are distended with electricity under the polyester.

Immobile as my body is, I think clearly. I think of the hole. The hole is secret. Therefore it is a miracle. On such miracles we live. The very thought of the hole will keep me for weeks. I hoard the secret of the hole as if the strip of sky in it is not the same sky I see above me in my courtyard. I am, I feel, privy to a knowledge that defies imagination:

The hole is the place where food comes from.

The hand that brings it shall be my avenue to the whole promontory. I vow to be awake when he puts the food through tomorrow.

But when will that be? Perhaps at dawn. I decide to go to sleep early and rise before dawn.

I place the plate just below where I know the hole is. I make sure the stones are loose so he can take them out easily. I wallow in the secret of the hole, how no one would know it was a hole with those stones. The sun has passed the purple point. I set my watch at nine, for the color of the sky looks like nine o'clock. I lie down to sleep. I realize that I am no longer thirsty. I have not thought of water since I discovered the hole.

When I set my mind to waking at a certain time, I can usually do it, even though I am beset by anxiety. It is the anxiety that makes me do it. I usually hit it within a radius of five minutes.

When I awake, it is still night. Cold. I try to read my watch but the moon has set, it is too dark. A few minutes later the night begins to bleach. A greasy pallor dims the stars. I look at my watch. It is ten minutes to five.

I sit up. I do not feel as if I had slept. Although I have no desire to drink water or do pee-pee, I am aware that I am surrounded by water. I don't mean the sea. I mean my skin. At the slightest movement of my body I can hear and feel a creaking, a slipping sound. Like canvas. The sky is pulling the teepee of my skin to an infinite distance above me, pretending to give me the freedom of day. But the pressure underneath my skin increases, particularly along my back. I am careful not to lean against anything.

By eight o'clock nothing has happened. The sun is high. I put on my blue hat to shelter my head. The cold of early morning has given way to a neutral temperature. Swallows are screeching in the copse chasing each other from the pine trees below to the cypress at the church. I catch glimpses of them now above the faces of the audience, but I pay little attention, for I am concentrated on the secret hole.

At quarter past nine there is a grinding sound. One of the stones wobbles. It is being pulled away from me. The first nostril is clear. The second stone withdraws, and the second nostril completes the hole. There is a clinking sound.

I feel my skin stretching. I do not dare move for fear it may give and all my life's liquid wash away. I wait for the hand.

But the plate appears first. It is chicken this time, not meat. The chicken sits in its bed of rice.

The hand carrying the plate is broad, tense with thick, black hair curling to its knuckles. But when it tries to set down the plate, it hits the old plate. It withdraws. There is nothing now except the hole.

The hand comes through seeking the old plate to take it away. I see the hand and the arm all the way to the elbow. The black hair curls up the forearm in a mat. The fingers are longer than I had thought at first, well shaped with curiously clean fingernails; the little finger has a long white nail. This is a disguise. The hand is a workingman's hand. It has the thick skin of old calluses. The palm is rough, and the wrist is massive, like a bull's neck.

The hand takes the old plate as nimbly as if there were eyes in its fingerpads. A few grains of rice drop off, and the plate disappears.

When the hand inserts the new plate again, I notice that the thumbnail is white from the burden of the plate's pressure. But the moment he sets it on the ground the blood rushes into it and it turns a robust pinkish-brown.

The hand is disappearing through the hole. I leap forward, mouth to the hole, whispering, "I want water." Then I think to say the word in Greek: *"Nero."* I cannot see the sky through the hole, but, as I watch, the sky slips back in place and blinds my eye with light. That means his arm is gone.

"Nero, parakalo!"

There is no sound. No shadow.

"I am thirsty!" The word in Greek sounds like a cat's yowl: *"Dipsao!"* I see a gourd of water being dipped.

"Mia stigmi," he answers.

In retrospect the voice telling me to wait a second was harsh, perfunctory, somewhat like a dog's bark. I wait more than seconds though. I see nothing through the hole but that strip of sky.

How many hours have passed since he said he would bring the water? Why is he taking so long? Did he have to go so far away? How easy it was to say: *Mia stigmi.* Stigmata. I listen for footsteps, for some sound. Nothing. Does he exist? I sit facing the hole, unable to touch the food. Waiting for his hand, I doze off.

Something wakes me. A voice? A bark? His hand comes through. He has brought water in a dirty, white plastic bottle. It has a red plastic screw-top. His fingerprints in mud mark the sides. His hand disappears.

I screw the top off the bottle, but my hand is trembling so I can hardly hold its mouth to my mouth. The water is cool. I want to drink in large gulps, but I cannot. How sweet water tastes! I had never imagined the sweetness. I smell it. I smell the earth in it.

For many hours, I sit with the bottle of water. I experiment. I pour some of it over my head and face, watching it drop into pools by my haunches.

It dawns on me what a waste! I have the whole sea for washing. I must use this only for drinking. So I sit and sip. I move to a spot shaded by the wall. I cradle the bottle. It is half-gallon size, the shape of a baby bottle, so I feel like a monstrous infant. Three hours later I have to do pee-pee. I go to the spot. My retchings have turned green. There are diamond-like flies buzzing over the pile. I do it. It feels like a large accomplishment. I return to the shade, pick my bottle up and drink again. The water grows hot but I do not care. Only after I have drunk my fill do I eat. I pick at the chicken. I get flesh from the thigh and chew. I sip water and eat the rice grain by grain until it is gone.

The sickness matches equally the force of my obsession. I am in love with the hand. I think of nothing but its black hair and brute wrist. The symptoms are a fever and aching. Now that I have water and food, now that I feel the physical flow of my juices, my blood, my pee-pee, my tears pumped through my veins and ducts, returned to me in concert with my breath and my heartbeat which, acting with the food and water, have produced them, this great, lopsided illness betakes me. I cannot move. I lie in the shade of the wall, groaning and delirious.

Though I had had a premonition of the separation, I had not realized that it would be volcanic and ecstatic. I live only for his appearance, and though I drink the water and pick desultorily at the bits and pieces of the meat, it would be nothing without my knowledge of him. I do not think of his face or body behind the wall from which he stretches forth his hand, for I know them without seeing them: they are embodied in the hand.

It is natural that I should love him, love the hand that saved me with water, love my keeper. The dangerous thing is that thick wrist. The difference between a man and a boy is the size of the neck. I knew Elias's neck by the size of his wrist. It is not convincing that that passionate woman would fall in love with a Hyppolytus with a neck the size of Anthony Perkins'.

I know Elias's forearm has downed regiments, lifted battalions of chairs and tables by one leg. It has done this coolly with, at the last moment, that faint trembling that proves him still mortal. This wrist has perhaps killed men with the right chop to groin or jaw, and I know those fingers, from the way he handles the plate, to be familiar with triggers well-oiled. I revel in his killing me in some brutal way, choking me, perhaps, suffocating me, or dashing me against stones.

My fever hallucinates my helplessness. I groan in revelry. Behind that bull is a peacock who will not open his colors. He remains a bull and in his girth, protected by the stones who watch with blank faces, I attempt to kill him. I throw large rocks at him, but they bounce off his shoulders or his chest without effect except for a stronger intake of breath, which like the trembling prove his mortality, but merely enlarge the girth. I hit him with my fists. I punch his face. With both my hands I try to hold his hand in back of him, to pin him to the ground.

"You've got to eat!" he barks.

How many days has he been telling me this? I have lost track of time in my ecstasy. It is not that I do not realize the gravity of my physical state. I tell him, but he blames it on my not eating. In this way he is child or idiot.

"You can't see me. How would you know!" I whisper hoarsely. "I may die of this fever and you'll be to blame."

He does not respond. I hear no crack in his armor.

Before, when I was dry, I had not been given sustenance for this ague. The elements were not right. But it is the water which he gave me which has done it. Burning demands liquid. Have you ever wondered that blood imitates fire in its molten state? I sweat. Then water forms dew on my rind, and I grow cold. I have lain on the ground too long. Chills.

"I am cold, you fool. Something horrible is happening to me!"

I need proof, an acknowledgment that the drum is leaking. This is the first presentiment of my rottenness.

The next time his hand comes through, the air is dusky although it is not dusk.

"Please leave the hole open and don't put the stones back," I beg, reaching to take hold of his hand with both of mine. He promises:

"En taxi."

I lay my burning forehead and chattering lips to the hairs above his knuckles so he can tell how sick I am. He presses my hands, squeezes them tightly. The feel of his hand is dry, hot leather. When I raise my head, tatters of skin like confetti are left in the black hairs of his hand. They are what were once my lips.

Something along my back moves. A seam rips from my shoulders to my wrists. The water I have drunk has thickened to a sludge. The sludge begins to leak through the seam.

"Help me! Help me!" I scream. "My body is coming off!"

"I want to make a telephone call to the United States," he said to a clerk at the long marble counter. His palms were sweating.

The clerk who wore glasses and had a mean mouth turned away from him to answer one of the telephones ringing on a desk behind him. "Well, why didn't you answer it then?" he said to someone on the line. The high brown ceiling echoed a din of ringing telephones and shouting voices. "I told you: Number Nine," continued the clerk growing angry. "Galveston." He repeated "Galveston," accenting the second syllable, but evidently the other person couldn't understand it, so he spelled it and then hung up.

"The United States," repeated Don. "How long will it take?"

"Maybe an hour. Maybe an hour and a half." The clerk pushed a pad toward him contemptuously. "Fill this out."

There were spaces for Party calling, Party called, and Domicile. He wrote his name, Philo's, the familiar number, and for Domicile: Home Pension, Valaoritou. The clerk gave him a paper with the words: "No. 11."

"Go to Number Eleven when your name is called."

He sat down in a row of black plastic seats. But he was restless. He decided to buy an *Athens News*. A sketchy plan began to form in his mind. He could go to Corfu and report to the police as the man they were looking for in connection with Annette Borlin.

A man got up from the black plastic seat opposite him.

Through the glass door he could see the kiosk, but the *Athens News* was not hanging there. You had to ask for it, they sold it under the counter. What if, when he opened it to "Greek News in Brief" he read: "An American woman tourist by the name of Kori Ellison was found by Samos gendarmerie—" An amazing thought occurred to him. He could, was free to, take the next plane to Izmir, pretend he had never met Cora, Zoe, Annette Borlin.

The man who was twenty-eight or twenty-nine, about the same height as he, black, receding wavy hair, stepped directly in his path, and said, "Will you please come with me?" in English.

"What for?"

"Just take a moment."

"But I'm waiting for a phone call."

"You have plenty of time. This is a frightfully dingy place and they've made a muck with all this water. The damp affects my sinuses."

He looked at the man, stared at the clean, white shirt buttoned tightly over his chest, and his kind smile, at his dewlaps, and said to him in a rough, malicious, threatening voice, "Okay, what do you want?"

"Why take such a tone? You're in a strange place and I thought I might show you some of the sights."

"No, thank you." He moved to pass.

"You're an American?"

"How could you tell?"

"The sneakers."

"I'm not buying."

"I'm not selling."

"All Greeks sell." He turned, reckless, to flush him out. "You sell your grandmother. Your country."

At that moment, a car drew up to the curb. Above the brass railing, newly installed to prevent pedestrians from walking in the street, the flower boxes, the geranium blooms, he saw the man at the wheel, swarthy, fat, with a Chaplin-type mustache.

"All right. Anything you want to tell me, you tell me right on these steps."

"You don't understand. I don't want to tell you anything. I want to ask you something." The man leaned forward, put a tentative hand on his forearm, and said in a low voice. "You're a friend of Anna Daimonides, aren't you?"

"No."

"You just came from her father's house."

He deicded to try something. "Anna Diamantes," emphasizing the name as he knew it, "is dead."

"No, she's not. You know that better than anyone."

The hand tightened. He felt the other hand before he could see what the man was doing, the pressure on his neck. The man pushed him down the steps. He tried to catch his balance, raised his arms like wings, but crashed into a couple of tourists.

"My friend is always losing his balance," jested the man into the surprised gapes of the Germans, captured him in a jocular embrace and rushed him into the car beyond the flower boxes. He could have ducked, feinted, gotten away. But he did not. "We'll be able to talk much better in the automobile," said the man, pushing in next to him and slamming the door. "Hi, Spyro. Meet my friend Adonis. He's a friend of Anna's."

Above the sparks of sun flashing off the gold molars of Spyro's smile, the light turned green. The clock over the Hellenic National Tourist Office said quarter to twelve. The Hillman packed into the lines of traffic, waiting at each light as it turned the corners around Síntagma Square.

They climbed up toward the old palace. His interlocutor stretched out next to him, opened the window, lit a cigarette. "Smoke doesn't bother you, does it?" Spyro drove with one hand, insolently. They were climbing up the side streets around Kolonáki. The motor knocked a little, metal rings beating against each other, needed a valve job. Spyro didn't gear down. He turned right, then left, left again, etc. Trying to make him lose his sense of direction. Succeeding. His hairy beef arm hanging out the window. Just as the interlocutor crushed out his cigarette, Spyro lit one, held it out the window with ringed fingers.

"See how high we are." They were on Lykabettos, headed for the Ring Road. "In a minute we can see Phaleron. Look! There's your Sixth Fleet. Turn right, Spyro."

As he pretended to relax, he tried to synthesize disparate details: The breeze spanking through the window, cool promise of May, incongruous to the threat. His interlocutor's British accent through teeth set on American idiom. The blood-red ring on Spyro's finger. The cigarette never inhaled, never tapped. The ashes sprouting off its tip. The pounces of wind which spread it like seed into his eyes whenever they weaved into another narrow street. The predictability of the promontory of Spyro's gut, which secreted a trough in the sheeny cloth of his white shirt, where sweat leaked through, a secretion of some inestimable force of body with muscles breathing. Spyro's oxen set of shoulders over the Hillman upholstery, with two brutal pouches of fat slung just under the brain pan.

They traveled for some distance on the Ring Road and then turned off at a grungy building, which looked like a bus depot. They drove through an area of new apartment buildings with orange-and-blue awnings. He was completely lost. Had no idea what part of the city. Were they in a suburb? The territory turned into an industrial area, empty lots full of trash.

"To the right, to the left," the interlocutor directed Spyro.

They passed a beer factory. He tried to memorize the route. It was the outskirts of Athens. They crossed a railroad track into a region of low crumbling walls and deep declivities. There were no buildings, except a few warehouses in the distance with peeling Fix ads in red and blue. Spyro pulled up by a deep gravel pit and turned off the motor.

"All right. It's quiet here, so you can tell us about Dimitri," said his interlocutor in a sweet voice, turning toward him, one arm stretched across the backseat.

"Dimitri who?"

"Fotianos."

"Never heard of him." When the hair on his head rose, the wound on his head throbbed.

"Come now, we have ways of making you talk."

"So that's why you bring me to a gravel pit?"

"You think you sprung him, you fairy patsy, but he's locked up in there tighter than a virgin's ass—" Spyro's voice was a grunt with wheezes and loose spots as if he had a gizzard and he had pulled himself at a half twist. His face was contorted. Personal passion.

·"*Skase!*" warned his interlocutor.

He took advantage of the mistake—they were rearranging themselves; Spyro turned back to the wheel, the interlocutor put his hands on his knees and took a breath—to scout the nearest building, the possibility of some passerby. Far away, too far to hear, two children with shaved heads were poking in some trash with a stick. At the same time, assessing what it was or was not he had carried, and the important thing he had learned, that it was an escape he had been involved in, they, Zoe had been involved in.

"Come on," said the interlocutor in an even more cajoling voice, and in a motion so quick no eye could follow slapped him open-handed across the cheek.

He felt the blood roll luxuriously down the inside wall of his mouth and mopped it with his tongue.

"You can't touch me," he said evenly. "I'm an American."

"Agnew love Papadopoulos." Spyro grinned, twisting back comically. "The American government and the Greek government." He rubbed two fingers together.

"Give me your credentials," he ordered his interlocutor.

The man pulled a plastic identification card from his pocket and flashed it just long enough for him to see a head—whose?—and writing in Greek. "Police," he said. "Security Division."

"Your names?" he demanded.

"Spyro Makris there. And my name: Stratis Babolas. Now it will be easier if you tell us right off. Any foreign national involved in criminal activity against the Greek Revolution is subject to Law Five-Oh-Nine."

"I can't."

"I don't want to do this," continued Babolas, sounding sincere, "but you were seen with Anna at that café in Naples, and we know you pretended to deliver that message to the parents only *after* Fotianos was sprung?"

"So he *was* sprung!" he managed before Babolas hit his face again.

His blood and dumbness thrilled Spyro, who turned around again shouting, "Faggot! You get women to do the dirty work and come up smelling roses. Are you too rich to get in the dirt? I know you, you little fairy with the Greek name. *Poniros* little bastard. Take a look at the bottom of that pit there. That's some good dirt there, and you'll be there a long time."

"What's the name of the organization?" said Babolas.

"I don't know."

"What do they call themselves?" Babolas looked strangely kind, his hand poised as if for a blessing.

"I can't tell you what I don't know, can I?"

In the front seat Spyro lifted one of his haunches up with his own hand and farted. Then he took out a package of chick-peas and threw them one by one into his open mouth, crunching and smacking. When he had eaten about ten, he put them back in his pocket. He opened his door and got out. He left his door open, crossed to Don's door, opened it. He grabbed his arm and twisted it in back of him.

"First of all, were you in Naples April nineteenth?" asked Babolas in the same kind voice.

"I never denied it."

He looked at the open front door, estimated his chances of escape against the ratio of pain and his excuse for suffering it, for *not* getting away from them before: information. Was Anna Zoe? Or Zoe Anna? Were they sisters? Had Fotianos escaped? Had he actually carried a message? And he knew that Spyro could break his arm in a minute.

"Did you meet Anna in Naples?"

"No." How much did they actually know? how much pretend to know? Spyro twisted.

"Then who did you meet?"

"Nobody."

The third twist brought him to a horizontal position on the backseat. Apart from the pain, he sensed his body at some remote distance reacting with a jagged spasm of muscles like a bolt of lightning. His head was embedded in Spyro's guts. His feet were pointed toward Babolas's balls. He folded himself up like an accordion and in a tremendous push of strength uncoiled and exploded a sharp kick in those testicles. Babolas recoiled and Spyro lost his grip in surprise.

He hurdled the front seat and jumped out the door. But Spyro reached and slammed it, catching his ankle. The pain ricocheted to the wound in his head. Spyro grabbed him around the neck. A succession of hard blows rained on his head, his face, and his chest.

The next thing he knew he was stretched out on the backseat and something was on top of him, suffocating him. He opened his eyes. There were flashes of fire, a smell of hot leather and closed breath. It was Babolas on top of him. His elbows pinned both his shoulders, his eyes looked deep into his, and his fingers, both hands gripped together, pressed down upon his Adam's apple.

"Okay, now talk," said Babolas.

He struggled, breathing hard, and at every move Babolas jounced, breathing hard also, as if in imitation.

His view of Spyro was upside down, for his head hung backward off the edge of the seat. Spyro had a rope in his hands. He made a loop. He put Don's third finger in the loop. He twisted the rope to the right.

He lost track of the reasons for his being here by a gravel pit on the outskirts of Athens in broad daylight: where were the passersby? the wonder of it; this thought roamed above his head—in pain. Acute, ingenuous, this systematic desecration of a finger with the twisting of a rope. It would fracture and in a moment break, but you can't die of a broken finger. He lost his idea of Zoe in the pain, and he lost all curiosity for the answers he was supposed to give. If he had carried the instructions for Dimitri Fotianos's escape, the law of correspondence decreed that that should insure his own escape.

The pain came in waves. It was accompanied by strange grunting noises. He smelled something. He opened his eyes. Spyro was farting and twisting the rope in unison.

"Damn you, he's bleeding. All over the leather."

The pain stopped.

He wondered what could be bleeding, when he felt the moisture under his head. The head wound.

When he opened his eyes, Spyro had his pants down. The white mass of underbelly spilled over a barbaric nest of hair where the half-alive worm wriggled. There were separate hairs inside the navel. Spyro was wearing knitted jockey shorts. He pulled the jockey shorts down around his ankles and placed his fist carefully in the crotch, like a darning ball, to expose the gleaming line of excrement. In a football squat he pushed the jockey crotch through his legs to Don's mouth.

"Lick it," ordered Babolas.

Feces. Holy poo-poo excreted from white half-moons of stranger-ass. Flash shot of Cora extending her lips to the cross. Bear the sacrament to me, O sensitive, sorrowful, holy goat. This is not a prescribed method of torture, not filth, not the shit of a human trying to degrade—it is the opportunity to ingest fear and perversity and conquer.

But the warmth was worse than the smell. He held his breath. There were thick yellow clots of paste in the middle which faded away at the edges to chips.

He began. Put out his tongue. Tasted. It was surprising. It did not taste like shit smells. It had a greasy consistency, like butter, and it was mild.

But Spyro wanted fight. Victory by passive resistance made him mad. He rammed it through his teeth and headed it back to his glottis moving it back and forth till he gagged. Spyro was furious at the bits of chocolate cake spattered on his shirt.

"American *pousti,* gangster, cheapie!" he shouted, jumping away. He meant "hippie." "You'll find out what it means to be a Greek, you fake tin-soldier American creep, playing around with these Commie bastards. You were born out of a whore's ass, and a whore's ass is all you know!" Spyro pulled up his pants and buckled his belt with a grunt of anger. Then he crossed in front of the car and got a billy club from the dashboard.

"Now talk!" he shouted, whacking him on the soles of his shoes. He beat him two more times, working himself up into a rage. Purple veins rose in his temples. "If you don't talk, you'll be executed!"

He beat him nine or ten more times. The strikes became progressively stronger, glowing like coals on the inside of the leather.

"We're not interested in you," crooned Babolas in his ear, pressing down on his throat.

"What do you want?" he gasped.

"Names. The name of the organization. The names of them. Names, that's all."

He felt wet. They raised him by the scruff of the neck, pushed him out the door, and held him up on his feet. They made him walk twice the length of the car, then they brought him back to the door.

"You're under arrest," Babolas said.

They pushed him back in the car.

Spyro got in the driver's seat again and drove away from the gravel pit and back onto the Ring Road. They passed through Fokianos Negri not more than three blocks from the house of Zoe's parents. His feet flared in pain, throbbing as the pistons clicked. A woman with packages in her string market-bag was buying gladiolas from a florist's stand while they waited for a red light.

"Where are you taking me?" he asked.

"To Police Headquarters," said Babolas.

Two Jehovah's Witnesses approached the junkyard gate. One was a black man dressed in a brown suit and polished shoes, the other a young white boy wearing a tie.

"Enter!" said Philo, as if they were long-lost friends.

At that moment the telephone rang.

"Pay no attention," he said, waving at it disgustedly. He thought it was Ann Marie. Such bad timing, just when he had an untried audience. She worried about him and kept track, the poor sourpuss.

The Jehovah's Witnesses were doubtful, abashed at a person who refused to answer telephones. They followed as he ushered them ostentatiously, talking over its third insistent ring.

"That's the Devil's instrument." He relished the moment that their spiel would begin. "Let's get away from it and go see the Lord's," and he led them down to the pen where Phryne, the goat, lived. The rings grew fainter, and Philo put out of his mind Ann Marie's concern. She patronized the old. Theo was busy with his baloney at the Puny Versity.

The Jehovah's Witnesses watched as he cut and stuck blackberry branches into Phryne's mouth. The telephone continued in the distance. He raised his voice to blot it out—trust her to let it ring twenty-three times; he imagined her thinking he was dead—informing them how he and his sons had rented out the goat's grandmother to the football games for a mascot, $6.50 per game, and how they had palmed her off as the Carolina Ram. The Jehovah's Witnesses did not laugh. He and Theo, Philo said, had designed a light-blue wool coverlet with four holes for legs and embroidered the letters UNC in blue and white, the same colors as the Greek flag, the significance of which was lost on people who had no idea of the origins of their culture. The telephone stopped.

He was free at last to get them started on the criminal Revelation of the Jews.

"Well, what can I do for you?" He could hardly wait for those superstitious scorpions' tails, the lambs with two-edged swords for tongues, the serpents and beasts beloved of all ignorami. "What are you witnesses of?" he asked.

They took out the Bible, inspired. "Have you read Revelations?"

"Have you read Plato?"

"But this is the Good Book," said the black man, "the first written book."

"Written by prophets?"

"Yes."

He led them back to the junkyard garden, told them to sit down on the folding chairs, and got the Jowett *Plato* down from the top of the refrigerator. He picked two of the best apples from a barrel.

"The prophets who wrote the New Testament got their ideas from Plato," he announced.

For a few moments they talked. They chewed the apples. They argued as to who should read which book first.

But the telephone started up again.

"I tell you what I will do," he bargained. "I will read Revelation if you will read Plato."

"All right," said the black man, standing up. "Aren't you going to answer the telephone?"

"Take it then," Philo said, handing him the book and ignoring the question. "Come back when you have read it."

The Jehovah's Witnesses walked with him back through the bridal bouquet to the gate, their footsteps beating time to the rings.

He said good-by lavishly and returned to the ringing phone, but when he picked it up, it was too late. Whoever it was had hung up.

Fotianos lay back on the sofa, his boots on the coffee table. He stayed in a stupor of drink.

"Was that Zoe?" he guessed.

Michalis, who had just hung up, said nothing about its being Zoe.

"Ah, Zoe's secret is that she cannot refuse faith or love or devotion. She has to give it back in spades." Fotianos was half in love with her, but it was a remark of disapproval.

She was phoning from right under their noses, disguised as a widow, black kerchief, from an office in the Commerce Department, and her voice had an edge of excitement. She had found out from the file clerk named Andreades that the American Tsambalis had been arrested.

A period of time passed which I do not remember now, nor do I want to. It could have been a day, it could have been five.

It seems to me that I was not lying outside on the paving stones anymore. I was inside one of the stone enclosures. There was a roof over my head. I no longer saw the sun. It was dark. I was lying not on stones but on a filthy mattress. I had both food and water, and I remember drinking, but I cannot remember eating. Cold compresses were placed on my head. Now I believe that the cloth they were made of were either slips or panties (mine) which had been soaked in water. It seems to me that Elias was taking care of me, putting the compresses on my head. I never saw him, no; but in the darkness I felt him there taking care of me, and I have a distinct vision of his hand turning the cloth over in a pail and then putting it on my forehead.

I lived in a world of pain. I gave myself up to it. But pain and darkness were synonymous. The only thing that tied me to life or to reality during this period was this animal presence of Elias. I gave my fate over to him. Whether he was really there or not is beside the point. My love for "the hand that feeds" had changed to a more wonderful thing, to a feeling of having let go to his presence in the darkness. I had confidence in him. It even seemed miraculous that the bull-necked prison guard had, by coming closer, become invisible. It is not that he touched me. I have no recollection of the faintest touch, not even the applying of the compresses. But I lived intimately with his presence, the changing of the currents of air as his body moved to different places in the room, with no more motivation, it seemed to me, than that of the goat upon whom I had done poo-poo that night. I loved the feeling of that animal in the darkness, of whose breath, motion, or motives I had not the slightest knowledge or curiosity.

My only other recollection during this period I can hardly explain to myself now, any more than I can explain the fact that I have come to consciousness here in his stone enclosure lying in the darkness *with no mattress nor any trace of a mattress!*

It seems to me I saw him! I saw him several times and for hours at a time. He was standing on the parapet watching me.

His standing place was to the left of the portal gate. It was too far away from me to shout. Even so I saw him with telescopic clarity. He stood feet astride. His torso, just as I had thought, was thick in the upper portion, massive neck and shoulders, and even a small hump of fat like a fighting bull. I was surprised how short he was, perhaps no taller than I am. But compact. His waist tapered in from the powerful chest. He was built stolidly upon stout loins and buttocks. At such a distance, his perfection had the laughable quality of a child's toy. I remember believing that rangy, cowboy legs were the apogee of male virility. My values change.

Dwight's long legs are a metaphor of mismatch. Dancing in the dark with him twenty-five years ago to the tune of the same name by a big band in Norumbega Park, I placed his masculinity at the brim of his eyebrows, though the knot growing harder in his slacks was at the level of my belly button. It made my consciousness slip downward, a thrilling streak of silk, to gather in sworls of promise between my legs or in my womb. He followed my consciousness with his hands, drawing them downward from my shoulders to my buttocks, arranging my hips against him. But then he bent his legs, crouching down and lifting me up as far as I could go on the dance floor, so that he could get the most for his penis out of my mons veneris. How unlovely! I thought with my unerring sense of grace. I am disgusted and saddened even now at the hypocrisy of it. He was embarrassed; I was shocked. I knew it was hypocritical then, that we were fooling ourselves. But his soft cheek and soft breath were a wonder to me, groping animals that we were. How could I have married a man with such long legs and such stunted emotions! He should have talked more and refused to let me create him.

Elias not only stood in this particular place. He also walked. Sometimes he walked toward me on the parapet as if to see me better. Other times he walked away, pretending he was not curious. If he had postured, I would have laughed. But his walk was not self-conscious. He wears a mustache. The back of his head rises in an arc to a peak of black hair.

The strange thing is I do not know how he got to his standing place. He simply was there when I looked, as if he had flown from the air.

I am much better now. But it is true there is no mattress. I notice that my clothes are hanging on me. Have I lost so much weight? I examine myself and see that there are two layers.

First there is my dress, a polka-dot blue, loose silk, which I have not worn for a long time. Below that, I am wearing something ugly, a limp material with streaks which looks like wet, white crepe paper. I feel of it. I always feel yard goods at remnant shops. It is slippery, like thick, cold nylon. It lifts off me in a thick sheet turning a dead-white color. It is then that I understand.

Certain sensations and images occur to me. I feel air in strange places, such as the roof of my mouth and along the veins of my upper arms. Wings are beating in me creating this air. I remember Don's horror of the albino butterfly-moth! He hated process itself. Yet he was born the officiating priest of it, being descended from Metamorphosis.

I hear myself scream. A ripping sound. I make little low gasps of laughter. I run out to see if Elias is on the parapet. He is not.

I am terrified, for I loved my shape in that former life, my romantic femininity which married its masculine replica, Dwight.

I go to the hole, as there is no other avenue to Elias. He is not there, but I babble anyway, telling him my secret. I have no notion of the time.

When he comes with my food he is shocked at me. He shouts contemptuously, "It's nothing! Just go down to the water of the sea and stay there until it comes off."

"How long will it take?"

"I don't know. Just stay there until it does. The minerals of the sea will cure you."

I run, I fly to the sea, feeling the wind blow through my strange tatters. I lower myself into the water. Water understands the secrecy of prehistoric places and seals wounds. The air stops fanning those unknown places.

I float as in a bathtub. I do not really swim. I tread water and move my arms a little. Perhaps, though, the force will pull it away faster. But I do not use force in my movements. I again become aware of the beauty of the sea and the unending beauty of the stone woman who lies so calmly upon it, her arms crossed. I regain my dignity.

How many hours I remain in the sea I do not know. I become waterlogged. That is why I do not feel it when it happens.

The sea becomes rougher, the Mediterranean being capricious. I have to move my arms more energetically because of the waves. A few moments later the wind subsides again. Or perhaps it is hours.

In any case, I am moving lethargically again, beguiled again, when I see the shape. It is floating two or three yards to my right. It floats like a balloon. The seams of the arms are split so it makes the forearms trail like wings. But from the shoulders to the haunches it is all of a piece. It is myself inflated by air! Myself cast off from myself and floating out to sea. It is horrible! I shudder.

Zoe met them at Herodes Atticus at nine. No precautions, no dark glasses. She had grown bold. The program was Webern. The Bamberg Symphony had not boycotted the colonels, but at that moment she could not have cared less, everything traveled on one sound, one sound, the sound of nature itself, or a man's voice or the speech of a gull, the only possible modern sound. In three years of France she had almost lost the feel of Greek honor, but, looking upward into the bright, endless night she felt a swelling joy, nothing had died, there was no scaffolding, Zoe was alive, could never die, just beyond her fingertips her mother and father were eating dinner, and not one of them could die, no more than could Socrates, who would certainly have understood how you planned one more escape in the endless chain of those refusing exile, of which Lampris would be only the latest. You planned it under the open sky on a note of Webern in front of them all, for they could not recognize you, laughter and defiance of death in the same breath.

After I come up from the sea with my new skin I have to protect myself carefully. For two days, I stay in the enclosed hut where I was ill. I huddle much of the time in a corner. I wear only a slip. My new skin born of the sea is afraid of the air. I don't even put the straps over my shoulders. I feel like a pomegranate, my kernels bunched and raw, each cell sparkling and bleeding. I do not dare look at my shoulders. They are pulp. I think of my old self often, floating out to sea.

Elias's contempt for my predicament gives me confidence. He treats me like an animal, and no one has ever done this before. It is because he is an animal.

Another thing happens to me. I feel pains in my ovaries and some of the pomegranate seeds bleed out of me. Trained into animalhood, I tear my robin's-egg-blue suit into pieces for menstrual pads. I feel the tenderness an animal feels for itself, both inside and out. I do not believe it is menstruation, however. I only use the word for lack of a better one. I no longer think in those terms, for I am a snake who has shed its skin. I am pupa. A ghost, larva. Change has occurred in my being which has nothing to do with event.

I get a craving for cereal. I put a towel over my shoulders, go out to the hole in the broiling sun, and wait for him. When he comes, I tell him I don't want the fish he has brought. I want cereal.

"Don't make trouble for me."

"Bring me wheat grain," I order.

He does not reply.

I refuse the fish, put the plate back in the hole, and return to my lair

215

where I turn inward and dream listlessly. In the afternoon, I rouse myself and go down to the sea to bathe. When I come back I am bleeding more profusely, but I cover myself with another pad, and, eating nothing, go to sleep.

The next day he is angry.

"Why didn't you eat?" he barks.

"I am bleeding, I don't know why," I tell him.

"Is it that time of the month?"

Something is peeled away from his self-righteous bark, and his voice has a note of awe, perhaps revulsion. I stifle laughter. My craving is stronger than ever, and I am hungry, but I vow I shall touch nothing until he brings me cereal. I put the chicken he has brought me back in the hole. I take only the bottle of water to drink.

The next evening I see him iridescent on the parapet signaling something to me. He has never been there at that time of day before. He is pointing to the hole.

Before I go to get the cereal I watch to see how he gets up and down from there. But he is suddenly gone from the spot. Like smoke.

Through the hole he hands me a white paper bag full of grain mixed with cinnamon, sugar, and pomegranate seeds.

"Funeral food," he tells me.

I am ravenous. I stuff it in my mouth with my fingers and drink water.

"Do you like it?"

It is like nectar. I tell him. He wants thanks. I thank him.

"Have you finished?" he asks. "I have another."

I smack my lips loudly and make noises of "Mmmm," so that he can be pleased.

There is a small ink-cross stamped on the bag.

"Who died?"

"A priest." He laughs. We now have a conspiracy. Whatever it is we are involved in is beyond us. It is lucky the priest died, because I had this craving. Anyway, he was a rotten bastard, he tells me, a cobbler as well as a priest, and he overcharged for new soles. He also overcharged for house blessings and baptisms.

"Did he die in the town where you live?"

"Yes."

"How far away is it?"

"About eight kilometers."

"What's the name of it?"

"Hora."

Every island, every province has a Hora. The word means "town."

"Elias," I begin, as if I were now going to say something important.

"How did you know my name?" he asks, as full of guile as I. But where I am exploring the realm which may be freedom, he is exploring me.

"I woke up knowing. I don't know how."

"I don't believe in miracles."

"Well, you know nobody's told me."

"Well, it's amazing." He uses the word *"mystiko."* "How did you know that the mountain was called Mount Elias?"

How could I answer?

"I'm never called Elias, though," he says, as if to disprove my powers, but I can hear his deference. "My name is Ioannis Elias and I am called Ioannis. My father is Elias."

"I'll call you Elias just the same."

"What is your name?"

"Cora."

"That means 'girl.' How old are you?"

"Forty-seven. And you?"

"Fifty-two."

There is an edge to his voice that tells me he is lying.

We explore the facts of these lives that we have on earth, and I tell him everything as I know it, holding nothing back, not only because I want to answer his curiosity but because I want to get it over with so I can get to my real questions. The fact that we cannot see each other makes us mysteriously more powerful to each other.

"Are you married?" I ask him.

"No."

"That is unusual, isn't it?"

"Why unusual?" he barks. "I am a poor farmer with one sister. My mother and father gave away much of our land for the dowry. Now I have to take care of my parents, they are old."

I ask him about his parents. His mother is ignorant, he tells me, but very smart, a good cook, and a prophet of weather. His father, Elias, reads

French and is educated. "Beautiful, civilized, generous, fair, and a fool," he calls him.

"Why a fool?"

"Because he can't make money. He is too good."

My scalp tingles. Whenever you think of a man alone, you think of his history, and the history of man is frail. And the individual man is frail.

"Why do you work for them?" I ask.

"Who?"

I don't know who he works for but I know how to get him to tell me.

"Who, the monopoly?" he repeats.

"Yes." It may be a monopoly which has put me here.

"I don't work for the monopoly. My father did, but they got rid of him. He ran the monopoly, and he was too honest."

"What does the monopoly do?"

"It is the government store for grain, oil, feed, and eggs."

"But I don't mean the monopoly. I want to know why you work for *them.*"

It is his guile, not his innocence that led me down this track.

"Do not ask questions like this. It is dangerous."

"Dangerous for who? You or me?"

"For you."

"And for you, too."

"For you, more than for me. What did you do that you are in here?"

"I don't know. I did nothing."

"Well, there's some reason you are here."

"I am innocent," I tell him, and I know I am. If I were guilty my prison would have ceilings.

"Well, you may be innocent," he says.

"But I am a prisoner all the same," I say.

The paradox of the wall in juxtaposition with the sweep of the sky gives me my intimacy with him. I insist that he confirm my words.

"I am a prisoner, aren't I?" I repeat.

He says nothing.

"And you are my keeper."

I have noticed that my senses are sharpened and when I concentrate through the hole like this, I project my voice in a way which exaggerates, like a soprano. I feel myself doing it more and more.

"How much do they pay you to keep me prisoner here and to bring my food?"

But I do not want to insult him too much, and I am aware of my sense of power. His silence gives off the smell of garlic and strong sweat.

I leave and go to the church. I speak to Elijah, the saint from whom he got his name.

"You can give me more information than he can," I tell Elijah.

But the face above his beard, when I examine it, is merely colors on wood. The artist was not good enough. Never having seen Elias's face, I believe that I could paint him as he truly is, a demigod. It should be in oil, though.

I decide to question him in a different way. But I take my time. I go to explore the dens and warrens in the northern part of the castle. They are broken down. Some of them have ceilings which are under the ground and covered with weeds. There is no water.

At the hole the next morning I ask, "Who brought me here?"

"I don't know," he says.

"Didn't you bring me?"

"No."

"But you saw me up close, didn't you?"

"What?"

"You took care of me when I was sick."

He does not answer.

"You put me on a mattress and put cold compresses on my head."

Why does he not admit it? His imperturbability is brutish.

That afternoon, he brings me a sweet, a cake made of lemon and sugar, and some wine made from bananas.

"I know you like sweets," he says, solicitously.

"But I cannot eat anything so delicious unless I share," I say, as if I didn't trust him. "You must eat a piece."

He eats. He smacks his mouth loudly so that I will hear the sound of sharing. We discuss his mother, who has baked the cake. I make him describe the outside fourno, and the twigs of grapevines with which she made the fire.

And then I begin again. "Is this an island?"

"No. It is a peninsula. There is a narrow strip of road, but you cannot see it because it is behind the half-moon beach which Mount Elias hides."

I am amazed that he tells me so much.

"Why did they put me in this fort?"

"They kept prisoners here in the War."

"What war?"

"You must have nine lives, och," he says.

There is no other war for them, that civil war which to them is more than the Second World War. I keep on asking the question.

"Why not in a regular prison?"

"That's where they interrogate prisoners."

"And no one will interrogate me?"

"Maybe they will, but—"

"But what?"

"But nothing."

"What will they want to know?" My innocence at last may have dawned on him.

"They will want to know what you did to be put here."

His voice is hard. I know what he is up to. He is only a jailer. He does not know why I'm here either, and he wants to.

"But you already know I have done nothing."

"You are a political prisoner," he says.

I suspect now he is testing me out. The tone in his voice is as tentative as when he said he was fifty-two years old.

"And what specific thing do they want to know?" The specific breeds the specific. "Questions about what?"

"The Omega." His voice is innocuous.

All the metaphors of my past congeal, and I cannot believe I have materialized this. That there is more to it than I had imagined, that he must be in league with a larger dimension.

What is the Omega? I want to ask him, but the time for questioning is stopped. I must think.

I cannot concentrate. The sound of the Omega possesses me. When I try to find the end of the sky, my will shrinks. Neither the questions I have asked nor this answer makes sense. Is Omega the territory I have abandoned by my own will?

"Home," says the sound.

"I want to go home!" I cry.

He tries to reassure me. He croons through the hole. He is shocked. He says my name, Cora, for the first time. He tells me that he will let no one hurt me, that he will bring me food and water, that I am safe, and that he will take care of me. But, having once made the sound of the word, I cannot stop. I keep shouting, "I want to go home."

*A*t a snap of the police corporal's fingers, a pimply private ran in from the corridor, looked at him as if at an exotic animal, and led him down a flight of stairs.

In the basement they went along a cement corridor with painted white doors. Each door had a number. But the private took him to a door without a number, put him in the cell and locked it.

There was no window, not a stick of furniture, not even a chair. A light bulb hung by a wire from a hole in the ceiling, its switch by the door. Everything was cement, except the door. It was metal with a round peephole through which they could watch him.

He felt that something was about to happen. Perhaps the pimply private would come back. He expected the door to open. He waited. He had felt a sense of relief at the idea of arrest. At last, something would get done. He had felt very American, citizen's rights, habeas corpus, freedom of speech, the power to elect governments, one arm California, one

Florida. Knowing by May 12 if M073112098C4 were not in Izmir, Turkey, the U.S. Army would start investigation. So he did not argue. In fact, his moral superiority had increased when the corporal had shoved the papers across the desk. Don filled out name, age, place, time of birth, etc., and gave him his watch and ID card without a murmur. He did not even ask what he was being charged with. The only thing he said was: "I would like to use the telephone to report to the U.S. Mission at Glyphada to notify them you've arrested me."

And when they said, "Later, the telephone calls; that will be taken care of when you're interrogated," he had leveled his eyes on Babolas with the smug smile of one who knows a mistake has been made, but Babolas was not looking at him. He thought of Zoe's mother and father finishing lunch while he was being taken to that carbolic, echoing limestone place.
the clock said 11:45 on the way to that carbolic, echoing limestone place.

But the moments wore away his feeling of expectation and separate pains, his feet throbbing, his finger, the base of his skull began transmitting through his synapses, reducing him to sensation. He sat down on the floor. The pavement was cracked and tipped inward from the walls to a declivity in the middle. He sat with his back against the wall, and this gave him a sense of finality. Everything in his life had come to this. So he concentrated on the corners of the room on the lines where walls met ceilings, where ceilings faced floor. He was on the inside.

Inside of what?

The tomb of his mother.

But he had imagined it lined with satin, not cement. He had put her in the secret room where life was eternal and safe, lit by his childish worship. Later, conditioned by Philo to deny her, he had sought out empty rooms, for you could achieve truth, he had read (in what book?) by speaking words in empty rooms. There was a good blank seminar room in the bottom of Peabody Hall. Also Gerrard Hall had been good. Protestant simple, touchingly pure. He had spent hours practicing words there, the pews creaking with sincerity. The words declared the power of the spirit, according to the book, and the authority of the moral sense, and the source of this power gained dignity from not being seen, from not being given a name, from being communicated with, not through the bread and wine of Christ's flesh and blood, but through thought alone. Saying the words was a form of worship. With Decker he had taken it to the mantra, but then came the limitations. Poor Decker turned inward, sly and paranoid. The bare, empty room was cold. It nourished hatred, repressed lust. Love was dried to dust.

"O," he said, taking Omega, from that point in Glossa where they had stepped on the stars.

"Know. *Gnorizo.* Roar. Blow. Olive. Omen." Nothing happened.

He started again at Omen.

"Omen. Moment. Home. Om. Omniscience. Know. *Gnorizo.*"

He felt the beginnings of excitement, for knowledge was the key. But where was it? Inside or outside? Everything depended on that relationship between in and out. Had his mother known In?

He thought back to when she was safe inside the satin box. It had been *his* consciousness. He had not thought of *her* consciousness. He was outside; all knowledge had been on the outside. Now he was in. But in what?

He took it from the cell. Outside the cell the corridor. The first floor. Three or four floors. The building. A street of buildings. He was *inside* block after block of buildings. Sewers, offices, schools, the Olympian Zeus, apartments piled on top of each other, stacked above subways, climbing up Lykabettos, stucco, churches, steel, pipes, electric cable, a funicular of edifices which extended topographically from the Agora to the Acropolis, chronologically from 1971 B.C. to A.D. 1971. He was buried inside a city with the name of Athena, the only place left for a pioneer in modern times, when male values, having achieved full triumph, have reversed themselves to destroy the context in which they have triumphed.

Yet it was not the Goddess. Only cement.

Then what had his mother known? The only thing he could think of was that she had *known* she was in his head. And what had *he* known out *there?* Something, surely. For he had conceived all knowledge to be farther out than the sky. Suddenly, he remembered how godly he had thought it to concoct an *inside,* a house, from an olive tree. Athena's olive tree. It led to the syllogism: What his mother had been inside his head, he was now in the Goddess's.

His mind split into two.

First, he thought of all knowledge. The idea of knowledge itself. It swirled around his ears and eye. Answers to the obvious questions: Where was Cora? Who killed Annette? Did Zoe know he was in prison? Had Zoe known she was putting him in danger? What was the connection between

Zoe and Fotianos. Et cetera. Beyond that, the knowledge that Cora knew (for Cora knew where she was unless . . .), or that Zoe knew (for she knew what was in the coufetta, she knew about Fotianos), or even that Spyro knew (for he knew with moral certainty why he was right to violate the flesh of another human being). And even beyond that: the knowledge of no moral import.

Suddenly his mind scrambled. He saw a doctor shining a light into Zoe's mother's eyes, saying, *"Someone knows."*

He caught himself, for he had to maintain the distinctions between thought, fantasy, and the reality of actual event. He reminded himself that it was only three hours ago that he had initiated the telephone call from OTE.

The next day the Jehovah's Witnesses came back. Philo was elated. "We have read the book," they said solemnly.

Too elated to question them as to how it was possible to read the entire *Dialogues* and *Republic* overnight. This time, though, he wanted no interruption. Ann Marie, it turned out, was not the one who had called. Neither had Theo. He led the Jehovah's Witnesses to the folding chairs and gave them apples immediately. They began to talk. The Jehovah's Witnesses said that Philo was right, that the Bible and Plato were really saying the same thing. Then they got down to narrowing the field. They turned to Revelation. The black man read about opening the fifth seal:

" 'I saw under the altar the souls of them that were slain for the word of God, and for the testimony which they held. And they cried with a loud voice, saying, How long, O Lord, holy and true, does thou not judge and avenge our blood on them that dwell on the earth?' "

Philo jumped at his opportunity, the world being full of assumptions and the only way to truth through holes:

"Oh yes! And listen to what Plato said about that same thing! 'A man came running up to another man and asked him: "Did you see a person pass by here?" "Yes, I did." "Which way did he go?" "Why do you want to know?" "Because that person is a criminal." ' Now if you were the man who was asked that question, what would you do?"

The Jehovah's Witnesses thought.

Philo decided they needed priming. "Would you accept that the person who ran was a criminal?"

The Jehovah's Witnesses chewed.

"On one man's say-so?"

The Jehovah's Witnesses took more bites. Philo made no move. All three sat thinking. The boy's teeth chewing sounded like Phryne's stone tongue.

"Would you tell him where he went, knowing he would beat him up or punish and kill him?"

They had chewed the apples down to the core. Philo was elated at the silence now that they were not chewing any longer. But they were holding their apple cores politely, as if they did not know what to do with them.

"Throw them down here," said Philo. "Maybe they will turn into apple trees." And he began to talk.

Eleanor called Corey at Wright Hall. Although it was exam time, it took her fourteen tries before she was able to break through lines occupied by adolescent palaver.

"What's wrong?" she began without preliminary.

"Nothing. Why?" he said, knowing she was talking about their mother. Eleanor was the one who always took responsibility.

"Well, have you heard from her?"

"No."

"I haven't either."

"But you got the watecolor picture two weeks ago."

"Three, and you *know* she always writes once a week."

"It takes longer to get a letter from Massachusetts to Washington now than it did when they had post-horses. And I read in *The New York Times* it takes five days from Moscow to Leningrad, one day longer than in Tolstoy's time."

"If I haven't heard by Saturday, I'm going to cable the embassy in Athens." Like their mother, Eleanor used melodrama to counter his irony. "And you be over here Sunday at one o'clock for lunch."

"Don't take your worry out on me," he said.

"Yes. I know your generational nostalgia for national catastrophe. You'd *love* the system to break down, just so you can hit rock bottom. You and Mother are just alike."

He ignored it. Eleanor could accept their mother only as some quaint cross between Rosalind Russell and Ethel Rosenberg. He tried to jolly her out of it.

After he hung up, he saw his mother as clear as day. It was ten years ago. The ape was wrinkling up its ugly face over the woman's shoulder making faces at the audience, twitching in its blue dress. His mother stared at it galvanized, and he thought she was going to grimace back. Then when they decided to grab the seats, she told him to run on ahead down those miles of balcony stairs, because she was puffing and couldn't go fast enough, so he was the one who established the beachhead.

But then she wouldn't let him sit in the ape's seat! *She* wanted to sit in it. For a moment he pouted, but such was the glitter of the chandeliers, the cake-frosting of the boxes, the excitement of the perfume, the gowns and tails and conversation, and such was the pink, rhapsodic splendor of his mother, that not only did he give way but he understood that he was in possession of an unspeakable secret. He laughed out loud in present time.

"You always know who you are," Steve had told him admiringly after his junior year in high school, the set-up for the joke: "Half-Greek and half-crazy."

He tried to make the cell fit his identity. He examined the expanse of wall to find a spot familiar enough to love. At first, it seemed blank, wishing him neither evil nor good. Then he noticed it was filthy, covered with spots either of blood or vomit. He pulled his knees up under his chin, refusing connection with hieroglyphics of terror.

A cockroach started up his leg. He flicked it off. It clicked on the pavement and scuttled into a crack. He heard Philo's voice coming out of the crack:

"But the ancients believed in man's goodness, and explored truth and beauty."

"What about Americans?" he asked.

"All Americans are Greek."

"Then what about other people?"

"Everybody is Greek."

The voice went on about organizations: cartels, subgovernments, the World Bank, the Mafia, Rockwell Industries, Good Will, the NKVD, electoral-reform committees, etc. "From each spot of the megalithic structure someone in power believes that his part is the whole. The structure becomes invisible, hidden by predicated enemies in pipelines. It is you who have multiplied matter while scientists tried to reduce the atom. The success of the Western world had led to myth, for the atom reduces ad infinitum. You have reduced words to consonants and vowels. But vowels swell into diphthongs. And behind consonants, the leaves whisper."

A perverse feeling of triumph crawled over him, cold sweat before a coma. For he was innocent. I am innocent, he thought, verifying the dead universe. I am forgotten forever.

A noise shattered him to consciousness, a scream of hollow metal, like crowbars being smashed against a tin drum. He jumped up so fast he skinned his elbow on the wall. Bone Atone, gonged the cell of his skull, a clock in which the artisans of hell and their child-apprentices beat time in copper and brass, hitting, scooping, scouring, a rhythm he had trouble translating outside his mind.

He went to the door to listen, to figure out where it was coming from. Directly outside his door? Or down the hall? At first, he thought it was pots and pans. Later, he thought it was chains. The location of the noise did not change, but its quality did. Sometimes a buzz saw ground through the gong-sound. Other times there was a ticking, as of stock on wood, like a scratch inside a bombardon. He shouted, "Shut up!" They were trying to disorient him.

After a while what he imagined to be the work of three or four people with different instruments acquired a personality of its own. It was one consciousness whose multiplicity lay in its different, unexpected sounds. Five minutes later, it stopped, but the silence was more sinister than the noise.

From that moment on the noise came at irregular intervals. It made him lose his sense of time. Yet he knew that it was calculated to do that. Gamesmanship. They wanted to terrorize, soften him up for the kill. Information was what they wanted. And they were working against odds. They could not torture an American with impunity as they could one of their own.

So he pitted his wits against it and exteriorized. Nevertheless, each time it shocked him. The noise separated itself from cause and became its own. Inhuman. A machine. It got to where it was more evil impulsion trying to get *at* him. Since it was his only relationship to nature, law, and time, he tried to use it. He began to interpret the intervals as days. He became degraded and acute. He counted. He thought he heard the guards change.

At the fifth interval, his nerves peeled away from his eardrums and he realized he had had no sleep. His muscles began twitching reflexively. Five days?

They brought him no food. Not that he was hungry. But his body began to undergo changes. He had stomach cramps. Then diarrhea. He banged on the door to be let out to go to the latrine. No one came. He shouted, but there was no answer. Only the silences, broken by the bangings.

He defecated in a corner, but it slipped down the broken cement and mired in the declivity at the center. After that, each time he had to go, he deposited in the middle of the cell, where it stank, and he went through periods of terror followed by physical weakness, trying to cling to the wall of the cell, afraid that he would roll down into it.

He had seen a car-wash cubicle at midnight once in Carrboro. Someone had stuck a quarter in and gone away leaving the hose jumping with the full force of water, a crazy dervish of a dance on an empty stage, the hose beating the walls in an orgy of spray, making the bricks drip with electric light.

At last, the door opened and a guard came, a boy no more than twenty years old. He had pimples on his face and dirty-blond hair the color of dishwater.

"Do you want anything?" he asked.

"Tea and a shower."

"You can't have a shower, but you can have tea." The boy grinned and left.

He was afraid the boy would not come back; that it was another trick. But he did come back. The tea was lukewarm. It was sweet. The minute Don drank it, the sugar hit his blood, and he began to itch all over, and realized mosquitoes had bitten him.

"How long have I been here?" he asked the boy.

"Eleven."

"Eleven *days?*"

"No. Hours. You came in last evening."

It was a lie. He knew.

"What is that banging noise?"

"What banging noise?"

"They bang drums out in the hall. Gongs. Chains. Or pots and pans."

The boy gave a sheepish grin, so that the pimples on his chin spread, pressing a whitish matter from the heads in squinch-dots.

"Oh, it's only a game," he chortled, as if embarrassed. "The boys are having fun."

The boy did not say this maliciously. He seemed well disposed toward him. It was even as though he were proud to have an American as his personal charge.

"You have to get ready," he told him.

"Ready?"

"You're going to be questioned."

He felt a slight thrill but armed himself against celebration.

"Look, my cell is dirty." He pointed. "Can you clean it up?"

"But I don't clean cells. I'm a guard," said the boy. "You'll probably get a new one anyway. They don't keep people in here long." The boy circled him smiling with a kind of tentative, shy, even respectful curiosity. "What are you? An American?" He began to imitate Americans. It was friendly. He made motions of chewing gum and snapping his fingers. "The Beatles, huh? The University of Michigan." It was a piece of fun stolen from his jail duties. The boy was coarse, ignorant, stupid and probably capable of beating up on people, but he had no penchant for sadism.

The boy led him down the corridor in his filthy clothes. He took him up the stairway to an office with a wooden door. A major with black hair and horn-rimmed glasses sat at a desk making marks on a stack of papers. A nameplate announced Major Mavros.

"You may close the door, Pano," said Major Mavros. The boy in a hush of respectful behavior backed out.

He waved him to sit down in the black, plastic chair.

"Will you have a cigarette?" invited the major, gesturing to a box. But he did not look up from the papers.

"I don't smoke," he said.

"Are they treating you right?"

What was he to answer?

Finally, Major Mavros looked at him. His eyes were cow-brown.

"I am Major Mavros," he said. "Is there anything you'd like?"

"A shower."

"You may have a shower when we get through talking," he said. And he consulted a set of papers in a folder. "Let's see." He sighed. "You have been in Greece sixteen days. You entered in Corfu on U.S. military orders. And in your spare time you were carrying the Anna Diamonides instructions for the attempted escape of Fotianos."

Fotianos had not escaped then!

"We are not interested in you," Major Mavros continued in a bored voice. "You have no reason for loyalty to Anna. We are perfectly aware of how you met her at the café in Napoli, and"—he cleared his throat—"that you were the stooge."

He let this sink in, and since Don did not answer, went on in a more attentive way. "Your best course is to cooperate with us fully, and then you can have a shower and be on your way." The major looked at his watch. "You'll be on your way, say, in an hour."

He fought the bait, one part of his mind admiring the consciousness of the euphemism, as if "on your way" was as natural as going out for a pack of cigarettes, the other focused on the substitution of Diamonides for Diamantes. So that he would slip, of course, and say the real name. Did that mean that they were not even sure of Zoe's name?

"To begin with," Major Mavros said, "who was the girl who drove the car for them?"

"What girl?"

"Come on. We knew she met you at the airport. The Belgian."

Major Mavros's eyes changed slightly registering the tremor of Don's shock. He improvised a scene with Annette and Zoe in the same room. He did not believe it. He went on the offensive.

"You had Annette Borlin killed, didn't you?" It was tantamount to admitting his part in a conspiracy. He felt a glory in it.

"Don't you adventurers know what happens when you play with fire?" Major Mavros was angry. "You imagine you're idealists. Only decadent countries produce this stupidity. You come here, hiding under hair and beards like sheep, carrying messages and explosives, and believe you're heroes. You don't know what you're doing. Shall I tell you? You're helping criminals and murderers escape."

Major Mavros was passionate, like Spyro. Justifying oneself to one's victim was the sincerest of stupidities.

"We know how many foreigners are in it and who they are: Annette Borgnes, University of Paris at Nanterre, jailed in 1968 for leftist demonstrations."

Again the name change. Deliberate? Was he acting? Had Annette really been part of it?

"You. On probation in North Carolina for demonstrations in 1968,

231

jailed in Jackson County, North Carolina, in connection with the trial of Lee Briscoe."

They must have gotten his dossier from the air force. He began to feel even better.

"Fotianos is a criminal. Don't you realize that?"

"I don't know who this Fotianos is. What did he do?"

Major Mavros changed his tactics. The anger disappeared from his face, and his voice became velvety.

"Let's get back to the point. The night Annette Borgnes drove the car for them, when she was pretending to be in bed with you, when she was waiting outside the walls—who was the man in the seat next to her? Next to the driver's seat?"

"Why do you ask me who she is if you know she met me at the airport and if you know what her name is and if you have records of all foreigners?" He trembled visibly.

"Who was the man with the green pullover?" insisted Major Mavros.

"Look, Annette Borlin *was* in bed with me all night! And just because I have a green sweater, which your agents must have discovered, since they stole my pack, does not mean that I was driving any car with Annette Borlin in any escape plan which I didn't even know about."

"So you're *not* the man with the green pullover," Major Mavros said sarcastically.

"I am not."

"You're ready to swear that under oath? That you're not the man with the green pullover who helped Annette Borgnes on the night of April twenty when she drove the car and parked it on the side street adjacent to the prison?"

"If you knew I was doing that, why didn't you pick me up right then?"

"Let's assume you didn't know what was in that little silver coufetta. That will be the basis of your case if it comes to court. But there's no way you can prove your intentions. You know as well as I do that Trigo turned evidence, and that you carried the alternative plan in that little cylinder when Fotianos did not appear. All right. So then, tell me this . . ." Major Mavros went on in a broad-minded manner, covering all contingencies academically: "Where did you go at four a.m., when Annette Borlin went back to your hotel room?"

He had said Borlin!

"She left you a note the next morning in your hotel room."

"She wanted me to meet her for breakfast. She got up before I did, and didn't want to wake me up." It was the wrong tack. He knew it, but innocence was choking him. Who was Trigo?

"And you're claiming that's all there was to it?"

"Look, Annette Borlin knew nothing whatever about any underground."

"So you admit *you* did."

"I never said that and that's not what I mean. All I did was to deliver a keepsake of candied almonds to somebody's parents. That's all. And if there was anything in that silver cylinder, I knew nothing about it. I know nothing about any underground. I never knew anything, and not until I started being followed, did I think anything about it—"

"Then tell me this. If you are as innocent as you say, and you knew you were being followed, why didn't you report it to the police?"

"Because I knew *you* were the police." He watched Major Mavros looking disappointed.

"You seem to think that we have made up our mind about everything. If that were so, would I be questioning you? Don't you believe you would be free if you were innocent?"

Major Mavros's sincere, cow-brown eyes implored him to answer.

"Do you believe we would keep you here for one moment if you were innocent? What kind of people do you think we are anyway? Tell me."

He tucked a corner of his mouth in his teeth so his smile became a leer.

"Why are you so hostile to our government? Why are you against the Revolution? You don't understand, you foreigners. You are the dupe of their propaganda. We are a group of honest officers. We're simply trying to make the country better. You don't understand Greeks. The majority are in our favor."

His silence stopped Major Mavros's sincerity. He knitted his failure into a scowl and said, "All right. I see you're not inclined to cooperate. Well, I'm not inclined to waste my time. We can wait. We'll put it off till next time."

Annette Borlin's aunt set the telephone down. It was the authorities saying for her husband to pick up a different set of papers unless the body was going to be buried there. She and her husband ran a small café in the working-class district up the hill from the North Central Station in Brussels, and though she had had a week to digest the shock of her niece's death, she did not know what she felt. She and Annette had never gotten along. Annette was always putting on airs and trading on sex. She'd worked at the café with half a mind, giving heifer glances to the Arabs, Turks, and other foreigners, and she couldn't be trusted. The aunt resented her; she let things go when she took the extra job setting hair three hours a day in the beauty shop. She didn't talk back, she just looked condescendingly vacant. So when she had left four years ago, it was a relief. They'd done the best they could. They'd had no kids of their own. It was her sister's child, Borlin had run off, Lilianne died in a car accident. They'd brought her up since she was ten years old. But, in a funny way, she wasn't surprised about Annette; she'd always had a feeling something bad might happen to her. She was too easy.

They'd gotten the intermittent postcard or two first from Paris, then from Lyons. The cards didn't say anything. She'd signed one "Good-by" in English. Mme. Papet's daughter, Solange, said Annette was in France illegally and was working in a sporting-goods store. Next thing, Annette wrote she was studying in the university in Nanterre. Surprise, if it was true, since she never made particularly good grades in school, but everything had changed; people had automobiles, went on strikes, and wandered everywhere, everything was Europe, they had the Common Market and foreigners, you didn't know anything about anybody. Now Giles had to go to Greece. He wouldn't take a plane because the railroad would give him a discount. He'd have to go through Yugoslavia to get there and sit up two nights. She was going to fill a plastic bag with sandwiches and chicken.

The police didn't say how she drowned. The Greeks claimed she'd washed up on a beach.

The bell rang. She was trying to fix her hair in the mirror. The dark roots were coming up and showing. She would have to get a new rinse job. She went through the curtains into the café to see if it was a customer. But nobody. The stew, the special for today, was boiling. It smelled of carrots. She opened the door to look out into the street, to see if it was kids—they were always ringing the bell for kicks. But there were only people strolling by. She had this feeling. She felt something vacant lurking in the street, nothing to do with the people walking by the ugly church or the ugly church sitting in the street.

They said she was on holiday and had been riding a red bicycle. She had been with some man, but the man was gone. You didn't have to go to Greece to drown. On holiday you were supposed to come home. You could wash up on some beach at Ostend if you came home once in four years.

The fact is that I do not want to go home. What is there there for me? I left home. I do not want Eleanor's life, nor Corey's. Sometimes, I feel sorry for the lives of my two children, whom I love forever and have dispensed with forever. I feel sorry for the surfaces of their lives, the paraphernalia which have rounded their corners and diminished their archetypes. They defer to the A & P with their station wagons and they cannot help being effect. They are as clean as carrots in cellophane. Once Americans had zest, now they are self-conscious. I imagine the letter I ought to write. I write it to Corey at P.O. Box 4801, Wright Hall, Clark University, Worcester, Mass. I write it on my art paper. I imagine myself maneuvering Elias into mailing it for me. I will write:

> Dear Corey,
> I am a prisoner in a castle. I believe I am in Greece. I do not want you to worry, though, because I am fine. In fact, the scenery is magnificent. There is a mountain to the south and a string of islands to the west, a place where people would pay exorbitant prices to—
> A string of weird coincidences—
> I do not understand—
> If you get this letter—
> Tell Eleanor for goodness sakes—
> Tell Eleanor not to—
> It may be political—

I cannot finish the sentences, so it would be pointless to write. I know in all seriousness that I should set down what is happening to me, because if I die, they ought to know how. A journal. But I hate journals. It is not that I am dead to my children, they are dead to me. Meanwhile, I feel this passion to live right here in this sun on these rocks where this wave is hitting my foot.

I hear the word "Home" again, seeing the Omega in it, but the sound is disembodied. I don't know where it's coming from. I look at the stone woman to see if she is the source of it. Is it the wind? I am back at the Big Pool.

I am seven years old. I have named the sections of the Big Pool England, Greece, Norway, Sweden, Europe, Spain, and Massachusetts. I don't know how long I have been here. Hours, summers collapse in the moving minnows. Above, far away, my father stops mowing the lawn. My mother is sorting out curtains with Svenga, the maid, on the porch. Tomorrow will be another day as beautiful as this. And the next day. And so on. A lifetime of days. I realize the secret of the universe: my life will reveal the secret. When I am fifty I will be able to name it just as I have named the sections of the Big Pool.

I am forty-seven years old. I climb down the rocks to the Big Pool. It is just before this trip. I am one of the few people whose home has not been ruined by progress. Rich people bought it after the Depression and still keep the North Shore private. The secret is familiar, just on the tip of my tongue, but I cannot say it. I think. Suddenly, I realize what it is. If I can remember the names of the sections of the Big Pool, just as I named them then, I will be able to name the secret.

The sound continues quite separate from the screech of the swallows and the flutters of the breeze on the grasses. I am sitting beside a sea-pool which mirrors the sky. Dark small shrimps flit, disturbing a cloud.

I look at the sea. It is past the zenith of afternoon, white, flat, dead. But the sun flashes on needlepoint waves. The more I watch, the more amazing is its pattern of signals. What is being signaled?

I have the sense, from these frantic points of light shining for a fraction of a second where I least expect them, of a lone engine, blindly, ruthlessly pursuing some course. It has nothing to do with this bleached gaze, without pupil, of the sea.

His mask!

Why didn't I realize before?

I rush to the courtyard to get the mask, then I rush back down to the sea again and I put it on. I hate the feeling. There is an ugly smell of black rubber. I remember how he put it on. The rubber lip goes above my lip. Do I look like him staring out from that Omega, priest-intermediary with this smokestack for a forked tongue? I try the mouthpiece. I can breathe through it. But I am bitted, in his guise.

I lower myself into the water, breathing carefully through the snorkel. I am afraid of suffocating if water gets in the snorkel. All I would have to do is take the mouthpiece out of my mouth, still I am nervous. The water is cold.

I paddle around for a few moments to get the feel of the mask. Then I lower my head into the water. The sight shocks me.

I see a world so dangerous and so deep I could never have imagined it. There are valleys and alps, weeds waving, sand, and rock, magnified like jewels. The water is thick and tenuous as velvet. It holds me in its breathing, moves me in its breathing until I see that, lying in its arms, I am moved by its breathing alone. And it is dangerous! For it is as vast as the upper world. Yet it is so slow that I can rise upon it a foot at a time, and I sink down near the peaks of the mountains. I see sea urchins with needles hiding beneath slow-motion seaweed. I swim. I go farther than I had ever imagined. I see those sea animals which I hunted so assiduously for that first day. I see a school of gray fish. They see me and turn, catching the light from above. It refracts upon them and rushes past me as a prism of pastels. I swim farther. Green beckons and darkens to a bold blue. There are weeds beckoning on the bottom. I follow and come to a region of black caves. They scare me. There are beds of stone inside, and fish there who look like tigers. They are small and fierce with brilliant gills.

At last, I see the most dangerous thing of all: shafts of pure light. They penetrate from those needle points above and plumb the blue like X rays. It is strange to *go through* pillars of light. I follow the straightness of their line, but cannot see to the bottom. I must be out far. I am.

Frightened, I head for shore. The columns materialize and dematerialize as the waves move above. I look upward at the surface of the water and see something as dull, as silky, as slippery as the skin which I have shed. At once, confounded by the implications of this, I notice that I hear the Omega no more. I hear nothing. I know only that it is beauty.

A week had passed since Propakis had brought her into Hadjis's office, where she lay drugged, the blood, the state of her robin's-egg-blue suit, the bits of thyme in her glistening black hair promising proof that beauty was alive. He had got the idea of taking her at once to his mountain home near Tripolis, but one of the corporals was whispering in an office two doors away. He got cold feet. That was the first place they would look, they who improvised with hate because he was rich, had silver hair, elegance, a reputation as a ladies' man, flirting with anything in a skirt, resented his affair with Angliapoulou, a vulgar bore in fact, but most of all resented the fact that he hated brutality and screened it out of his consciousness by putting on feasts and entertainments and being generous, when he could be, to some of the political prisoners. Even those good Christian *vlachoi* patriots could be iconoclasts, given the right icon. So he did not give them a chance. He had had a better idea. There was nothing to hold her for. He had gone through both her suitcases himself—Propakis had already searched them. No indication of anything that connected her to Naples, or even to the American, so they let the American free to track, and her they brought to him.

"We're letting her go," he said in a loud voice, dismissing Propakis. But with a dig: "What kind of work is this, roughing her up? Hell, what a mess!"

And later Hadjis pulled the file so there would be no record. He called the Charybdakises, his old school friends who owed him a few. They could either put her in their villa or in a hotel. He didn't want to know. He sent her in a government limousine across the Peloponnesus. The driver was a clam. He trusted him. And now, in another week, she would be ready for him. It was like keeping something in cold storage, not too cold, he hoped, imagining the tryst which would—indeed, now that she was just another non-event in the office of a bureaucracy—take place precisely as he had imagined by the swimming pool next to the cypress tree. Something pleased him about keeping a prisoner outside the bureaucracy. He had foiled the hegemony of plebeians in a regime where generals took orders from colonels, and beauty had to be imprisoned to survive.

The next session they took him to a room with a wooden ceiling and walls of cement. It was on the roof of the police building. He had to walk across a dazzling cement pavement with a full view of Athens, apartment buildings, sky, and streets full of automobiles below. Panos escorted him.

On the roof next to the cement block which housed the room was a large Harley-Davidson motorcycle. It was suspended like a piece of sculpture on a cement pedestal, its wheels hanging two inches in the air.

Once Panos closed the door, he could have been anywhere, five stories up or five stories down. There was no window. It was lit by one light bulb. The only hint it was on a roof was the heat of the sun which beat on the low ceiling and made it stifling.

But the room had equipment in it. There was a table in the middle of the floor with three or four chairs. Implements hung from hooks in the wall. A pair of manacles. Two whips. A thing that looked like an egg-whisk

239

which was a stick with bare wire ends. On the end wall, there was a crude machine in the shape of a coatrack, constructed of two perpendicular beams with iron rings at the top, like the rings in gymnasiums.

"Take off your clothes," said Panos.

A thrill of cold inserted itself between his skin and his muscles.

Even then he did not believe he would be tortured.

He thought the word "Torture" while he took off his sneakers, socks, and shirt, and deposited them in a pile on the floor. But it did not make sense. Even when he was totally naked. He smelled himself and looked at himself, his chest and shoulders and the hairs on his thighs, and he stank, he was filthy. I am a body, he thought. When you have no clothes on you are nothing but a body. This is a Torture Room, he thought. But it was too unreal to believe. He picked up his clothes from the floor and put them on a chair.

"A doctor is coming to examine you," Panos told him. "Go and lie down on the table."

He went to the table and sat on it, but he refused to lie down. He could feel the grains of wood against his bare butt.

Panos was pacing the floor by the coatrack, humming absently but in time to the worry beads behind his back. After a while he said, "Be sure you call him Doctor."

He did not take the connection between Torture and Doctor as irony. You had to take off your clothes for both. Both worked on bodies. Doctors to cure, torturers to hurt.

But I am not a body, he thought with the beginnings of terror. He wanted the Goddess back. Her reality as he had had it with Cora. He thought how his body, this one, had merged with Cora's body while the Goddess was present, and he did not understand it.

He straightened his spine. He began the sound. He sucked in a breath, held his stomach as near to his spine as possible and followed the wire inward from his eyes. He pursued it inward as he breathed the sound, backward along the black corridor growing thinner and whiter, until nothing was left inside the Torture Room and he felt light. But it was not the same Omega sound. An "h" aspirate was wheezing behind his nose. It sounded like "Ohm," the sign of the unit of electrical resistance.

Two people came into the room. Panos shouted for him to open his eyes. One was a man with an attaché case. The other was Spyro Makris.

The man with the attaché case said, "I hope you will be cooperative this time."

"Which one do I call Doctor?" he said. He looked at Spyro because he was familiar. He knew Spyro's body, he knew his rhythm, he knew his smell. He was glad he would have Spyro, since he was the same one. He would not have to learn someone different. He wished the other man were Major Mavros.

Spyro knocked him a blow that sent him horizontal on the table.

"Let us understand each other now," said the man with the attaché case mildly. His skin was very smooth. "If you answer these questions, you will not get hurt. But if you don't, it may go very rough on you." He did not spell out the things with instruments. He set the attaché case on a chair, put one foot on the chair, and leaned on his knee.

"What is the name of the organization Anna Diamantes belongs to?"

"I don't know."

"Come on."

"I don't know."

Spyro clamped a cable over his chest and upper arms and over his ankles, so that he was strapped down.

"Now tell us the name of the organization."

Even when it began he did not think of it as Torture, although it was different from the gravel pit because of the room and the method. Spyro beat him with his fists, altering the position of each blow so he never knew where to expect it. He clamped his mouth together and made the sound. The Goddess could not be contingent on his body, even though her reality was most palpable when his body was indistinguishable from Cora's. The "h" said the name of the nineteenth-century German physicist. He was in an exercise room and his balls were hanging out. What you resist, you become.

Theo placed the cookie cutter on the leather and hit it smartly with the hammer. Theo was always a sucker for Philo's schemes. It was ladies' handbags. You cut the pieces out of leather and they fit together like puzzles. Philo promised they could subcontract somebody to line them and sew in the zippers.

"I don't know."

"All right then, we'll move to something you *do* know. How many people were with Anna when you met her in Naples?"

"Six thousand a year," said Theo. Philo was more modest about how much they would make. They worked for five weeks cutting, and when the pile of bags was in the shed, Philo couldn't find anybody to line them. Wyvono Ethridge's wife had a job in Lenoir Hall and she didn't want anybody else to use her sewing machine. Theo had been up till two every morning working on the bags and trying to make the dean's list. He felt betrayed.

"How many were there? Talk!" said the man with the smooth face.

"All you do is talk. You make us do the scut work and you just sit around like a goddamn hippopotamus!" Theo said.

"Filthy cheapie." Spyro was working himself up. He rolled up his shirtsleeves. In his hand was a blackjack that looked like a sectioned, rubber penis. He beat him with it on the soles of his feet. He alternated this with pokes in the stomach. His fist was sweaty. Drops of sweat blistered his face. "Ass-licking creep! Lunatic Christ-killer trying to bring decent people down!" He continued his stream of epithets. The filthier they grew, the more inspired he became.

Philo laughed. "Theo can do anything!" he boasted, strutting around Chapel Hill. The next business was making office safes from broken refrigerators. "He's like Heracles, a genius with his hands."

"How many?" insisted the man with the smooth face.

He was compelled to consider that his part in the cosmic sound involved resistance.

"Five," Don said.

"We're going to incorporate."

Theo chopped round holes in the refrigerators with a metal cutter. They used a blowtorch on the locks to weld them in.

"Six!" Any number except the right one.

They sprayed them with white paint. Two, they sprayed powder blue.

A blue worm in Spyro's temple wriggled. It was as intimate as fucking, but centrifugal. It lacked center. The only reward for Spyro came with each blow. Each blow had to be a blow for God, decency. . . . Make the anti-Christ squirm. There was no orgasm to work toward, only confession (nothing to do with the act) or death.

"First you say five and then you say six. How do you explain the inconsistency?"

He heard himself coughing.

"Now which was it, five or six?"

"Five."

"What were their names?"

"I don't know."

"Cóme on now. You can certainly remember one or two."

Nobody. Nobody wanted a safe made out of a refrigerator. Wrong. Nick Spathos, proprietor of Nick's Grill, known as the Armpit, bought one. Also the occult bookstore bought a powder-blue one. But nobody else.

"They talk about recycling, but they don't want it," Theo said.

"Nikos who?"

"Spathos!"

"They want brand names."

But the two main questions they wanted to know were: "What is the name of the organization?" and "What name did Anna Diamantes use?" The man with the smooth skin kept alternating the questions to mix him up, and the blows came too fast. He lost the sense of light and dark.

"You want him to stop? You have only to say the name and he'll stop."

"The Omega."

"You know as well as I do the Omega isn't the name of any organization. It's the symbol of the Resistance."

He had no intention of resisting. What you resist, you become.

"I know how you could make a million dollars" said Philo, inspired.

"How?" said Theo, falling for it again.

"I don't consider that you have been cooperating at all. You've been inconsistent. You've lied. I don't want symbols. I want names. Dates. Facts." The man made some kind of signal to Spyro.

"By creating plastic Parian marble!"

Spyro was wiping his sweaty hands on his pants and the clamps around his chest and his feet were loose.

"Now we have ways of getting information out of you. Nobody can hold up under such pressure."

"Of course, you have to learn the properties of resin and cooling techniques. And we need somebody to invest a little money."

"I don't think you understand properly."

Electric prod to his nipples or genitals. Or, cruder, attach a string and pull his balls off. If you beat a backbone in a certain place it affects the spine; later you become paralyzed. These were the standard measures called Torture. They hoped to scare him by talking about them.

Philo was buttering Mrs. Schonsveldt of Haw River Realty who believed in the occult. "I was sitting," he began dramatically, "and suddenly the streaks of marble rose out of the stone and the hieroglyphics formed a message: 'If Man can understand the properties of marble, then he can make it.'"

He knew he was part of a fool's apparatus. It would fail like all the other businesses had failed. But Theo was hooked and delivered. He learned the techniques from a Siamese man named Spoy, who made Fiberglas catamarans in Durham. Mrs. Schonsveldt didn't invest any money, but Philo did—three hundred dollars. For two weeks Theo experimented, boiling the liquid in an old kerosene barrel over a bonfire.

"What are you defending Anna for? She used you."

The light danced on the leaves and upon the pine slabs of the shed, a heart beating in a vast forest of ignorance. They had not even figured out what they would make with the plastic Parian marble.

"Maybe you were in love with her."

There was a terrible stench.

They took him off the table, turned him upside down and hung him like a piece of meat from the coatrack. The rings were not for hands. They were for feet. If the Goddess is contingent on the body, then what is she?

Lamp bases was one possibility. Coffee tables was another.

"She used you. Maybe she didn't plan it, but maybe the moment she saw you, she realized the kind of person you were, and saw a good thing. A way to get the plans into Greece."

People came from far and wide because of the stench, a thick sulfuric, rotten-eggs smell. The black people, Spoy, even the sheriff came. They made jokes about the smell, but they were fascinated.

"You owe her no loyalty. If you're innocent as you claim, what misguided sense of loyalty would keep you from telling us her name?"

Because he had imagined gulping death for her as his heart was cut out, a piece of cake, not being kicked with shoes upside down.

Theo stood in his shorts stirring the liquid with a wooden paddle. His torso glistened with sweat. It was hot in the night, so hot that Philo turned the hose on Theo to cool him, the jet of water shining in the firelight like a caress, ennobling the son and ennobling the father too.

It was Cora who had seen the Goddess, not he. The moment she had seen it, she had decided not to come to Athens with him. Up above the wooden paddle was smacking his genitals.

The molds were ready.

"What are you protecting her for? She knows you're here!"

He felt the blood pouring up his chest into his armpits and eyes. Red with cream swirls. Maroon with whipped curds. Aquamarine agate with foam horses. Philo's adoration for Theo spilled over onto him, and because Theo was too near the fire, pouring, to touch, Philo touched him. He felt his kisses on his cheeks, he felt his hands caressing his chest and shoulders.

"Don't get him bleeding too much."

"It's a failure," said Theo.

But it was only that batch, and Philo used them for tabletops, bird feeders and chair seats, it looked like a Disney Toadstoolville. The next batch was good. They made lamp bases, fire-blew them together, drilled small holes for the wires.

"Go out and get orders," said Philo.

His mouth was dry, but he discovered when he went to lick his lips that they were chewed up from his biting them against the pain.

"What was the name you knew her by?"

Gaynor Mae Ritchie, the manager of Rose's, thought they were crazy, two high-school boys trying to sell Parian marble lamps. They went to Arlen's, Sears, Grant's, and Kress's.

"Listen, Philo!" said Theo. "We're amateurs. Business doesn't work like this. You've got to have a factory, an assembly line, a company in New York. Business isn't for education. It's for profit. You made a laughingstock out of us."

"She knew you for what you are, a sucker, on an ego trip to do good. She knows you now for the same thing. While she's out there, you're here refusing to say her name. Why?"

"I don't want to sit around all my life in a goddamn junkyard hearing you preach education. I want to make money!"

It was he who made the decision, he who stood her up, he who decided to take the coufetta on his own time, his own terms. Philo's face froze in his mind through the broken window of that Rolls-Royce carcass. It was his first realization that Theo was going to mutiny.

"I know what we can use them for!" breathed Theo. "We'll only need one mold. They'll never wear down in the rain, and there's an everlasting market."

"What was the name?"

"Tombstones!"

"You're marketing death," said Philo.

Theo left, stuffed his junk into a duffel bag, and strode past Philo's beseeching arms.

"I put more than a thousand dollars into that invention of his!"

Philo lined up all the automobiles in straight lines, his answer to Theo's condemnation of his life. When Theo got the job at Powell-Peters as a part-time automobile mechanic, Philo said, "A smut job. They burn you out before you can turn around. They exploit you. Tell him to get a job in the library, clean work where you can study."

There was a sound of screaming. A motor started up, a metallic and grinding roar that swallowed up the scream.

He sat in a chair in Theo's room gazing around fearfully. Philo had sent him bearing figs. It was an old rooming house on Ransome Street run by a woman they called Flirty McDirt who had bile-colored curls. How could he live in a common street after Philo's domain? He studied him to see if he had changed, as if the place itself could do it.

"He kicked my balls."

"Tell us what name she used."

"He crapped on me. He killed our mother, devoured her."

"The name!"

The motor swallowed up the scream.

"I believed him. And now he's bribing me!"

Theo lifted the figs, as if they burned his hand, and from a distance of eighteen feet made a perfect drop-shot into the toilet. It was a thud rather than a splash, and he was on the floor.

Something cut him loose. As he fell, he threw Philo out of his skull. He had started with Philo and had gone past Philo. Philo was only a diversion from pain. Such pain belonged to the merciless force. The Goddess was not beautiful, but horrible.

Spyro let him lie there for a few minutes. There were terrible, gluey bulbs on his groin. The sound of the motor began.

The fact that I have the mask changes my relationship with Elias somehow. He saw me swimming with it yesterday. At the hole, he asks me about it.

"You were swimming a long time yesterday, longer than you have been in the water before. Where did you get the mask?"

"It belonged to a friend of mine, the friend I was with before I came here. He must have been captured too. They searched through my luggage and messed everything all up, and put his mask in my bag." I say this accusingly.

But he ignores it. The only thing he says is: "Did you see many fish down there?"

I tell him nothing about the plan that I am formulating. I do not think that he suspects anything.

But there is another side to it. I have a new world which he cannot share now. I find myself so awed by it that I want to tell him about each thing I see. I want to talk about it, like telling the plots of movies.

"Have you ever looked under the sea with a mask?" I ask him.

"Lots of times," he says. And he tells me about a large fish that he caught with a spear gun.

"Where was that?"

"Out beyond the last island."

He means the stone woman. I did not catch him. He mentioned no names.

My enthusiasm, in fact, disguises the plan of my escape. I spend many hours in the water. I notice a curious thing. That the larger a fish is, the uglier and more suspicious it is, and the more fearful. It lurks in the dark caves at the steepest places. I meet a particular fish which lives beneath the huge rock that I saw the first day. I happen to meet this fish in a way that frightens me.

I am floating above the great rock, without making any movement at all, just looking. I have been looking for a long time, perhaps five minutes, when I realize that this huge and monstrous fish is lurking beneath at the edge of the darkness looking directly at me, nothing moving but a wave of his gills. He has been looking at me for five minutes too!

In the moment of recognition I make a move; I kick my foot, frightened. This frightens the Big Fish. He makes a pull on his leviathan tail and with one whack he sails beneath the rock and disappears.

Later I am drawn to the rock to see if he may be there. Carefully, I approach without making any sudden moves of my arms or legs. I float against the swell, motionless, and he takes shape clearly against the bed of stones.

He does not see me. I understand that the huge rock is his house and that the bed of stones is like a front porch upon which he sits in the sun. I stare at him for a half an hour, fascinated with his sleepiness and the yellowish-brown cruel bones back of his head as vicious as barbed wire. At last I am bored, and I make a move to swim on. This move apprises him of his danger, and he takes one look at me and flees.

While I am telling Elias of this I realize that I'm identifying the Big Fish in my mind with him, so that I believe that Elias looks like the Big Fish. Yet the circumstances are entirely opposed, and I am looking at the Big Fish from high above, just as Elias has been looking at me every day from the parapet. And though I can go into the cave rooms and escape his gaze, just as the Big Fish goes under the rock, nevertheless, we are in the relation to each other, of witness, even of jailer.

"Where does the Big Fish live?"

I begin to tell him. But I have trepidations. "If I tell you, you will not kill him, will you?"

"No."

"You must give me your word."

"All right. I promise."

I believe his promise and tell him.

An hour passes. I write to Eleanor and Corey on my art paper, telling them that I am in a place called Hora, Greece, where there is a big castle, and I describe some of the things that I see under the surface of the water. I do not mention that I am a prisoner. And I tell them that I will be moving, so that they are to write to me when I write them next time, since I have no fixed address.

I hand this note to Elias through the hole and I ask him to mail it for me from the Hora post office, just as if it were a natural thing to do.

He actually takes the note in his hand, and after a moment of silence says in a choked snarl, "You must be crazy if you think I would actually mail this."

"Why not?" I ask. "It is only to my son and daughter. I don't want them to worry about me. I don't mention my being a prisoner at all, and I even tell them not to write to me until later." And I repeat what I have said in the letter. "If you don't believe me, ask some friend of yours who understands English."

"I do believe you, but have you no conception of the trouble we can get in, if I mail it?"

"Who is going to know, if you don't tell?"

"They have ways of finding out."

"Who are *they?*" I ask, with edge.

"I don't know." And his voice is strangely hollow.

Two impulses push and pull us.

Later that day, I say gratuitously, "I don't believe you are a real jailer, Elias."

"I am the keeper of this fort."

"What hold do they have over you? In addition to that?"

He does not answer.

The very fact that we have arrived at some kind of mutual trust, for I believe he will not kill the Big Fish, just as he believes that I have written what I told him and no more, makes us more suspicious of each other in a hidden way.

I sense that something is going on in his psyche. He acts strange to me. It feels as though he is thinking something over. I do not ask him if he has mailed the letter. I feel that he is ruminating, stewing, as I believe that the Big Fish does when, spotting me, he now refuses to propel himself into the cave.

At the same time he becomes more sharp and suspicious of me in a new way. It has to do with Don.

He wants to know about the man to whom the mask belonged. Was he a husband to me?

I stall. He was twenty-five years younger than I am, I tell him, exaggerating slightly.

"What has that got to do with it?"

"Do you mean was he my lover?"

For the first time in my dealings with Elias I am tempted to lie. It is as much my confidence in him as anything. But have I arrived at that point with this one person who, so remote, so close, will spur me to minimize myself for human feelings? My loss would be Elias, the God.

"Yes, he was."

He does not answer. I believe I am through with it. I go down to the water's edge and cast myself in.

Twenty minutes later I see an octopus. As the Big Fish had materialized out of elements I took to be seaweed, so the octopus formulated its essence in my eyes out of the toadstool formations in a part of the rocks not excessively deep. It is the first time I have ever seen an octopus walk. I have always believed my mind capable of understanding what it sees, but in the case of the octopus, I am galvanized by an inability to understand its rhythms. It walks along the bottom. It stretches its arm as far as it wants to cross a chasm. Then it uses a third arm. But there is no pattern, and while three of the arms are walking, stretching themselves to the desired length, the others dangle tentatively, or curl. I keep thinking of them as legs.

I am afraid, for it sees me, and I am not sure that it will continue along the bottom. Can't octopuses swim in a jellyfish manner and wrap their arms around you and squeeze you to death? But this octopus is not large, and as I have now accustomed myself to the sea in the manner of a familiar, I do not move. Innocuous and huge I hover above him watching until he slides out of sight below a great rock.

Hours, or was it days later, they took him back to the roof. Despite the beating, he could walk. This time it was to a different room. The man with the smooth face was there. Also Major Mavros. It was a waiting room with chairs and a table, but there were no instruments and the room had a window facing out on the roof. They told him to sit down. He could see the door of the Torture Room twenty feet away. There were two doorways beyond it. The cement block obscured the bepedestaled motorcycle, so that only part of its rear wheel showed, catching the sun on its spokes like a halo.

He tried once more to feel the Goddess, but he felt nothing. She might have been alive or she might have been dead, he simply could not feel her Presence.

"We've got Anna," Major Mavros told him.

He did not believe it. He stared at the sky.

"See for yourself," said Major Mavros in an offended tone.

A few minutes later, footsteps sounded on the cement and two guards appeared pulling her along between them. He was not sure it was Zoe, because they had hold of both arms and it distorted her walk. But she was wearing the black jersey and her shoulders were hunched over her breasts. She pulled her arm away from one and walked almost slowly, with a measured step, almost calculated. He looked carefully. It was her walk.

But he could not see her face. It was in profile and too far away. Her hair, a little longer than he remembered, fell in its irrepressible wave on her forehead. In a moment they opened the door of the Torture Room and she disappeared.

"Now it's up to you," Major Mavros told Don. "If you tell us the name of the organization and the name she used with you, it will go easier on her."

The Face became quite clear on his retina. But it was a mask as if the suffering was withdrawn or done internally so that nothing was left for the outside.

The man with the smooth face got up and left. He crossed the roof and went into the room where they had Zoe.

A sound began like rope slapping water.

The Face changed and there was less beauty than he had thought. He saw the real Zoe. Her features were more flagrant than the Face in his mind. The curve of her eyebrow from the bridge of her nose conjured the fight, the rebellion which the tail of her eyebrow denied, as though everything started with the struggle and the course of the eyebrow followed a single strand of music and gave in to the tragedy of life, became synonymous with it, swelling upward at its end, tracing the possible course of a transcendence.

They stopped slapping and used fists. Perhaps sticks.

But in this rendition of the Face the eyebrows were static. It was a modern face. The eyebrows did not have that swirl; it was unable to be transformed.

They could have been punching a mattress; pucks, plumps. It was like being in a movie but being unable to see, only to hear.

Major Mavros asked him a question.

The answer came to him that this was the Goddess as opposed to the Face. The reason he could not feel the Goddess was that he was locked into her. He was separated from human emotion. Emotions rise out of insufficient union. Pity can only exist when you are *outside* the object of your pity. Even hate, which appears as a singular and separative emotion, arises out of an inability to incorporate what is hated, and when it rises for attention, the perfect mechanism of denial makes the hater strike out to kill. The inconvenience in a murder is that it is irrelevant to its goal, which the hater cannot understand. Its goal can never be accomplished, and the hater is left with an even stronger ambivalence, wanting to deny, and wanting to incorporate. Even love is divisive, insisting on cataclysmic union in terms which will never satisfy it. And it produces new vessels of passion.

She screamed. It was not loud. He remembered how it wrenched his heart to hear a sound like this from a human. He thought of human decisions: hers to resist, which had brought her here; his to take the coufetta, which now gave him a second decision—to betray her and save her from pain.

All the icons he had used to find the Goddess, of which he had been so afraid—even the Face itself had appeared interminably as an intermediary—flaked off the insides of his skull. The screams exploded them to orange fragments of light.

It was not that he could not have told what he knew, nor that he intended to resist, nor that he had any sense of the nobility of man, nor that he wished to spare or not to spare Zoe. It was just that if the Goddess left him anything in this cosmic numbness, it was the ability to *not* speak.

A motor started up, blotting out the screams. From the blue smoke on the terrace he realized it was the motorcycle. They used the motorcycle to keep the screams from being heard by people in the street below.

In late afternoon when the sun's glare begins to glow more from rocks than from the sun itself, Elias appears in my courtyard. I cannot believe it is he, yet I know him.

It is in precisely the same way he appears on the parapet that he appears before me. Out of nowhere. I now see that the Big Fish and the octopus have appeared to me that way too. Out of elements which I have thought to be something else.

Since it is by his torso that I know him . . . ah, I'd know that walk anywhere! . . . the faint strut, the massive shoulders, the smooth, gliding arms, the compact march of the legs on solid loins, the thick chest . . . I stare at his face, his head. I am amazed.

His brow is wrinkled and massive. His hair has receded but is thick as lamb's wool, black, cropped close to his ears and his neck. His eyes a greenish yellow and his mouth is as cruel as a wolf's. But the wrinkles around his eyes and the corners of his lips are such that they could either express the vicious indignation which leads to revenge, the triumph of a bayonet slash, or the stunned laughter of one who recognizes God Himself.

He stares into my face as if I am a ghost.

"I knew you would come," I whisper in spite of myself.

But instead of responding he takes hold of my forearm. He is predatory. His fingers dig into my flesh and I pull back from him in pain.

"Lie down," he orders.

"You want to take me by force?" I say, ripping out of his clutch, and I laugh contemptuously.

I feel justified because of his shirt. It is of very soft knitwear, a cheap version of American. The very softness of it, like baby-wool, its cleanliness, its close fit make it a ludicrous costume to wear for rape.

He does not attempt to get at me again. We circle each other, but so slowly that it is the world which is revolving around us. I am fierce. As fierce as he. I look at his eyes and I see no trace of humanity there. I do not care if he takes me or not. Pinned by his eyes, I feel that human part of me as history. It may be five miles down a backroad behind my head, and if there is a trace, it is small.

"Life, it is nothing," he says.

"Nothing," I answer.

He spits.

I laugh again. There is dazed admiration in his eyes at my laughter. I see he wants to laugh, too, but he is on another track of this passion.

"We live one day, and then we are dead. As my spit dries there in the falling sun."

I imagine, looking down the V of that cheap, soft shirt to the bronze, silky skin, so surprisingly without hair, his chest, of the feel of him, slippery against me. He is hardly taller than I, and stronger than any man I have ever known. Though his face is igneous, as hewn as rock, his body is smooth as a fish. I wonder what I look like now that I have become fierce in looks as well as soul. I have not seen myself in a mirror. I have entered the only mirror that was present, that opaque milk of sea, Don's gaze, and broken the way to my freedom.

"What do you want?" he asks.

"I am not a whore to be asked questions like that," I crack like a whip in his face.

It is his turn to laugh.

I could have answered: "My freedom," but I do not want my freedom, for I have it. I want to get down to brass tacks. I want to be specific again.

"Do not threaten me," I say, going on the attack. "I am not like you, with something to lose, something to protect. I cannot be bribed or blackmailed. I have nothing to lose, not even my body now. And I cannot lose my soul."

The fury in his face is terrible. He wants to kill me, to slap the boldness from my eyes. Instead, he puts his face near to mine, and without touching me repeats again, but in a mechanical, almost idiotic way, as if he were screaming across a transatlantic telephone cable:

"What-Do-You-Want?"

I do not apologize for misunderstanding him. If it had not been for Don's mask, he would never have come into my precinct. He would never have asked me this question.

"I want to know who captured me, and what is so horrible that they can blackmail you to hold me here."

He says nothing. But it is like tying knots, the decision of the moving wrinkles as he ties them with his nose, mouth, ears. He turns his back, walks out of the courtyard toward the church, and disappears.

I am disappointed.

That night, thinking of the threats, of the smoothness of the skin of his shoulders curving over the bulges of muscles which could have killed me, I cannot sleep.

Early in the morning I rise and go down to the sea.

For a long time I swim along the shore. I turn at the point of the fort. I swim very far, perhaps two miles, following the coast. I do not raise my head at all. I keep my eyes trained on the deep, lost in the dramatic world of rogue palaces and fishes. At one point I come to a sheet of rock, so near the surface of the water that the seaweed brushes my breasts as I swim over it. On its farther side there is a steep drop, and the water is foamish blue and calm. Far below, upon the bottom, the stones are smooth. The water is warmer. I am in a deep lagoon whose borders are cliffs on either side which penetrate fathoms. I swim inward, following the left-hand cliff. The water becomes shallower. The two cliffs widen. It is like swimming into an embrace.

I lift my head.

I am upon a perfect, triangular beach, a half-moon strip of sand which is the lip of a mountain, hidden from the outer sea by the angle of the small aperture. I walk on the sand. Cicadas sing. Pine trees climb a cliff. I sit down to rest, and for many minutes I gaze around in the deep and brilliant silence speculating upon that narrow aperture, which not even a boat could cross and which renders the privacy of this place as secret as the Garden of Eden.

Suddenly I notice a donkey tethered to a tree. I am not, as I had thought, alone and private; this means that there is someone near. Someone who owns the donkey. I look upward at the mountain and realize that I am beyond the walls of the fortress, that I have come out upon the mainland of the peninsula, and that just beyond my vision on the other side of the mountain lies the road to Hora.

There was no change of outward expression on Thea Vasiliou's face, although a wisp of her white hair, unloosened when she slipped her wrist free of the cloth some hours before, made a slight tremor. She did not take another breath.

"He does not know anything," Major Mavros told the three officials in the third-floor office.

They took him to the corporal's desk in the lobby and gave him his wallet and watch back. They were polite. They told him he was discharged. Panos even gave him a grin and a mock salute as he walked down the steps.

When he got into the street, he kept going until he was out of sight. He came to some flower shops on Agia Sophia. The smell of chrysanthemums made him want to vomit. He sat down in the frightening gas fumes on the curb where shining traffic roared.

There was a hippie-freak, dyed-blond hair and dyed-purple T-shirt, leaning against a tree. "Hey, man," he said, "you sure look strung out. Where'd you come from? I just came in from Israel myself."

He stepped into the line of traffic for a cab.

"What is the date?" he asked the cab driver.

"May eleventh," said the driver, shooting him a curious glance. Don had the feeling he should go and report to the U.S. Mission. There would be an army liaison. Six days he had been in there!

When he reached the second floor of the Home Pension, Mme. Guaracci, roused by the groan of the elevator cable, was peeking out of her doorway to see who it was.

"Give me a bar of soap," he ordered. Report what? They would court-martial him for working for a foreign government.

"Oh," she breathed, backing into her room like an elephant. In a second she returned, staring impressed from her painted lips and her small hard eyes, holding out the bar of green Camay from the narrow opening.

"Leave my key on my table. I do not want to be disturbed."

He took a shower. Just before he passed out on his bed, he looked around and missed his knapsack and thought: They took it and I forgot to ask for it back.

Hours later, there was a loud knocking on his door.

"Mr. Tsambalis, you have a telephone call."

The telephone was on the sideboard in her room. He had to squeeze past her crepuscular flesh, through knickknacks, hairbrushes, old calendars, and teacups.

"Adonis?" said Zoe's voice.

"Yes," he said. "Who is it?"

"Zoe."

"Yes."

"Do you trust me?"

"Yes."

"Come to the Kentrikon Theater on Voucourestiou, just around the corner from where you are. The performance, with Elli Drachopoulou, begins at nine and finishes around eleven-thirty. Come to her dressing room after the show. Everything will be taken care of."

"I give my name?"

"Yes. You'll be expected. But come to the performance. Can you sit through a performance?"

"Yes."

"All right then." She hung up.

He felt no surprise that Zoe was alive, not dead, nor that she was in Athens. He went back to sleep, but awoke on psychic cue.

257

He walked slowly through crowded streets. Voucourestiou was dark, and the theater was not well lit. The play was *The Bad Seed.* Elli Drachopoulou played the mother of the evil little girl. It took place in Kansas, but there was a part for a Negro gardener, played by a black man who drawled like Rochester in Greek. At the end, his muscles were frozen in the contour of the theater seat. He threaded through a crowd backstage. There were bangs, hushes, and laughter in the dressing rooms. Somebody was dragging the bed from Act II along a cement corridor.

He found Elli Drachopoulou's dressing room. The door was open, and it was large and dark, with many people milling around inside. The actress was standing in front of her mirror, lit by little light bulbs, her hair pinned up, giving off blue highlights. She turned toward him with a warm smile. She shook his hand.

"Ah yes, we've been expecting you!" she said. She turned to a youth at the far end of the room. "Manoli!"

"Ela?" He was short and muscle-bound and came on as a faggoty, young tough.

"Will you take our friend, please?"

Manoli took him through a door at the end of her dressing room which went down some creaking wooden steps into a basement.

"Nasty place, huh? But it could be nastier. Just follow me."

They passed another doorway with letters saying Blue Pension, and then went up stairs that led to the lounge of an American-style bar called the San Francisco. There were blue lights, and a pink Schlitz sign in the window. It was full of Sixth Fleet sailors.

"Come on. Have a drink." Manoli paid and alternated between looking at sailors and looking out through the Schlitz sign to the street.

He barely had time to down the whisky, when Manoli ordered him up. There was a car outside, and a man driving whom he introduced as Sotiris.

"Okay," said Manoli, and he went back into the San Francisco.

He leaned back against the upholstery of the car while the lights of Athens went by. Sotiris parked by a block of old apartments. They entered a dark foyer with a wooden floor. They climbed two flights of stairs, and walked along a balcony to an adjoining block of flats. The floor changed to tile. A rubber plant sent leaves along the balustrade of an enclosed passageway. There was a white door with a nameplate: Falkonis. Sotiris rang the bell.

Zoe came to the door.

Her eyes turned on him from a peremptory greeting to Sotiris, a long gaze full of intensity into which he was drawn as into an embrace. She took him into a living room which had been converted to a half-bedroom, half-study. It was well furnished with a couple of Oriental rugs and a Steinway baby grand. The bed in the corner was made up with a Turkish print, and a large, inlaid French desk covered with papers stood against one wall.

"I must go. Good-by, Zoe," said Sotiris, kissing her.

She continued to gaze at him walking through the room. "I think this will be comfortable. There's a bathroom through here. Now, sit down. Have you had anything to eat? I'm going to bring you some avgo-limono soup"—a contemplation which transfixed his sense of the vastnesses of his losses and gains in connection with her while he took in his new condition on the periphery.

In this rendition the Face was more tentative, more mobile. Too human for Tragedy to be glazed. She wore her hair slightly longer, the wave was somehow lighter. But there were reckless dots of pale green in her amber pupils.

"No, you'd better lie down." She'd gotten a fix on his physical state. "One of us is a doctor. I'm going to get him—"

"You are here. You are in Athens."

"Yes."

"Why are you here?"

A cloud passed through the amber. She made no attempt to answer.

"How did you get here?" he asked.

"Illegally."

"By plane?"

"Yes, to one of the islands, and then by regular ferryboat."

"Why are you here?" he repeated.

"I can't tell you. Something is going. to happen."

A euphoric assumption which he had not clearly formulated dictated his questioning, but it had to do with Cora. Although he was curious, he did not want to know what was going to happen. He was adamant for the other thing.

"Did Fotianos escape?"

"Yes."

"Who planned it? You?"

"Yes."

"You make all the plans?"

"Yes, but with the help of other people. I coordinate details."

"Because you are the leader?"

"Yes, because I am the leader of this part of it."

"There's another part?"

"Yes, of course, the organization, whatever you want to call it as a whole. I don't tell you the name because—"

"And I was a decoy?"

"No."

"Was I carrying anything in the coufetta—plans, contingency plans? Things I was suspected of carrying?"

"No."

"Then it was a mistake?"

"A mistake. I should never have given it to you that day. They were watching."

She ran her hands once up and down her arms with the suggestion of a shudder, but he was adamant, for the transaction was beyond guilt or recrimination. Everything else was arbitrary, his decision to take the coufetta, her obligation.

"A mistake," he said, easing himself down onto the sofa.

She made an involuntary move toward the door.

"No, don't get the doctor yet. We have to talk."

She paused, doubtful.

"I'm all right, don't worry, I'm okay." He made her sit down and went on: "How did you find me?"

"We knew when you were released."

"And you knew when I was arrested?"

"Yes. Routine information. You were on the list of people detained that day. One of us works in the deputy assistant's office and sees the lists."

"Then you know about Cora Ellison."

"Yes."

He was not surprised, but he had a feeling of shock.

"Where is she?"

"She was never interrogated, either in Vathy or in Athens. Our contact found a dossier under the name Kora Ellison, spelled with K, indicating she was brought in for questioning by an officer named Pantelis Propakis. Later, the dossier disappeared. There were insinuations that a general named Hadjis took her on a kind of unofficial arrest to his private house in a cypress forest outside Tripolis, but she never got there."

He had never imagined the name *Cora* on Zoe's lips.

"Is she safe? I mean— She's all right? Not—"

"I think so."

"And you have no idea where she is?"

"We have an idea she's on the Peloponnesus, or on some island off Kythera."

"How do you know? You have somebody tracking?"

"Hadjis has some old cronies who went to school with him and own a lot of land down in Messenia somewhere; we think they've taken her there. It's not as easy as with *records,* but I don't want you to worry. Yes, we have someone down there. We had to call off too much asking around in offices. You have to be careful. Greeks talk to amuse themselves, to make jokes, but too much and you blow everything. They're *poniros.* We got on to Hadjis because they're jealous of him; he has a reputation as a skirt-chaser unpalatable to the colonels. Under the guise of gossip, you can find out a lot."

He went back to the beginning, leaving unanswered the question of the name Pantelis Propakis whom he suspected was Richard Burton.

"I saw you being tortured yesterday in that machine of truth."

She took his hand.

"No, you didn't see me."

"I heard you! But I saw you walking."

"It wasn't me."

"Who was it then?"

"Somebody who probably looked like me."

"It was real though. You screamed."

"They have not got me. I am here."

"Have you ever—" He bit his tongue back. She squeezed his fingers with more pressure.

"So it was pantomime," he said.

"Tricks. Yes, tricks." Her knuckles were white.

"Why did you come to the Service Club in the Hotel Grili?" he asked.

"Sanchez," she answered. "He was the pilot that got Fotianos out."

Of course, he thought, rue drifting down his throat and out his eyes; Sanchez would know how to fly a plane.

"But he hates leftists."

"But he loves exiles and money."

"And Annette?"

"Annette?"

"Annette Borlin." Was it possible to draw a blank?

"I don't know any Annette Borlin."

"Wasn't Annette part of the organization?"

"No."

"But she was killed," he said.

Now the transaction predicated that Zoe be interrogated, even blackmailed by him to do that for which they had been brought together. But first he had to tell her everything.

He told her what he knew. She told him what she knew. They matched information, detail for detail.

While he was talking, telling of his movements, Corfu, Kalamata, Cora, the islands, Samos, her eyes roved over him. But she showed no emotion. He recognized Zoe the administrator. Her rhythm was as quick and cool as his backhand.

In another room, there was the noise of a typewriter rat-at-tatting and a voice in an undertone mixed with coughing, wheezing sounds. A squeal like a siren. A high-powered radio, he guessed. He tuned it out. Put off the *cost* of the lost manhood, the numbing of the soul. *He did not want to know.*

"They thought that Annette was driving the car when Fotianos escaped and that I was in the car with her dressed in a green sweater," he said.

He noticed some change in her eyes, yellow dots abstracting in the amber, as if she had made some connection.

"Akou, lipon," she said. She told him the facts of the Fotianos escape. It had not been planned as a single action. There was to have been another escape that night, from a prison on Aegina, a middle-aged man named Evangelis Lampris. Both actions were coordinated so that Sanchez could make two landings, one on Corfu, the other on Aegina. But what should have been the simplest, the escape of Lampris, did not work out, because Lampris was sick, diabetes, and unable to get outside the wall. While the difficult job, Fotianos's escape, did work. Trigo, the guard they had bribed, turned out to be unreliable and told what he knew to the Security Police the day before. So the police knew there was going to be an attempt. Still it went off all right because of the contingency plan.

There was a tunnel, which had taken months to dig, from an old fourno inside the prison to a garage some distance down the road. Fotianos, during a toilet break, had left the corridor, gone into the fourno, pulled the metal back over its mouth, and crawled through the tunnel to the garage. He had waited there for Lefteri, a girl named Aphrodite, and a Dutch friend who were to pick him up.

Lefteri had left Naples on the nineteenth of April, the same day as Don. He had flown by Avianta to Brindisi and there had met the Dutch friend, who had a car. Posing as tourists they took the car ferry.

"The same day as I did?"

"The same day of course, but he must have gotten there seven hours later at least."

Lefteri was on a fake passport. They did not know Trigo had betrayed them, so they were operating in terms of the first plan. They picked up Aphrodite, and then they switched drivers. Aphrodite drove to the assigned spot outside the prison wall. Fotianos failed to come. A suspicious car stopped around the corner. Knowing something had gone wrong then, they moved off. The car followed them, but Aphrodite outmaneuvered it and got away. By that time it was late. They went straight into the second plan. They drove to the garage. Fotianos had been waiting more than an hour. They picked him up and sped to an abandoned fishing village where Sanchez was supposed to land. He had been there for hours. By this time it was past eight in the morning, and it was light, so they didn't dare drive the car, which could be identified. They abandoned it. Because of Trigo and communication from Naples, the Lampris escape was out, of course, so they flew back to Italy with Sanchez.

"Then they thought Annette was Aphrodite," he said.

She nodded. In the silence his mind ran forward, for it did not explain why Annette was killed, or whether they had killed her, even. Why, too, had they continued to follow him? The coufetta? And two weeks later going through Cora's cases?

"Why didn't they arrest me right away?"

"They wanted you to lead them to us."

His mind took a different turn.

"When did you know I was arrested?"

"Five days ago."

"And you did not know this man had followed me from Corfu? You didn't know that until right this minute?"

"No, I knew that five days ago, because the moment we saw your name on the list of arrested people we tried to trace down what happened. The man you're talking about is famous in KYP. His name is Kostas. They call him Kostas the Cheeks."

So that's how it is, he thought. How easy to accept words that had been mere affectation before: "Contact" "KYP" "Our People" "Betray" "Informant."

In the silence he was contemplating how many more strands of information they had to tally, when he noticed the concern on her face.

"I'm going to get Grigoris," and she got up in a rush.

"No, wait."

But she kept on until he stopped her at the doorway:

"Anna."

She turned.

"Are you Anna?" he asked.

"Yes."

"Who was Zoe?"

She didn't answer, she looked at him a gaze that was half-naked, half-guarded.

"Was that her picture on the sideboard? Was she your sister?"

"Yes."

He held the transaction ruthlessly over her.

"I have so much to thank you for but so much more to regret," she whispered formally, her voice on the edge of trembling. "You told those bastards nothing—"

"Is your father deaf or what? Did he mislead me?" he barked.

"It is painful," she said.

"But you will tell me."

"Yes, I must tell you."

At least she didn't say "owe."

She sat down again. Her voice was calm, even languid.

"Zoe was an architect married to a classmate, Ioannis, also an architect—Zoe, my sister, yes, my sister—and they had three children. Before, in Karamanlis's time, Ioannis did his national service and she was managing the office. She went up every other weekend or so to Kavalla to see him. One weekend when she got there, Ioannis was dead. He had been shot. At first they had said, the military, that he was a member of some plot that had been discovered, and that he had shot himself in disgrace.

But there were discrepancies. She got a lawyer and threatened to make an exposé. A week later, they claimed she had hanged herself from a roof joist on the site where Ioannis was planning an installation. There was another suicide note, in her handwriting this time, pleading infidelity. I had to go identify her like that."

He no longer had hope for a vocabulary to distinguish between the Sergeant Brills and the Zoes.

"How old were you?"

"Seventeen. She was five years older. It was the year after I came back from Tennessee."

She was mechanical but didn't mince words. She looked like a marble statue.

"Does your mother know what you are doing now?"

"She suspects but doesn't know. She's seen things."

"What?"

"Things. Police."

"At your house?"

"Yes."

"What did they do?"

"Insult. Knock things around. Vases—"

"Knock you around?"

"Yes."

"Why did you take Zoe's name?"

"So she will live through me."

This time she got up and looked at him with a glittering expression that was almost derision.

"Enough," she said. "This is enough now."

"And you, then, Zoe, whom I can't call anything but Zoe—"

She leaned forward and felt his forehead.

"You have a fever, you know." He felt strange, that touch, remembering her laying-on-of-hands on the camel's hump. "Stay here. I'll come right back with Grigoris."

"—Zoe, you will help me get Cora Ellison free."

She nodded.

The sun beats fiercely upon me, and I think now of climbing the mountain. But I am barefoot and naked. The donkey and the thought of any incipient meeting with the person who owns it and must be nearby terrifies rather than reassures me. I skirt the mountain at a distance from the donkey, to get high enough to see on the other side. I reach a promontory. A declivity in the ridge enables me to see a cart track.

From that moment, I begin to make my plan, for I cannot leave now. I must be prepared. I shall swim here not in the morning but in the late afternoon, long enough before the sun goes down to gain the beach, climb the cliff, and reach the road. I shall tie shoes and a dress around my waist. At sunset I shall reach the road. Dark will close me in, and I shall be on the road at night when no one can see me. By morning I shall be far away.

I hurry back down the cliff, past the eyes of the donkey, who stares at me as if nothing were unusual. I am terrified lest I be discovered, and gaining the beach, I enter the water.

It is at the zenith of noon when I climb into my courtyard. He is there.

"I have found out," he says.

"What?" I ask.

At first I believe that his words are an accusation, that he has found out about my secret beach and my plan for escape. Even when I look full into his face I do not think he is speaking about who captured me.

He answers, "The name."

"What is it?"

"Hadjis."

"Hadjis?" It means nothing to me.

"Someone fat and high-up in Athena," he says, "who did not want to put you on any books as prisoner, who wanted you as a guest. You understand?"

"No."

We are standing again in the sun, but near the portal gate where the breeze comes up from the sea waving the beads of the grasses and casting their shadows, a million black dots jumping over our feet. I am locked in his eyes.

He has a smirk on his lips, but his brows are knitted in a scowl so intense that I do not believe he is saying what he actually says in words. He is bronze, but under the searing light of the sun his face is in shadow, and his black sheep's curls are so tight they look like iron.

"He wanted you for himself."

He wants me for himself, I translate. His scowl garners such an intensity that it wants to break, to throw these facts to the wind. More important is the frame of the portal shadowed on the ground, setting him apart from me in the patch of scathing sunlight, like the center icon of a triptych. I step back, aware that the sun is moving, and that the frame is going to arch to its highest point, and I see that the ceremony will take place in a patch of soft, brown thistleless grass at his feet. I face the sun. But I wonder how he can bear the heat.

"Don't you understand how things are done in this country?" he shouts at me. "The right hand does not know what the left hand is doing. He gets an aide to put you under some sort of house arrest. Who knows what happened? *Telos pandon.* The aide puts you in someone else's hands, and you are some kind of hot goods, dynamite. They are afraid, attracted. You get lost from the very source that wants to keep you. Some idiot made a mistake. You were supposed to be in somebody's villa eating sweet cakes and drinking Coca-Cola all day and beer and banana liqueur on silk pillows like some pasha's harem, until the heat was off, but the underlings did it wrong, and you end up here with me, and I have my instructions. They are not interested in what you know. They are interested in *you!*"

I can scarcely believe this, but it is irrelevant. For myself, I am free, having already escaped via my secret beach.

But saying this breaks whatever it was in his face. The smirk. The smirk breaks into a dangerous smile. The scowl jumps into spokes aimed from his eyelashes as straight as X rays.

"I asked these questions, muddied the waters. I am *poniros,*" he says, screwing his forefinger into his temple at the very moment that the sun edged to make the black triptych perfect straight angles. "But now they've got wind of someone's interest, it makes it very dangerous. Dangerous!" He mouthed this in a whisper with a gleeful expression calculated to make me not step back.

I step back in spite of it. For he needs the entire space to himself, locked into Her eyes through me, to realize.

I am a fool. He did not need space. He did not even need me. And the sun is not in his face as it is in mine. It is back of his head, entering him from the one aperture, the mouth of the tuning fork in back of his neck that he cannot see. It seems to me that his face is bleached out, but it may be that my line of vision is now blinded into whiteness from the glare. Only his eyes have any meaning at all, green slits spitting and laughing, liquid with sun.

Freedom, of course, does not exist without danger.

He throws all of it, all the facts, and all reservations away, and just as he screwed his finger into his temple, now he screws it into the whole world. He throws it down in an imaginary gesture on the ground, like a gauntlet.

"The sun never stays in the same place," he barks, and stamps upon the base of the shadow on the ground with style.

That opens it. I step like a queen where his hands describe the chariot of the sun.

Surprisingly, all the bronze turns into the silk that I had imagined. I, who have grown vast enough to be invaded within by Elias's fire, have grown the different skin without to bear it. I feel soft, immobile, am surprised by the coolness, by the smoothness of his skin which I had only imagined. The one other thing that has any meaning are his hands. The black hair on them now seems tightened wings, but inside, they are white, in great contrast to their great, hard, clawlike backs, even the calluses smooth. We take off our clothes, lie down in the spot on the grass. I am liquid as rain, but hot. He is smooth as sand, but cool. All around us the jagged rocks of the prehistoric earthquakes rise into the sky, and the walls of the castle, made by men, abstract into mere lines across the vastness of such a thing. I do not know what he did to me in the course of that lovemaking, in which only his eyes and his hands were alive to make me come to orgasm so many times. I remember, after the seventh or eighth, thinking that I might die, for I am past forty, and I screamed this to him. It made him laugh. "I am past forty, too!" And at last I become mere cataclysms and dying falls at a greater strength than his, and yet aware of a very powerful extension of a spine which pushes me where I respond.

The paradox of rockhood assaults me. I realize that rocks are the freeze of the world's erection. The world caught in the apex of orgasm is a constant reminder of the holy state. And yet the more I inhabit rock, the more living and warm I have become. The more I inhabit them, the higher, faster, farther I can inhabit the follicles of my own flesh. Through the surface of the woman's skin the action takes place. The more gentle the caress, the deeper the feeling that penetrates. When it reaches the center, it affects the surface again, and the center cannot be reached except through the surface. In such action the center cannot be located because everything becomes whole.

I arrive at a point past desire, though these separate orgasms merely asked, beyond mind or emotion, for the next one, ad infinitum, and I know too that the physical body can bear only so much. I fall asleep, feeling smoky.

Or perhaps I passed out. It is only when I awake, as the sun is going down, that I become aware of distinct feelings.

He is gone.

I want him, not because he is the sun anymore, but simply so we could laugh at the gifts of divinity we have been given. I desire to smell something other than the jasmine which is now overpowering. I try to remember it. Brine, but human brine, the smell of his sweat traveling on the air. I would have put my fingers on his neck for the first time, and even traveled with my finger to that sacred mouth hidden by the head of his hair, the bones of his skull where the spirit enters us. How did he have strength enough, I wonder, to pull himself up away from me and go?

But I do not have strength enough to maintain these animal wants. When I turn over, I pass out again.

Grigoris, the doctor, was a tall, stooped man, ascetic and homely, with a long, Ichabod Crane neck and watery eyes which swam through gold-rimmed spectacles.

He lifted the bedsheets. He pushed Don's balls gently to the right and to the left.

"Can you feel this? This?" The pressure broke the crust slightly. He felt pain. Something leaked.

They were healing. Terrible-looking.

"Will I be able to fuck?" he asked.

The pale curls on the nape of Grigoris's neck jiggled. Grigoris was scared, he saw. The doctor had a heart tender as meat.

"Will I be able to fuck or am I castrated?" The words squeezed out of his throat louder than he intended.

"No. No," said the doctor. "Castration means taking the testes. This is a massive assault to the organs. It all depends on how extensive the damage is."

So that's how it is, he thought.

He could see Grigoris, the doctor, fucking; he would be one of these deeply inhibited, totally committed heterosexuals, an intellectual who picks an intellectual, some shy, wool-smelling, inhibited girl student, his replica, and waits ten years before doing it in some terrible place like a coal cellar or urine-soaked doorway, getting it off sweat-soaked but standing, his pinched emotional life having rendered him violently awkward but once having started not being able to stop, repeating it inordinately, repeating it inappropriately, pumping his acne-covered face into the girl's neck in time to his prick, sobbing with love, and even then not limp, stumbling back to the library to tremble and study, a phallic iconophile like all steeple-people, poor stele-haunted, cock-ridden male-kind.

In the blackness of sleep he accepted the charge laid on him.

"You can use my thirty-thirty," offered Theo. Theo was awed, even frightened at his brother's courage. He shrank from him. He stared at him from odd places like thresholds and the windshields of the junk cars.

He knew the .30–.30. He had shot it out back of the shed at trees, his eye and arm magically lethal. He remembered one tall maple which did not change expression, shuddering only slightly when the blast tore through its trunk, exploding shreds of its bark. It kept on standing, looking at him.

"Get rid of." Why were he and Theo so literal? Why did they not consider the other possibilities? Because the veterinarian was a decadent evasion of the difference between animals and humans. Now there was a new litter of eight puppies and Leo suckled them back of the Frito's truck. Philo evaded him. Theo went so far as to back down, pleading: "You don't have to do it." But it was his dog. He would kill it. Gratuitously, he accepted the mantle.

But not with Theo's .30–.30. It was a matter of honor not to kill Leo with a family gun. He borrowed Tyrone Odom's .22.

"Hey, Leo, come on, boy!"

Leo jumped up from the puppies, overjoyed to take a walk.

"You stay with the puppies," he ordered Theo, "until I get back."

He headed for Merritt Mill Road, as if black people would understand shooting a dog better than white people. Eleven years old. He held the gun like some unimportant stick. Leo galloped, looking now and then to his face, tongue slung into the air joyously. And now and again turned back toward where he had left the puppies which they would sell later. Suspecting nothing.

He knew where to aim, at that small hole formed by the two legs at the back of his neck. The medulla oblongata. He could have made him heel or sit, and shot him point-blank, but he could not push his betrayal that far. He had no feeling that he was going to do it until he did. Leo was ahead of him walking along. He aimed. Just as he was about to pull the trigger, the dog looked back and for a second of incredulity his eyebrows questioned him and his lips lifted off his teeth. Before the shot he uttered a horrible whine and took off.

It missed and hit him in the back of the spine. He screamed, sprayed upward, a crazy bolt of fur, and fled spastically through some weeds into a ditch and underneath a ghetto house. Don chased him, holding out the gun to kill him dead and right.

"Hey, what you doin' with that yeah gun?" cried a man, running out on his porch.

He skidded down the dirt, aiming. Leo was cowering under the porch next to a chewed-up green-and-yellow plastic scooter. But, seeing, the dog fled yelping down the row of houses and disappeared.

"This yeah's a peacubble neighborhood!"

It was pitch-black. He screamed waking in a great sweat, thinking it was night.

"I'm killing my dog!" he shouted, beside himself.

Zoe ran in. She was wearing a short denim skirt and a cotton blouse and she threw her arms around him to comfort him. She rocked him like a child, repeating some word over and over, and he felt the voltage of her energy ingesting every decibel of his loss. He had never found Leo. Never found any furry stiff to confirm death.

When he grew calm, he opened his eyes and looked at her in wonder, thinking: Who is this human being holding me in its arms? Why should it do this? Slits of light penetrated through a venetian blind which had been closed. It was not night. It was noon. He looked up from the physical embrace into the speechless edge behind her amber eyes. She had little to do with the Face, this new Zoe, his accomplice. From now on, what he knew of her and she of him was in the context of this moment, the wound he had first evaded in her and which she now nursed to life.

He thought about how he needed a gun for when they went for Cora and the irony of what made him practical at last was not lost on him.

The next day I do not rise till noon. There is no sign of him. There is no sign even when the sun begins to go down in the late afternoon. I am starving. I go to the sea to swim, but I do not stay long, for he must come soon.

When I return to the courtyard, he is there.

"Pack your bags," he orders me. "You must leave here." There is not a trace of acknowledgment. He has brought me bread and cheese.

"Why?"

"Because something's up. I don't know what. Maybe I have made them remember you and now they want you."

Who wants me? His use of the word *they* puts it into my mind that he is deceiving me, that he may be acting in behalf of Hadjis or perhaps of someone else. I sit down on a stone in deliberate disobedience. I eat the bread and a large piece of the cheese. I swallow. I want to ask him contemptuously, "Whose instructions are you following now?" But one look at his face and I see the sun flaring out of it. He is in earnest.

I begin slowly, methodically dismantling my Robinson Crusoe existence. Putting my clothes, my shoes, the mask and snorkel which are now mine, back into the suitcase. But I pack in my own way, carefully, gently, still retaining that habit from my past life.

He watches for a while. Then he says, "I will be back for you in three hours."

"Why?" I ask. "Why not now?"

"Because we will be seen. It must be after dark. Past darkness when everyone is dead to the world."

I am packed, about to close my suitcases. He is gone. It is my last chance to escape. To escape all of them: Hadjis, the police, or whoever it is here under whose hegemony he operates. The timing is just as I had planned it: to leave at sunset, arrive upon the secret beach at night. To wait for moonrise, which I know will not occur until two in the morning, and to begin then, so that I shall be on a road past Hora when morning breaks. I will then put on my dress, and perhaps I can catch a ride in some tourist's car, some truck, before the authorities know. Wily, I can leave him a note: "I do not wish to risk your life or the welfare of your family."

Michalis picked the phone up, and Zoe said, "It's go." She was using this bastard-American-astronaut-deteriorated language from a pay-telephone in HEN, she told him, the YWCA on Amerikis Street. He knew the purr of the fourth gear where her being was floating on Lampris's escape, the details taken over by fate. Was she wearing a black wig? He felt something strange in her tension, tight and deep as rocks on the sea's floor. A recklessness in her voice.

He asked her about the weather.

"Sunny, hot, eighty-nine degrees," she told him.

He asked if she had been to their favorite café. No. About their friends: Bebe?

"She's grown fat," she answered.

Andreas?

"He's fat too. Making money."

But there was something she was leaving out.

All those alien's questions he asked her, jealous that she was there instead of him, hearing her disillusion, eaten up with love for her. He rubbed his chin, felt the sweat, though it was only fifty-one degrees in Paris and raining, and he whispered his love for her.

"I love you, *agapi mou*," said her familiar voice. "Don't worry about me."

For the next three days the Lampris affair was going on. He could feel it. The whole household was built around it. There was an inordinate amount of laughter and gaiety alternated with hushed interludes.

At first a blackness enshrouded him. He could not breathe. He had fever and he found himself outside his head beyond the blackness in some perimeter far away from his body, far away even from the earth, looking at himself and what he had experienced. He was numb.

Zoe brought papers to his room and worked at the desk. He looked at her, too, from far away, accepting her presence as a stranger for whom he felt little, save curiosity. Everything was supernaturally clear and destined. Every step he had taken, every thought he had thought from the moment her face had fused with his in the aluminum water fountain, had led to this fact of Adonis.

Male genitals are complex discriminators. Balls, root-testes are the gateposts which determine the elements allowed out onto the highway of the penis. Sperm makes new blood of your blood as oil makes fire. It melds you into the race of men, making you small as an individual to create you large as a race. But your highway also carries the element of water. That is the paradox of potency.

The power by which he had so indiscriminately and parsimoniously made all those bargains with all those cunts: so much semen for so much knowledge of the source, was now stopped in him. His balls were turned to stone. They were gateposts closed in upon him and they guarded the urn he had become now that the altar by which he had worshiped was useless.

He saw this clinically. But in the darkness he feared the nameless element of water. He feared that he might, his gateposts turned to stone, like a dam, rise and spill over as water. At times he wanted to be dead. But then something in the room would change.

She brought him a slice of tiropeta. It was noon. He was not hungry.

"But I make the best tiropeta in the world!"

He turned away.

"Try. You must eat."

He looked in her eyes and believed he saw an emotion kin to his. It was not whether he needed to be unlocked of the Goddess or whether Cora needed to be freed. The question was one and the same. It was that you couldn't get a person into such a thing and not get them out.

So he tried to eat. He took each bite studiously. He breathed in once and choked on the crumbs in his windpipe, and his balls hurt as if they were not stone.

He slept a lot.

He woke up—he had dropped off for only a few minutes—and found her looking at him inquisitively. Her expression made him feel that he was in an inner sanctum. He was an outsider in the center of this house. He had no grief, merely the clarity of rightness, no love, no worship, no care, and no indignation left. Outside the door he could hear noises, the clink of dishes, of silver, a rush of low voices, and sometimes he had the feeling that whoever paused and whispered at the door, was careful not to betray one detail.

"They like my tiropeta," she said. "They're gobbling it up!"

They? Who? Was it a slip? He imagined the guard bribed, the automobile scheduled, the whispered password, the plane synchronized, and she, helpless, now that the operation was under way; she could only sit and wait. Was this why he was specially favored? Was it his room into which she escaped from the tension?

He felt she was stepping into his gaze like entering a broken shell. He tried to imagine what she got from him. Some cypress heart betrayed by the Greece of automobiles? Guilt? A new friendship from Esso Country?

He was looking around the apartment, and she followed his gaze, as if she were trying to identify herself by what he saw. It was rich, even pretentious, as though a stage designer or gallery-owner had stolen the starkness of peasant walls to justify the gold-embroidered upholstery of the Louis Quatorze chairs, the patterns of the Braques, the Panasonic sound system, its gold brocade stretched against mahogany, cantilevered at angles from the ceiling.

"Who does this place belong to?" he asked.

"A friend. Georgopoulou."

"I know that, but I don't mean who. I mean what."

"An opera singer." She laughed ruefully, as if she defied connection with such a way station.

Certainly the rhythm of the goings-on was at odds with the elegance. The balcony overlooked an open-air movie theater, its blank, cement screen adorned with laurel forming the blind wall of an apartment house lined with cypress trees. Across the street stood a massive, bulging church. The people he heard came and went at all hours, disregarding night and day. He knew it was an encampment whose equipment, from typewriters to sleeping bags, could be folded up and taken away at a moment's notice, like nomads' tents.

"Have you told Michalis about me?" he asked.

"How?" She was stalling or testing him.

"By telephone. Or by the short wave."

"No."

"Why not?"

"I am used to automony."

Unsatisfactory answers. But it made clear to him the distinction between his goal and hers. He blocked out all thought of the Lampris affair. He did not want to know. He wanted to know only about Cora.

That evening, while she was out of the room, he got up and walked around. He did exercises.

She walked in with a meal on a tray.

"What are you doing out of bed?"

"I can't stay in bed. I have to get myself back in shape."

For what? And he thought ironically of the Izmir Finals on May twenty-first.

"Rest, for God's sake, for a few days," she said, setting the tray on the desk. She had brought Coca-Cola for herself. She drank it from a coffee cup. She sat down in the chair at the desk and lit a cigarette. She inhabited her body in a strange way, half-reckless, half-languid, disguising the quickness of her movements and thoughts. He caught her gazing over the brim of the cup at him. She was tiptoeing around his dead center. Was it his impotence that attracted her? Or did she smell his obsession, the single-minded white heat that was crystallizing, forming a pearl out of what had once been Cora? He felt she had a desire to tame him, to find that hard core, or what she believed to be the Greek heart of him. He felt as if she were living off this dead center of him. What was it?

He saw then. It was the newness of his despair. She recognized in him her own cry, and she wanted to make him cry it, circling like a gull. This was the only thing that was keeping her alive.

But my mind can support neither the insult to my experience nor to Elias's sacred offering, so I go to spend my last hours in the church. I face the wooden icon, and I speak to it, the first words I have ever addressed to it out loud. I thank him for the fire he has given me in which was wrought this opportunity to participate in one of the fiercest harmonics of life's existence. I am assailed by fears and doubts which I recognize to be human. I pray to Elijah that his vision remain with me and with Elias, and then I take a sprig of the jasmine which now begins to saturate the world, place it on the iconostasis of Jesus Christ and ask him to leave us. I even speak aloud to him, acknowledging that were it not for him, the church would not have been built. "But let it be a world now which has no need of you anymore."

I go back to await Elias.

That night while he was alone, a sad, dark girl came to bring him some tea. In contrast to her black hair, she had extremely white skin and pale lilac eyes behind pink harlequin glasses.

"Where is Zoe?" he asked.

She did not answer. He took the steaming tea.

"Will she come?"

She nodded. Her fingers were translucent as milk glass. She watched him drink. She made creepy, sympathetic gulps every time he swallowed, and she gave off a sweet, damp, sticky smell.

"Soon?" he joked.

She nodded again.

"When?" he baited her. He was repelled by the harlequin glasses, her smell, and her extraordinary beauty.

But she did not answer. She merely smiled, and when he had finished, she took the cup and left.

An abhorrent sensation lingered in the room. He felt vague terror. He wanted Zoe. In fact, Zoe was the only thing that was real to him. Their relationship was a passion, like love. It was compounded by the fact that she—or they?—did not want him to know what was going on, any more than he wanted to know, and he began to be filled with curiosity. He desired to confiscate her out of the Lampris operation—the Lampris operation was the lie—to get at the truth of her. But what was that?

About four that afternoon she came. He was half-asleep. He opened his eyes in a state of calm, like a mollusk, his pearl-colored hardness of purpose secreted in his shell. From her expression, he suspected something had gone wrong.

Her face was white, strained, and the circles were deep under her eyes. She walked with her arms akimbo; her skirt was too skimpy and in the half light from the small lamp she looked unwieldy and large of limb, like a kangaroo. As she looked at him, he saw something break in her eyes like a burst dam. She threw her hair back in a gesture which made the shape of movement inside her bad posture seem graceful. She threw some things she was carrying—clipboard, keys, a Samsonite case—on the desk, lit a cigarette with a lighter, and exhaled as if she had made a decision.

"Don't tell me anything. I don't want to hear one thing!" he said in a threatening voice.

She looked stricken.

"What's the difference between an American and a Greek?" he asked to divert her.

"What?"

"An American forgets he's an animal because they clean the shit off the eggs for him. A Greek cleans the shit off the eggs because he knows he's an animal."

She took a drag of the cigarette with only a hint of a smile.

The core of their relationship, their embrace, was a duel, a holding operation, strength for strength.

"You should stop smoking," he went on relentlessly. "You'll die at a young age."

She smiled coolly. He tried other subjects. He asked about Tennessee. But the question was too far away from the tension. So, as a joke, he began insulting her.

"You like expensive things, don't you?"

"What expensive things?"

"Leather. Cowhide. You carry around that leather purse. Best leather there is. And look at that Samsonite." She cocked her head at it with mock admiration. "And a gold fountain pen. You're nothing but a filthy capitalist snob passing yourself off as a revolutionary."

She broke down and laughed.

The forbidden universe of their exchange loomed over their conspiracy. Was she grateful to him for stopping her? It was what they did not tell each other that counted. When he thought of what he knew, he felt that she was blind, and he was sorry for her blindness, greater than his own, which made what was going to happen terrible. She was about to become the servant of the cosmic. Everything he had imagined when he had first met her: that mission against death when he would become human at last, was about to take place.

She sat down and took some apples out of her purse. She began peeling. Her motion was quick and deft and she kept the cut ribbon intact, watching it grow longer, thinking about something. He remained silent not to interrupt her.

"Tell me about my mother," she said at last in a shy voice. "How did she look?"

He felt the same suction on his skin as when her mother had asked about her. Her eyes hung on every nuance. He had seen photographs, he told her. He described how she had looked at thirteen. He quoted what her father had said. As he talked, he felt close to her. He felt that he was beginning to know her.

"Why don't you telephone them?" he asked.

"The phone is tapped."

He kept silent. He had to keep it peripheral. He did not want to skirt too close for fear he would find out something about the Lampris part.

"It's an irony," she went on. "If you call from Greece, they're liable to make a trace."

"Even from a pay phone?"

"You never know. Besides, I don't go out now."

Was she really revealing nothing? He doubted her. He knew the multifaced life of the fugitive.

"It's an irony," she repeated, "that I can talk to my mother any time from France. In France, we don't have to worry about a tap. Not until things are finished." She looked directly in his eyes. "Ah, in seventy-two hours, I'll—" and she broke off.

He could only believe that the slip was deliberate, that she wanted him to know the timetable. Was Cora included? Forty-eight hours for Lampris, twenty-four for Cora? Or the reverse? He felt jealousy, reasonless and sharp. He did not want her to think of the Lampris affair; he wanted her to think only of Cora.

Yet he felt embarrassed, as if the forbidden had broken through inadvertently. He even felt she was attacking something hypocritical in him. And at the same time he felt opened up.

"Are there many of you?" he asked in a low voice.

"Many," she said, keeping it general. "From cobblers to opera singers, as you see. Lots of people from the arts, of course. But most people are afraid. You cannot expect people to lose their jobs or health, or to die."

At that moment there was a knock at the door. She reared nervously like a horse.

A man's voice said, "Zoe."

She put the apple on the table and left. The door was ajar. He heard their voices but could not make out what they said.

When she returned, she pulled the door till the latch clicked. She picked up a section of apple on the point of the knife, holding it out to him.

"What I was about to tell you before you showed how little you trust me—"

"But I *do* trust you, Zoe," he said quickly.

"—was that they have located Cora."

The silence raised the hair on the back of his neck, not the less for his realization of her coolness in foiling him than for his thought of Cora.

"She's being kept in a fort off the tip of Messenia, a place they kept World War Two prisoners." She held the rest of the apple, its flesh palpable in her fingers.

She had brought a map. He went to sit next to her at the desk, looking where she pointed. She had "a friend" who worked in the town of Gargalianos, where Agnew came from, taught there in a *frontisteria*, a private school, which taught English for profit. They would visit him. Then they would take a trip to Nestor's Palace.

She put her half-eaten apple on the desk, took the Samsonite case and placed it on his lap.

"Open it."

Inside he saw the pistol.

"You *do* deal in weapons," coolly, but fierce with gratitude. She delivered. He took it out, opened the safety catch.

"It's loaded." Her voice sounded sarcastic.

Now that he had it, he knew he wouldn't use it. It was the same thing as his backhand with which he had defeated Sanchez in Naples.

Inside the case there was a change of clothes and a plastic bag from Condor Air Lines which contained washcloth, toothpaste, and soap. He put the things back in the case and zipped it up. Her arm remained against his. He took her hand, held it tightly, and kissed her.

"You need sleep," he said.

"I never sleep," she scoffed. "I don't need more than three hours a night."

"Who is that girl? The one who brought me tea?" He picked up his apple.

"Aphrodite."

He had known it.

"What's wrong with her?"

"She has no tongue."

He laughed. Pieces of the chewed flesh of the apple sprayed the air.

"She bit it undergoing torture in Corydallos and it got infected and had to be amputated." She said this gravely.

It was this expression of gravity that gave him the clue to what it was he wanted to know.

"I love her very much," she was saying, as if that explained everything. Then she threw her arms around him.

His own arms tightened to hold her in his grip and he breathed her odor of salt and nicotine. They stayed in the embrace for a long time.

It had to do with the head. Turn away from the head. The head was not where the knowledge of God had entered Adam. The head was not where the wound was taken in.

It was the solar plexus. He saw the Chinese mystic and understood the ecstasy in his eyes.

For the power of the Goddess can be understood only when you know how to be killed by her. He wanted his death to be an orgy, the death throes ecstatic. He must gulp death as a demand for holy air. Ex stasis. Pure kinesis, a prodigious, ecstatic upheaval where you, as the dier (whether or not you were germinator, stud, or sacrificial king), swallow heaven. You take in bliss. You take in bliss *before* you are able to understand the new, unfamiliar place; and your last sensation, the ricketing and clicking of your eyes, is the only thing left for the world, because your heart, receiving the wound, arrives in heaven first.

To Tasia, who found Thea Vasiliou's body when she came in from the fields, the familiar human stench of the room was an enormity.

*H*ours pass. It seems to me that I hear strange footsteps in the wind, mechanical and quick. And then it dies. An hour later I hear his shoes scuff upon the paving stones and I rise.

He is filled with the recklessness that he uses against a world with which I am now totally unfamiliar. He picks up both my suitcases, saying in that same familiar bark with which he announced the water an eternity ago, "Follow me." He brushes away my attempt to take the small suitcase.

I follow him up the staircase which leads to the parapet. It leads into the room of the guardhouse at the land corner of the castle. A room I have been in many times. He places the suitcases on the floor, opens a door to an empty air shaft. It is across this air shaft that I have to jump to enter the passageway. He heaves the suitcases over first, hurls them across the six feet. Then he jumps the distance himself, turns, holds out his hand, and orders, "Jump!"

I do this, perfectly aware that the drop, if I fall, will kill me. But he takes my arm in midair, and with a flying tug, propels me in a perfect interval, so that my foot lands squarely on the doorsill.

It is pitch-black.

"Hold on to my shoulder."

For a moment he flicks on his cigarette lighter, just enough to see the way, and, following like a blind woman the propulsion of his muscles, we descend a heavy, hot, earthen stairway which circles and circles. I am glad I cannot see. A half an hour later we are on the rocks at the lip of the sea. There is a boat tied to a pine tree. That was what I had heard.

He puts the suitcase into the bottom, taking care not to let them get splashed by flopping fish. I sit in the bow.

"You caught fish?" I say, amazed.

"Yes." But he pays no attention to my surprise, gives the outboard motor a pull by the rope which sets it into that staccato put-putting that had seemed some quick and nervous footstep to my transition. The waves take us as we head out into the blackness, the moon not having risen yet, but I am familiar by now with all their whimsicalities. I wish I could see where we're headed. But I am lost in the vastness of galaxies. I cannot even distinguish his head. The motor is a mere insect upon space. I smell the gas fumes, despise and forget them.

"Is this your boat?"

"No."

"Why did you go fishing?"

"So I can sell fish tomorrow."

He has contempt for my questions. So I have to figure it out myself. The excuse. What story will he give for my escape? He has been night-fishing.

For an hour, we travel. Then he brings the boat to a coast lit up by the light created behind the mountain. It is the incipient moon trying to pull out of the earth. I long for it, until at once I see that it is a race against its light. He ties the boat, pulls me out in one jump. I have become light on my feet. A motorcycle is there. He ties the suitcases on the back, orders me on. I straddle it. For the first time I straddle a motorcycle, pulling my dress up to my thighs, and with a motion as abrupt as when he had started the motor of the boat, he guns the vehicle until it whines in the night. It is a big one with a German motor.

For a half an hour I hang on, the sky hurling the stars past my hair as I push myself against his back, the shriek of the pistons slamming our bones like hammers. I do not like the sensation. It has too much hate, too many foreign bodies, too much metallic matter mixed with the fire. I prefer to wing, without such a jagged knowledge of earth.

When the moon pushes out of the mountain on our right above the olive heads, he swears. I retreat. I have contempt for such freneticism. We are plummeting into a valley and from then on we wind around the next mountain, past shrines, past water faucets where gypsies camp, to the first vestiges of human habitation that I have seen in weeks. We climb in tiers into an ugly town, the pale faces of the houses gaping upon us blankly. In the shadow of a big stone schoolhouse he stops, motioning me into the shadow. He cuts the motor. For a moment, his head bent, he listens to the spark of silence, I realize he can hear, supernaturally, because of the talent of the moon.

Beckoning, he leads me down a stony lane, through rivulets of water from the outside spigots, under the black shadows of the bodies of trees, until we come to a portal in the unforgiving walls which block us out.

He lifts the latch.

"Where is this?"

"My house."

"But—"

The crow of a rooster cuts me off. Is it dawn? No. It flaps its wings, restive in some outside building. He locks the gate behind me and tells me to follow. I follow the suitcases bobbing in his grip, up a rotten, creaking stairway.

He whispers, "It is the last place anybody would ever look for you. Would they believe I would be fool enough to bring you to my own house?"

The door squeaks. He mimes me to be quiet, points to his mother and father's room, and takes me into the largest room in the house, which will be my room from now on. The bed is made. The moon, streaming through a crack in the closed portal, shows me a ghostlike wardrobe and large bare walls upon which hang the photographs of ancestors in fezzes. I smell livani.

Something coughs.

"The horse," he says, pointing to the floor. And when I listen through the cracks I hear its heavy breathing.

"Welcome to my house," he says, setting the cases down. "It is yours."

Abruptly, he leaves me. I hear the key grind outside. I listen. Yes, he is gone. I hear the portal gate open and shut again, and the sound of his footsteps dying away in the darkness. I listen for the start of the motorcycle at the end of the lane, where he left it. But nothing.

All about me are the thick sounds of night-breathing, the heavy silence of the moon-crowned town. And there is nothing now to do but to go into the bed.

How long has it been since I have been in a bed? The sheets smell of wheat grain, and the softness is as dizzying as the sea while I am falling to sleep.

Later on, far away in the darkness, I hear a sharp, metallic sound, and I wake. I see only the top of his head in some dusky light. And then the bed is filled with his weight and his brine. Suffocating, I turn away. He lies behind me, his arms encircling me like wings enticing me from the smoke of my sleep. He does not touch the surface of my body. But I feel the air from his hands. He is circumscribing the shape of my body in the air. My surfaces distend for his touch. At the first stroke, he barely touches my breasts—my nipples incrassate. The blankets are gone. He takes me the way he took me in the sun, but with larger, increasingly larger and profounder explosions, until at last, exhausted, we are ready to fall insensate into sleep.

"Where were you?" I ask.

"I had to return the boat to the fishing village where I got it."

"Then you walked back to the motorcycle?"

"Yes. And in two hours I shall go to sell the fish."

"Where?"

"I will hawk it in two or three villages in the mountains. And you will be asleep here. In the afternoon, I shall return. Do not be afraid. I have told my father and mother, and they will not disturb you."

"What will they think?"

"They will think nothing."

"They will think what you tell them to think?"

"They are free to think what they want to think. They will think that it is merely life."

The feeling of repugnance continued to dog him. He was caught in contrary emotions. At times he avoided thought. He dreaded the element of water. He feared lest Aphrodite come in his room again, but he did not tell Zoe, for it was her love for Aphrodite that he distrusted, was repelled by, being by extension the same thing as her passion for him. And he longed to deny it. But he needed Zoe, because she was his only link to reality. When she was in his room, he dreaded the moment she would leave. When she was not there, he waited for her to come.

He had not seen her since morning, and now it was late. Getting dark. He had a premonition that Aphrodite would come in that moment, so he did not turn on the light. If she thought he was asleep, she would not wake him. He had no idea of the time. Out the window, past the blank movie screen, the church was lit, and he saw people all dressed up going in.

He fell asleep and dreamed of the Aphrodite of Milos. She was alive, and instead of being armless, she was tongueless. A voice, which was supposed to be Zeus's but was really Philo's, said: "Which is to be a hero? To know the risk you take and in taking it suffer? Or merely to suffer?" The tongueless Aphrodite tried to answer but couldn't. Philo was prompting her, saying, "The first has two assumptions: one, that you *can* know the risk, but of course you can't; two, that you believe in cause, effect, and good result." The tongueless Aphrodite grew so perturbed at this prompting that her marble turned into flesh, which grew red, whose veins in neck and temple popped. After a terrible effort, she let out a sound which he recognized as the final "doo" of the rooster, and he woke up.

The questions were wrong. He had the feeling fate had turned full force upon him because he had been *trivial* in seeking the Goddess. With thought, with will, like a course in anthropology with a sex lab. Even as he thought it, he was framing new questions for Aphrodite: "What did it feel like when they cut it out?" But that was not the right question either, and he imagined them making her look at it, held up between some strange thumb and forefinger in the air. "Why did you do it? Is *anything,* anything on earth, worth having your tongue cut out for?" No. Nothing on earth. But if she came this minute, he would study her assiduously, as he had studied Thea Vasiliou. His mind was sharp; his will was good. Embrace the loathed; do not repudiate.

He remembered an American secretary he had seduced in Calcutta in 1967, a civil service GS-7 with the USIS, who had said during their postcoital discussion of the starving millions: "Mother Teresa is a horror. She actually loves people to be diseased and dying so she can pick them up and thrive on it. They call it sainthood, but in my book it's evil." And he, desperate for a palliative even then, countered with a fit of patriotism: "What about the Phallus of Liberty? Don't we offer refuge for your sick, your huddled, and your poor?" "Well, at least we don't call it Mother America!" she had cracked.

Through the window he heard the chanting of a liturgy. Oil lamps flickered in the church making its windows jump like heartbeats. He heard her name being intoned three times, Cora Ellison, Cora Ellison, Cora Ellison, and it took him more than a minute to realize they were singing the Kyrie Eleison.

It was about eleven when Zoe came in.

"She has been moved from the fort to a private house," she said, turning on the desk lamp.

He got up from the bed.

"That's bad then, isn't it?"

"No. Curiously, that makes it better. We know exactly where it is."

She had a hand-drawn map on her clipboard. "See?"

He followed where she pointed. There was a field here, the sea was in this direction. You approached from an alleyway leading from a school. They could leave the car here where it would be mistaken for a tourist's on a visit to the museum.

For a long time they talked. The only thing she did not know was *when*. He understood tacitly it was to take place *after* Lampris.

She had organized it in detail. They were to drive to Gargalianos in one car. They were then to take her friend's car from Gargalianos. They would park where she had pointed. They would walk to the house and get her. Then they would drive to the village of Roumanou, where they would leave the car for the Gargalianos friend to pick up. A boat would be waiting to take them to Zakynthos, from where another boat would take them to Brindisi.

Since they did not know what to expect at the house, they would assume that it was as ordinary as going to any house to find a friend.

"We will knock," she said, "and when the door opens we'll ask for Elias."

"Elias?"

"Elias, the name of the keeper of the fort, whose house she is in."

"And if there are police?"

"There are no police. No guards. The police don't know where she is."

"You sure?"

She scoffed and went on: "We will not say her name until we speak to Elias. There's no reason to expect resistance. They may lie, deny she's there, but the element of surprise is on our side."

"And if they lie?"

"We must be persuasive, but not use force."

If they resist, he thought, he *would* use the gun.

"You will be carrying a gun?"

"No," she said, "I won't carry a gun."

"Why not? Have you killed someone?"

"No, but I shot a man in the leg once, and I won't use one again."

The words were banal, borrowed, even artificial. They did not belong to them, but to some formality of the medium. The nexus of their intimacy being built on distance, each respected the payload of the other's life: "I don't know why you do what you do, but I love you for it." The thought of automobiles, guns, maps, houses, assaults thrilled him *because* of their artificiality, and the thought that his life depended on them was unreal. It had been inevitable since Naples.

"You're dead on your feet," he said.

"No." She brushed back her hair with one hand.

"Come on, Zoe. Lie down."

"Ah, *matia mou.*"

To his surprise, she took his hand and lay down on his bed. He lay next to her staring down, studying her. Her eyelashes were very black, and the flesh of her lids as pale as the eggs in the coufetta, alive though, encapsulated amber. He speculated on the Face and wondered at its disappearance in this warm, breathing face. He wanted to know, did she believe in God? If not, how could she risk her life?

She slept only a few moments, and when she awoke and found him there, she put her arms slowly around him, and they clung together in silence.

"Do you love Cora Ellison?" she asked.

"Yes," he said.

She moved to get a cigarette. Her purse fell open on the bed and during her motion of striking the gold lighter, a small plastic card fell out of her wallet. It was the size of a BankAmericard, but it was a picture of a stained-glass Omega.

"What is this?" he asked.

"The symbol of the Resistance."

"You carry it around with you?"

"Yes."

"But it's willful. What if they catch you?"

She shrugged.

"What does resistance mean?" he asked.

"Conscience."

So we are all in the habit of ethics.

"Listen, Adonis *mou.* I'm going to tell you something. Remember it for the rest of your days." She began quoting. The words were like the automobiles, guns, maps, houses, assaults, but she had that look that people have when they have committed something to memory. The words were George Mangakis: "We are no longer . . . simple . . . not a belief in a single truth—not because we no longer have any truths to believe in, but because in our world we do not experience these truths as absolute certainties. We seek something more profound than certainty, something more substantial, something that is naturally, spontaneously simple . . . hope . . . this hope concerns our humanity which cannot be annihilated no matter how much it is persecuted on all sides: this is why there can be no purpose as serious, as noble, as to commit ourselves to its safeguard, even if we must inevitably suffer for it. A humiliated people either take their revenge or die a moral and spiritual death. In other words, you situate the meaning of your existence in this strangest, this most dangerous and unselfish of all struggles which is called Resistance."

He was touched but weary. What struck him was her knowing it by heart, but she was walking around in the forest of *Fahrenheit 451,* reading.

After she left, he thought how strange and natural that people use the word "hope" when things are going worst, and he fell asleep where she had lain, the bed still warm with her, knowing that Lampris was probably doomed, the word "noble" flitting against the glass.

Something woke him up. Zoe had returned, and believing him to be asleep, was tiptoeing. She looked at him a second and sat down at her desk. She was leaning forward, her chin on her hand. Her profile, polished by the slit of light from the half-open door, was a perfect semblance of despair. Having let so much time pass without speaking, he continued to watch her with eyes wide-open.

A shadow passed the door. It was Aphrodite. Zoe did not know she was there. She came into the room, one arm outstretched. When she reached Zoe, she stroked her hair. Zoe turned and leaned forward against her. Aphrodite lowered her cheek to the silhouette of Zoe's cheek. For a long time they rocked back and forth in this position, like a ballet.

He felt strangely excited, for they were attached to each other by that network of arm and cheek in the same spectrum and with the same delicate grace as the tangerine-lace fish. He felt he was swimming in the sea. What was it of Zoe that had released poor, creepy Aphrodite from albino mothhood?

From this moment my life becomes confinement and explosion. Where before I ranged sky, sun, and sea in command, now I am bound by dark walls. It is like living in a photographic negative. Everything is the reverse of what it has been. The scowling, barbaric valor of dead strangers is my jailer. From infinite horizons of space, from dazzling light I am reduced to the peeking light which sneaks through the closed portals of the windows. Instead of rocks I am surrounded by embroidery, buttons, and the colored, raggy scraps of cloth which his mother has woven into country rugs. I live entombed in the center of this agricultural village, locked in, guarded by these two ancient people whom I have never met. Everything is soft and thick. Instead of wild hard thyme and brine I am surrounded by the smell of smoke-fires, cooking, the incense of churches, eggs, and manure. I am in an atmosphere thick with breathing, and with only a hint of the sky above.

I wake. Is it noon? I am numb with luxuriance. I am an egg in a nest. I am warm, and I look at the gray light which hints the flaming world outside. My room is large and dignified. The ancestors keep watch. The ceiling is made of ancient beams which support a trellis of bamboo upon which the tiles are fastened by mud. At least four feet of stone separate me from the outside. There is a large table, a chair. The floor is rough and silvery with age. From below comes the soft cough of the unexercised horse. Some other animal responds with a stamp. I listen to them. Where before my compatriots have been the shrieking starlings and the crabs and fish which lived the endless prehistory of sea-depths, now I am with animals tamed by man.

I rise. My body feels the weariness of my escape from the light to the dark. How many hours has he been gone? I look through a hole in the floor to see if I can locate the eyes of the horse. I cannot. I see nothing below, for it is dark, or grayish. I see nothing but some bags, hogsheads, and a scythe. I have to pee. Through the hole which I have just looked to find the horse, I aim my pee-pee. I hear it sprinkle domestically upon some earthen floor where the horse urinates. Swish, it splashes against straw. I lift myself from my haunches and go back to sleep.

Later in the afternoon he comes. I know it is he. I recognize his footsteps. There are voices. Hens cackle. And then all becomes silent.

An hour later the key turns in my lock. I rise up from the bed to greet him. He bears the sun with him. It sparks from his green eyes, and all the wind, the dust, and the strife of the road is etched in the cruel lines of his face. He undresses to his undershirt and pants, folds his dusty clothes neatly on the chair. Standing by the bed he picks up my hand. He looks at it, his eyes traveling up my inner arm to the concave of my elbow. For a moment, it is as if he were making some kind of choice. Then he buries his mouth, his chin in my forearm. He lets my arm go and gets into bed, climbing above me to the space against the wall. He goes to sleep at once.

It is my monstrous privilege to watch him sleep. Monstrous, because my eye, now taught by the sun, dares everything. Though my gaze is as unfettered and less human than the barbaric scowls of his ancestors, it understands nothing. I do not understand this man. Despite his B.V.D.'s, the bulge of his sex against the white cloth, he has no quality of nakedness. He is as tight as his curls. His muscles spiral upon each other under the smooth skin. His wrinkles are an iron grille. He may be made of scales or armor. He is as dry and hard as a snake. He makes no noise breathing. His nose is as sharp as a beak. And the jutting of his lower lip, a wolf-trait, keeps guard even from sleep. There is only one thing that hints of the mystery behind this armor. Below his eyelids are bedded something as alive as animals, and his eyelashes curve, as dark and shiny as a woman's.

I do not feel love, for nothing since my queendom of air and sky can chasten me to those longings and rushes that belong to mankind. The one emotion that has not been bleached out of me is the sense of wonder. I am struck with wonder for this species of man-god beside me. All the more so because of the liquid seeds of eyes secreted behind guard.

I honor his work, his travel, his wardenship of me in the castle, his hawking of the fish. I honor the hours he has not slept. And I am his guard now against the world of waking. As he is submerged in the world of sleep,

I am like him when I was immersed in the underworld of the sea. How did he have the strength to go all those hours without sleep, to cover the tracks of my escape from the castle?

Yet, asleep or awake, I have no true interest in his psyche. He might as well be a god or a wolf. But not a man. I am not interested in his egoism, his pride, nor even in his love for me.

I have the pride of my guardianship of him in the waking world. I have wonder for the beast that I guard. And I have my knowledge of his powers now, since he has become my one contact to the world of the sun which I commanded when I was his prisoner in the castle.

I realize in these hours of watching him sleep that my freedom is more boundless than before. Now, detached from my body, it roves an endless night in the heart of people and animals. I am out of sight, unknown, yet living in the midst of people. I am not murdered. I am not even prisoner. I am guard! And for his sake I cannot let my presence be known!

At sundown he awakes. Without a word he rises, dresses, and leaves the room. I hear the talking again. Then again the silence.

I arise. I understand that my moment has come. I am to be introduced. I am to receive my orientation to the new life.

The door opens again, and an orange light penetrates. I stand in the middle of the room. I see that my door opens to a hallway which leads onto that rickety balcony where I entered so long ago. The house looks to the west. I see the setting sun.

The old people enter my presence, a fat old woman with one eye and wattles. She groans at each footstep, and when she approaches, I see that she has brought a stool upon which she sits. She raises her head and looks at me. And I see that his face is hers, for she has also the lip of the wolf. She winks her eye in a hard stare, and unexpectedly chortles, rising up, with her hand outstretched to me, conspiratorial:

"Welcome to our house, *kyria mou*," she says, wagging her wattles.

The old man is gentle with silver-white hair and liquid brown eyes. He too welcomes me to the house. He is sacred and debonair at once, and he knows a world which neither the son nor the mother knows.

He says, "You shall feel like a daughter in this house," and gives me a look from his brown eyes which signifies that I inhabit a place which has no name in modern life.

We sit down to a meal the old woman has prepared, steaming fish stew and sliced tomatoes. There are dark olives in a bowl. The old people watch me eat with a curiosity in their eyes to match the strange sensation I feel at sitting once again at a table.

I am not married to Elias; yet I am his wife.

I am above Elias, because I am a guest, a stranger, in fact, a queen, who shall be waited on.

My power is threefold: First, I am educated, what they call *morphomeni*. I read books, the privilege of men or the well educated. I have read many books, painted many pictures. I know more than Elias, and more even than his father, whose refinement and education have failed to save him. Second, I am a foreigner. I am privy to a great world which controls destinies. And, third, I am the danger with which they must live.

"You see this spot?" says Elias afterward. "You are never to go beyond this. You are not to go out on the balcony in daylight, for the neighbors can see from their balconies. You can eat in the *kouzina,* but we will close the blinds when you do."

"But the sun," I say. "I must see the sun."

"The earthquake room," says Kyrios Elias to his son.

There is a confabulation. The three speak excitedly together.

Conspiratorially, they lead me into the hallway, and from there into a farther room whose walls are broken. On two sides the holes give forth to the view of a field and far below the mountain, the shining sea.

"The walls of this room fell down during an earthquake," says Elias. "This is where you may see the sun. But never step over this line"—he draws a line past the bags of wheat and hay, past a clothesline hanging with herbs and raisin candies like cigars—"for your head will be visible." Kyria Maria and her children live in the next house. They must never suspect my presence.

I fall into a state of hilarity.

"Anything you want, anything, you are to tell my mother," says Elias.

The first thing I request the next morning is a bath. I am not accustomed to being waited on, but now my tenure behind portals of secrecy demand obeisance to service. The mother brings a washtub and fills it with steaming water and cold, with oil, and with sweet-smelling olive-oil soap. For a whole hour I luxuriate. I bathe in sweet water for the first time since my new life. I wash my hair. I go out to the earthquake room to drv it in the sun.

Every whim of my existence is attended to by the two old people, and when I try to help the mother, she draws her breath in with a sharp, electric sound.

"You will be seen! You will be seen!"

Late in the afternoon Kyrios Elias and the mother bring sweet coffee on a special tray. I take the watercolor paints out of my suitcase. We sit, the three of us, on the special parlor chairs in my salon, and we sip the coffee.

They scarcely breathe as I begin my first watercolor portrait. As the lines of Kyrios Elias's head form, I remember the thundering icon of Elijah in the church. I speak of the icon. Kyrios Elias brings out the Book of Saints and, as I paint him, he reads the story of Elijah the Saint for whom he and his son are named.

A bond gathers between us, and we formulate the mode of behavior in which we will exist during this dangerous tenure. I may paint. I may speak with Kyrios Elias about the saints, about French, about world politics. But I may not cook. I may not sweep.

That night, when the mother is outside in the cookhouse and Kyrios Elias is feeding the animals, I ask Elias, "What happened to my letter?"

"I have it," he says.

"You did not mail it?"

"No. If you want it, here it is," and he goes to the kitchen table and opens a drawer. There, lying carefully next to a sprig of thyme, a pair of shears, needles, thread, a large pistol with corrugated handle, and a pile of ancient coins, is the envelope exactly as I have written it. He puts it in my hand.

"What good is this to me?" I ask. "It must be mailed."

"It cannot be mailed," he says. "No ripples must go out."

Yet he takes the letter back. I sense its importance to him. It is as if, having carried the letter around for two days, he will carry it around forever. It is a talisman of his love for me, all that of me which he knows and cannot have, my former life and my future life.

That evening at the supper table I know that my request for the letter has opened a rift in his mind. He sits abstracted. The mother drops the information first:

The Charybdakises will be told if anyone sees me. All reports get back to the Charybdakises. Who are they? I ask. They are the family who run the town, three brothers and a sister. During the German occupation, one brother was the chief of police. Another ran the monopoly. A third controlled the lands and was the mayor. After the war, a band of hooligans came through the town, collected the mayor and his brother who ran the monopoly and kept them in a room over the town square. Kyrios Elias, who was known to have *andarte* leanings, was the intermediary for the lives of the two Charybdakises. He paid over all the money the monopoly had collected for the lives of the two brothers. But something went wrong during the exchange, and the mayor was thrown off the balcony and killed. Two years later, the chief of police surfaced and threatened revenge. First, he dismissed Kyrios Elias from his job. Then he had him indicted for embezzlement. For the very illegalities that Kyrios Elias had committed for the lives of the Charybdakises, he was now made to pay. They took away his vineyard and threatened him with jail. And it was at this point where I came into the picture, for I see now that in some former time one of the Charybdakises, probably the police chief, had been a henchman of Hadjis, or if not, some cohort of Hadjis who palmed me off on the son of Kyrios Elias. I fit the picture together. Elias was doing it for his father. He did not work directly for the Charybdakises. His job as warden of the *castro* was a part-time affair.

After supper, I begin a portrait of the mother. In the kerosene lamp it is difficult. The lines of her wattles move on the paper.

"What politics do you believe in?" I ask Elias.

"None."

"Do you believe in Papadopoulos?"

"Who is Papadopoulos?"

"Were you an *andartis?*"

"Who were *andartes?* Communists? They said they were Communists, and they come and bam bam bam, they kill all the people with money in the town. Then the people with money kill them, bam bam bam. My father, the peacemaker, crucified by his own peacemaking. And the very people whose lives he saved now want to hang him and use me to do it."

Kyrios Elias listens to his son say this without comment.

"But your father is afraid," I say.

"He is afraid for no reason."

"And you are not afraid?"

"No."

"What do you believe in then? What do you have allegiance to?"

"No human being."

Kyrios Elias's silver brows lace in a delicate scowl over his nose and his eyes glitter far away.

At five-thirty the next morning, when the gray light of dawn peeks in the window and the town awakes, Elias gets out of bed and leaves. The noise of hooves, of donkeys, of carts, and the grinding of tractors screams against the cock-crows, for the people are starting their trek to the fields.

At nine Elias returns. He stands in front of me—I have taken my morning bath, am dressed, and have begun on the picture of the mother again— A scowl and the thrust of his lower lip is the only sign. He holds my letter out with a piece of paper.

"You are free now," he says. "This is a bus ticket to Patras. A bus leaves at ten o'clock. You may take it and deliver this letter to your children in person."

"But how will you explain my escape?"

"I will say you found a secret beach and escaped by sea."

I am startled. Had he known all along?

"But how will I have taken my suitcases?"

"You will leave them here and take only a small woolen bag, with the mask and what you need."

"But the Charybdakises . . ."

"A chimera."

That you kept me for, I think. But I say nothing, and I let him think it is possible. I think of the sacred ceremony of our nights, the turns like an arrow in the flesh. At the same time I think of the country I have come from, the language that I once spoke, and I am leaving a perfection of dumb glory which is sustained by my imprisonment and his danger, for that dead world.

Nevertheless, I follow him to the portal gate, the woolen bag he has given me in hand. Once again we circle each other.

I say to him, "Why do you want me to go?"

"It is you who want to go. It is you who speak of the children to whom you want to send the letter."

He lifts the bar of the portal gate and stands holding it.

"I have not said good-by to your mother and father. Shall I not tell them good-by?"

"No," he says fiercely.

"But they will recognize me, the police, those on the lookout."

"Ah, Cora, no one will recognize you now," he says, and I realize for the first time how I have changed.

In the brilliant sun tears are running down his cheeks. "When you leave my door, I say, 'Cora, my Cora, you are gone from me forever.'"

I am shocked. For the operatic glory of the sun reflecting off his tears and the bargain I make for a few days longer cannot obscure that he is tamed. I cannot bear his human pain.

For his pride's sake I say, "I am not ready. I have not finished the picture of your mother."

And I go back into the courtyard calling for his mother to come out of the cookhouse and pose.

When she came to him it was past one in the morning, and he knew that whatever it was had happened. He had not slept, but had lain wide awake in the darkness. Once the harmonica had played, and there had come a heavy buzz of voices. He knew something was wrong, for there were no more squawks from the equipment. Then the harmonica began again, and someone began to sing.

She took her clothes off one by one until he saw her naked in the streetlights. The next moment she was in bed beside him warm and smooth. Though he touched her eyebrow, now at repose, stroked her hair, her skin, it was she who made love to him; he who lay prone. At first she was gentle, as if he were herself whom she was discovering, tracing the bones of his face, the curvature of his lips. But there was a rage in the control of her hands, and in the reversal of his role he read each stroke, each touch. These hands had caressed every person she had loved, and they had been legion. She was masterful in love, both active and passive, and she made no distinction of sex, or age. But behind the control he felt unassuaged need. Her fingers explored the one they had chosen.

She kissed the corners of his lips, the curve of his chest, the bones of his shoulders. She separated each hair on his chest, according each one a message. She kissed his neck yearningly.

He suspected her of trying to rouse him, to prove once and for all the hegemony of his phallus. He thought: What unregenerate hubris!

But the intensity of her caresses became so splendid that he had awe of them, appreciation, and he understood that something else was going on. She was practicing on his body the litany of their alliance. In each tender, demanding stroke he recognized her rage for their act.

He became aroused. It was not physical. But it was not a mental sensation either. It was the element of water. The oil and fire, unable to go through the closed, stone gateposts, were changing to water. They rose like water as pity and hate, melted him as they climbed toward his heart, distended him in their power. They crushed the question of whys and wherefores. He no longer needed the source.

Even as his emotions spilled into the spiritual sphere, she was somehow abstract, as if the water which had climbed the inside of his body to his heart were released through pores to the surface, or that he had grown speculative breasts and shores which could rise infinitely for her to coast upon. She was his waves and the walls of his mind shores that he could strew at will, making him feel infinite. He thought: So this is what Cora felt like! and recognized that the semen which he had aimed upon the reflection of the moon had come full circle back. But because he could not aim the Presence or travel out from the quay, he became witness to Zoe's passage. It moved up from his center, half-revenge, half-redemption, since one cannot exist without the other, distending him with power, certifying the deed demanded of him. To find Cora was equivalent in a hopelessly small human measure to liberating the Goddess to all men's knowledge. The moment he recognized this, her hunger came unleashed. He lay there while she dug her fingernails into his flesh. Her voracity was frightening. He tightened his hold on her, and he felt he was about to strangle her. She cried, "I pour." He put his hand on her cunt.

"Lampris is dead?" he guessed.

"No, Lampris is free." And she laughed.

Afterward she lay smoking and they exchanged confidences. She said how once she had gone to a certain village in the north. "The people are simple. They are great. You should see the caves where we had the meeting, all lighted with candles. It was beautiful. They're herdsmen, small farmers. They give you their hearts." He noticed her voice had tones like bells in the upper register, and since this was the first time he had noticed it, he reckoned she was happy.

After a while he said, "Go to sleep. We've got to get up early tomorrow."

"Ah, Adonis *mou,* you are relentless, you American bastard." She smiled.

They left at four in the morning. By five they were at the Corinth Canal. They stopped for coffee. She cocked the visor of her cap against the rays of the red-rising sun and looked at the cut in the earth.

"You look too spectacular with that hat."

"Don't be a warthog." She meant worrywart. "I look like any common Italian woman. We're tourists."

She did the driving. It was a small Triumph, and she drove fast, with one hand, chain-smoking, languid. The windows were open and by seven-thirty they had eaten up the first leg of the mountain road beyond Argos. The wind, quite hot, was whipping her sun-burnished hair. In minutes they had covered territory it had taken him and Cora days to traverse. The shape of the act, too, skidded at the top of his consciousness, for it had no connection with what it was. There was a façade of gaiety. It was the reality that was unreal.

The plans had changed slightly. They were not going to use Petros's car, the friend from Gargalianos, but one which had been rented from Germany by a pharmaceuticals company. Another contact.

In addition, they would park outside Elias's house. It fronted one of the east-west streets, though the only door, a small grain entrance, was blocked, and they would have to walk half a kilometer to the parallel street and down an alleyway to get to the entrance.

At Tripolis she took off the hat and threw it into her bag. She looked at him, took his hand and held it. "Sing 'Ta Roda ta Triandafila,' " she said. He sang, feeling the triple entendre, pure melody, no harmonica, no dimensions. For a half an hour they both sang songs.

They were in Gargalianos by ten. The coast was alluvial, fertile. The towns they passed through sprawled against the mountains, dirt roads, stone walls, low stucco houses, and country warehouses. They met Petros at his office.

"Ah, Zoe *mou,* darling!" he cried, wrapping her in an embrace. He was a slight, very ugly man with black kinky hair, moody eyebrows, and a thick nose.

"Meet my friend, Adonis."

"*Harika poli.* Now come, let's go to my place and eat."

He didn't want to go to his place. He wanted to be gone, get the pharmaceuticals car and move.

"Ah, yes, we're starving," cried Zoe.

They left the Triumph parked by a restaurant in the middle of town. Petros took them to his house, a new building. There was a black car parked beyond, an expensive-model Volkswagen. They ate on a balcony in the spanking breeze from the sea. Zoe piled keftedes in her mouth, and she and Petros laughed and chattered loudly. Don felt the pistol not because he would use it, but to remind himself what they were doing. Zoe flung her arms in the air with wide gestures, but she drank only one small glass of retsina. When she finished, she poured a drop of wine on the floor of the cement balcony, like a libation.

"*Lipon, paidia,*" she said. "We'd better get on with the lesson."

It was about the boat. A fisherman, Petros told her. There were no tourist boats in Roumanou, nobody there till July. A friend of his from Kythera, pretty far away, but no matter. And yes, he'd bring the pharmaceuticals salesman over after siesta to pick up the car. Leave it at Tourkakis's. "It's only a stone's throw from the beach."

Petros wrapped her in his arms again, slipping the key of the Volkswagen into her hand.

"Ah, Zoe *mou*, Zoe."

"Take care, *matia mou.*" She was moved.

He drove the last leg. She sat next to him, subdued. The road was full of potholes. They jounced up and down. How cool she had been there, under full sail, attention on everything from jib to ballast. He was afraid of her pensiveness. He looked at her.

"What are you thinking?" he asked.

"Greece, and my mother," she answered saying "mother" with that open voweled "ah" sound that made her vulnerable.

He was thinking of Cora, but did not say so. She turned to look at the map. Below the long loop around the mountain there was a gorge. He drove into the town. There was a sign saying "Museum."

"There won't be a problem if we keep it cool," she said. "We're on a visit, and we're not a threat to him."

"Are you thinking of me? The gun?"

"Turn left here."

He turned left around a huge, peeling stucco church and steered the car down a bumpy thoroughfare, past a square. The sea stretched far below in the distance, the same Messenian Gulf upon which he had looked from Thea Vasiliou's, but from a different angle.

"Zoe *mou*," he said softly. "The last thing I shall ever use is the gun."

"Forgive me, *matia mou*. The contingencies. I was thinking of it being your first time."

He was touched, but he wanted to laugh.

"Here. This is it."

She pointed to a large, old stone house. He parked at the base. It was tall, like a façade except for a low, unpainted door. It was like a citadel with one wooden window below the high tiled roof.

"Let's leave the bags in the car. We won't need them," she said.

"Shall we lock?"

"No."

They walked back to the cross street and through to another dirt street until they came to the schoolhouse, where the alley began. It was a narrow alley with high walls. It smelled of donkey droppings and thyme. At a village faucet, there was an opening where you could see the sea.

At the bottom they came to a portal gate, and she knocked. There was a long wait. She knocked again and an old woman lifted the rusty latch and peeped through.

"*Mana mou*, we have come to see Elias. Is he home?" asked Zoe.

"*Christos kai Panagia!*" whispered the old woman, dropping back out of sight. The old gate creaked open. Inside, in the sunlight of the courtyard, chickens squawked.

Zoe stepped inside tentatively, and he followed. He looked, but the old woman had disappeared. Perhaps she'd fled into the cookhouse. A rickety bulwark of stairs led up the unrelenting walls to a porch, but except for the commotion of the chickens, the *aulis* was empty.

I am sitting on the wheat bag in the earthquake room staring across the furry field to the sea. It is late morning. I remember how I tried, in the *castro*, to hoard the irrecoverable colors of the sky, how I had to rely on my memory. This allied me to the hours in my day. I learned when it was one o'clock as opposed to the hour of noon. By those needle points of sun on the waves. It is past twelve, but the deadness has not yet come upon the sea, the time of glass. Although I am hypnotized, I become aware of something below in the courtyard. It is the chickens. They are squawking. A different signal than I had expected. This stir means someone has come. I go to see. I know how to keep myself just beyond the periphery of eyes, how to be there and yet not seen. It is an invisible line. But when I see Don standing with the woman I recognize immediately as the Face, I step forward.

He saw Cora up through the rotten steps of the stairway, although she looked nothing like his Cora. She was thin as a cadaver, bones. All the fat he had loved was vanished. Gone the lightness, the insubstantiality which had made their lovemaking spiritual, elusive, flimsy as his mother's embrace. Her hair was bleached white, not a thread of black left. Her ice-blue eyes streaked fire out of a skin as hard and brown as a crocodile's.

The frame of her body was so small and old it shocked him. Her shoulders were narrow. Her back was slightly bent. Her arms and legs were the only fleshy part of her left, little brown sacs like wings on her upper arms. Brittle! Frail!

It has happened to her too! he thought, for he would not have recognized her old version, he saw. So that's how it is; we see from where we come.

She started out of the room. The way she moved, the way her arms and legs circumscribed the air was the same old, strange, floating way that belonged to her fathood. It filled him with such a rush of love, the inappropriateness of such movements to this new, condensed version, that he headed for the stairs.

On the porch above there were loud footsteps, but he had started up.

"Don't!" she cried to whoever it was. She was teetering on her legs and her nosebone stood up imperious under the crocodile skin.

But the man—it was Elias—came stamping past her with a Browning .30–30. He paused at the head of the stairs, came down two steps, and took a position so casual that it was at odds with the fierceness of his peasant mustache and the musculature of his bull-body. He propped the rifle on the railing, cradled it through one elbow, and aimed directly down into his face.

"He isn't the people you think. He's the friend I told you about!" Cora cried, raising both arms in the stance of the Goddess. She looked down into his eyes; it was such a straight gaze the thought flashed in his mind that losing her fat had make her able to focus. "I know him!" she yelled.

He wondered how he could have thought her frail a moment ago. Everything condensed and distilled in her. Everything congealed to a white power. "I know him" extended through the tendons of her neck, out the nerves of her arms, passed from her fingers and eyes in a direct transference into him, although she stood distinct, separate, and terrible.

But he kept going upward in a fit of euphoria, for looking up the length of the barrel, seeing her there, he understood that as in the case of Meandrios, humans see *because* the citadel end is blocked.

Beyond or because of my saying: "Don't! A friend!" is Elias's distrust. It is greater than my voice or any woman's voice in warning. Elias acts as if a gun is more reliable than the promise of life or its negative corollary the danger of death.

I know the man toward whom Elias points the gun, but Don is something from the past. He has changed. His olive skin is lighter, his eyes bluer and deader. He has walked a lifetime. How amazing that one can travel an inch and go miles, whereas another can travel miles and go an inch. That is Don. I know him. I know what he thinks. He thinks that he is Adonis. It is irrelevant what he thinks, this almost-knowing which has led him here. Do I need saving?

The gun point moved from his face to his chest, the perfect position for the ultimate wound. But he had no fear. Everything had led to this, where the cake could be sliced and served. He went up a step until he was close enough to reach out and push the barrel aside. There was a deafening blast. He heard the bullet rip the empty air behind him.

It is a roar which splits the skein of space within time. I feel glory—Don's movement trips Elias's finger on the lever, an error which releases the safety—the glory of the Goddess erupted, doing away with all the small dislocations of motive. Triumph without content. It is a great, black-painted laugh. Anybody could have seen from the beginning.

The expression on Cora's face made him turn around. Zoe had dropped down on the courtyard floor, having taken the death that had never been his, despite his daring and dreams.

Minutes pass, during some seconds of which we sway like children in the game of Run and Freeze. Then someone calls out from the next house. I swear I see a look of collusion between Elias and Don, and in the silence— the chickens have been silenced—I see Elias's rifle rise slowly, aiming for a bird splashing upward on wings from the laurel tree. There is a second blast, and Kyria Maria and her children, unable to see the dead woman lying in the courtyard obscured by their grape arbor, follow the explosion of feathers and the downward drop of the bird.

"*Ay na hathisi!*" cries Elias in triumph.

"It took you two shots!" says the youngest.

"Go and get it, Lambroula," Elias tells her. "You can eat it for supper!"

The woman and children run back into their house. A moment later the children run out their back door toward the place beyond the cookhouse where the bird has fallen.

Elias strides past Don, who is bending over the woman, his mouth upon hers, trying to breathe life into her. Elias chops the air with his hand, hissing to his mother, who is peeping out of the cookhouse, "Get back inside!"

She waddles across the courtyard, groaning.

Elias bends by the wall. He picks something up.

"Leave off! She's dead," he barks to Don, holding the bullet between his thumb and forefinger. "Take her in there." He points to the bowels of the house where the animals live.

I see Don lift and carry her. Her legs are jouncing. I see the shiny whiteness of her upper arms flashing like the signals of the sea-waves. I think of the spot on the hay where my pee, aimed through the hole, has fallen, and I rush to tell him not to lay her there.

"We have a car in the street," Don whispers to me. English sounds strange. He lays her on a pile of canvas which they use for drying currants. "There's a door that leads outside."

I recognize the words Vivien said in a dream, and I know I can stay here no longer. Fools! Goddamn fools! The arrogance of all the dreams of nobility which lead them to slaughter!

"What are you doing here?" Elias screams to me, grabbing my arm. He forces me past the woman. I am staring at the hole in her blouse, ringed with faint pink, at the piece of flesh caught on a stick of straw on the canvas. Elias pushes me toward the outside stairs.

"Cora!" Don says.

"I will come, then," I say, although he does not yet realize he has asked, any more than Elias realizes I am going.

Elias follows me strangely with his green eyes as I go up the stairs.

The old woman is sitting on her stool. Kyrios Elias is sitting at the table, lips moving over the Book of Saints.

I hear them below. My present home has been broken apart. I am a kernel laid open to all. Yet I am unseen. There is a bonk. The horse groans. Something scrapes across the cement floor. Something else falls.

My woolen bag is ready, the one Elias packed when he was determined I should go free. Fools! My freedom is mine always and has always been. I walk the four corners of this room, once more the dark heart where I have hid and burned in the night. I say good-by to my two white suitcases at last, and imagine the time past this time when he will take them to the police station.

I hear Elias's footsteps on the stairs. When I turn, he is gazing at me with disbelief, yellow on the periphery of his green eyes.

"It is not safe to stay here now," I tell him. He cannot speak, for though he had not thought of it until I say these words aloud, he knows.

"I will take your cases to the police as we planned," he says.

"Yes," I answer. "And you will hear from me."

"From America?"

"Yes," I tell him, for is that not where I shall be? Where shall I be? Can I speak in geographical terms? I go past him into the room where his mother and Kyrios Elias still sit. I thank them for their hospitality. The mother makes a chuffing sound.

I make sure that the people next door do not spot me going down the stairs. I see the sea once more as I descend. Under the house, the horse looks at me with a baleful eye. Don and Elias have moved the hogsheads. I thread my way through strewn tools, across the cement floor, past an opening where bags of wheat had stood.

"Cora!" cries Elias.

"You will hear from me," I repeat. I do not say good-by.

There is a car parked in the street. The dead woman is lying on the backseat, her head pillowed like a doll's on her leather purse. She looks alive. But someone has closed her eyes. Don is poised, one hand on the steering wheel, one foot on the street, the car door still open.

"Get in," he says.

I put the woolen bag on the floor. The metal is hot, the car stifling.

A glint of sun annihilates Elias's face. A door slams. It's a Volkswagen. The motor starts. I am jerked past Elias's face. The road passes white houses and turns to dirt at the edge of the town. We jounce down a mountainside toward the sea. The sun is in our faces. Olive trees thrash the horizon. We head for the sea.

There is a fork in the road. Don pulls the wheel to the right. We don't speak. The thickness of the sun fills us. We are dumb. We clatter a mile or two through vineyards. Don looks white, suffering, concentrated, like some dead, male complement to my psyche.

We are entering a village. He stops the car in front of a store. The motor idles. Two men come out of a coffeehouse and stare curiously through the back windows.

"Wake her up. We are here," Don tells me in a loud voice, and he puts the car in first gear and pulls away from them toward a beach at the far end of the village.

There is a fishing boat waiting there, similar to the boat in which Elias took me from the fort. We bounce over the small pebbles of the beach toward a rock quay where the fishing boat is bobbing up and down, pushing against an old rubber tire on a rope. There is a man looking through the salty pane of the windscreen. He comes to the bow, smoking a cigarette. Don pulls the brake, turns off the motor, and gets out to meet him. Don says something to him in a low voice from the rock quay. The man balances on the deck and lets his cigarette fall overboard.

Don returns, and takes her out of the car in a kind of embrace, dancing her as if in a waltz, her head on his shoulder, to the bobbing boat, and I see for the first time that the wound where the bullet came out through her back is a red hole the size of my fist.

Someone hauls me over the gunwales into the boat. There is water inside, up to my ankles. She is lying on a bunk in the cabin. Don is leaning over her.

I look out to see the Volkswagen squatting on the beach, one door still open.

There is the noise of an explosion as the motor starts, and the floorboards vibrate as the fishing boat plows out against the waves.

Don comes out of the cabin saying, "Cora?"

Fools! I think.

Beyond his head I see the *castro*. We are heading for my stone woman, and from the boat bashing in the sea, I look at the foam churning around her, beating, spitting. There she lies, bosom pointed toward the sparkling sun, and I reflect with some satisfaction how she will be there long after I am dead.

Although he put up a fight in the gamesroom of the old Hotel Atlas in Izmir, he lost to a poker-faced Minnesotan whose smashes seemed to him curiously soft, like a click not a roar. He looked up after each of these expecting an afterreport.

In his mind, he knocked at the door of 9 Barka Street, but never got the right sequence of words. He should have gone and told Zoe's mother himself, but he could not. He called Michalis from Brindisi. He saw Cora off on a plane to Geneva. With no credentials he reported in to the navy which flew him direct to Izmir. Twenty-four hours after he lost the tournament, he was back in the old routine in Ruislip and three and a half months later was separated from the army.

He took a trip across the country. He felt as if he had become more solid, garnered a strength around himself like gristle around bones, become fully healed. He had an affair with a girl in Portland, Oregon, totally reassured that he had not lost it forever, came back across the Canadian Rockies and into the States through Vermont, and, with some trepidation, looked up Cora.

She was working in a stationery store—not in Chelmsford, but in Concord, Mass., in a mall not far from where the embattled farmers stood. Her skin had pinkened a little with the milder weather and there was a hint of her old roundness, but she looked at him with the straight gaze. They did not talk about what had happened. She was as enthusiastic as ever, and she acted as if it were perfectly natural that they should meet this way. He found himself staring, obstructed by a case of small file boxes and leather cases, as she told him about having gotten the job in this place. "I absolutely dote on paper," and he had the distinct feeling, like a discovery, that she was insane.

When he left, they kissed, and he walked out of the door and down the street feeling not empty, but as if something he had had in his shirt pocket were missing.